parched

GEORGIA CLARK

Holiday House / New York

Text copyright © 2014 by Georgia Clark

All Rights Reserved
HOLIDAY HOUSE is registered in the U.S. Patent and Trademark Office.
Printed and Bound in February 2014 at Maple Press, York, PA, USA.
www.holidayhouse.com
1 3 5 7 9 10 8 6 4 2

Library of Congress Cataloging-in-Publication Data

Clark, Georgia.
Parched / Georgia Clark. — First edition.
pages cm
Summary: Feeling guilty after her mother's accidental death, sixteen-year-old Tessendra Rockwood leaves the abundance of Eden to fight for survival in the drought-devastated Badlands, but when she joins the rebel group, Kudzu, to fight the tyranny of Eden's government, she is in for some big surprises.
ISBN 978-0-8234-2949-3 (hardcover)
[1. Science fiction. 2. Droughts—Fiction. 3. Survival—Fiction. 4. Revolutionaries—Fiction.] I. Title.
PZ7.G5449Par 2014
[Fic]—dc23

2013022884

For Mum and Dad,
for always being my biggest fans

Acknowledgements

I am extraordinarily grateful for my lovely, enthusiastic agent Chelsea Lindman from Greenburger Associates, who has been excited about "the robot book" from day one. I'm indebted to Sylvie Frank and her obviously excellent taste for ushering *Parched* into Holiday House in the first place. Huge thanks to everyone at Holiday House, especially Sally Morgridge; my wonderful editor, Julie Amper, for guiding me through the process with such expertise (I just have a few more changes—is that okay?).

Special thanks to Pascuala Ortuzar, whose initial passion for this story inspired me to keep going and whose scientific/medical knowledge is second to none! Thanks to Ora Colb and all the students in my Gotham Writers' Workshop courses who offered feedback, especially my teacher, Michelle Knudsen, whose insights were invaluable. I also tip-tapped away at the incredible Martha's Vineyard Writers Residency—twice!—thanks to the kindness of Justen Ahren. Everyone I met there; you are all fantastico!

Danke bolshoi to John "I speak a thousand languages" Tillet and Nat Fong for helping create Malspeak; what a fun, nerdy treat.

Thanks to every reader I strong-armed into looking at a draft, particularly Will Hines for excellent naming suggestions, Lori Goldstein, Ryan Williams (you *can* have ponytails without ponies!), Danielle DiPaolo, and Jen McManus. Ally Collier saves my life on a daily basis; *never, ever* leave New York! And what would I do without Nora "Nozzy Pants" Tennessen or Dan "Hello ladies" Fox? High-fives to Book Club and the Amalfi Crew while I'm at it.

Cheers to my little team at Showtime (best day job in the world!), especially Adam Waring, for genuine interest and support in my other life as an author. Also a shout-out to the Upright Citizens Brigade Theater in New York; I wrote this book while doing a ton of improv with my teams Dreamboat, Kinsey and Cash Fur Guns. Everyone at UCB is great. That is all.

Huzzah to the passionate, supportive community of readers at Goodreads, in the blogosphere and working at independent bookstores and libraries; you're the reason I'm here!

Finally, thanks to the Clark clan. My brother William, for being a lovable nutbag. My smart and generous Dad, for never raising an eyebrow at my antics and cheering me on every step of the way. And my loving, kind, pioneering Mum, for too many things to list here. Reading this book to you over Skype was always the highlight of my week, and not just because I love the sound of my own voice. It was because you thought it was flawless. Love you guys.

part 1

chapter 1

My eyes snap open with familiar panic. *Bang*. Awake.

There used to be a time when waking up was a gentle seesaw in and out of dreams, safe in a cocoon of warm blankets. Back then, the word *sleep* perfectly matched what I was emerging from: a long, drawn-out, sultry affair: *sleeeeep*. These days, I jerk awake with all the subtlety of unexpected vomit. This is because I live in the Badlands. And more specifically, because someone is pinching my big toe.

Heart leaping, I fumble for Mack. My bone-handled hunting knife is still under my pillow, never more than an arm's length away. Before I can even bring the room into focus, I'm shoving Mack out in front of me, and in the direction of...Mileka. My landlord's ancient skinny mother, crouching at my feet. My shoulders slump in relief as she opens her toothless mouth and laughs at me.

"Yes, funny," I mutter, yanking my foot out from her thumb and forefinger. "Glad to see my abject terror is a source of such hilarity for you."

My room—well, really more of a hole in the wall—is in its usual state of bomb-went-off disarray, managing to look messy despite my meager possessions. I drag myself up from the lumpy bedroll and pull on a pair of loose black pants that fall mid-calf. Like almost everyone in the Badlands, I sleep in my underwear. Too damn hot not to.

Mileka cocks her head to one side. I'm speaking English. She doesn't. Out here we speak Malspeak, a mangle of English and old languages like Spanish, Mandarin, and Russian. Dialects from a time when the land was defined by many borders. Now there's only one that matters. And I am on the wrong side of it. *"Ni me pugat."* I tell Mileka she scared me.

"Zhukov," Mileka replies, grinning her strange, toothless smile at me. *"Quiere the fangzu."*

My heart manages to sink and shoot into my mouth at the same time. Mileka's son, Zhukov, is my current landlord and boss, and he wants his rent. The five dollars I owe him for the pleasure of staying in this flea-bitten hovel of a room for another week, I don't have. Again.

"Donde nar Zhukov?" My attempt at sounding unconcerned when inquiring as to his whereabouts fails.

Mileka shrugs, ducking her head to retreat to the low doorway. Sharp eyes watch me as I slip my arms into my sun robe and try to tame my sleep-crazed hair. I'd been routinely shaving an undercut since I'd gotten out here to keep it off my neck. I scrape what's left into a long black ponytail. This includes three thin plaits threaded with speckled feathers that snake behind my left ear. A local custom that helps me blend in.

A bellow from below answers my question. *"Donde nar ella?"*

Mileka and I widen our eyes at the same time, so quickly it'd be funny if I weren't in a stack of trouble. Finding a new place to sleep would be a major hassle. Plus, I like Mileka. Maybe one of these days I'll even tell her my real name.

"Lillith's nyet là!" Mileka screeches, covering for me.

"Mentirosa!" Zhukov roars back, not believing her. The stairs wheeze and creak under his weight.

Mileka presses a worn silver key into my palm, voice low and urgent: *"Zhuan ban ba al bar."* She's offering me her shift at the water bar. If Mileka pretends to leave for work as usual, Zhukov won't look for me there.

I hook the worn straps of my backpack over my shoulders and breathe a quick thanks, *"Danke bolshoi."* I find a hard chili candy in my pocket—Mileka's favorite—and toss it over. She catches it neatly and rewards me with another gummy grin, waving her hands at me to go, now.

As Mileka disappears to face her beast of a son, I push open the dirty glass window. A whoosh of dry heat hits me in the face, momentarily sucking the air from my lungs and burning my eyeballs. I blink fast a few times, squinting in the glare. Then, after hooking one leg over the open window, I shimmy expertly along the narrow stone ledge and start climbing down the bone-dry drainpipe. My boots kick up tiny puffs of red dust as I land squarely on my feet.

The narrow street shimmers unevenly in the relentless heat, empty but for some barefoot kids playing stones. Over a hundred degrees and it's still early morning. After only a few steps, I have to pull up my sun robe's hood to stop my hair from feeling like it's melting.

Welcome to Kep Sai'an. Population: who the hell knows.

Zhukov's water bar is only a few blocks away, and by *blocks,* I mean a few twisting back streets of rundown shacks and gutted buildings housing dozens of families. Some of the shacks are alive with noisy chatter, crying babies, even the occasional waft of cooking food. But many are quiet, no signs of life at all. Some have been quiet for weeks.

It was kind of Mileka to offer me her shift. If I'm lucky, I'll scrounge my rent together in tips. But it's unlikely. What little money the locals have is not being spent on the guarded girl who serves them the crappy *aqua ferro*—iron water—that dribbles from Zhukov's taps. It's being spent on the aqua ferro itself.

But before I start serving out said water, it's time for breakfast. Breakfast used to mean eggs and coffee and creamy yogurt swirled with fat berries, all fresh and organic and harvested in the Farms. Now it means *pourriture.*

I suppress the urge to gag.

The compact little stall I've been eating at in Kep Sai'an is sandwiched tightly between two buildings whose tall walls provide coveted shade. This one tends to get my business because it's slightly less horrible than the hundreds of others littered around town.

I find a seat between a silent old man with a face like a gnome and a couple of women wearing colorful patchwork dresses and conical straw hats. They all ignore me.

I nod at the *pourriture* mama and hold up one finger. She ladles a spoonful of gelatinous gray porridge into a wide plastic bowl and drops it in front of me. A little slops over the edge, and my stomach turns in disgust. Lifting the plastic spoon—reused, no less—I let the cheap millet stew drop in globs back into the bowl. It's as slimy as snot and the color of snails.

Eat it, I command myself. *Eat it!* It may not taste good, but it will fill me up for the day. I swallow mouthful after mouthful. Just like yesterday, and the day before that, and the day before that.

The women next to me are gossiping intensely in Mal. *"Un mes,"* one woman insists.

The other disagrees, shaking her head vigorously. *"Un semana."*

I can guess what they're talking about. Water. And how quickly it's going to run out.

The old man next to me rises like a ghost. *"Danke."* His thanks to the pourriture mama sounds painfully hoarse.

After I finish, I leave a couple of copper coins on the table and head toward the bar. I'm almost looking forward to a quiet morning; maybe I can crash out for a nap if there are no customers. I'm stretched thin with exhaustion, and not just from the heat. I haven't had a good night's sleep since, well, since my life fell apart and I ended up stuck out here. But as I round the last corner, I see that I won't be alone at Zhukov's water bar.

Dozens of local kids, their dark eyes wild with dehydration, are gathered silently around the entrance. There are more every day, ever since they lost their jobs in the Manufacturing Zone. Their coat-hanger bodies hunch on the unpaved street. Their limbs look as gaunt as the dead trees that shoot up from the hard, red earth.

Even after a year of seeing kids like this, I still feel a flush of something raw and sad. But I can't help them. There are too many. I'll just have to deal with dozens of pleading eyes staring me down. Or maybe this time they won't just be staring. I've heard rumors that water bars are being held up for even the tiniest amount of *aqua ferro.* Maybe today these kids will work it out that together, they could overpower me.

Another bad day in the Badlands. Is there any other kind?

I draw in a deep breath of dry, searing air and remind myself: this is the way it is. I move confidently through the crowd. Thankfully, they scatter to make way.

The metal shutter rises with a screech, spilling light into the dim, dusty bar. A long wooden counter runs along one wall, facing a few mismatched tables and chairs that sit unevenly on a packed dirt floor.

I toss my sun robe and backpack under the bar, then begin twirling Mack through my fingers. Casually enough so it won't be mistaken as an invitation to fight, but fast enough so the kids outside can see I know how to use it. I traded my scratch for it the first week I was here. Technology won't protect you from being attacked for fresh water. A badass blade will. Back in Eden where I grew up, the closest thing to knifework I'd experienced was cutting up a loaf of warm bread. Last night, I'd gutted a wild prairie chicken after scaling a rock face to find its nest and slit its throat.

What a difference a year makes.

The knife handle glides through my fingers, under and over in a fast figure eight. It's a neat trick, and easier to learn than you might think. Easy, that is, if you have a lot of time on your hands and nothing to distract you.

A shadowed figure appears in the doorway, blocking the sun. I whip the handle into my palm.

The figure steps inside.

A girl.

My age—sixteen—maybe a pinch older. I relax my grip. She doesn't look like a threat. Her sharp, almond-shaped eyes move around the dingy bar with the precision of a tracking beam. On seeing me, she double-takes, eyes pulsing in a split second of what looks like recognition.

Apprehension shoots up my spine. My fingers tighten around Mack's hilt.

Without breaking eye contact, the girl slides onto a stool at the end of the bar, loosening her copper-colored sun robe. Her look is typical Badlands: a loose-fitting, hand-sewn dress constructed from mismatched scraps of material and leather boots as brawny as a bull. A few stripy feathers are woven into a handful of tiny plaits. But there's no hiding the sheen of her thick, black bangs or the plump swell of her cheeks and arms. Her sun robe's not nearly as stained as mine.

"*Poká, coméstá?*" She greets me eagerly in Malspeak, but it lacks the confidence of a local.

"*Poká,*" I murmur back.

"*Un acqua, qing beaucoup?*"

"*Shì.*" I drive Mack's blade into the soft wood of the bar where the kids can see it while I tend to the girl. The aqua ferro that trickles from the faucet runs opaque yellow, dribbling like syrup. It smells like wet dog.

"No." There's a light, if frustrated, laugh in the girl's voice. "*Acqua azul.*" Lake water. Eden water.

"A dollar," I challenge. "And you owe me ten cents for the *ferro.*"

She slides a red ten-dollar note across the bar. "Keep the copper."

I grab it before the kids catch sight of it: ten dollars is a week's wages around here. She's a tourist, then. Slumming it in Kep Sai'an to regale wide-eyed friends back in Eden with a daring anecdote or two. Time to show her some classic Kep Sai'an service.

"Hey! Robowrong!" The substitute that'd been standing motionless at the far end of the bar jerks its head up. Flat, mechanical eyes aim themselves in the direction of my voice. "City girl wants a city water."

The large, ungainly machine rolls bumpily toward us. It's a head shorter than me and stout, like a dirty bronze troll. I cross my arms, a satisfied smirk creeping across my mouth. Being the world's biggest cheapskate, Zhukov has the world's shoddiest substitute.

Eden is full of sophisticated, beautifully designed substitutes, but in this backwater part of the world, we have the oldest, clunkiest subs around. It would take this hopeless hunk of metal five minutes to hand the girl a bottle of water. She knows it, but if she's annoyed, she doesn't show it.

"I haven't seen that model of substitute in a while—a Builder, right?" She gives me a quick, deliberate smile. "Did you make the modifications so it could work in here? You strike me as someone who might know her way around a substitute." Her eyes are all questions that she already has the answers to.

She knows who I am.

Time to change tack. I give her a big, dumb smile, and force a chuckle. "You've certainly got me pinned wrong. I don't know the first thing about all that stuff." I cock my head, the too-friendly smile still slapped on my face. "You're not from around here, right? You know, there's a pretty decent *pourriture* stall nearby. I eat there all the time and have never gotten sick—"

"I'm not here for travel tips," she interrupts. "My name's Ling Sun-Yi." She sticks her hand out. I don't shake it. "And you are?"

"Lillith." My fingers find the sharp tip of the small gold sword dangling from my necklace and press into it, hard. A nervous gesture I can't shake.

Her dark eyes practically swallow me whole. "Wasn't Lillith the woman who was cast out of Eden? According to myth?"

My skin shivers but I keep my eyes and voice hard. "Ping, was it?"

"Ling," she corrects.

"Here's a travel tip for you, Ping." I frame my words like a question, but they sound like a statement. "Why don't you get out of here before I tell those kids to roll you for all that spare cash you have."

The girl's eyes drill into me, unblinking. "Are you sure your name isn't *Tess Rockwood*?"

Despite the heat, I freeze.

Ling's fist pops the bar in triumph. "It *is* you! You're hard to find,

Tess. I've been looking for you for a month!" Her words are lit with excitement. "Got a tip-off at a trading market an hour north. They remembered the tattoo. Not many people around here have electronic ones."

My fingers move automatically to my tronic, the glowing scrawl of text implanted on the underside of my left arm, from the crook of my elbow to the bottom of my palm. Four words: *No feeling is final.* I'd never guessed it could be used to track me down. "I know my rights," I say. "It isn't against Trust law for Edenites to be in the Badlands."

"Tess—"

"Leave." My fingers hover over Mack's hilt. "Or I'll be forced to get persuasive."

"It's taken me a month to find you," Ling says, incredulous. "I'm not leaving."

"You can't make me come back with you," I all but yell. "I don't care what you do for the Trust!"

"I don't work for the Trust!" She takes a deep breath, eyes burning bright. "I'm part of a group called Kudzu."

That stops me short. "Kudzu?" I stare at her in shock. "You guys actually exist?"

I'd heard of Kudzu. Or, I thought I had. It was years ago now.

It was winter, when the temperature in Eden is dropped into the high forties, cool enough to warrant wooly scarves and morning mugs of hot apple cider. Our Year 7 teacher, the endlessly enthusiastic Ms. Hutchinson, had taken our entire class ice-skating. I remember careening forward, legs wobbling, breath steamy in front of me. I remember feeling like I was flying.

And then I remember the rats.

Hundreds of rust-brown desert rats, suddenly skittering on the ice. Instant chaos. Kids were screaming, falling over each other, scrambling to get out. And that's when sheets of paper tumbled from the sky like snowflakes. I'd only ever seen paper in collectibles like books and posters, never like this; rough and slightly uneven, as if it was hand-made. But what was stranger was the message it contained: KUDZU RATS OUT THE TRUST. It had to do with the Badlands. Something about people having to live on scraps like rats. I remember words like *desperate, drought-stricken,* and *dying.* I was stunned by this different take on the Badlands—after all, we all thought of the Badlands as exotic, not dying.

But everyone knew dissent created instability, which was why it was against Trust law. When Ms. Hutchinson snatched the paper from my hand, I didn't argue. In fact, I felt relieved.

That night, a news stream explained the rats as a freak infestation. There was no mention of Kudzu. When I asked Ms. Hutchinson about it the next day, she looked pained, then patted my shoulder and told me not to worry about it. And not to talk about it.

After that, I'd heard vague rumors of other stunts over the years. Poisoned grass in a park spelling out *Untrustworthy* in thirty-foot letters. A painted ladder on the inside of the city walls, all the way to the top, and the word *Welcome*. But no one ever talked openly about Kudzu. My best friend, Izzy, didn't believe in them, and made me feel babyish the one time I brought it up, saying it was like believing in the tooth fairy. In the end, I assumed the group wasn't real.

"We definitely exist," Ling assures me. "We're a nonviolent collective working to undermine the Trust and free the Badlands. Once the Trust is exposed as lying and corrupt, we believe Edenites will do the right thing. Open the borders. Save the Badlands." Ling lowers her voice with deliberate control. "Kudzu is going to destroy something called Aevum."

I hesitate, curiosity trumping caution. "What's Aevum?"

"Aevum is being developed by Simutech," she replies. "It's their second attempt at creating an artilect."

No. No. No, don't say it—

"You might remember the first attempt." Ling smiles cannily. "Magnus."

Magnus. The word punches me in the stomach. I struggle to keep my voice even. "That's impossible. After Magnus—Simutech shut it down, his programming was destroyed. Artilects are over, they're *done*."

Ling rocks back on her stool, looking relieved. I realize too late I've just confirmed everything she thought she knew about me.

"It's not over." Ling leans across the bar, her voice barely a murmur. "The Trust restarted everything six months ago. It's just top secret this time. No information is public."

Dread prickles my body like a rash. "Then how do you know all this?"

Her smile is sly. "We're not the public."

I realize I'm clenching the edge of the bar. I drop my fingers, not wanting her to see the full effect of what she's saying to me. My heart-beat is crashing in my ears.

Magnus.

A black volcano is boiling up inside me and before I can stop it, Mom's face shoots into my mind, her brilliant blue eyes wide with horror. The memory of my voice, alien in its terror: *"Get away from my mother!"*

Frantic, I push the image away. I push everything out and away. Disconnecting.

"Aevum is completely outrageous," Ling continues. "The Trust shouldn't be funneling resources into a stupid science experiment. They should be fixing the problems out here."

I can't believe this is happening. It's been a whole year. I changed everything. I speak to no one. I have nothing so that nothing can hurt me.

"C'mon, Tess. You, of all people, can see how bad things are getting, especially since the dam was built." Ling's voice swells with insistence. "We've been monitoring the project and believe it to be in the final stages. We have to act *now*. You, of all people—"

"Stop saying, 'You of all people' " I choke out, spinning back around. "I am *not* involved in—"

A crash cuts me off. I whip around. Shards of glass fall from Robowrong's metal fingers. It had gripped the bottle too tight. At the sound of the breaking water bottle, the kids outside jerk to attention, like pack animals picking up a scent. A few of the braver ones dart forward but stay beyond the open doorway.

Ling looks at me pointedly. "Not involved? Those kids'll be dead in a month if Lunalac runs dry."

"Don't be so sure," I snap. "Badlanders are more resourceful than the Trust gives them credit for." But even as I say it, I know Ling is right.

At over ten thousand square miles, Moon Lake keeps Eden flush with clean water. Until a month ago, it also fed a sizable river in the Badlands called Lunalac, which provided a limited but livable supply of water for the locals. The Trust changed that by building a dam to block off the aqueduct. Now, Moon Lake suckles the shining city exclusively, leaving the Badlands to fend for itself.

Damming Moon Lake wouldn't kill everyone in the Badlands right away. The survival instinct of two hundred million people is too strong.

We're already making a day's worth of water last a week. But millions will still die without Lunalac. It might take a year; it might take ten. But it'll happen.

Ling draws in a breath and lets it out slowly, as if to help distill everything she's saying to me. Her words come with calm control. "Kudzu are going to destroy Aevum to draw attention to Moon Lake being cut off from the Badlands," she says simply. "That's the whole point of the mission—*No new life until all life is equal.* But we need your help."

I know why.

For years, Simutech had been trying to make an artilect, a different kind of substitute that could think and feel and reason. Artificial intelligence. Magnus was the first attempt. The reason Ling had left the safety of Eden to track me down was because Magnus had been created by, and then had killed, my mother.

According to the official story, Magnus killed Dr. Francesca Rockwood accidentally: a test went tragically wrong with no one to blame. The true reason for her death was something only my mom, Magnus, and I knew. And I am the only one of those three still alive.

Ling swats a fly away. "We have information that they're working with a combination of robotic and biological technology."

I blink and refocus, the words coming more on instinct than by design. "Robotic neurocircuitry."

Recognition sparks behind her eyes. "That sounds familiar."

"The biological side of things is to make sure it has a nervous system."

Ling wrinkles her forehead. "Why does Aevum need a nervous system?"

"So it can feel things, respond emotionally to what's going on. That's a part of being alive." I feel like I've stepped outside my body and am watching someone else reeling off facts as easily as breathing. I can't believe I remember all this. Listening to my mom, reading her reports, doing my homework at Simutech surrounded by scientists—it seems like a lifetime ago. "The processing speed of the singularix would have increased exponentially."

"The singu...What?"

"Singularix." I pause. "Their brain."

"Tess, you know more about this than any civilian out there." I can almost taste the passion in Ling's voice. "More than any of us, that's for sure."

"I sold my ID for iodine. I can't get back over the border."

"I figured as much." Ling unzips a hefty-looking bag slung over her leg and pulls out one of the shiny red ID cards every Edenite is supposed to carry. For a moment, I'm mesmerized by the five-second loop of me—the old me—that plays on the card. My eyebrows slowly rising, then a smile that's more of a smirk, followed by a toss of silky blond hair. The way Izzy taught me to take a loop. Looking at it now, I almost see my best friend's face instead of mine. I barely recognize myself. The loop ends and starts again, thin eyebrows rising in an endless cycle.

The name, however, is not mine.

"Carin St. Clare?" I ask.

"Completely fictional," Ling assures me. "I'll prep you on her background so you can pass border control. That ID will pass a DNA scan."

"How did you get my DNA?" I ask, alarmed.

"I didn't say we had your DNA. I just said it'll pass a scan." Ling leans toward me intently. "I can get you back over the border. But we have to leave now."

I could go with her. Part of me knows I should. "Why do you think you can trust me?" I ask. "What makes you think I'd want to help?"

Ling holds my gaze unflinchingly. "Because I read about what happened to your mom. I know Magnus killed her."

And just like that, the itching, driving urge to flee takes over. I pluck Mack out of the bar and drop him into the leather sheath on my belt, then slip both arms into my sun robe. My backpack pulls down on my shoulders. "Thank you for a fascinating conversation. Let's never do it again."

As I head for the door, I feel undone. Angry at Ling for tracking me down. Angry at Zhukov, at the Trust, at everyone. The barefoot kids part for me as I stride through them. I don't need to join Kudzu to help them. I spin back to the small crowd and call, *"Acqua azul, à porte! Dalé!"*

They just stand there, staring at me in dumb disbelief. I gesture at the open doorway. *"Dalé! Dalé!"*

One darts inside. The rest keep staring at me, and I nod encouragingly. *"Acqua azul,"* I repeat, pointing at the bar. "Lake water." Another kid follows the first. Then another. Then en masse, the kids rocket inside the bar—a dam bursting. I watch them scamper past Ling to jump over the wooden counter, shouting with delight. My anger disappears, flipping into amusement. My mom always said my impulsiveness was my best and worst quality. Right now, it feels like the best. Satisfied, I spin around and head up the street.

The sun turns everything into hot metal, even the shadows. After half a minute, I hear Ling call after me, mocking, "What are you going to do, Tess? Keep running?" She's chugging behind me on one of the bulky solar floaters most Badlanders ride. The castoffs from Eden hover a few inches off the ground. This one has faded red-and-yellow flames painted on a silver body that has definitely seen better days. "How's that working out?"

"Perfectly," I snap. But the truth is, I'm not even sure how I'll get a ride out of town. I'm about to celebrate a year of aimless backpacking. I've spent everything I had on pickup rides, tasteless food, and thin bedrolls in airless rooms. I don't even have a floater. No possessions, no plan.

Maybe this whole Kudzu thing is an option. Head back to Eden, where life is lush and sheltered and easy. Take a shower for the first time in a year.

Meiyou—no. I squash the idea before it can bloom.

Ling's voice is urgent. "Tess! You *know* this is important. Come with me!"

I spin around to address her directly. "Ping."

She scowls. "It's *Ling*."

"You're looking out for the Badlands. That's great. But you know what I'm looking out for?"

She squints at me. "What?"

"Myself."

"*Scucha!*" A huge, angry voice cracks up the street. A swarthy, shirtless man with a long ponytail made of real horsehair fights off the riot of kids looting his bar.

Zhukov. The kids are scattering, but it's too late. Dozens already have armfuls of expensive *acqua azul,* because I let them steal it.

He points at me, yelling at someone to bring him the *fuega.* Not someone—some*thing*. Substitutes. The two old Divers Zhukov had repurposed as his own personal security emerge from the shadows, motors sputtering into action.

I swear loudly.

Divers could haul me back to Zhukov in a heartbeat.

"Get on," Ling urges.

"No." The Divers begin gunning up the empty street toward me, their three large wheels zooming easily over the unpaved roads. I can see their weird, open mouths from here, set in a permanent O to suck out floodwater that no longer exists. I start to run but the Divers are gaining ground.

"Tess, get on!"

I hesitate for a nanosecond before swinging my leg over the floater, leaping in front of Ling and shoving her down the seat. "I'm driving."

"Hey!" She barely has time to grab on to my backpack before I shoot us forward.

"I know the streets better!" I yell over the roar of the engine.

We race jerkily up the narrow, twisting street, weaving around men lugging canvas bags of spare sub parts and barefoot kids playing chase. Zhukov once gave a local boy a black eye for refusing to pay for a bottle of lake water. I shudder to think what he'd do to me now.

I take a turn so tight we tip to one side, so close to the ground my ponytail skims the earth. My stomach rockets into my mouth. Ling lets out a little shriek, but I manage to pull us upright, heart drumming furiously in my chest.

We pause at a cramped cross street. Left or right? In a roar of twin engines, the Divers appear at the far end of the street to my right. They whip themselves in our direction. *Left.*

"We have to lose them!" calls Ling.

"You don't say!" I call back.

Red dust sprays out on both sides as if we were cutting through water. We curve left, then right, shooting up streets as squiggly as noodles. Through an upcoming archway, I spot a flight of stairs. My teeth chatter as we hurtle up them and I almost run straight into a woman with a huge basket of pots and pans. The basket goes flying. She curses at me furiously over the oddly musical sound of metal clattering down the stairs.

"Sorry!" I yell over my shoulder.

At the top of the stairs, I pause. We're on the second floor, which overlooks a square interior courtyard. A handful of young girls are playing in it, amid trash and debris. "This used to be a school," I tell Ling quietly. "But people live here now."

Slowly, I begin chugging us down the corridor. Dirty clothes are strung up between gray concrete pillars. Most people can't afford water to wash them, but sunlight gets rid of some of the smell. Through the open doorways, we pass classrooms repurposed as one-room apartments. Some are jam-packed with dozens of makeshift beds, some contain no more than a bedroll and a bucket. Looks of surprise morph quickly to anger, and within a minute, we've attracted a trail of men and women yelling at us to get the hell out of their building.

"Tess?" I hear Ling say uncertainly. "I don't think we're exactly welcome."

"We'll just be a minute," I mutter. I need to stretch out our hideout as long as possible.

In a familiar roar of engines, the Divers appear at the top of the stairs behind us.

I power us forward at full throttle. *"Yídòng, yídòng!"* I shout at the Badlanders coming out of doorways in front of us to see what the fuss is. I hear Ling gasp as we take the first turn. The dull buzz of the Divers behind us echos around the corridors. Another turn. Another. Then we're in the final stretch. "Hold on!" I yell to Ling as we careen back down the stairs. The woman with the pots and pans is standing in the stairwell entrance chatting to someone. *"Yídòng!"* I yell, and she does, just in time.

Back in the streets, my foot jams on the accelerator. "Are they behind us?" I yell to Ling. I feel her body twist as she turns to look.

"Yes!" she calls. "Gaining!"

"C'mon," I mutter anxiously, scanning the storefronts for a way out. An alley. I wrench the floater into it, barely keeping us horizontal. We fly toward the bright light at the end and burst out onto a market square.

Hundreds of men, women, and different kinds of junky substitutes—Divers, Sweepers, Strongs, Mulchies—crowd around us. Beat-up old floaters laden with cages of cackling prairie chickens are crammed next to guys haggling viciously over livestock and solar bars and barrels of aqua ferro. I almost laugh in relief. We're saved.

Amid a chorus of honks and beeps and yells, we start blending into the ragtag crowd. After a few minutes, I'm sure we've lost the Divers. Eventually, we pass all the way through and emerge on the other side. With no particular destination in mind, I join a throng of floaters heading for a main road.

"There's another reason you might want to come back," Ling calls from behind me.

"Oh yeah?"

"The new head of Innovation at Simutech is Dr. Abel Rockwood!"

I'm stunned. "My uncle? That's not possible."

"What?" she calls over the roar of hundreds of old floaters.

"He split—quit!" I call back. "He told me himself he'd quit Simutech. He promised he'd destroy Mom's research!"

"Guess they made him an offer he couldn't refuse!"

My *uncle* is the head of Innovation? The position that got his own sister killed? I wouldn't have picked Abel as a career-hungry grave digger. The idea tastes as bad as *pourriture*. All my fear and panic and guilt begins to solidify into another emotion, as clean and pure as a flame. Anger.

"That's why we need you, Tess!" Ling continues. "Dr. Rockwood is our best way in, and you're the only person who knows what to look for!"

Going back to Eden means getting close to secrets—horrific, ugly secrets that I've worked hard to bury. But if I don't *really* get involved with Kudzu and Simutech and Aevum, those secrets will stay where they belong—unknown, and then lost forever. I can pretend I'm interested, take the free passage, then disappear as simply as smoke clearing.

"Okay!" I yell. "I'm in!"

"Then I guess we're heading the right way!" Ling points to the hand-painted sign we're passing under. It has one word on it: *Vuelvol*. Airport.

I'm going home.

chapter 2

It's a three-hour flight to one of four crossings into Eden. A decrepit cargo ship flies us the thousand-odd miles to the Western Bridge. Like the floaters, Badlands cargo ships are also Eden hand-me-downs. The soft passenger seats have been stripped to make room for as many people and things as the fast-talking captain can cram in. This means we can bring Ling's floater with us, but it also means I have to be sure the hungry goats in the cage next to me don't make a meal of my backpack.

After taking off, we circle back over the Manufacturing Zone, which most people just call the Zone: miles of stifling hot factories, where people aged seven to seventy used to do everything from recycling glass bottles to building talking tennis rackets. But there are no human workers there anymore. In the last six months, the Trust switched over the entire workforce to shiny new substitutes. There's a tired joke about it—the Zone was the only place in the Badlands where you got good service. Everywhere else, the substitutes were a notch above junkyard.

It's obvious why the Trust made the change. Substitutes are more efficient. Plus, subs don't need bathroom breaks or fresh water or shelter. Even though many are human-shaped, they're not sentient. They're just robots. Ex-Zone workers were left to starve like everyone else.

When we clear the outskirts and begin to head east, the earth becomes more uniform. Glimpsed through the small, dirty windows is endless dry, red clay. Occasionally we pass over forsaken villages, or larger cities stripped of everything useful. The land, once a compact grid of people and parking lots and ninety-nine-cent hot dogs, is now empty.

Ling and I sit with our backs pressed against the side of the plane. I toe my backpack farther from the cage of goats and say, "I assume you have some proof to show me."

Ling checks that her floater, which is parked directly in front of us, obscures us from everyone else's view. Then she unzips her backpack and pulls out a folded piece of scratch. The gold computer is paper-thin, but made from a durable, flexible material that you need a knife to cut. That's one of the good things about scratch: you can cut it if you want to share it. You can even meld together the same generation if you want a bigger piece for bigger holos. At the cinematheques in Eden, they use scratch the size of houses for holos just as big. It makes you feel like you're in a completely different world. Ling's scratch is the same kind I traded for Mack. When she presses her thumb and forefinger into one corner, it begins glowing a familiar deep amber.

"Show me the Simutech file." A silent holo materializes between us—a colorful, shifting cloud. There's no mistaking who's in it. Uncle Abel is speaking passionately with a man wearing a flowing yellow robe. I recognize him instantly: Gyan, leader of the Trust. Abel waves his hands emphatically as he talks, while Gyan's fingers are clasped behind his back, gaze directed straight ahead. They're heading into Simutech itself; I catch sight of the company slogan glowing above the imposing main entrance: *How the Future Feels.*

With a small wave of her hand, Ling flicks the holo to pause and the two men freeze. "It was recorded a few weeks ago." Specks of red dust drift through the crystal clear holo of Gyan. In his yellow robe, our charismatic father figure is unmistakable. I can see every smile line around his piercing blue eyes, every hair in his full, thick beard. He looks, as usual, powerful without even trying. On the other hand, Abel's shirt is untucked and his hair is mussed. They're both surrounded by a clutch of attentive Guiders—blue-robed community officials who uphold the will of the Trust. The Guiders are all looking at Gyan, even though my uncle is the one speaking.

Ling pulls open another holo. "And then there's this."

I skim the tight black print scrolling before me: *Work Choice Reassignment for Dr Abel F. Rockwood.* Abel's signature is scrawled at the bottom of the page, floating just above my knee. "How did you get a copy of this?" I ask incredulously.

Ling shoots me a look of amusement. "Child's play. Actually, this is what tipped us off in the first place. Achilles, he's our tech guy, intercepted some correspondence and managed to decode it. A classified stream they don't think we know about."

I scan the text with small swishes of my fingers. It looks official enough, detailing Abel's relocation from Animal Cloning to Innovation.

"See, right there," Ling says, pointing at the hovering text. "All the resources in Innovation are being directed to Aevum." She shakes her head in disbelief. "That's insane. Those resources need to be directed out *here*. That's why Kudzu wants to stop this thing."

I frown at the text before me. "Why would the Trust want to make another artilect?" I mutter, more to myself than Ling. Cutting off Moon Lake fit the Trust's overall agenda of keeping Eden lush with life, as did replacing Zone workers with substitutes. But Magnus was a spectacular failure. I chew on my lip, thinking aloud. "If the Trust wanted more power and control, they'd just invent more substitutes. They do what they're told, take fewer resources to run, and are way less risky." I glance at Ling, still frowning. "Artilects are unpredictable. They're supposed to be able to think for themselves, that's the whole point."

"You really know a lot about all this."

"Artilects?" I give her a sardonic smile. "Child's play."

Ling looks deep in thought for a long minute. "It's interesting," she says eventually. "When I first heard about Aevum, I thought it was a massive waste of resources and a good target for a high-profile mission. But hearing you talk about it…" Ling widens her eyes for a second, then shakes her head. "I'm just doubly glad that I'm bringing you back."

I nod, scrunching the scratch into a tight little ball and squeezing it, hard. *But I'm not coming back for you.*

"C'mon," Ling says, gently taking the wad of scratch out of my hand. "Time to become Carin St. Clare."

I concentrate on memorizing Carin St. Clare's backstory, which I'll need to know perfectly to pass border control. I feel like I'm cramming for a test again, only if I fail this one, Ling and I will be banished from Eden permanently. Or worse.

As the hours pass, the land below becomes more and more populated with makeshift cities. Then Ling nudges me, voice low and slightly strained. "There it is."

Through the dust-streaked windows of the ship, I see it: Eden, the powerful city of shining abundance. For a second, I forget how to breathe as the long, white walls rise up from the horizon, ringed by a wide moat of black water. Home. Where the clear dome that arcs from the tops of the walls filters the awful heat into pleasant, safe sunlight.

When I was born, we'd been in a drought for over fifty years. I wasn't alive when the planet first fell into a marathon of endless natural disasters. That was closer to two centuries ago now. As substitutes rebuilt one city from a hurricane, a tsunami hit another. People scrambled to re-create homes that the planet seemed intent on destroying. As Earth's resources began to dry up for good, the remaining cities began an ugly fight for survival. First came food and energy limits. Then rations. City walls. A desperate race to create renewable sources of power as the old mining industries finally bled the land dry. Solar energy replaced fossil fuels. But eventually, everything was sucked into one place, one stronghold, one last beacon. My ears pop as our ship begins dipping back to earth, just a few short miles from the gleaming white walls.

The late afternoon is alive with prehistorically ugly dragonflies the size of desert rats. The soupy air is something of a relief from the full force of the midday sun, but I still feel like I'm burning up. I have to focus hard on getting us the final few miles to the border crossing. I guide Ling through the teeming throngs of Badlanders, past ad hoc stores selling sun robes, smoky desert-rat skewers, and ridiculously overpriced water. She's surprisingly street savvy for an Edenite, ducking out of the way of kicking camel hooves and floaters zooming recklessly through the crowds. A tiny old man with a face like a wrinkled prune makes his way through. He carries a tray of small paper bags. *"Grillos fritos! Grillos fritos!"*

"Good, I'm starving." Ling waves him down. "What are you selling, señor?"

The man opens a bag to show us a fistful of dry fried crickets.

Ling screws her face up. "Ugh, gross."

I nod to the man. *"Cuánto copper?"*

He flashes his open palm twice—ten cents. I drop some coins into his palm, and he gives me two bags.

Ling blanches. "You're not seriously going to eat those, are you?"

I tip my head back a little and somewhat theatrically drop the biggest cricket into my mouth. Ling makes a small sound of disgust.

I crunch the sharp, very salty cricket loudly. "Funny what you get used to out here," I say, turning to rejoin the crowd.

Ling shakes her head in disbelief as she walks next to me. Then, as if the movement reminds her, she unties a necklace that's hidden under her dress—a thin red piece of string with a tiny silver charm in the shape of a K. For *Kudzu,* perhaps? She notices me watching her. "String breaks easily," she says. "In case we're caught, we can throw it away." She tucks the small charm carefully into the lining of her dress.

I grind up pointy cricket legs with my teeth. "A risky fashion statement."

"It's not a fashion statement." She smiles dryly. "It's a sign that I belong to the thing that matters to me the most."

I shrug, thinking abstractly that it might make a good trade. "When do I get mine?"

Ling raises her eyebrows at me. "When all of Kudzu votes on you joining. When you prove you're one of us."

I tighten my sun robe. Whatever. I wasn't sticking around long enough for that to ever be a possibility. I stride ahead with purpose. The sooner we cross the border, the better.

"Was it a surprise for you?" Ling asks, keeping pace with me easily. "To see what it's really like out here?"

It certainly was. But not the fun birthday kind. More like, hey, the government lies and everyone here is really thirsty. "Sure."

"You really had no idea?"

I shrug again, fishing in the side pocket of my backpack for my water bottle. "How would I? The streams all downplay it."

The streams are the way we access all knowledge and entertainment. And the streams are all connected—we call it being on-cycle. If you searched the streams for the Badlands, you'd see holo after holo of smiling, colorfully dressed locals living simply in exotic locales. You would not see kids with xylophone bodies or dead dogs in dry creek beds.

"You must've known the Trust controls the streams," Ling says. "They censor them. And they change things. Did you know that?"

I drop a couple of iodine pills into the bottle to make the foul liquid a little less toxic. "That was another part of the surprise," I admit. It was only from seeing the Badlands firsthand that I understood just how much the Trust manipulated Edenites' understanding of the place.

"Did you hear about the Valley of Spines massacre?" Ling asks.

I glance at her sharply.

"Apart from Lunalac, that's all anyone's been talking about," she adds.

Rumors of the massacre had reached my ears too. A Builder killed ten men in a bar in the Valley a few weeks ago. No rhyme or reason. It just slaughtered them all. But substitutes can't harm humans. Not just because it's against the law, but because they're designed that way. No substitute can be programmed to harm a human, let alone kill one. "Don't believe everything you hear out here."

"It spooked me," Ling says with a shudder. "A substitute killing people like that." When I don't say anything back, she adds, "Did you feel the same way? Or is that one of those things that you get used to?"

"Ling." I pull to a sudden stop. "Look. I'll help you stop Aevum. But I don't want to . . . Y'know—" I wave my hands at her.

"What?"

I look at her deliberately. "Bond."

Her reply is interrupted by yelling. A crowd of Badlanders presses forward into a water bar, craning their necks to see something inside. They seem royally pissed off, heckling loudly. *"Scucha. Dim pasó?"* I ask a woman near me what's happening.

Her reply is sour. *"Gyan habla guan yu Lunalac."*

"What is it?" Ling asks me, eyes wide.

"Gyan's explaining why they cut off Lunalac."

The dimly lit water bar reminds me of Zhukov's: a low ceiling and packed dirt floor. But unlike Zhukov's, it's packed to the rafters with hot, jostling bodies.

Gyan's deep voice warbles in and out. His image quivers up from one of the earliest versions of scratch, which is dull brownish-gold and as thick as a rug. "For many years, Eden has been mother to her boisterous child, the Badlands," he intones. "But now, it is time for our child to grow up. To learn to crawl, walk, and finally run free, as we here in Eden have done. We have created our Arcadia, our utopia. Now it is time for the Badlands to define their Eden for themselves."

Ling and I exchange incredulous expressions. I used to think Gyan's speeches sounded enlightened. Now they sound straight-up insane.

"This is why we must stay firm in our decision to cut off Moon Lake as a permanent measure." Gyan's voice is barely audible above the howls of protests from the angry Badlanders. "Just as a mother must one day free her babe from her breast, now we must free the Badlands."

Ling's face is twisted in anger. "What total *bullshit*," she spits. "Any fool can see Eden has a *responsibility* to—"

But her words are swallowed up by the curses coming from the increasingly angry crowd. In the din, I keep hearing one phrase over and over again: *"Gyeong-gye de fronteras! Gyeong-gye de fronteras!"*

Border crossing.

"C'mon!" I grab Ling's hand and pull her into the swell of people.

Leaving Eden a year ago had been so easy, I did it in less than ten minutes. It's a different story getting back in. Hundreds of people crowd the border crossing, a mash of rickshaws, floaters, and angry Badlanders on foot. Chants rip through the mob. Empty water containers filled with stones rattle hollowly in the dying light.

A line of ragtag subs—mostly Divers and Strongs—patrol the border, stretching out in both directions. Tranquils, the fully armored human guards of the Trust, wander among them, razers at the ready. A direct hit from their white laser guns can kill you, and everyone knows it. The Tranqs' bulky white uniforms bear the emblem of their employer: a swirling white *T* encased in a blue circle rimmed with yellow. Yellow for enlightenment. Blue for liberalism. And white for peace.

Two Tranqs man the entry gate. Their brandished razers keep the crowds at bay. Words hover above the gate: EDENITES ONLY. MUST HAVE VALID ID! The whole desperate scene makes my stomach clench.

"Let's go," Ling says, but I caution her back. This is about to become a riot, and if we aren't careful, we'll get caught in the crossfire. I tell Ling to use her sun robe to hide her body and hair, and I do the same. If the crowd suspects we're both actually Edenites, someone's bound to try stealing from us—or worse.

The crowd is forced apart. A circle of Tranquils protects a Guider making her way toward the gate. I wonder briefly what a Guider is doing out of the city—Guiders look after Eden, not the Badlands. While she's trying to appear calm, fear flits across her pale face. Her body tenses at every yell.

A rake-thin man in a ratty animal pelt is screaming at the Tranquils as they work their way through. "My family—we're dying! We need fresh water! We're all *dying*!" He shoves the Tranquil, who stumbles.

The Tranq's deep voice is tinny through an armored helmet that prevents us from seeing his face. "If you don't have ID, we can't help you."

"Soon we won't be asking for your permission!" the man yells, his words ringing out over the swollen crowd. "Soon we will take your precious city without asking!"

"Get out of here!" the Tranq snaps, sounding almost panicked.

"No!"

"Fine!" The Tranquil smashes the Badlander in the face with the butt of his razer. Blood arcs from his nose and mouth, a bright, wet spray of red. My vision swims. The man crumples to the ground. His skull hits the dry earth with a sharp smack.

All hell breaks loose.

I grab Ling's arm. "Now," I hiss. As the mob turns on the Tranqs, I pull Ling toward the entry gate. We flash our IDs, and two sets of strong arms lift us clear of the crowd.

The border control official is all straight lines and hard edges, suspicious before I even open my mouth.

"Name?" Her question ricochets around the bare interview room like a gunshot. I barely keep from flinching.

"Carin St. Clare."

"Address?"

"Forty-six–ten Mountain View Road, Liberty Gardens."

Her eyes drop to the square of scratch in front of her. It's on the 2D setting, and angled toward her, so I can't see what's shimmering on the flat gold surface. My answer evidently checks out, because the next thing she says is, "Education?"

Stay calm. You know this. "I went to pre-education in Liberty Gardens, but I attend education in West Charity."

"Where?"

I swallow. What was it called? All the education centers are named after Greek gods, and Carin's is the goddess of intelligence and the arts…"Athena."

A flash of recognition, and the woman permits a smile. "My son goes there. Grey Myerson. Head of the philosophy club. Do you know him?"

Her left eye twitches. Ling shifts next to me, almost imperceptibly. She's lying to me. "We don't have a philosophy club at Athena," I say carefully.

The border control official's face hardens once more—I was right. "Why did you leave Eden?"

I draw in a deep breath. The pain in my face is real, but not for the reasons I'm about to give. "My boyfriend died protecting the Trust. His work choice was a Tranquil. He was attacked and killed in a riot at the Zone." I lower my eyes and shiver. "I just…needed to get out."

Again, her eyes confirm her belief in this sad story, cleverly patriotic in its lies. This time when her face loses its severity, it seems genuine.

"I'm sorry to hear that," she murmurs, then turns her attention to Ling. "Name!" she barks.

Ling is an impressive liar, maybe even better than me. She plays the role of the concerned best friend, eager to save me from the nasty Badlands and help me get my life back on track. She uses her real name, but I think her entire background is fake. I wonder if Kudzu maintains fictional records for all their members. I wonder if this even extends to monthly allowance usage. Do they use their allocated credit to collect Goods and Sustenance? If they didn't, it would draw attention to themselves. I remind myself to ask Ling about this, before remembering I'm not getting involved with Kudzu. In less than an hour, I'll never see this girl again.

"Your reentry is approved," says the woman, before pausing. Her gaze shifts between us both. I feel myself straightening. "I don't need to remind you," she continues, in a voice that is somehow both soft and hard, "that undermining the Trust is a crime which can result in allowance reduction, community service, or in extreme cases, banishment."

Ling and I exchange a quick look of bemusement. "Yes, we know," I hedge.

"It's important you are extremely judicious over how you relay your experiences out here," the woman finishes.

She's telling us to keep our mouths shut. Maintain the fiction that the Badlands are not being slowly strangled by the Trust. A sick sort of anger boils up inside me, but before it can spread to my face, Ling nods eagerly, all bushy-tailed enthusiasm. "Oh, yes, ma'am. We understand." She drops her voice to a murmur. "Personally, I'd prefer it if the Trust just killed the whole lot of them in their sleep. The sooner we get out of here, the better."

The woman nods approvingly. "Welcome home, girls."

The sun hangs low over the horizon by the time we guide Ling's floater onto the smooth concrete bridge for the final ride to the white-walled city. Behind us, the sounds of the protesting Badlanders begin to fade.

We ride fast, the only ones racing along the empty bridge. The last rays of the setting sun glint brilliantly off the dark water in the moat that surrounds Eden, making it look as if it's on fire. They say there are strange types of sharks in that moat, swimming in the tar-black water.

The low drone of the thousands of air filters that are set into the high, white walls becomes louder as we get closer. By the time we reach the walls, the roar is so loud we can't hear each other even when we shout. Ling pulls the floater to a stop. A small, all but invisible doorway set into the pristine white walls slides open. As soon as we're through, it slides shut behind us.

We steer the floater along a darkened, echoing throughway—the musty interior of the walls. The roar of the air filters is barely audible. As we putter forward, the temperature drops. Stifling heat becomes comfortably warm. I catch the zesty scent of lemons.

Two more Tranquils scan our IDs. A final set of slick white doors slides open.

And suddenly we are standing at the edge of a lush, sprawling park. The air is fresh, with just right amount of early evening chill. The soft *chk-chk-chk* of sprinklers arcing across the velvety green is the only sound that fills the pale purple twilight.

Eden.

chapter 3

The air is cool and clean; it *smells* like water, the way it does near a gushing fountain. The oppressive dry heat that had exhausted me for a year is gone. In its place is freshness so pure, I find myself gulping it in. I fight the urge to sink into the deep grass to smell the moist, healthy earth.

No one is waiting to get into the Badlands. There's no border control on this side of the wall. If it weren't for the two huge shiny doors, and the couple of silent Tranqs standing motionless on either side of them, you'd never guess it was a way out.

Ling parks the floater, then ducks behind a bush and turns her dress inside out. The lining used to be cream but it's now stained yellow with sweat and smeared with red dirt. But after belting it and pulling the feathers out of her hair, she at least looks more Eden than Badlands. She also has an outfit for me: a delicate slip of a dress that leaves me feeling uncomfortably exposed. I try to wipe my face clean but I'll need a shower to get the red dust out. *A shower.* None of this seems real.

We cruise slowly through the park. Several young girls in white dresses cartwheel in the soft light—a pre-education dance troupe rehearsal, perhaps. Their bare feet twist in the grass as they spin and whirl, so light and lovely they look like dandelion puffs.

The other side of the park gives way to a quiet street. Through the ground-floor windows around me, families make dinner in kitchens lit by a cozy golden glow. A whiff of simmering onions makes my mouth water. Buzzcars zip high above us, the compact little aircrafts as charming as fireflies in the dusky light. Through the clear dome high above me is the same night sky I used to see in the Badlands. But the light from the city dulls the stars.

Ling knows my uncle's address and takes us on a twenty-minute ride through Liberty Gardens, the pretty neighborhood that spreads out from the western entrance.

Eden's shaped a bit like an ear. Lakeside bulges up in the north, dominated by Moon Lake. In the northeast are acres of pleasantly rustic Farms, where trees hang heavy with fruit and fields are filled with crops. In the easternmost part of Eden, spinning windmakers create the light breeze I can feel now. The thin, U-shaped Moon River forms a natural barrier all the way around the curved, shining skyscrapers of the Hive. I always assumed this was named for the number of buzzcars that dart in and around the heart of Eden, which is located more or less in the middle. The comfortable homes of Liberty Gardens fill the west, and the younger, hipper Charity is in the east. The squiggly streets of the South Hills rise over it all.

And beyond the South Hills, perched at the highest point overlooking Eden, up where snow dusts the tops of the Smoking Mountains, are the Three Towers. The home of the Trust. The trio of curved buildings looks like the spikes of a jester's hat. Gyan's private quarters are located right at the tip of the biggest of the three buildings. It's the only structure that offers views over both sparkling, beautiful Eden, and farther south, over the barren red earth of the Badlands.

For the first fifteen years of my life, everything in Liberty Gardens—from the wide, green parks to the burbling water fountains—seemed normal. Now it is beyond surreal.

We pass a young woman chatting animatedly in between bites of bright red apple. Is she talking to herself? No, a delicate silver comm decorates one ear. I'm struck by how impossibly perfect an average Eden outfit looks to me now. With her light bodysuit and mane of loose golden hair, she looks like she belongs in an entertainment stream, not on a sidewalk. She'd probably assume someone like me wanted to rob her. I catch myself—no, she wouldn't. I'm back in Eden now. Being held at knifepoint is not a daily possibility here. The woman tosses the apple core into a sleek white compost bin on the street corner, and it chimes.

Two men push a stroller with a chubby baby. One man touches the other's back as they talk quietly. Presumably, they are partnered. Edenites are permitted two children per partnership or one if independent. No, I correct myself again. *We* are allowed that. Now, I am an Edenite again.

"Hey, Ling, stop for a sec!"

"What's wrong?"

"Just pull over!"

Before we've even come to a complete stop, I'm off the floater and racing to a curved white water fountain. When I lived here, I must have passed a dozen of these every day. Now they look like a beautiful miracle.

I close my eyes and open my mouth. Nothing happens. Then I remember: my ID. I need to scan it to record my water usage, even from the public fountains. All Edenites are permitted monthly Lake Allowances, albeit generous ones. Can I use this fake ID?

Ling answers my question by waving hers in front of the scanner with a grin. "Mine works. Yours won't."

Water shoots from the fountain. Cool, fresh, clean lake water. It fills my mouth, running down my chin, onto my chest. *Water.* I drink hungrily, in great gasps and lurches. I'm grinning like an idiot, delirious with happiness.

I'm home. I'm actually home.

The flow of water stops with a small chime. When I open my eyes, two young boys astride whisper-soft floaters are staring at me. Their twin looks of horrified fascination make Ling and me burst into laughter. I run back to the floater, and we take off again.

Ling drops me around the corner from Abel's modest two-story home. By Badlands standards, the houses look enormous. The softly curved architecture creates soothing, undulating waves that remind me of air and wind and water.

"Get settled tonight. See what you can find out, but be careful. Don't blow your cover," Ling instructs. "I assume you don't have any scratch?"

Oh no. She's going to give me her scratch. "You assume right."

"Give me your knife." She pulls out her roll. Mack slices through the scratch like butter, cutting it neatly in two. She hands it to me. "Try it."

I hesitate. "I don't really want anyone knowing I'm back." Not only that, but I haven't been on-cycle in over a year and I left sort of . . . abruptly. The idea of five billion messages all asking where I am? Pass.

"Kudzu uses only off-cycle scratch and comms; you can access the streams anonymously," Ling assures me. I hide a flicker of surprise—I've heard of off-cycle scratch, but I've never used it myself. She adds, "Be careful around subs; most of them are on-cycle these days. Just stay off-cycle altogether."

"Why?"

"Because the Trust can access everything that happens on-cycle," Ling says patiently. "It's important you stay anonymous from now on."

Smoothing out the blank scratch, I press the corner of it with my thumb. It glows gold before a tangle of noisy holos spring up between us. Notices of local meets, sign-ups for open-air art classes, and a recipe for quinoa-crusted lemon tofu all scramble for my attention. I try flicking them to mute with my eyes, but I just end up making them louder.

"Out of practice." Ling smirks. "I'll send you a missive via a Forest-Friend tonight, after we've confirmed a dead zone to meet in."

I give her a look. "You're certainly not stingy with the jargon, Ping."

She grins, her eyes whipping through the holos. "Dead zones are places off-cycle, where the Trust can't see us. And ForestFriends are something kids use to send messages to each other. You can program your scratch to alert you when one's coming, even when it's off. Here. I just sent you one." She folds the scratch in two, shutting the holos off, and gives it to me. A second later it begins pulsing and making a peeping sound, like a baby bird. "Open it." She nods.

I do, and a holo of a baby bird flies out, adorably tiny and sweet. It has bright blue wings, a puffed-up yellow chest, and big expressive eyes.

"Cute," I admit. It circles around my head and lands on my shoulder, peeping into my ear. *"Kudzu loves you!"* Then the bird disappears.

"Kids send a million ForestFriends a day, so it's a good way to send messages on the down low," Ling explains. "The Trust isn't monitoring this kind of stuff. Once I send you one, you can answer it with one of your own."

"So if you don't send me one, I'll have no way of contacting you."

Ling looks at me as if I'm profoundly stupid. "I didn't spend a month looking for you only to disappear after getting you back, Tess."

I scrunch up the scratch and shove it in my backpack, fighting a flush of guilt. I'm about to completely double-cross this nice revolutionary who'd bought me a cargo ship ticket and saved my butt from a couple of Divers.

Ling fights a yawn. "Oof, I'm exhausted. I'll see you tomorrow."

"Aye, aye, Captain." I salute.

She smiles back. "You're doing the right thing, Tess." She chokes her floater back into gear, words barely audible above the motor. "And remember, you're back in Eden now. Dissent's against the law, so watch what you say." Her foot presses the accelerator, and she zooms off up the empty street.

For a few seconds, I just stand there. Alone. Even though I've been on my own for so long, it feels like forever since I've actually been alone. Unable to hear, see, or smell other people. Everything around me looks so ordered, so safe. Even the tangled front gardens that brim with plant life look perfectly composed. Considering I'd woken up on a dirty bedroll with a knife under my pillow, it'll take a little getting used to.

Movement.

I flinch reflexively.

But it's just the dark shape of a bird flying low over the street. *You've got to stop that, Tess, if you're going to fit back in here,* I chide myself. I swing my backpack over my shoulder, turning in the opposite direction from my uncle's house. I'll sneak into a Longevity Hub, clean myself up, then work out what to do next.

But I can't move.

I can't believe he's doing it. And I'd thought, or at least I'd tried to believe, that I didn't care either way...but I do. I have to know. If it's true, and Abel really is doing this, then he lied to me. He lied about destroying the research for a project that ripped our lives apart. My uncle. My ditzy, brilliant, *completely harmless* uncle. He could never be involved in something so wrong, so dangerous. Could he?

I give my head a hard shake. No, I tell myself fiercely. I don't want to know. I don't want to get mixed up in this. The past is the past and the members of Kudzu are all probably on a fast track to getting banished or getting themselves killed.

I will not go to Abel's.

I absolutely and unequivocally *will not go.*

Abel's front door is just how I remembered it: a pane of smoky gray glass that warps my reflection into something unrecognizable. There's a scanner for those with IDs on his home access list, and a white round doorbell for those without. Familiar and foreign at the same time.

The doorbell chimes faintly. I hear my uncle's voice ring out. "I'll get it, Kimiko."

His voice, distracted and slightly surprised, sends a shiver of recognition up my spine. Moments later, I am face-to-face with the famous Dr. Abel Rockwood.

Appearance-wise, we make a fine match. The man who created the much-lauded *Toward an Understanding of Artificial Consciousness in Advanced Bio-Cybernetic Systems* stream looks, as usual, like he was dressed by monkeys. Color-blind monkeys. His pants don't fit, his collared shirt is buttoned unevenly, and I'm fairly certain his peach-colored housecoat was originally intended for ladies. I can't help noticing how weathered his face is. He's unshaven. Sleep-deprived circles cut under hazel eyes, which I watch shift from curiosity to recognition to deer-in-the-headlights shock.

"Tessendra?"

My full name: the one no one except my family uses. I have the urge to hug him. Or more accurately, let him hug me. It's been so long since anyone has hugged me. Instead, I rock back on my heels. "Yo, Uncle A. What's up?"

He stares at me, completely dumbstruck. "But I thought . . . I thought you were—"

"A blonde?" Without waiting for an invitation, I stride inside.

I'm expecting to see Aevum everywhere—charts, holos, streams, reports—just like Magnus had been last year. But the spacious living-cum-dining room that the hallway opens out into is unexpectedly . . . tidy. In fact, it looks suspiciously like a regular home. Colorful cushions are neatly arranged on an overstuffed sofa. The orange tiled floor is spotless, dotted with rugs that actually match the sofa cushions. An immense wooden dining room table plays host to a bunch of poppies, rather than stacks of circuit boards. The smell-conditioning is set to fresh-baked bread. Or perhaps Abel is even *baking bread himself,* a concept even more far-fetched than me getting back over the border unscathed. Did Ling have the wrong intel after all? Or was Kudzu trying to set me up? My plan to confront Abel falls limply at my feet.

"Tess!" My uncle almost trips in his hurry to follow me. "What—Where—When—"

"How, who, and why?" I finish. The emotion on my uncle's face causes my throat to squeeze, and I cough. "Thought you science types answered questions, Uncle A."

"You're alive! I can't believe it. *You're alive!*" Abel grabs me in a hard hug, words tumbling as if they can't find a place to land. "I can't—I just—I hoped, I did, but I never really thought—" He squeezes me into his chest and my defenses shatter.

"I'm sorry," I hear myself saying, my voice muffled against his neck. "Abel, I'm so sorry."

"Oh, Tessendra." Abel chokes. Eyes wet, he pulls back to study my face. As if it's the most important question in the world, he asks, "Are you okay?"

I nod, and am about to tell him "I'm fine" when I catch movement from the corner of my eye. A tall, slender boy stands near us, just a few feet away. Adrenaline bangs through my system. I shove Abel behind me and whip Mack from where I'd hidden him in my boot. "Who the hell are you?"

"Tess!" Abel's shocked voice is girlishly high. "Oh my, what in heavens are you doing with a knife like that?"

I'm not sure who is more startled, the boy or my uncle, both of whom evidently know each other. In the awkward pause that follows, the inappropriateness of my actions becomes painfully clear. I drop Mack to my side.

"Give me that." Abel pulls a handkerchief from his pocket and I let him gingerly extract Mack from my hand. Unsure what to do with the blade, he crosses to the dining room table and puts it down delicately.

The boy stares at me, unblinking. Everything about him is sharply defined, from the straight edge of his nose to the cut of his gaze. He says, "You said Tessendra Rockwood was dead."

"How do you know who I am?" I ask, hackles up.

My uncle quickly maneuvers himself between us, one eye still on Mack. "Tess, this is my assistant, Hunter Adams."

"Your assistant?"

Abel fingers his collar in a daze, flitting his attention from Mack back to me. "Yes, I'm still teaching neural engineering at a post-education center in the South Hills. Hunter is one of my students, and yes, a very good one." Abel turns to face the boy. "Hunter, this is my niece, Tess."

"I've seen your image on-cycle," Hunter says, stepping around Abel to offer me his hand. "You've changed your hair."

His handshake is efficient and doesn't linger. I can't talk to Abel about Aevum with a stranger in the room.

Abel coughs, inclining his head toward Mack. "Can you explain, er, that?"

I draw in a deep breath. "I've been living in the western part of the Badlands, in the outskirts of the Zone."

Abel and Hunter stare back at me.

"I was living near the Salt Flats and ended up helping this guy ride a bunch of camels to Potkamp, which is farther west. Rumor had it there was a freshwater spring there. But we didn't make it—long story—and I ended up in Kep Sai'an, working in a water bar..." I trail off, clocking how overwhelmed Abel looks. Maybe he didn't want that level of detail after all. "Real nice place," I finish lamely. "If you like death and dying and stuff."

Abel's eyes search mine. In a voice as soft as it is serious, he asks, "Why are you back?"

"I'm back because—" I catch myself twisting my hands together anxiously, so I drop them to my side. *Don't be nervous.* "Can I get a glass of water?"

"Would you like me to get that, Dr. Rockwood?"

I spin around to see a sleek, white substitute gazing at me politely. It's a much newer model than Robowrong. Its two spindly arms end with five dexterous-looking fingers, while its bottom half widens out into a bell shape. Above bright silver eyes, two white eyebrows slant up to give the impression of curious and helpful. A panel in its chest displays the time, the date, the temperature, and more. Below the panel, the word *Simutech* shines in mother-of-pearl. It would've come from Innovation, mom's old department.

Abel speaks noticeably slower to the substitute than he did to Hunter. "Kimiko, this is my niece, Tess Rockwood."

Its smooth, silicon body isn't distinctly male or female but it has a modulated female voice. "Tessendra Rockwood, niece." It whirs quietly. "Missing, presumed dead."

This time I almost laugh. "You should teach your little fembot better manners, Uncle A. Am I going to get that every time?"

"Why have you come home?" Abel repeats. "Why now?"

I meet my uncle's gaze with complete sincerity, aware how important it is that he believes me. "If I stayed out there any longer, I would've died. Fresh water's impossible to find, and I am so over eating *pourriture* for every meal. I missed real food and showers and my friends. And," I add, "I missed you."

I watch him process this, no idea if he believes it or not. "Well, where are you staying?" Before I can answer he goes on, "After you left, your home in the South Hills was reassigned. Everything was redistributed." He frowns doubtfully. "I can inquire as to getting some of your things back—"

"I don't want any of that stuff. I want—I need..." *I need to know if Ling is telling the truth. Are you really creating another artilect called Aevum?*

"What do you need, Tess?" Abel asks gently.

I take a deep breath. "A place to stay."

Abel's face relaxes into a smile. He comes over to grasp my shoulder, his eyes a little moist, his voice a little gruff. "I can certainly help with that."

"Dr. Rockwood?" Kimiko interrupts politely. "It is eight P.M. You are currently ten minutes behind schedule."

"What?" he asks, looking confused.

"Your staff meeting," Hunter says. "We need to go."

"Good heavens, yes. I'll have to cancel."

"No, that's okay," I say quickly. "You should go. All I want to do is shower and then sleep for a week."

"Absolutely not, Tess!" Abel exclaims. "I can't leave you alone. We have to talk—"

I cut him off by yawning like a jungle cat. "Talk? Sure," I say, affecting a sleepy tone. "But, later. Tired. So tired. Go to your meeting. I'll be fine."

Abel stares at me as if I've just started speaking Mal. "I'm not leaving you alone, Tess. Not after—" He shakes his head. "Kimiko, I need to reschedule. Go to the study, we'll comm from there—" Abel's voice breaks off. I catch a quick glance directed at a red door on the other side of the room. The door to the basement. It has a computerized lock on it, the type that requires a password for entry. That's never been there before. A basement door with a brand-new top-of-the-line lock stinks of top secret. Maybe Abel does have something to hide. Weirdly, I feel both thrilled and crushed by this.

I glance back at Abel. He's looking right at me—no, through me. I freeze. *He knows the real reason I'm here.* "What?" I ask nervously.

"You're your mother's daughter, Tess. No one can tell you what to do. Just like her." His mouth forms a small, sad smile. "Just like Frankie."

A spike of pain drives straight into my heart. I keep my face frozen.

"I'll be back in a jiffy," Abel continues, hands fluttering in front of him. "Hunter, wait here a moment. We still have to go over tomorrow's lecture." Then, calling over his shoulder to me: "Hunter can catch you up on what you've missed!" Disappearing through the living room and into his study, he leaves me alone with Hunter Adams.

Hunter clears his throat. I lift my eyes to his reluctantly. He offers a cautious smile, but it's more like an impression of a smile than the real thing. "Is there anything specific you want to know?" he asks.

"No." I drop my gaze to the rug in front of me and concentrate on finding patterns in its geometric design. A long, uncomfortable pause follows.

"Can I get you something?" he tries again. "A glass of water?"

I shake my head. The long, uncomfortable pause decides to put its feet up and stay awhile. Where is Abel? I thought he was in a hurry.

After a few more moments of awkward silence, Hunter wanders over to the table where Abel left Mack. He considers my knife with his arms folded in front of him, as if it might bite.

"So," he says thoughtfully, "you like knives."

The way he says it, so considered and without trying to be funny, actually makes me laugh. Hunter glances up, looking surprised but pleased at my outburst. "It was unexpected," he says. "Your entrance."

I bite my lip, smiling in spite of myself.

Hunter picks up Mack curiously, running long fingers over the worn, cream handle. His eyes flick back to mine. "What was it like out there?"

I can't articulate that to someone I've just met. "I don't know," I mutter softly.

He cocks his head at me, intrigued. "You don't speak English out there, right?"

"No," I say. His look of expectation morphs into a look of confusion, I assume at my inability to hold a normal conversation. "Malspeak," I tell him, somewhat unwillingly. "But we just call it Mal."

"You said you used to eat *pourriture*. Is that Mal?"

I nod, surprised he picked that up. "It's this disgusting porridge stuff."

"It's a portmanteau word, right? From the French?"

I frown. "What's a portmanteau word?"

"It's when you combine the meaning of two words into a new one." He furrows his brow, thinking aloud. "*Pourri* means 'rotten' and *nour-riture* means 'food.' So *pourriture* means 'rotten food' or 'bad food.' "

"That's right," I say, a little impressed. I guess it's meant to be ironic because French food used to be the best in the word, and *pourriture* is definitely the worst. But no one speaks old languages like French anymore. I only know the meaning because some local boy told me, tracing the words into the red dust with the tip of his finger. "You speak French?"

"Yes," he says, as if this isn't unusual. *"Pourriture. Pourriture."* Hunter rolls the word around his mouth with satisfaction. "That's so clever."

"You'd be less enthusiastic if you had to eat it," I tell him, and now it's his turn to smile. This time, it looks closer to the real thing. His curious, darting eyes seem to exude intelligence. A fast brain, my mom used to say. No wonder my uncle picked him to be his assistant.

Hunter places Mack back on the table, and I'm pleased to see he does it carefully. "So, why'd you leave?"

"What?" I ask, although I heard him just fine.

"Why did you leave Eden?"

I suddenly feel light-headed. "I, um..." My palms are sticky with sweat. I wipe them on the front of my dress. "Why did I... What?"

Hunter's eyebrows twitch down. "Are you all right?"

I swallow hard, glancing around. "It's just hot in here. Don't you think it's hot?"

"No." He eyes me uncertainly.

"I should go," I say, backing away from him. "I'm sorry, I have to—" My leg catches the edge of an end table, knocking a photogram over.

"What's the matter with you?"

I try to regain control of my voice, but it's wavering and unstable. "N-Nothing. I just should go unpack—"

"Okay, done!" Abel bustles back into the living room. "Managed to reschedule. Now, Hunter, why don't we just work from the study. You don't mind, do you? Tess, towels and sheets are—well, you know where they are."

I pull myself together and nod staunchly. "Sure."

Hunter's on his way to the study. From the corner of my eye, I see him cut me a sideways glance. I don't return it.

Abel turns back to me. "If you need anything, anything at all, I'll be right in here. And Tess?"

"Yes?"

Abel's smile is genuine and loving. "It's so good to see you again."

I wait until I hear the study door close. Then I fall into the sofa and press the bottoms of my palms into my eyes. I want to be swallowed up by the blackness I find there. Now that Hunter and Abel are gone, I can't hide from the memories.

I've sunbathed in the courtyard out back. I've burned ricotta pancakes in the kitchen that's tucked away around the corner. The old me is in this house. My mom is in this house. The past seems so close I could reach out and grab it.

C'mon, Tess. Get it together. Remember why you're here.

I make myself look over at the red door. If Abel is working for Simutech, he'd have a home lab set up. If the project is as classified as

Ling suggested, the lab would be behind lock and key. My uncle's security measures were always pretty predictable—I might be able to guess the password. But even the thought of doing that makes my blood feel icy.

Instead, I find myself picking up the photogram I knocked over on the end table. My eyes find my own. The framed three-second loop of Mom and me cuts through everything else. I remember when we recorded this. I can hear my mom's voice as clearly as if she were here now.

"Oh, Tess, you look beautiful!"

"Mom!" I spun around in surprise. My red dress whirled like a cape. "What are you doing home so early?"

"I only have a minute." She brushed my cheek with a kiss, before heading over to riffle through the mess on the dining room table.

"Should I wear this or the white one?"

"Red. You look like Joan of Arc."

I made a face. "'Dead martyr' wasn't what I had in mind."

Mom laughed. Her comm beeped, and she switched her attention to unrolling some scratch. "Is that boy taking you?" She wiggled her fingers as if trying to conjure up his name. "Matt . . . Zinney?"

"You mean Mark Manzino?"

"Right."

"He's taking someone else." I replied flatly. Of course he is. "I'm flying solo." Of course I am.

"Good," my mother said, with unexpected gravitas. She stopped fussing to meet my eyes, assessing me for a long, cool moment.

"What?" I asked. "Why are you looking at me like that?"

"I'm going to tell you something, Tess," she said. "Something important."

"Okay," I replied apprehensively. This was not Mom's typical parenting style.

"If you want to be happy in this world, you have to learn how to survive on your own. You don't need a partner."

I rolled my eyes. "It's my choice, I know—"

"I mean, you'd be better off independent," she said emphatically. "If you only rely on yourself, you'll never be let down. Partners

weaken us. Oh sure," she continued with a wave of her hand, "love is grand, love is flowers and sunsets, but love fades, Tessendra. Love is just a chemical called dopamine and that doesn't last."

I was stunned. She'd never said anything like that to me before. I felt confused and oddly embarrassed. But if she noticed the effect her words had on me, she didn't show it. In a flash, she was back to fussing around and getting ready—as always—to leave. "Honey, I have to go. Magnus is being particularly difficult today."

"Sometimes I think you love that dumb robot more than me," I said sourly.

"He's not dumb. And that's just ridiculous, Tess. I could never love anyone more than you." Her lithe fingers danced through the opaque clouds of nonsensical science jargon, moving them around at lightning speed.

"Let me put the white one on real quick," I pleaded.

"No, I have to go." She threw her arm around my shoulder, holding the scratch in front of us. In photo mode, it reflected our faces like a mirror. "Say Camembert!"

I'm half scowling through the three-second loop that follows, but I can see why Abel has it: you can't tell we were fighting seconds before she started recording us. I mutter *Camembert,* but then Mom elbows me in the ribs and I yelp in surprise, which looks charming. Then it starts again: just a flash of what looks like a loving if typically dysfunctional mom and her grumpy teen daughter, hamming it up for a photogram. Mom looks vibrant, as always—she was always more photogenic than I. She's wearing the necklace I wear now—the light catches the intricate hand-cut gold sword. I look so young in this loop. It's hard to believe it was only a year and a half ago. Young and naive.

Death started the life I now recognize as mine.

A scorching wave of tears rushes up and a painful, strangled gasp escapes my throat. I clamp my hand over my mouth. If I start crying now, I'll never be able to stop. I stare at the loop, at my mom's face. She was so beautiful. So bright and so alive.

"I'm sorry," I whisper at the loop. "Mom, I'm so sorry."

"Are you all right, Miss Rockwood?" I jump in fright. The eerie substitute is standing next to me.

"Y-Yes," I stutter in shock.

"Can I assist you with anything?" It rolls a little closer.

I scoot farther down the sofa. My voice shakes. "I'm fine."

It rolls closer still. "I'm detecting tremors in your vocal pattern, indicating discomfort. Can I assist you with anything?"

Irrationally, my heart is racing. My instincts are telling me to flee. *"Meiyou!"* I snap, slipping into Mal. "You stupid *fuega!*"

I'm cornered at the end of the sofa, having scrambled back as far as I can. Kimiko leans over me, a few inches from my face. "I'm sorry, I'm having trouble understanding you." Her creepy silver eyes drill into mine. Her voice seems to warp in my ears, coming from a mouth that does not move. "Can I assist you with anything?"

Terror seizes me. The eyes. The fact that she won't stop, even though I've told her to.

Magnus.

The ghostly echo of the day that changed everything; distorted, drawn-out words that feel like terror itself: *"Get. Away. From. My. Mother!"*

A cry escapes me, a shuddering release of fear. I push the thing away, knocking it over. I grab my backpack from the floor, snatch Mack from the table, then bolt for the stairs.

The guest room is dark when I fumble my way in, slamming the door behind me. My hands are shaking so badly, it takes forever to lock the door. *It's just a substitute,* I tell myself, over and over and over again. *It's just a stupid robot.*

I allow myself one, two great sobs, and then I steel myself. I make myself as cold and hard as a blade.

A noise. I stiffen, my body still clenched. A chirrup, like a bird. Kudzu. They're trying to send me one of those forest things. For a few seconds I just stand there in the darkened room while a high-pitched *cheep cheep cheep* cuts through the otherwise quiet night.

Then I'm moving. Unzipping my backpack. Pulling out Ling's scratch. Shoving it between the mattress and the base of the bed. Pushing it in deep, where the heavy mattress drowns out the bright, insistent sound.

These movements, unplanned, as if someone else is controlling my body, tell me with perfect clarity what I already know.

I will never join Kudzu.

I don't care about Abel's involvement.

And I want less than zero to do with this thing called Aevum.

chapter 4

I sleep like the dead, my body surrendering completely to ten hours of dreamless slumber in the most comfortable bed I've been in for a year. When I wake, my hand's under the pillow and scrambling for Mack before I remember where I am. I don't need to defend myself or hit the ground running. I'm back in Eden. I'm safe.

By Eden standards, the guest bedroom is sparsely furnished. But the flowing curtains that let in clear morning light and the soft carpet my feet sink into feel embarrassingly luxurious.

Towel in one hand, I uneasily face off against the shower. The neat guest bathroom is evidently rarely used, as a fine layer of dust lines the shower's ribbed floor. Thumb-sized bottles of shampoo, conditioner, and cleanser squat on a silver ledge.

A warm, gushing waterfall cascades around me. The water hits my skin in all the right places, like an all-over massage. I can't help groaning with pleasure as it drums into my shoulders, my back, my chest, my neck. I close my eyes and turn my face to the spray, letting it fall over my cheeks and forehead and scalp. I soap up my skin with an opaque goo that smells like ripe peaches. Layers of dirt and sweat and grime disappear in the bubbles. The sweet smell of peach mixes with the steam. I never want it to end. I want to stand here forever.

But as the dirty rivulets swirl down the drain at my feet, the pleasure starts to sour. This is more water than anyone in the Badlands gets in a month. And it feels good—*damn, it feels so good*—but I can't help feeling a little guilty. And then I can't enjoy it anymore. I dry myself with the soft, fluffy towel, feeling clean and refreshed and like I've done something wrong.

I comb my hair into something passing for neat and change into the dress Ling gave me. I wonder if the Tess of a year ago would've liked this dress. It feels like trying to recall memories that aren't even mine. I know for sure Izzy would love the way it *only just* covers my butt, which means I probably would've liked it too. The foggy bathroom mirror reflects the old me looking at the new me looking at the old me.

I do a terrible impression of myself.

"Ah, screw it," I mutter, and change into some Badlands clothes I have stuffed into my backpack. Loose black pants and a dark red tank top, both lousy with stains and sweat. I don't look entirely Eden, but if I get new clothes and a haircut, it shouldn't matter too much. This outfit only breaks social conventions, not actual laws.

I twirl Mack through my fingers and consider taking him with me, but I don't need his protection anymore. And besides, carrying weapons in Eden is illegal. I leave my old friend on the bedside table, looking decidedly out of place next to the cheery yellow lamp.

When I come downstairs, Abel is already at the dining room table. "Tess!" he exclaims eagerly. "Your heightened anabolic state has come to an end."

I translate this as "you're awake." He's flicking through a busy morning news stream, one hand curled around a cup of tea. Little clouds of stories about sports results, a buzzcar crash, and the set temperatures for the next few days hover about cheerfully. All so nice. All so normal.

"Morning," I say.

"Sleep well?"

"Like a baby with a hangover."

"Like a what?" he asks, thrown.

"Sorry." I smile, biting my lip. "Badlands expression. It means I slept well."

"What a colorful phrase," he says diplomatically, before stifling a yawn.

He has bags under his eyes. "What about you?" I ask curiously. "You look beat and it's not even nine A.M."

His fingers tighten around his cup. "I must admit, having you back is somewhat surreal. I didn't sleep a wink."

"Sorry," I mutter softly, sliding into a chair across from him.

"You don't have to apologize," he says. "It was hard for all of us, but it must've been hardest on you." Abel peers at me, eyes bright despite the bags. "Are you sure there's nothing you want to talk about?"

My nails dig into my palms and I smile tightly. "Nope."

"Well, how about some breakfast?"

"Sure."

"Kimiko!" he calls. "Our guest requires some breakfast."

The fembot zips around my backpack toward me. "What would you like to eat, Tess?"

I blink fast a couple times. I'm back in Eden now. These sophisticated, silver-eyed substitutes are just something I'll have to get used to.

The fembot repeats itself, "What would you like to—?"

"I don't know," I cut it off. I haven't ordered breakfast in a year.

Abel answers for me. "Just some fruit is fine."

Lucky for me, robots don't hold a grudge. Kimiko rolls off to the kitchen without another word.

"I was thinking we could have dinner together tonight," Abel says.

I raise an eyebrow. "We haven't even had breakfast yet."

"I mean, a special dinner. To celebrate your homecoming."

"Okay." I nod, trying not to feel wildly overparented.

"Kimiko will do the cooking. The kitchen isn't really my forte. She's been a real addition. Very helpful." Abel begins chattering blithely about Kimiko's make and model: she's called a Companion, very articulate, designed to be socially intelligent and synergistic with everyday life. . . . I nod politely, trying to gauge the subtext of what's going on. He seems nervous. The shock of my return? Uncertainty about our future? Or guilt about his involvement in something that sent me to the Badlands in the first place? I suppose it could be all three.

I eat Kimiko's fruit salad obediently, savoring the sweet slices of nectarines and plums. Good, healthy food was a part of my old life. As I crunch a green grape between my teeth, I almost swoon. *Showers. Soft beds. Fresh fruit. Why did I ever leave?*

And so when Abel asks me what I'm going to do today, I don't hesitate.

"I'm going to see Izzy."

Izzadore Lucy Williams and I met on the first day of pre-education. I'd been busy stealing all the coveted golden building blocks from the communal stash in order to make a castle. When the teacher finally worked out that someone wasn't playing fair, she gently suggested I show her what was under the basket behind me. When I did, nothing was there. The blocks were gone. Izzy sat a few feet away, a pint-sized picture of adorable innocence. Under her cute ruffled skirt hid a treasure trove of gold. We split the blocks, then worked a two-man scam on Alby Peterson for his milk and pudding cup. We'd been partners in crime ever since.

Part teddy bear, part shyster, that's how she'd always been. I'm average for my height, but Izzy clocks in at five foot two. Her enormous dark blue eyes rimmed with ridiculously long lashes give her a look of perpetual naïveté, which we often used to our advantage. She commanded male and female attention effortlessly and collected broken hearts for a hobby. She was excellent.

Izzy's father is a Guider, which means they live in one of the South Hills houses that have a killer view *and* a pool. Even though every house in Eden is supposedly as good as the last, some are simply more advantaged, and people who work for the Trust are always given the "advantages." We'd spend our weekends soaking up the sun by the pool, workshopping our love lives—hers: colorful, mine: nascent—and starting rumors about people we didn't like.

But then Mom died and I left. I have no idea how she'll feel about seeing me. Betrayed? Ecstatic? Furious? For all her wickedness, Izzy is, at her core, a total sweetheart who always had my back. I didn't even say goodbye.

"I'm heading out!" I call to Abel, who'd disappeared into his study after breakfast. "I'll see you later!"

"Tess. Greetings." Abel's assistant, the tall boy I met yesterday, emerges from the study.

I've completely forgotten his name. Harrison? Hugo? "Hey, um—"

"Hunter," he supplies, unfazed at my faux pas. Physically he's neither particularly good- or bad-looking—mop of dark hair that looks uncombed, typically pale Eden skin, thickish eyebrows above eyes that could be gray or green. It's his unselfconscious focus on me that's the point of difference.

"Hunter, right." I laugh, shifting awkwardly in his gaze. "Sorry. Bad with names. Surprised you remembered mine."

He cocks his head at me. "Tess Rockwood, the missing niece who returns after a year in the Badlands? That tends to make an impression."

I wince. No wonder he's staring at me. Most Edenites never leave the city, even for a night. "What's up?"

"Abel said to come say hello," he says, inclining his head toward the study.

"Abel said to come say hello," I repeat in confusion. "Why?"

An embarrassed smile colors his face. His gaze drops to floor. *"I wanted to come and say hello,"* he corrects himself.

"Oh." I nod. I'm momentarily unsure of how to react to this level of social awkwardness. My fingers worry the gold sword on my necklace. "So, he's got you working weekends, huh?"

"Yes," Hunter replies. "He's a gauche slave driver who is guileful and malevolent in nature."

I blink. "He's a what-now?"

"I was being sarcastic," Hunter clarifies quickly. "Or trying to be, I guess."

And suddenly, a new level of awkwardness has been reached. "Well, have fun with that," I say, edging for the front door. "I'm going to get a makeover. An Eden makeover."

His eyes examine my face as if I were a science experiment. "You don't need a makeover."

I hook up an eyebrow. "Sarcasm and you do not a fine match make."

And it's his turn to blink in confusion, just for a second, before his face clears into understanding. "I wasn't being sarcastic," he says simply. "See you later, Tess."

"Bye, Hunter."

"You remembered!" I hear him call out as I head down the hallway. I roll my eyes, a faint smile teasing my mouth. What. A. Weirdo.

Joggers huff and puff past me, lightly sweating in all-white exercise suits. I scan their faces intently. Izzy never used to miss her Sunday jog: *How can I demand physical perfection in others if I'm not committed to it myself?* My foot jiggles with nerves. I feel a bit sick—lucky I didn't have a big breakfast.

Just as I'm about to give up hope, I see her. She's changed her hair. An elegant pixie cut shows off her heart-shaped face and makes her look a few years older. She's chatting with a cute little sub that hovers next to her as she runs. It's soft and cuddly, with snow-white fur and eyes as big as hers. Izzy always did prefer the adorable designs to the more functional types. She's just about to run right past when I call out a tentative "hey!"

She glances up and promptly stumbles to a stop. Her eyes widen as she pants, catching her breath, face frozen in a comical mask of shock.

I wave an unsure hello. "Never thought I'd see Izzy Williams lost for words."

"Metabolism slowing," chirrups her sub. "Continue jogging to achieve—"

Izzy hushes it. It buries its head in her neck, purring. She waves it away distractedly, eyes locked into mine.

"Tess?" Her voice is deep with disbelief.

"In the flesh." I nod, swallowing. *Please be happy to see me.*

Her eyes race frantically around my dyed black ponytail and shaggy undercut, my grimy clothes, my dirt-caked boots. "Where have you been? You just—Tess, where have you been?"

"Away?" I offer tentatively. "But I'm back now." I exhale a breath I didn't even know I'd been holding. "It's really good to see you, Iz."

"You're...you're so skinny," she says. Then her eyes bug. "You got a tronic?" She flips my wrist to get a better look at the four words that glow under my forearm: *No feeling is final.* "*You* got a tronic?" She sounds equal parts disbelieving and disappointed. Izzy and I were going to get electronic tattoos together, the day we graduated education. We'd spent hours arguing over what to get: a heart, a leaf, the word *beautiful,* the word *true.* But whatever it was, it would be the same.

I make a noncommittal noise, tugging my arm out of her grasp.

She blinks, words stumbling, hands waggling. "You look so—"

"Disheveled, tired, scraggy, wild?" Izzy's sub buzzes helpfully, hovering at her head like a friendly ghost.

"*Different,*" Izzy finishes. We lock eyes. A huge, excited, overwhelmed smile bursts onto her face. "*Tess!*" She squeals, leaping forward to kiss me flush on the mouth and throw both arms around my neck. I go to hug back, but before I can, she pulls herself from me. Her face is screwed in disgust. "Oof. Tess, you *stink.*"

"Oh." I smile, giving my top a sniff. "Yeah. Guess that's part of the story."

I see a clutch of white-suited joggers heading toward us, and instinctively move off the path, drifting into the trees behind us. Izzy trots along next to me, eyes unable to leave mine. As we walk, I start with her small questions: I'm fine; I'm staying with Abel; yes, you're the first friend I contacted; no really, I'm fine. Then I answer the big one. "I've been in the Badlands."

The news cuts through her like an electric shock. "The Badlands?" She gapes. "As in, the *Badlands* Badlands?"

"Yup."

"On your own—for the whole *year*?"

"After Mom died, I just needed a change."

"I never got the chance to tell you how sorry I was to hear about her." She shudders, stopping to face me. "So awful, Tess. I can't imagine . . . I mean, the thing she was working on. What was it?"

"Magnus." The word is an unwilling whisper.

"That's it. I had no idea it was actually dangerous." She stares up at me, expression pained and pitiful. "Are you okay? I know it was ages ago, but . . . I wished you'd commed. You just left. You were just gone—"

"I know," I say. "I'm really sorry." I grimace. "Can we change the topic?"

Without skipping a beat, Izzy says, "Sure." The air is warm around us, heavy with summer scents and the light trills of birds. We're heading toward a more populated part of the park. Around us, families are out picnicking and tossing Frisbees. Izzy links her arm into mine, a gesture so familiar it's almost automatic. "So," she says, trying for upbeat, "what are we doing today?"

"Actually," I say, "I need your help."

Izzy wrinkles her nose. "I hope it's help with your dirty clothes situation."

I laugh. Already I'm feeling lighter. "It is. Your father's still a Guider, right?"

"Daddy dearest surely is. Day off today, though."

"Which means he's working in the garden?" I guess.

She nods, grinning, pulling me closer to her. "It's like you never left!"

"Excellent." I grin back. "Now, I don't exactly need to break any rules . . ."

"Just bend them into pretty new shapes?" She blinks coquettishly. "Luckily, I am in a *very* flexible mood."

I tell Izzy I lost my ID in the Badlands, and the border control official said to get a new one when I was back. I tell her I want to see her dad because that process takes days, and I want a new ID now. The truth is the panel of Guiders I'd have to present this story to at a local meet would see through it in a heartbeat.

Izzy's house is just as light and airy as I remember it, all stainless steel and sparkling glass. I'm a little winded from the walk up, but the view across Eden still takes my breath away. The curved glass skyscrapers in the Hive catch the light brilliantly, as do the glittering solar panels on the roof of the house below. I can even glimpse parts of Moon Lake way up in the north, shining like sunlight on a mirror. It really is a stunningly beautiful city.

Izzy dismisses her sub, who burrows into a sofa like a white furry cushion. I wait next to it while she changes out of her exercise suit. I used to love coming to Izzy's house. Compared to mine, it was so clean and perfect. Their pantry was always full and her mom was always whipping up snacks: cheese and spinach triangles or homemade lemon gelato. But now it feels different. Empty and too quiet, like I'm waiting for someone after everyone else has gone home.

Izzy emerges wearing a floaty yellow dress and heeled sandals. "Pretty," I say, and in response she curtsies, smirking at me. Then we head out to the back deck to look for her dad, who'll be lost in a maze of flower beds and potting mix. The crystal clear water of their pool sparkles invitingly. As always, it's a perfect day for a swim.

Izzy cracks her knuckles. "Want me to do the talking?" It sounds more like a statement than a question.

"I can do it," I reply.

She throws me a sideways glance. "You sure? I don't mind."

"I'm sure," I say, spotting her dad raking an empty flower bed. "Ready for a big reaction?"

Izzy bought my story unquestioningly, but her dad is more suspicious.

"You're not supposed to be able to cross the border without ID." He frowns. Izzy takes after her mom; Mr. Williams is long-limbed and wiry—a man-sized toothpick. He wipes a dirt-stained gardening glove across his brow, leaving a dark smudge. "Maybe I should comm them to make sure. Which crossing did you say you came through?"

Izzy opens her mouth to jump in, but before she can, I fix him with a sincere gaze. "Mr. Williams, I've been away from Eden for a year—a year too long. I just want my old life back. Please? I wouldn't ask if it were't important."

"Yeah, *c'mon*, Daddy!" I should've known Izzy wouldn't be able to keep her mouth shut. "I mean, look at her! It's criminal such a hot girl is forced to look this way."

He chuckles nervously. "All right," he acquiesces. "Just this once."

Whereas Abel's study is all dark wood and dust motes, Mr. Williams's study has floor-to-ceiling windows and a long clear desk that's perfectly spotless. He pops open a drawer to reveal a roll of bright blue scratch. Guider scratch. Their exclusive portal to the Trust.

"I'll take a new loop for you," he says. "But I need to actualize the ID alone." He means print it, in a special 3D printer that can produce official objects for Guiders. And he means alone because only Guiders are allowed to open blue scratch. We're not even allowed to watch.

"Thanks, Mr. Williams."

He smiles at me fondly. "Only because I know I can trust you, Tess."

Of course. If nothing else, the Trust has taught us to trust: in them and in each other.

I smile back at him.

The Hive feels... sanitized. I don't mean everyone's walking around like they're lobotomized. People chat or laugh or look bored as they go about their business. Substitutes of all shapes and sizes glide, whiz or stride to keep pace with their owners. But there's no underlying urgency. When a buzzcar backfires in a vertical ascent, I'm the only one who cowers. It's as if no one ever told Edenites that life can be dangerous.

What strikes me the most is the sound. In the Badlands, people play handmade instruments—upturned bins for drums, a piece of metal strung with string. When we danced, it was barefoot, stomping our feet into the hard dirt in raw release. It was music that defied, music that celebrated, music that kept us going. In the Hive, classical music drifts from unseen sources. It's as elegant and precise as fine china.

Shimmering holos of Gyan are everywhere. Pearls of his infamous wisdom ripple under the image of our bearded, beatific leader: *Freedom for the self is freedom for the whole. All are equal, equal is all. Evolution, enlightenment, en masse: Eden.* Each of them bears the Trust logo: the swirling white *T* enclosed in a yellow-trimmed blue circle. Either more appeared after I left or, more likely, I just didn't notice how many there are. As we pass through one, the hard flash of light makes me shiver.

In order to begin my much-needed makeover, Izzy drags me into her favorite new boutique. We'll use my new ID to collect clothes. Because I haven't used my Goods Allowance in a year—the Allowance we have for everyday, essential items like clothes, homewares, education supplies—I have a ton of credit.

Izzy marches inside like she means business. I trail behind. Funny—this used to be our old dynamic. Even though I always thought of us as equals, ultimately Izzy called the shots. I was always along for the ride. It never used to bother me. It's just the way it was. But it's different now.

"*This* is cute, and so is *this* and *this* and *this*!" Izzy emerges with an armful of dresses—swaths of pale, pretty cloth. "You *have* to get this one, it's just to *die* for."

"Actually," I say, "I'm just going to try these on."

"Pants?" She reacts like I've held up a clown suit. "You don't wear *pants*."

"I have a top too," I argue, holding up a black V-neck.

"Very...utilitarian." Izzy shakes her head, unable to compute. "You can get anything in this store, and this is what you want? Seriously?"

"I'm not really in a dresses mood right now."

"But these would all look amazing on you," she insists. "You *have* to get at least one."

I used to buy whatever Izzy suggested. I realize how unused to following orders I am now, even orders from a friend. But I don't want to upset her.

"I just have so much to do now that I'm back, and dresses aren't as practical," I say in my most reasonable voice. "Next month, for sure."

She sighs, relenting. "Fine." Then, with a consoling grin: "Guess I'll have to try this on myself."

The pants and top fit well, both made from a fine hemp that feels strong and resilient. And I like how I look in them too. *Capable* is the first word that comes to mind. How weird—that's never been an adjective of any importance to me until now. The tag inside both the shirt and the pants says, "Made in the Zone." No wonder they're so well made. Substitutes sewed these strong seams. For a moment I consider not getting these clothes as a protest, and collecting clothes from someplace else, before I realize there *isn't* a someplace else. Unless I want to make my own clothes, I have to get items created in the Manufacturing Zone.

"Hey, Tess?" Izzy calls out. I peek out from behind my curtain. Izzy stands in the center of the fitting rooms wearing the flimsy dress she'd wanted me to try on. And nothing underneath. She twirls provocatively. "How does it look?"

Where I'm flat and sinewy, Izzy's got more curves than the South Hills. She's hot and she knows it. I give her an unimpressed shrug. "It's fine," I tell her with deliberate boredom. "Bit frumpy."

"Bitch!" she exclaims with a grin. She goes to swat me but I duck out of reach. She starts giggling, which makes me start giggling. "I'm getting a second opinion."

And with that she flounces out into the store, basically naked. I shouldn't be surprised, but I am. Izzy has shock value down to a fine art. She wouldn't last five seconds in the Badlands.

I end up getting five tops, three pairs of pants, a black jacket, and a random selection of socks, undershirts, and underwear. I stopped wearing a proper bra in the Badlands because no one else wore one. Now they feel too restrictive, and I'm too flat-chested to really need one. At the last minute, I let Izzy switch my black jacket for a blood-red one, which actually looks pretty badass. As a delicate-looking sales assistant scans my new ID, I tell her I'll wear my new clothes out of the store.

"Sure thing," she says, nodding at the Badlands shirt and pants in my hand. "Do you need a bag for your old clothes?"

"No," Izzy answers for me flatly. She's behind me, fully clothed and fiddling in her purse. "You can burn them."

"Oh, c'mon," I tease her. "Don't you want to keep them?" I wave the clothes in her face. "They'd look great on you."

She smacks at my hand. "Get those away from me."

I blink. "C'mon, Iz. I was kidding."

"Well, I'm serious, they're disgusting. I can't believe—" She catches herself and shakes her head, just once. Her eyes are flashing with a hardness I've never seen before. "Never mind. Let's go."

Without another word, she turns and strides out.

The clear sound of two bells rings out across the Hive as I hurry to catch up with her. Two o'clock. I'd been hungry for lunch but now my appetite is gone. When I reach Izzy, she addresses me with a cool, no-nonsense expression. "You should use your Pleasure Allowance for a cut in Charity." She means getting a designer cut with a stylist, instead of using my Goods Allowance for a standard style at an ordinary barber.

I nod, wanting to make peace. "Should we take an airbus?"

Home to most of Eden's artisans, the colorful and charming Charity oozes an effortless hip feel. Post-ed students squat on wooden crates in the coffeehouses to discuss art and philosophy and poetry. Street healers offer everything from reiki to aura cleansing. Storytellers tell tall tales in underground performance spaces, while dancers spin through the plazas, silk ribbons rippling out behind them. By the time we jump off the clean, spacious airbus, being back in our favorite part of Eden has cut the chill between us. Izzy's fingers curl into mine, pulling me into the salon she's chosen.

My stylist's name is Starfish. He's well over six feet tall and skeleton-thin, with large, luscious lips that curl down in a permanent pout. Bangs flop over one eye. The one I can see regards me suspiciously as I sit down in front of the mirror, black cape around my shoulders to protect my clothes. "Sooo, what are we doing today?" Starfish has a habit of drawing out his vowels.

"Cut and color," Izzy answers. "For the cut, I'm thinking something girly, sophisticated, definitely cute, a little bit sexy?"

"Okaaaay," drawls Starfish. "And color?"

Again, Izzy takes the floor. "You wouldn't know it, but she's a natural blonde."

Starfish feels the texture of my coarse black hair reluctantly, speaking to Izzy via the mirror I'm sitting in front of. "I can use henna to warm this into a nice chocolate brooown."

"Perfect." Izzy nods.

"Do I get a say in this?" I ask, half amused, half annoyed.

Izzy rests her hands on my shoulders. "No offense, Tess, but the decisions you've been making lately have been pretty freakish," she says sincerely. Then, as if speaking to a child: "Lucky you've got me to help guide you back to the world of the sane and the stylish. Oh," she adds to Starfish, "and lose the weirdo plaits with the feathers."

"No." I pull back, my fingers moving to my Badlands plaits protectively. "I like them. Leave them."

Starfish frowns. "But I need to unbraid them for the color—"

"I said, leave them."

After washing my hair, Starfish wraps the three plaits in tinfoil, not bothering to hide his distaste. Then he mixes the color and starts working the cool, sticky mixture through. I'm not in a talkative mood, so I let him tell a long-winded story about a fight he'd gotten into last night with his boyfriend that involved a disagreement over a gray scarf. Izzy flicks through a fashion stream using the salon's scratch, one eye on me, one eye on a flashing carousel of woven straw purses.

Washing the henna out seems to take forever. I'm overly conscious of the amount of gushing warm water Starfish is using. As it gurgles into the basin behind me, I find myself calculating what I'd do with it if I was still out there. Wash everything I own. Bottle it and keep it somewhere safe. No, sell it in Zhukov's bar and live like a king.

Back at the mirror, Starfish unwraps the plaits and then starts drying my hair with a hair dryer. Wet, it looks the same color as before, but as it dries it looks...pretty, turning my ordinary brown eyes the color of rich milk chocolate. When I run my fingers through it, it feels as soft as lamb's wool. Starfish swats my hand away. "No touching the masterpiece until I'm finished."

Even though I like how it looks, all the water needed for this whole production gnaws at me. The more I think about it, the more flat-out ridiculous it seems. I make the mistake of mentioning this to Izzy.

"Yeah." She nods, swishing through a collection of light pink tops. "Totally."

"Izzadore." That catches her attention. "You're not listening to me. This is a waste of water."

"No, it's part of your allowance," she corrects me. "When you get your hair colored, that uses some of your Lake Allowance, right?"

Starfish nods in agreement. "Sooome."

"That doesn't change the fact that I just used a week's worth of water coloring my hair," I say. Then, after Starfish's look of confusion, I add, "A week's worth for someone living in the Badlands."

"I don't think so." Starfish sniffs. "Not a week's worth."

"It's true. I was just—"

"Tess," Izzy warns.

"I was just there."

Starfish glances at Izzy, and for the first time, I see something real and human on his face. Alarm. Izzy's lips are pressed together so tight that they're white. Starfish clears his throat uncertainly. "So, your cut. Let's start by losing these." He twists his fingers around my three thin plaits and gives them a sharp tug.

"Ow!" I exclaim. "I said leave them." I jerk away from him. My face is hot. I feel sweat on my brow. In a voice that's unexpectedly loud, I blurt out, "Edenites should be using less water. And it was wrong of Gyan to cut off Moon Lake."

The salon goes dead silent, as if everyone has frozen at once. Izzy's mouth drops open. Starfish laughs nervously, high and weird. I glance around. The other customers click their gazes away quickly, but two older women with heads full of tinfoil glare back at me with ugly disapproval. Publicly denouncing Gyan is a crime against the state. Plus, everyone has a comm, and everyone has scratch. Everything I just said could've easily been recorded. The air feels like it's alive with electricity, the tension so palpable I can feel it on my skin. The thought repeats itself, giddy, elated, and panicked. *I just broke the law.*

Izzy is staring at me, her chest visibly rising and falling. "We should go," I say, whipping the cape off my shoulders and grabbing my bag of clothes from the boutique.

In what has to be a first, Izzy is silent as we book it out of the salon. And the only thing she says when I say we need to talk is, "Where?"

Animal Gardens are the extensive grounds that form part of Eden's Central Zoo. Animals that don't need to be locked up are free to roam in habitats curated especially for them, making the gardens educational as well as beautiful. I lead Izzy to the glass-enclosed rain forest.

Here, the air is humid and sticky-warm, alive with the ringing chorus of tree frogs. We move along a slatted wooden walkway, deeper into jungly scrub. The vines overhead form deep shadows. We're the only ones here, the steamy air proving too unpleasant for most Edenites. It's also completely off-cycle: the educational streams that defined plant species, bird calls, and animals had to be taken out a few years ago after the humidity kept corroding the scratch.

My feet move soundlessly along the damp wooden walkway. Izzy lags behind. We haven't spoken since the salon. Even though I'm wired, my brain playing what I said in the salon on repeat, being here is taking the edge off. I don't want to fight with Izzy. I want to talk. I breathe in the smell of fresh, wet green and blow it out through my lips, trying to calm the insistent *tap tap tap* of my heart.

Through the trees, I glimpse a tall, ungainly bird pecking around a tree trunk. It's a dodo. Years ago, Abel worked on bringing the once-extinct bird back to life. There's something distinctly comical about its tiny eyes, bulbous beak, and oversized feet. I go to point it out to Izzy, but she's too far behind. By the time she catches up, the dodo is gone.

Eventually, the path widens to form a deck overlooking clear water rushing down wet, mossy rocks. Fine spray dampens our hair and clothes.

Izzy turns to face me, her voice raised to be heard over the burble of tumbling water. "Look, I get it. You've been through a lot. You're not thinking straight." She sighs, placing one small hand on my arm indulgently. "I forgive you, okay?"

I frown. "Iz, I didn't bring you here to apologize."

She blinks and drops her hand. "You didn't?"

I take a deep breath. "I need to talk to you. About the Badlands."

Izzy freezes. Her voice drops a full octave. "What?"

"What I said in the salon, it's true. It's—"

But Izzy cuts me off with a raised palm. "Tess," she says, swallowing hard. "I am really trying here. Okay? I am really friggin' trying. But this, this Badlands stuff? I just cannot—" She spins away from me for a second, just a second, before whirling back, eyes glittering. "I thought you were dead, Tess. I thought you were friggin' *dead*. And then you show up, and you're like, 'No, I'm fine, I was just in the Badlands'—the friggin' *Badlands*. And you're acting like, like I'm not supposed to freak out, like we're just going to go back to normal." She's pacing before me, words pouring out of her. "And at first I felt like, great. Yeah. Let's go back. Because I loved the way things were. I friggin' loved it. You were my *best friend*." Izzy's voice cracks and she struggles to keep it even. "I don't get it." She stops to face me, mouth working. I know she's trying hard not to cry. "I don't get what is happening."

I stare at the waterfall, at the tumbling, endless water gushing into the rockpool. "People are starving out there, Izzy," I say. "They live on a bowl of *pourriture* a day. Kids, Iz. Kids live like that."

She shakes her head in confusion. "What's *poo-rita*?"

I shake my head, trying to arrange my thoughts. "It's not important. Look. All *this* exists because people out there are dying and the Trust is letting it happen. They're *making* it happen."

Izzy rolls her eyes. "Don't be so dramatic. It's not that bad."

"I'm telling you it is," I explain incredulously. "*I was there.* We have to do something about it."

"Do something about it?" Izzy repeats scornfully. "What are you going to do, Tess?"

I shake my head, caught out. "I . . . I don't know. I only know I have to change things."

Izzy looks at me with gentle pity. She sighs, and softens her voice. "Tess, this is just the way things worked out. We ended up the lucky ones." She puts one hand on my arm and gives it a reassuring squeeze. "Look, I'm not totally heartless. I care about the Badlands, sure I do. But we're in Eden and they're out there. You can't change that. So you may as well just enjoy it."

I twist my arm out of her grasp.

Izzy just stares at me. I know she doesn't care. I know because I didn't used to either.

Then, after a few moments, Izzy says in a voice as small as a ladybug, "I feel like I don't even know you anymore."

Suddenly, I am overcome with exhaustion. "I feel like I don't know me either," I say blankly. I sink down onto the wooden bench and lean my head back against the railing. A family of spider monkeys swings through the tops of the tall trees above me, a canopy of endless, tangled green.

Izzy sits down next to me. "*I* know you," she says. "The old you. Tess Rockwood: fun and loyal and up for anything. *Tess Rockwood:* smart, way smarter than me." She draws in a deep breath, gaze dropping to the wooden walkway under our feet. "I've been thinking a lot about you since you left." Her eyes find mine again. "Maybe I stopped you from doing stuff you wanted to do?"

"What stuff?" I ask.

She shakes her head, overwhelmed. "I don't know, all that science stuff. You were always so into it. Maybe I was...mean about it, sometimes?"

I'm stunned. Izzy doesn't apologize, and more importantly, I'd always thought she had little to no self-awareness.

"Maybe," I say hesitantly.

She takes both my hands with hers. "I won't be like that anymore. I'll be...whatever, supportive. Just forget the Badlands, Tess. Please. I missed you so much."

I always thought Izzy was the most rebellious person I'd ever met. But now I see that we weren't rebels at all. I pull my hands gently out of hers. "I'm sorry," I say. "I can't."

When I get up to leave, Izzy doesn't try to stop me.

chapter 5

When I wave my new ID over the scanner next to the front door, it swings open with a chime. Abel either forgot to take me off his home access list or recently added me back on. I'm betting it's the former. The smell of rich and pungent cooking greets me as I wander down the hallway. "Hello? Uncle A?"

Kimiko whizzes out from the kitchen. "Good evening, Tessendra."

"It's Tess," I tell the fembot curtly. "Only my family calls me Tessendra, and you ain't—"

But my words are cut off by the sight of the dining room table. It looks ready to host Gyan himself. Abel's best silver cutlery spreads out from gleaming china plates. White linen napkins nestle inside red mechanical bolts that have been upcycled as hip napkin rings. Curls of butter sit in shallow glass dishes made from the bottoms of wine bottles. A large white candleholder carved with intricate floral detail holds no less than seven handmade candles. They flicker gently in the middle of the table, making everything feel positively regal.

"Tess!" Abel glances up from a news stream he's watching and quickly lowers the volume with his eyes. His face is gray with exhaustion, but the sight of me inspires a smile that looks genuine. "You're just in time. You didn't forget about dinner, did you?"

I had. But the smell of food cooking makes my stomach rumble loud enough for us to both hear and I realize I haven't eaten since breakfast. Dinner sounds pretty good right about now. "Course not," I tell him, before gesturing vaguely in the direction of my room. "I'm just going to...wash up."

In the darkness, my yellow room looks like it's painted in black and white and shades of gray. I sink down on the edge of my mattress, grateful for the quiet. It's hard to believe it's only been twenty-four hours since I crossed back. I lie back on the bed and let my body settle into the softness. I wish it could pull me under.

Things aren't exactly on track. My plan to not see Abel? Fail. Plan to become an Edenite again? Double fail. Plan to reconnect with Izzy? Triple times a million fail.

Did I overreact with Iz? Was she right, that this is just the way things are? Is Kudzu a real alternative or just a bunch of deluded kids on a one-way street to being banished?

Kudzu. I stood Ling up today. I picture her confusion, then her anger. The scratch she gave me is still buried under my mattress. I wonder where the dead zone is. Maybe I should check.

I can tell she's sent me more than one of those holos because of the sound: a menagerie of beeps and chirrups. When I smooth it open, I'm accosted by half a dozen baby animals. A feather-tailed squirrel races up my arm. An owl swoops around my head while a goofy-looking badger ambles onto my thigh, all talking to me at once.

"Meet behind the old filtration plant in Lakeside, thirteen-hundred hours."

"Where are you? Meet behind the old filtration plant."

"Tess, is something wrong?"

"It's sixteen-hundred. I'm leaving."

And then, delivered from the same adorable blue-and-yellow baby bird Ling first used, the final message: "You'll regret this."

The holos all disappear, leaving me alone in the dark.

You'll regret this. Is it a threat? Is Kudzu coming after me? Or does she just mean my own conscience will punish me? Somehow, that prospect feels even worse.

"Tess!" Abel's voice floats up from downstairs.

Ling said this scratch was off-cycle. That means I can use it without being recorded. Even if I never see Kudzu again, I am still curious about Abel and Aevum. I don't even know what that word means. *Magnus* is Latin for "great;" the name of ancient kings, powerful dukes, and noble saints of the past. But *aevum?* I don't even know if it's a real word.

I could enter the streams to find out.

"Tess?"

"Just a minute!" I call back.

The gold scratch glows bright, ready for action. I take a deep breath. Then, in a quiet, clear voice, I open the streams. "Show me *aevum.*"

The streams burst into light around me, a dense but lovely web of objects and text and information. The holo of a smiling, neatly presented woman settles in front of me. Her tone is modulated and pleasant. "*Aevum*, Latin, meaning 'age' or 'everlasting time.'" As she speaks, separate bubbles appear to show me the word, spinning out into the meanings that continue to load. I catch unfamiliar words like *aeon* and *aeviternity*. "Ancient philosophers believed the aevum was the temporal experience of angels and celestial beings," the woman continues. "Societies of the past believed that unlike God, who experienced time as infinite, and humankind, who experienced time as finite, the aevum was how angels experienced time and the world." The woman continues to talk as the streams spin and whirl to show me angels—some rosy-cheeked cherubs who loll languidly, some tortured-looking men with eyes raised to their maker above.

I'm not used to being in the streams off-cycle. If I'd been on-cycle, I'd already have dozens of people sharing this with me; my friends trying to pull me into a concert or a random party, or strangers wanting to chat about all this weird medieval stuff. Everyone's avatars would be bouncing and spinning around me—Izzy's was a purring kitten. Mine was a tiny thunderstorm, complete with lightning and rolling black clouds. Being off-cycle feels a little lonely. But it also feels safe.

Now original texts scroll before me. Black letters squash together unevenly, primitive in their awkward imperfection. The language is foreign to me, but *aevum* is helpfully highlighted with a soft glow. I wave my hand over the pages. The woman flickers for a moment, then starts explaining. "Here you see the first mention of the aevum in a treatise written in the thirteenth century by the saint Albertus Magnus—"

What? I swish my fingers to start it again. But I didn't mishear. Albertus *Magnus*.

"Tess!" Abel's voice rings out for the third time, shorter and more annoyed.

"Coming!" I call impatiently.

Aevum is how angels are supposed to experience the world. According to myth, angels are special, powerful, inhuman. All words that could be applied to artilects.

I hate to admit it but the idea of Aevum as the code name for an artilect is Abel to a tee. Clever, cerebral, based in the classics. Plus the fact it was created by someone called Magnus, that it *came from* Magnus, just as the second attempt would inevitably be born from the first. The connection seems inevitable.

"Tess." He's right outside my door. Quick as a flash, I scrunch the scratch into a ball. The aevum stream disappears a split second before Abel sticks his head into my room. "Dinner's ready."

Abel smiles at me from across the table, pulling the napkin from its red-bolt ring and shaking it out over his lap. "So, what did you get up to with Izzadore?"

"I, ah, got some clothes," I say. "And dyed my hair."

"Ah, yes," he says, squinting at it. "Very fetching." I am 100 percent sure he cannot make out any noticeable difference.

"What about you?" I ask, toying with my fork. "How was your day?"

A grimace flares across his face. "Trying."

"Hard day at post-education?"

"Yes," he agrees. "Hard day at post-education."

Or a hard day at Simutech. I eye him, trying to work out if he's telling the truth.

"Speaking of education," he says. "We'll have to reenroll you for your final year. It's very important you finish education before deciding on a work choice next year—"

"I'm not going back!" Back to education? To classes and homework and fresh-faced Edenites with no concept of how the world actually works? The thought hadn't even crossed my mind. Abel frowns in disapproval. "I mean, not right now," I backtrack. "I need a few weeks to get…reacquainted."

My uncle looks as if he's about to disagree, but fortunately, the moment is interrupted by the arrival of Kimiko.

"Dinner is served," the fembot announces, carefully placing our meals in front of us. "Wild mushroom risotto with tangled salad greens."

Before me is an enormous mound of steaming risotto that smells like butter and garlic. Slices of crumbling golden cheese ooze in the soft, sticky rice. Next to the risotto is a clump of dressed arugula salad, dotted with cut cherry tomatoes and paper-thin slices of cucumber.

"I can't believe you remembered," I mumble, eyes round and mouth watering. Mushroom risotto is my favorite meal, hands down. And what Kimiko has prepared looks like it could be the best I've ever tasted.

"I programmed her myself," Abel says proudly.

I pick up my fork, unsure whether to savor every bite in a luxurious slowness or cram as much as I can in my mouth at once.

"I'm about to turn into an animal right about now," I warn my uncle.

He chuckles, pleased. "Go for it."

I aim my fork at the rice, about to strike, when I hear something. Distant yelling. I glance up. It's the news stream Abel was watching. Floating in the lounge room is a holo of a group of Badlanders. They are running as if their lives depend on it. Their faces are strained and terrible. My fork clatters to the table. "Kimiko, turn that up!"

The sound of the crisp news stream fills the room: "—was attacked today by illegal immigrants from the Badlands. More than thirty outlaws stormed the Northern Bridge border crossing—"

The Guider's voice fades in my ears as I stare at dozens of Badlanders racing across the empty bridge toward the white walls of Eden. Bare feet hit the concrete. Some leave stamps of blood. They are being chased by a dozen black-and-silver substitutes, running with inhuman speed. With a sharp charge of fear, I recognize them. "Quicks."

Abel nods, face impassive. "Quicks."

One of mom's colleagues in the Innovation department—a bald man with a turned-down mouth whom I referred to as Frog—was working on the design of these new substitutes before I left. I didn't like Frog and I didn't like the designs. I'm sure he only showed me the floating schematics to frighten me.

At six feet tall, with two arms and two legs, they're the most lifelike of any substitute I've ever seen. Unlike Kimiko, who looks cute and helpful, these powerful substitutes are terrifying. Their eyes gleam bloodred. They move like lightning. They are meant for disaster relief— even though there hasn't been a natural disaster in decades, Eden isn't immune to house fires or buzzcar crashes. Quicks are supposed to help people, and they do it, as their name suggests, quickly.

It looks like border patrol also falls into their skill set.

The Quicks overtake the Badlanders on the bridge. Their metal bodies interlock to form a barrier, an impenetrable fence of black and silver. The Badlanders are at an impasse. Before any of them can begin climbing over the solid wall of Quicks, a dozen Tranquils catch up. The first brings his baton down hard on a man's leg. A bloody shard of bone sticks through the shin. Another Tranq has his gloved hand around a woman's throat while she claws at it in horror, choking for breath. My hand clamps over my mouth, stifling a sharp cry. She looks like a younger version of Mileka.

The voice-over continues impassively. "The outlaws made it approximately halfway across the Northern Bridge before they were detained by Tranquils."

Detained? Yeah, right. I wonder how many of the Badlanders were beaten to death by the Tranqs, right there on the bridge. Substitutes can't kill people. But Tranquils can.

"Gyan called today's incident a victory for all Edenites."

The stream cuts to a meeting of Guiders. A life-sized holo of Gyan stands at the front in his bright yellow robes. He enunciates every word with perfect diction: the voice of a born leader. "Once again, the Trust has ensured that all Edenites remain safe and secure. We will not stand for attacks by criminals determined to undermine our freedom."

I feel sick. Those people on the bridge weren't criminals or terrorists. They were scared, desperate, and dying.

Gyan continues, "I know some have already called the Badlanders in question terrorists. That's open to debate, but I can say that thanks to the swift action of the Tranquils on duty, Edenites can sleep well knowing that these criminals are kept far away from our children and our homes."

"Is this attack a consequence of cutting off Moon Lake?" an unseen person calls out.

"Yes, it appears so," Gyan answers gravely. "The Trust was hoping for a smooth transition as the Badlands became its own sovereign state, but the Badlanders have let us down. We are exploring ways of dealing with the situation, but please, rest assured that our top priority remains the protection of Eden."

"I used to feel sorry for those people." The stream cuts to a woman standing in Orange Grove Plaza, the large town square in the middle of the Hive, ringed by orange trees that perpetually bear fruit. "But it's obvious I should be afraid of them."

The report switches back to the host. "And that's the latest on the thwarted terrorist attack. And now, the temperature. We can expect another beautiful day tomorrow—"

"Switch it off," I growl to Kimiko.

Gyan is clever, I'll give him that. He never said outright that Badlanders were terrorists, but even claiming that others called them that is enough to plant the idea.

"They're not taking it lying down," Abel says. I look up, refocusing. "The Badlanders," he continues, rubbing his eyes tiredly. "From what I hear about security at the border crossing, they did well to get as far as they did."

The words of the man who'd been hit across the face, the day I crossed the border, come back to me: *Soon we won't be asking for your permission!* Abel's right. They're not taking this lying down. They are fighting.

But maybe Gyan planned for that. Maybe our clever and calculating leader knew that the Badlanders would have no choice but to act recklessly in the struggle to stay alive. Then the streams can recast them as criminals. But to what end? To justify retaliation? Edenites believe in peace. They'd never support a Trust declaration of war. Would they?

"Tess." Abel breaks my reverie. "It's getting cold."

I look down at my food. It's more than an average Badlander would eat in a week. I push my plate away. "I can't eat this," I mumble, feeling sick with shame. The long showers. The soft bed I sleep in. The salons, the boutiques...

Abel eyes me carefully. "It's already made."

"I can't eat this," I repeat, louder, more sure.

"We don't eat like this every night, Tess," Abel says gently. "This is a celebration—"

"Yeah, that I'm lucky enough to get back over the border," I cry. "You don't get it, Uncle A. I was out there for a year, I lived like that! I can't go back to all this like it never happened!" I shoot the chair away from the table, the legs screeching. Hot tears fill my eyes and my voice splinters and cracks. "We have everything and they have *nothing*—"

"Hello?"

My head whips around.

"Hunter!" my uncle and I say in unison.

I'm panting. Both hands are balled into fists. I want to kick the wall or throw something across the room.

"What's wrong?" Hunter asks, sounding alarmed.

Abel clears his throat. "Nothing's wrong. Tess was just exercising her right to an ethical decision, albeit loudly."

Hunter's face works with confusion. "Should I leave?"

"That won't be necessary," Abel says. "Kimiko, please clear Tess's plate. I'll take it for lunch tomorrow."

"Yes, Dr. Rockwood," Kimiko replies smoothly. She picks up the offending meal and whizzes off in the direction of the kitchen. I fold back down into my chair, which is now a good few feet from the table. My anger is ebbing; in its place, the slow throb of mounting embarrassment. I can't believe Hunter just witnessed my meltdown.

Hunter clears his throat uncertainly. "You wanted to go over tomorrow's lecture, Professor Rockwood?"

I wipe at my nose and look up to see my uncle watching me.

"Yes," he replies faintly. "Yes. Hmm...I'm sorry." He blinks, turning back to Hunter. "What did you say?"

"The lecture," Hunter replies patiently.

"Oh, yes. Yes, the lecture!" Abel rises to his feet. "Go ahead to the study. I'll just be a moment."

As soon as he's gone, I lift my eyes to my uncle's. "I ruined dinner."

"No," Abel says, and I'm surprised that he says it kindly. "You actually made it much more interesting."

I give him a watery smile. "You're not going to report me to the Guiders?"

"Report you? Of course not!" he exclaims. "Tess, you're my niece. And besides," he adds, dropping his voice to a stage whisper, "I'm not completely unsympathetic to your point of view."

I straighten, stunned. "Really?"

Abel sits back in his chair, dabbing absentmindedly at his mouth with a napkin. "How was it seeing Izzadore today? Really?"

I stare at him, wondering for a few wild seconds if he'd somehow seen me in the salon or at the Animal Gardens, in person or on-cycle. It's certainly possible, but I don't think that's what he means. I think he just knows, somehow, that things are different. "It was...not good, actually. Actually, it was pretty bad." And suddenly I find myself telling him all about it—about the uneasiness with using so much water, how frivolous Izzy seems to me now, even though I still care about her. I leave out Kudzu, obviously, but I tell him everything else. "It just feels like the Trust"—I suck in a big breath, psyching myself up to say the words—"doesn't care about the Badlands at all. Like they want everyone to starve. And that's just so horrible and wrong."

I eye my uncle. My heart is racing. He could report me for dissent. I pray I haven't just made a colossal mistake.

"It is unfair," Abel says quietly.

I exhale, sagging with relief. "It was just so hard," I say. "Being out there and seeing these skinny kids every single day and knowing I couldn't do anything about it." My throat tightens. A tear slips down my cheek, and I quickly wipe it away, embarrassed.

"Well, you were living there," Abel says thoughtfully. "It's one thing to have a philosophy. It's another to have an experience."

I nod. "Yeah. Yeah, it is."

"You look tired, Tess," Abel says. "Why don't you get some sleep?"

"Okay." I take a few steps in the direction of the stairs before turning back to him. The light from the candles flickers around his face, causing deep pools of shadows under his eyes. "And thanks. For everything."

Abel smiles back at me, looking wistful and distracted. His eyes shift away for just a second, and even without following his gaze, I know where he's looking. The red basement door. "No, Tess," he says, meeting my eyes again. "Thank you."

I can't sleep. The harder I try, the more impossible it becomes. I toss and turn for hours. Deep down I know why. After my conversation with Abel, it's absurd to think he's really working with the Trust. I believed him when he said he thought what was happening in the Badlands was wrong. I have to know. I have to see what's beyond the red door. I have to break into the basement.

A single lamp lights the otherwise darkened living room. The clock on the wall reads just after three. I cross to the basement door quickly, feeling like a thief.

"Can I assist you, Tess?"

I squeak and whirl to see Kimiko behind me, her bright eyes cutting twin paths of light in the darkness. "Be quiet!" I whisper furiously.

"Can I—"

"No, you can't assist me with anything," I mutter irritably, gingerly moving behind her. Creepily, the top half of her body swivels around with me. "Stop moving. I'm trying to turn you off." I just hope these new models aren't so sophisticated they don't have an off switch.

"Dr. Rockwood never turns me off."

"I'm not Dr. Rockwood," I reply, finally finding the switch with relief. "Bye-bye, Kimiko."

"But why would yooouuu..." The lights in her eyes power down. Then a series of tiny beeps begin chorusing from around the house. The air- and smell-conditioning, the sole lamp—they all begin turning off. The time on the clock disappears. Moonlight casts the whole house in ominous shades of silent gray. Huh—that's different. Apparently substitutes now control all the electrical stuff, like a central computer. Maybe Kimiko was even linked to the lock on the red door. No, no such luck—it's still active.

My fingers hover over the keypad. I know Abel. He's sentimental and he's lax with security. My guess is he'd choose a loved one's name. My first guess: Pascuala. My aunt who died when I was five. *"Password denied. You can make two more attempts."*

I bite my lip, heart beating fast. I enter *Tessendra*.

"Password denied. You can make one more attempt."

I exhale in frustration. I could try Tess, But I don't think that's it. *You know who it is.*

I have to enter her name. Her nickname. The one only Abel uses. Frankie. My mother.

"Password accepted."

The basement is pitch-black when the bright red door swings open. My heart is kicking against my ribs as I slowly descend. Then, in flickering shards of pale light, the basement laboratory is revealed to me: an unhinged, sprawling mess.

Holos of DNA, strangely beautiful twisting ladders, spiral slowly in the air, beamed from glowing gold scratch. Streams of complicated algorithms are everywhere, as are holos of dark pink neurons, like webby spiders aching to connect. I see one, two, three floating models of the human brain, all slightly different, all shot through with light and wires and whirls of movement. Confusing mathematical formulas flicker as holos in the musty air. My eyes travel the cracked spines of ancient books—actual *books*—on philosophy and consciousness and free will.

I know what all this is for. The familiar-looking tropes of science's next frontier.

Artilects.

Ling was right about Abel.

Abel, the kind old man who actually teared up when I arrived on his doorstep, the man who just agreed that what was happening in the Badlands was unfair. *No,* I tell myself. *The man who's in the pocket of the Trust. The man who lied to me. The man I have to stop.*

Amid the mess on a long, stainless steel table, I notice one of Abel's Simutech security swabs. The pliable, palm-sized silicon swab would get me into any restricted access areas in Simutech itself. I push it into my back pocket. Abel usually has two or three because he keeps misplacing them—he might not even notice this one is gone.

I pick up the model of an arm, cut through to the bone so you can see all its layers. Dermis, epidermis, muscles, bone: the strange, otherworldly ecosystem that pulses beneath our skin. Next to it is a bone-shaped piece of dull gray metal, about as long as my arm. It is as hard and cold as death itself.

Then I see him.

In the corner. Standing upright.

Magnus.

It takes me a full ten seconds to accept that the dark gold, human-shaped artilect is just a dead, harmless shell. His eyes, once a burning silver, are now black. He stands at over six feet tall, as broad as a football player but so much stronger.

My own horrified voice rings in my ears, the distant echo of a ghost. *"Get away from my mother!"*

Perversely, I find myself moving toward him. Something deep inside me wants to feel the exact texture and temperature of this weapon. To feel beneath my own hand the brilliant death my mother made for herself. My fingers hover above the space where a human's heart would be. I realize I am holding my breath.

"You're teaching him to do the dishes?" I slouched against a stainless steel counter in the Simutech break room, brightening my obnoxious blue manicure with another coat of gloss. I was there because I was grounded. Again. I blamed Izzy. It was her idea we take a swim in a plaza fountain.

"Handling something as fine as a plate requires the complex coordination of many joints and muscles," Mom replied, hovering around Magnus, whose hamlike hands were plunged into a sink. "We need him to be able to mimic this level of control. It's part of his motor training. Plus, I haven't programmed him to do this. He observed me, and now he's doing it all by himself, which means—"

"He's a constructivist system—a system that learns," I parroted, blowing on the wet gloss. "You've only mentioned it five billion times."

"I don't understand you, Tess." Mom sighed. "You used to have such an aptitude for this."

"For painting my nails?"

"For scientific study."

Magnus was awkwardly maneuvering a soapy plate out of the sink—a boy learning to keep house. Around us, streams hovered and whirled to record the constant conversations of his synthetic synapses and neurons. Magnus was rarely undocumented, the constant center of everyone's attention.

"A little respect, please, Tess," Mom tutted. "His processing speed is ten to the thirty calculations per second."

I shrugged. So what?

"Humans only process at ten to the sixteen, Tess."

"So, he's good at math?" I guessed.

Mom all but ground her teeth. "Good at—Tess, at those speeds, he is math. He's calculating algorithms in a trillionth of a second that took me years!"

"Who cares? He can't even catch." I wave my hands at him. "Magnus! Catch!" I toss the nail polish at him. His arm moves up, but his reflexes are seconds too slow. The little bottle hits him in the chest with a sharp clink, then falls to the floor and smashes. Polish spills everywhere, like a messy puddle of blue blood.

"Tess!" Mom exhaled in annoyance. "You'll have to clean that up. Interesting, though..." She can't help swishing a note about it into one of the streams.

"I apologize, Tess," Magnus said.

"That's all right, Magnus," Mom answered for me. "Please keep trying to pick up the plate."

His hands plunged back into the sink. "So, how human is he, anyway?"

Mom blew air through her lips. "The human body inspired his physical design. He's beginning to display free will. No empathy. Not sure about morality, it's too early to say."

"But, he's alive, right?"

"Depends on who you ask."

"What do you think?"

"Personally?" Mom narrowed her eyes. "No. I don't think so. Not yet."

"I am experiencing difficulty." Magnus's deep voice was somewhere between human and machine. The plate slid out of his hands and plopped back into the soapy water.

I rolled my eyes. "I'm experiencing boredom."

"Try this one." Mom handed Magnus a champagne flute.

"I am not able to guarantee the safety of this object."

"Try," Mom urged.

"I am not able to guarantee the safety of this object."

"Just try—"

A high, almost musical, crash. I jumped, startled, as thin shards of glass scattered across the floor. "Can you not do that?"

"I am sorry, Tess. I do not like upsetting you—"

Mom sighed, addressing the artilect. "That's okay— Wait, what did you just say?"

"I do not like upsetting Tess."

"What? Why?"

Magnus paused. It almost looked as though he was thinking. "Because I like her."

Mom squealed with excitement, flinging her scratch into the air. "You like her? He likes you! I can't believe it! Tess, do you know what this means?" Mom curled an arm around Magnus's bicep, looking starstruck. "He might actually be feeling *something!*" She giggled hysterically, feet crunching over the glass. "Tess. He likes *you!*"

This is what I remember when it comes to Magnus. Things that break. Now, back in the present, my hands find his cold, hard body. Rage wells inside me. My hand clenches into a fist, about to snap back— but then it falls to my side.

I'm not angry. I'm devastated.

I grab a sweater hanging over the back of a chair. When I scream, it's a wail that's primal and painful. I cry for everything: for my mom, for the fact that I will never, ever see her again. I cry for having to always pretend that I am okay, that I am tough enough to survive this. And I cry because I am so completely alone.

After the worst of it is over, I let the sweater drop, my throat sore, my face hot.

I have to get out of here.

Outside Abel's house, I gulp in cool night air and try to slow the hammering of my heart. Breathing deeply, I focus on making myself feel numb.

But it isn't working. And then I realize, I don't *want* to feel numb anymore.

I am hurt and I am ashamed and I am scared. But I am also motivated. And alive. And angry.

Because now I have a purpose. Now I have a way of making up for what I have done. A mix of revenge, sadness, and anger funnels into a decision that's so simple and neat, it could fit my pocket.

I will help Kudzu destroy Aevum. Just like Magnus destroyed my mother.

And then, standing alone on the silent street that smells of fresh-cut grass and safety, I begin to smile.

chapter 6

I wake with a gnawing, anxious sensation squeezing my stomach, at once painful and familiar. Hunger and adrenaline. Just like a Badlands morning.

"Tess." Abel glances up from his morning tea with a pleasant smile. "Your suspended sensory activity is complete." The steam from the cup drifts and curls as fluidly as a stream.

"Morning." I'm unable to add a *good* in front of it. I sit down to a plate of lukewarm scrambled eggs and begin shoveling them into my mouth.

Abel studies me from across the dining table. I guess as far as he's concerned, last night bought us closer together, not farther apart. "Is everything all right?"

I almost laugh. Everything might get close to being all right, however, if Ling shows up to meet me today. It didn't take long to work out how to reply to her slew of friendly forest folk. I chose a baby deer wobbling on toothpick legs to tell her I'd be at the filtration plant at noon. I have no idea if she'll show.

"Everything's just great," I tell Abel, speaking through a mouthful of food. "Peachy as peach pie. With extra peach."

"Good to hear," he murmurs. He's watching me. It takes all the willpower I have not to glance at the red basement door.

Instead I meet his gaze, and swallow. "What?"

"I've been thinking about my plan for you."

A tiny chill skids through me. "Sounds ominous."

His gnarled hands jitter in front of him. "I mean, our plan for what you'll be doing. If you're not going back to education today."

I relax a little. Of course. It's Monday morning. "I've been thinking about that too," I say, licking some egg off my fork. "I think I just need a few weeks to get back on my feet. Eat. Sleep. Exercise at a Hub. Check out some art, spend some time at the park. Then I'll reenroll."

He nods slowly. "Sounds like you've put some thought into this."

"Children are the future, Uncle A," I say innocently. "Gyan said that himself. I need to take my future seriously."

He can't tell if I'm being sarcastic. "Yes. Of course."

I resist the urge to lick my plate clean and instead scrape my chair backward. "I'm out, Uncle A. See you later—"

But Abel stops me with a raised palm. "Just a moment. Until you go back to education, I have some requirements of my own."

I sit back down with slow caution. "Oh yeah?"

"I'd like Hunter to tutor you," he says. "In the evenings, after he's done at post-education."

"What?"

"Tess, you've been out of the education system for a year," Abel continues calmly. "That puts you at a considerable disadvantage to the other students."

"This is a joke, right?"

"Hunter's very responsible, very bright—an excellent teacher. And he lives right around the corner. You'll be able to review what you've missed. I dare say you'll be caught up in a matter of months—"

"*Months?*" I spit hotly. I'm on my feet. "I can handle a knife, I know how to defend myself, hell, I even know how to kill and cook a damn prairie chicken. Those kids should be learning from *me*—"

"No one is questioning your... abilities, Tess," Abel says, "but this is not up for debate."

"What if I say no?" I ask, daring him.

"If you want to live at my house, then you will have to obey my rules," he says with surprising authority.

He's got me. I don't have anywhere else to stay. Abel barrels on hurriedly. "Right, he'll be here at seven o'clock tonight and every week-night for the next month. He has access to the house. I might be here, I might not. Kimiko can fix you dinner." He pauses, eyeing my reaction.

"Fine." I groan. "But, can we start tomorrow?" I have no idea what's supposed to happen at Kudzu, assuming I even get there. I don't want to cut anything short because I'm being babysat.

He nods. "Oh," he adds as I turn to skulk out. "One more thing. Did you turn Kimiko off last night?"

I freeze, eyes popping wide. Then I relax my face and turn to face him sheepishly. "Yeah. I came down for a snack and I didn't want her to wake you."

"Next time, just put her to sleep. Shutting her down resets everything in the house."

I look at the man who's constructing an artilect from the blood of my mother. The man who is working for the Trust. The man who keeps his sister's killer six feet below us in a secret basement. I smile, sweet as syrup. "Sure thing, Uncle A. Whatever you say."

At first, the Trust kept Moon Lake clean with a large-scale filtration system. A few years ago they developed a microorganism, a simple bacteria that cleans water a hundred times more effectively. Bioremediation. They trumpeted that breakthrough on the streams for months: "That's what you get for putting your trust in the Trust!"

Eventually the old plant will be turned into offices or housing, but for now, it's abandoned. If it weren't for the bright sunlight and high twitter of unseen birds, it'd definitely feel a little spooky. Some of the glass windows are broken, spiderwebbed with cracks. Giant black pumps, once endlessly sucking and spitting water, are now motionless, sprayed with dark red rust. My footsteps echo from the high concrete walls. It's just before noon. I find a concrete ledge to perch on, and I wait.

At 12:30, I wonder how much longer I should stay.

Then I hear it. A low drone, growing louder every second. I stiffen. A floater.

Ling rounds the corner. She's wearing tight white pants, sturdy boots, and a loose white sweater. Even though it's a typical Eden outfit, she still looks like a badass. Maybe it's her eyes, which are narrowed suspiciously at me beneath blunt black bangs.

The hovering floater zooms straight past me. At the other end of the plant, Ling circles around, looking every which way, scoping the place out. Then she rides back to me and stops a good ten feet away.

I slip off the ledge and take a couple hesitant steps toward her. *"Poká. Coméstá?"*

"Empty your backpack," she orders.

"Huh?"

She glares at me. "Now!"

I shrug it off my back, zip it open, and shake everything onto the ground. I don't have much: the scratch she gave me, a muesli bar, a bottle of water, and Mack.

"Is that the scratch I gave you?" she asks.

I nod, holding it out for her to see. "Yeah. Look, Ling—"

"Shut up." She putters forward on the floater to snatch the scratch from me. She smooths it open and spends a minute swishing through some streams. Satisfied, she scrunches it back into a ball and shoves it in her pocket. "So," she says, "where were you?" I open my mouth, but she cuts me off. "You know what? Let me guess." She presses her fingers to her temple like a mind reader. "You bought clothes in the Hive, then took an airbus to a salon in Charity. Pretty fancy one too. Later, you took another airbus back to your uncle's from the Animal Gardens."

I gape at her. "You were following me?"

She gives me a withering look. "Your new ID, genius. Way to lay low."

I'd forgotten how hooked up Kudzu were. Of course they could trace my ID. "Ling, I can explain—"

"Save it," she says, turning her floater around. "We don't deal with traitors."

"I'm not a traitor!" I cry. "I'm not!"

"See ya, Rockwood," Ling calls over her shoulder. "As in, never again."

"Ling, wait!" I race to catch up with her, throwing myself in her path. She pulls the floater to a stop, inches before it crashes into me. "I'm not a traitor. Okay, so I got a new ID. I freaked out when I got to Abel's. I didn't think I could handle it, that being an Edenite would be better. I was wrong. I want to join Kudzu, Ling."

"Why should I believe you?"

"Because..." I rack my brain for a way to make her believe me. "Because yesterday at the salon, I told Izzy and the stylist and anyone else listening that we all should be using less water, and that I don't think Gyan should've cut off Moon Lake!"

I'm expecting Ling to be won over by my revolutionary zeal, but instead she just stares at me, horrified. "You broke Trust law? In front of other Edenites?"

I'd just made it worse.

"This isn't only about being able to scrape by in the Badlands, Tess," Ling says hotly. "We're revolutionaries. When we break the law, we do it anonymously. Not with an audience."

I'm still standing there, dumbstruck, as Ling starts maneuvering her floater around me, muttering insults under her breath.

"*Ling!* I'm new to this. I made a mistake. I'm sorry, it won't happen again. You want my ID? You can have it. I won't need it anymore. Because I want to join you. I want to stop Aevum. I want to help."

She sits, unmoving.

"Why did you even come if you didn't trust me?" I ask, taking a few steps closer to her. "You know I'm legit, deep down you have to know. What you're asking me to do is huge. And I've already started. I broke up with my best friend, and I broke into Abel's lab—"

"What?"

"That's right!" I pounce on her interest. "I broke in last night. Magnus was down there. Abel is working on something, you were right."

"Of course I was right." She sniffs, but I can see I've hooked her. She's listening.

I pull my new ID from my back pocket. In this new loop, my expression is cool and unyielding. Taking it in both hands, I snap the glossy card in two. I hold the pieces out to her. "You can trust me."

Ling and I ride north through the gentle slope of Lakeside. Unlike the shady, oak tree–lined streets of Liberty Gardens, the relaxed and easygoing Lakeside boasts breezy palm trees and squat bungalows with water views. It's kept a few degrees warmer than the rest of Eden, making it balmy all year round. We pass girls with long golden braids walking barefoot in short shorts and old men playing checkers in shirts splashed with bright flowers. I catch snatches of Moon Lake between the houses, winking in the sun.

We keep heading north until we clear Lakeside altogether and are on a single road surrounded by trees and scrub, heading toward the uppermost tip of Eden. The farther north we go, the higher the white city walls get, until it feels as if they're about to topple down on us. It's so strange—I never used to notice the city walls. Now I feel as if they're watching me.

We veer off onto a side road, then a side road off that, then what barely amounts to a dirt track. Finally, we slow to a stop, seemingly in the middle of nowhere. It's peaceful and quiet except for the hopping song of a few birds.

Ling guides the floater to a small thicket. She grabs a piece of green canvas that's covered in leaves and twigs and flips it back. About ten floaters are nestled underneath.

"Why don't you use buzzcars?" I ask, watching her park her floater next to the others. "Be a lot faster."

For a second I think she isn't going to answer me, but after a beat she does. "Buzzcars are all on-cycle these days. Too risky. Floaters are the safest way to move around Eden."

After pulling the canvas back, she heads off into the scrub. Her sturdy leather boots find footing in a steep pathway that snakes endlessly up through the tangled vegetation. She moves with the certainty of someone intimately familiar with this all-but-invisible mountain trail, anticipating which rocks are stable and which ones aren't. "Just follow my lead," she calls over her shoulder.

"I spent a year in the Badlands on my own, sister," I reply, using Mack to slice away at some of the thicker vines. "I think I can work out how to—*oof!*"

A second later, I'm on my hands and knees, banging both kneecaps on sharp stones. Ling is grinning as she leaps back down the path to offer me a hand. I don't take it, which makes her laugh. "I've never met anyone as stubborn as me," she says, watching me get awkwardly to my feet. "You're going to fit in just fine."

This land technically belongs to the Trust, but it's overgrown and uninhabitable, and thus, unmonitored. As we hike, I ask Ling what exactly she expects me to do today. "You'll speak at an afternoon briefing," she says. "About artilects."

"What about them?"

"Explain what they are," she replies. "Why they're dangerous. And how we can destroy them."

We climb steeply for over an hour. Despite Eden's climate control, it's uncomfortably muggy. Unlike the Badlands, this heat is thick and wet. Sweat crawls down my temples and back.

"Up here!" Ling calls, waving from the top of the path, then disappearing over the ridge.

"Yeah, yeah. So where's this—oh."

I stop in my tracks, stunned.

Moon Lake.

The morning sun plays on the gently rippling surface—a vast reservoir of clean blue water. Vegetation grows right up to the edge, verdant and brilliantly green. Swallows swoop above it, catching invisible insects in the air. It is living, this lake. *It is life.* "It's so *beautiful.*" The words come in a whisper.

"Yeah, never gets old." I hadn't noticed Ling squatting on the ground near me, taking a sip from her water bottle. "Hard to believe it used to ice over in winter."

"Really?"

She nods. "Back in the Age of Excess. As in, really ice over, not climate-control ice like the Smoking Mountains."

Wow. The planet has changed so fast. Sometimes I try to imagine what it would've been like to live back in Excess. They didn't have allowances then. They had money, like in the Badlands, and if you had enough of that you could do whatever you wanted. And even though they knew the earth was dying, no one really cared.

Ling arches her back in a stretch, chin tipped up toward the sun. "C'mon. We're nearly there."

We troop down toward the water. Ling explains that like the filtration plant, a filtration office was also shut down after the Trust switched systems.

"We found it last year," she says. "Perfect, really. All unmonitored, lots of supplies, and we worked out how to switch the solar back on." She stops abruptly, gesturing proudly. "This is it. Home, sweet home!"

Partly overgrown with foliage and tattooed with moss is an unassuming coffee-colored building. The single-story construction has a flat roof and is set with small, square windows. It is devoid of personality or any signs of life. This is the headquarters of the underground rebel force, Kudzu? It's like popping a bottle of champagne to find it full of Badlands water. Ling takes one look at my raised eyebrows and laughs. "Not so impressive from the outside, I know. We don't want to draw attention to ourselves, in case some lost hiker comes by. But it's pretty great inside. C'mon!"

She heads up a path through the foliage toward the front door and goes to push it open.

"Wait a minute," I say. "Who else knows? About the ID thing, and standing you up yesterday?" If I have to deal with a thousand people all as suspicious as Ling had been, I want to be ready.

Ling sighs. "Just me and Achilles. Everyone else thinks you're a superstar robot girl, here to save the day."

I cringe. "Why would they think that?"

"Because that's what I sold you as," Ling says matter-of-factly. "Look, grudges are for whiny bitches, and I'm not a whiny bitch. I'm willing to forget about the past twenty-four hours if you are."

"Definitely." I nod, sticking out my hand. "Friends?"

She gives my outstretched hand an amused look. "We're more than that now. My life's in your hands, and vice versa."

I roll my eyes. "Just shake my damn hand, Ling."

She laughs and grabs it, eyes dancing. "Welcome to Kudzu, Tess."

part 2

chapter 7

The heavy front door swings open into a dimly lit room. Filling the three hefty tables that line the walls are mountains of mismatched equipment—different generations of scratch, snakepits of black cable, devices I don't even recognize. Little lights blink unevenly, while non-sensical data stream from different pieces of scratch. Amid the computer gear are superhero figures, dirty coffee cups, a dead plant. It smells like somewhere unwashed people spend a lot of time, mixed with the woody scent of incense. Old posters are tacked to the walls, crowded next to silly happy-snap photograms, ripped stickers, and graffiti.

Someone had carved KUDZU LOVES YOU! onto the wall next to me, and underneath it, in a different script, THEN WHY WON'T HE COMM?

The wall to my immediate left, next to the doorway, is filled with a huge piece of glowing scratch. It looks like a patchwork quilt. Impressively, some brainiac has worked out how to meld different generations of scratch together. Usually you can only cut and meld the same generation. But the very first kind of scratch—an inflexible dark brown type about half an inch thick—is fused with the paper-thin kind Ling gave me. The patchwork scratch is on the 2D setting, showing flat, ever-changing images of quiet stretches of water. The workers here must have had access to the Trust security streams set up around Moon Lake. I guess Kudzu had worked out how to access them after they left. Handy.

In the center of the room is a large conference table, lit by a single overhead light. Empty chairs are scattered around it. I glimpse a few pieces of scratch beaming tiny holos of familiar names: Aevum, Simutech.

"Tech-room-slash-meeting-space. This is Achilles' territory," Ling announces, gesturing at an authoritative-looking red swivel chair, currently empty, presumably Achilles'. "You'll meet him in a sec."

"So, he's the one in charge?"

Ling blows her bangs out of her eyes. "Of this stuff, yeah. Cracking an uncrackable security system is all he ever wants for his birthday."

"No," I clarify. "Of you guys—of all of Kudzu."

"Oh no!" Ling says with a laugh. "No one's really 'in charge.' We're a leaderless collective. Everyone has an equal say."

This surprises me—Ling acts so much like an alpha. "So why did *you* come and get me?"

"If you have an idea for a mission and the entire collective votes that it's a good idea, you can call for volunteers and run the mission yourself," she explains. "This is my mission, so I was the one who went to get you." She waves her hand back at the room. "We'll do the Aevum briefing here after lunch."

I follow her down a narrow corridor that hugs the left side of the building. The maroon concrete floor is littered lightly with dog or cat hair and the walls are covered with bold graffiti art showing blue-haired girls pouting dreamily next to strange, spacey animals that drink from martini glasses. In spiky purple paint, I read the words: OUR MINDS ARE BETTER. OUR HANDS ARE FASTER. OUR HEARTS ARE STRONGER. WE ARE KUDZU.

"That's kind of our motto," Ling explains, somewhere between proud and embarrassed. "Still waiting for a chance to really use it. Apart from the leaflets, I guess."

Piles of multicolored paper are stacked against the wall. I recognize one pile immediately: KUDZU RATS OUT THE TRUST. The rats at the ice-skating rink. What did she call this? A leaflet? "Why paper?" I ask Ling. "Seems a little last century."

"Untraceable," she replies simply. "For us, and Edenites. But this mission, we're stepping things up." Her eyes flash intently. "After we destroy Aevum, we're releasing a whole stream about artilects and what's happening in the Badlands."

"But the Trust controls the streams," I point out. "They'll just shut it down."

Ling shakes her head, looking smug. "Not if you're sneaky like us. The Kudzu stream will be totally anonymous, totally untraceable. Just like paper."

An unauthorized stream. Something that tells the truth about the

Badlands, the truth about the Trust. "That could really wake people up," I admit.

"It *will* wake people up," Ling says. "That's why this mission is so important. Stunt plus stream equals real change."

The smell of something warm and rich and tomatoey drifts up the hallway. A booming woman's voice calls out, "Chicken? Is that you?"

"Henny!" Ling calls back.

I follow Ling as she bounds into a cluttered kitchen. Wooden shelves nailed to the walls hold stacks of mismatched plates, mugs, bowls, and saucepans. Wire baskets full of fruit hang from the ceiling. Potatoes still covered in dirt are heaped in the sink, next to big bunches of fresh basil and parsley. Something bubbles on a stove, wafting the warm, salty smell of roasted tomatoes mixed with fragrant herbs. Every bit of space is used, and there's enough food in here to feed an army. Or at least, a bunch of hungry revolutionaries.

From the open doorway, I watch Ling hug a big woman with a pile of yellow-and-black leopard-print hair. Then Ling swings her backpack onto the floor, unzips it, and hands the woman a bottle of dark yellow cooking oil, a packet of flour, and three large blocks of chocolate wrapped in gold paper. The woman squawks with excitement. "You did well, chicken. You did well." She glances in my direction. "Seems we have a visitor."

Ling gestures at me proudly. "Tess, this is Henny. Henny, Tess."

"Hey." I give a small wave.

"No, that won't do," says Henny, barreling toward me. "Everyone gets a hug hello from Henny."

Before I know it, she has wrapped me up in a huge hug, squeezing me hard. I just stand there stiffly. She smells like onions, but in a good way.

"Not much of a hugger, huh?" Henny says, letting my stiff-as-a-board body go with a bemused smile. "We'll soon change that. All right, let's get a look at you." She gives me a slow once-over. "Looks pretty tough," she says to Ling approvingly. "Nice tronic."

Ling takes a wooden spoon from the large pot of stew on the stove and licks it. "Yum. Did you make the strawberry thing for dessert?"

"I wanted to, but those darn rabbits got into them again."

"Rabbits?" I'm surprised. According to the Trust, there's no pest or invasive species in all of Eden.

Ling nods, her nose wrinkled in annoyance. "They live in the woods. Fair game if you can catch them." Then, to Henny, "When's lunch?"

"Ten minutes," she replies.

We head farther down the corridor. Ling gestures to some more workrooms, storage spaces, and a small bathroom, before the corridor opens into a space about twice the size of the tech room and three times the size of the kitchen. It's a riot of blankets, backpacks, and boots. All four walls support handmade wooden bunk beds. Several of the bottom beds hold double mattresses, presumably for couples. Every bed has a box or some shelves built onto the end of it; they are piled with clothes, toiletries, and knickknacks.

"Ah," I say, turning in a slow circle. "The famous Kudzu Procreation Palace."

Ling jolts with alarm. "Is that what people say about us? Procreation... Palace?"

I grin and give her shoulder a light sock. "Relax, Ping. I'm kidding."

A golden Labrador retriever lies on one of the bottom beds. On seeing Ling, the dog's tail thumps happily. "This is Carlos." She gives him a scratch between the ears, and he whines. "He's kind of all of ours." She points to one of the double beds. "That's mine."

"You all sleep in here?"

Ling nods. "You sound surprised."

"I just thought there'd be more of you," I admit.

"We're growing," Ling says. "But it's hard to find people we all trust." She gives me a quick smile then inclines her head toward the back door. I can hear chatter and someone playing a guitar. "C'mon. Everyone's dying to meet the famous Tess Rockwood."

"Then meet her they shall," I say, affecting a touch more bravado than I actually feel.

The large backyard is filled with a couple dozen people, all roughly my age or a few years older. The person playing the guitar is a gorgeous boy with coal black skin. He smiles broadly as he strums. Next to him are a couple of pixieish girls who are messing around with stream design, beamed up from a square of scratch. They both have strawberry blond hair cut uneven and shaggy, and thin arms covered with swirling tronics. One has a lip piercing, and the other has silver rings threaded through both eyebrows. Their fingers draw jagged red lines that hang in the air like frozen lightning.

A faded yellow hammock has been strung up between a huge tree to my right and the corner of the house. A gangly boy with short dark hair and olive skin lies in it. His fingers swish in a busy stream featuring maxed-out muscle men pounding on what look like wolves with wings.

Behind the tree, a half dozen fat chickens peck around the edges of a sprawling vegetable garden. A guy in a pair of overalls and rubber boots is tying up a vine that's heavy with ripe red tomatoes. Nailed to a wooden post nearby is a pockmarked dartboard that another guy is using. Darts whiz fast to the bull's-eye. Beyond the veggie garden, I can see empty fields full of sunlight. The air smells sweet, like honey—I wonder if they have beehives somewhere.

On the other side of the backyard is a medium-sized shed. In front of it sits a muscular, tough-looking girl with dark, hard eyes. Her head is completely shaved and a hand-rolled cigarette is pressed between her lips—the kind you can get in the Badlands. But that's not why I find myself staring at her. She is oh-so-casually tinkering with a razer. I've only ever seen razers in the hands of Tranquils.

Kudzu HQ is a hotbed of rule breakage. For starters, they're growing their own food. No one cares if you have an herb garden or fruit tree, but large-scale gardening throws off the equal distribution of resources. Not to mention the weapons (double illegal), and that they're presumably all undocumented and operating without IDS (triple times a million illegal).

"Ling!" The two pixie girls spot her first. They abandon their stream and run over to us.

"Hey!" Ling laughs as both girls throw themselves on her, light as birds. Like Ling, they have red string necklaces with little silver Ks on them. "Everyone!" Ling calls, extracting herself from the giggling pixie girls. "I found her!" She gestures at me grandly. "Meet Tess Rockwood, the robot girl!"

At once, every person in the backyard is heading my way.

"Hi!"

"Hey, Tess!" The pixie girls bounce in front of me eagerly.

"We've heard so much about you!"

"Pretty tronic! Does it glow it the dark?"

"Uh, thanks. Yeah, sort of." Everywhere, eyes are on me: curious and excited.

"Gem and Kissy," Ling introduces the pixie girls. Gem's the one with the lip piercing, Kissy's the one with eyebrow piercings. "Sisters, obviously. The guy in the garden is Tomm—"

Names and faces blur around me. "Hi," I keep saying, shaking hands and bumping fists. "Hey, how's it going?"

"Did someone say 'robot girl'?" A boy's voice rings out from way above me. A pool of rope falls from the sky. The sound of friction—*vvvvvvvip!*—and a grinning blond boy lands squarely in front of me.

"Benji!" A voice calls from around the same point, high up in the tree's branches. A second rope drops down. "You were supposed to wait for"—*vvvvvvvip!*—"me!" A girl lands confidently. Golden-blond hair spills out around her shoulders.

These two look different from the overall vibe of Kudzu. Blue-eyed and supremely healthy-looking, their lithe bodies are free of tronics and piercings. I would've assumed they were brother and sister, except the girl has a lilting accent that makes every *s* sound like *z*.

"Nice." Benji grins at her.

"Thanks." She grins back, and they high-five.

"Should've guessed you guys would want to make an impression," Ling says. "Tess, meet Benji and Lana."

"Nice to meet you," Benji says, shaking my hand. He's wearing thick black gloves lined with a bumpy grip.

"Welcome to Kudzu, Tess," adds Lana. Her handshake is just as strong and assured as Benji's.

"Thanks," I say. "Happy to be here."

"We're psyched to have you on board," Benji adds, running a gloved hand through his short blond hair. "This mission is going to be awesome."

"For sure." I try to sound as self-assured as they do.

Benji grins at Lana. "Race you back up?"

Lana frowns. "No, it's nearly lunch—" But before she finishes, she leaps for her rope. Gripping it expertly with her feet, she begins moving up it lightning fast, like a spectacularly attractive monkey.

"Hey!" cries Benji, racing to do the same.

I turn back around to see the guitar player sidling up behind Ling. He circles her waist with his arm and plants a loud kiss right on her ear. For some reason, I assume the tough and competent Ling would be put off by this, but instead she squeaks in surprise and whirls eagerly into his arms, kissing him hard on the mouth. She grins at him happily, then turns back to me. "This is my boyfriend, Bo."

"Hey." I smile, stepping forward to shake his hand.

"Welcome," he says with an easy grin, then steps back to consider me with mock disapproval. "So. You're the reason my girlfriend was running wild in the Badlands all month."

"She'd probably be running wild no matter what she was doing," I say, and they both laugh. I breathe in the warm fragrant air, so sweet it makes me crave chocolate. "What smells so good?"

"That's the milkwood." Ling gestures to a row of white flowering bushes that line the left side of the backyard. "Actually, that's what we call this place. Milkwood."

Milkwood. I roll the new word around in my brain. This place does seem like a Milkwood. Pleasant and peaceful, but strong and solid.

"Okay, kids!" Henny materializes behind me, her voice booming over the backyard. "Lunch is served. Get it while it's hot, chickens."

Everyone begins moving past me to the kitchen. I glance at Ling, half hoping she'll help me navigate lunch, but she's dragging Bo off around the corner of the house and out of sight.

"Coming to get some lunch?" Lana asks. "Henny is an incredible cook."

"I, um, ate before," I find myself saying.

"Okay." Benji and Lana smile at me again, then head inside.

I'm not sure why I lied like that—I am actually starving, and whatever Henny was cooking made my mouth water.

I take a seat in an empty folding chair and try to organize my memories into some sort of narrative for the meeting. I think I know how to destroy an artilect. Obviously it wasn't anything Mom told me directly, but I was around enough that I do have something of an idea. I remember the way Mom's eyes would glaze ever so slightly when describing how science could make the world a better place, as if she were looking inwardly at her own private utopia.

Kudzu begin filtering back outside, carrying bowls of soup and hunks of fresh bread. I fish the muesli bar out of my backpack. Nibbling on the corner of the hard, dry bar is like eating rocks. I can barely bring myself to swallow one bite. Giving up, I toss the stupid bar in the direction of the scrub.

"Hey! What are you doing?" The girl with the shaved head picks up my muesli bar accusingly. "Did you just throw this away?"

Mortified, I stare at her. Even though she's a full head shorter than me, she is completely terrifying.

"My family is starving to death in the Badlands and you throw away a whole bar?" Furious, she holds up the uneaten bar for everyone to see. "I knew you would be trouble!"

"I—I'm sorry." A deep, hot blush crawls up my cheeks. The entire Kudzu contingent is looking at me and the bar.

"It's just a bar, Naz," someone mutters, but she cuts him off decisively, growing angrier by the second.

"*No*, not just a bar. This is proof she *doesn't* think like we do, she *isn't* Kudzu—"

"Naz!" Ling reappears from around the corner of the house, hair slightly mussed. "Calm down!"

"She doesn't know how to live like we do—"

"Oh, shut up, yes she does," Ling snaps, striding toward us. "She survived a whole year in the Badlands; she can take care of herself." Ling snatches the bar from Naz's hand. "Now unless *you* want to walk us through Aevum, keep your mouth shut."

Naz scowls, muttering a low *fuega* at me before stalking off. She speaks Mal—doesn't surprise me. She's got Badlands written all over her.

Ling exhales angrily, rolling her eyes. "Sorry about that. She's a hothead."

"Yeah," I say. "She's very . . . spirited."

Ling laughs. "Right, spirited. You should see her with one of her tricked-out razers. Spirit central."

"I thought Kudzu were nonviolent," I say, watching Naz disappear into the weapons shed.

"We are," Ling says. "But sooner or later, the Trust will come for us. And we want to be ready."

"So, Naz—she's weapons gal?" I clarify.

Ling nods. "Best in the biz. She's also got opinions. You'll see." She frowns at the offending muesli bar in her hand. "C'mon. Let's get you some real food."

After lunch, everyone converges in the front room. Among the jostling, chatting bodies, I recognize Gem, Kissy, Bo, Tomm—the gardener in the rubber boots—Henny, and, of course, Naz, looking as surly as ever. Carlos lies curled at the feet of Benji and Lana, who sit right at the front, holding hands. After scanning the room, I count twenty-one people. I sit close to the front, but on the side, against the wall.

Ling stands before the group, eyes glittering in the semidarkness. "Aevum," she announces, quieting the chatter. "I'm finally ready to give everyone the full briefing on Kudzu's next mission."

A small volley of whoops and whistles follows.

Ling continues, "This mission is both a stunt to draw attention to the unfairness of such a resource-heavy undertaking while the Badlands are dying, as well as a way to stop the Trust from creating a powerful, self-aware being."

"Why should we care about that?" Naz asks.

"If the Trust creates an artilect," Ling explains, "they're basically the artilect's parents, right? The Trust can tell it whatever they want. Like it needs to keep them in power forever. Who knows what it might do then." Everyone is listening attentively, nodding in agreement.

I catch the eye of the olive-skinned boy who'd been lying in the hammock. He is sitting comfortably in the large red swivel chair, which I assume makes him Achilles, lord of all things tech. He gives me a quick, confident nod, as if to say, "I'm on board." I nod back, then refocus on Ling.

"As most of you know," Ling says, "we have someone helping us with this one—Tess Rockwood. Tess's mom designed the first attempt at an artilect, Magnus." A flash of pain cuts through me. "She knows Simutech, she knows artilects. We're lucky to have her on our side."

"All right, Tess!" Lana grins.

Ling gestures for me to take her place at the front of the room. The room is a sea of eyes, heavy with expectation.

"Okay, so I'm not exactly sure what I'm supposed to do right now," I begin, half joking.

"Tell us about this stupid robot, Rockwood," Naz drawls sarcastically. "You're the freakin' expert."

I bristle, suddenly filled with a sharp desire to prove myself. "First off, it's not a robot. It's an artilect; an artificial intelligence. A machine that can think and feel like we can."

"How is that even possible?" Bo asks.

"My mom was aiming to create something with free will, morality, and empathy," I explain. "Basically what the science types agree could constitute a living machine."

"Why?" Achilles asks.

I shrug. "She was idealistic. She thought a new life force could make things better—see the world in the different way, and try to fix things."

"So, why does the Trust want one?" asks Benji.

"Yeah," adds Achilles. "The Trust doesn't want to make things better. They think they've already done that."

I shake my head. "I really don't know why they want an artilect. It doesn't make a lot of sense to me, either."

"How do you make one?" someone calls.

"Robotic neurocircuitry," I reply. "They'd have an artificial central nervous system, with an artificial brain called a singularix."

"What's the difference between an artilect and a substitute?" asks Tomm.

"Artilects are alive, substitutes aren't," I explain. "We control substitutes, right? We tell them what to do. Artilects will be able to think for themselves and make decisions on their own."

"Substitutes just emulate emotions," adds Achilles, "instead of really having them. Right?"

"Exactly." I nod. "But Magnus could feel things, and Aevum, theoretically, can too. Hypothetically, they'll be capable of wanting things, and then acting on their desires to get what they want. Free will. As well as having a sense of right and wrong, a sense of morality."

"Morality created by Simutech, and the Trust," Ling says.

"That's right," I say.

A ripple of understanding filters through the room.

Achilles taps his fingers together, looking fascinated. "Will it look like a person?" He has a clipped, quick way of speaking.

I shake my head, feeling my confidence grow every second. "That would require human cloning, which has never been done successfully. Plus, it's against the law. Aevum will almost definitely be human-shaped, with a head and arms and legs." I flash on the cold piece of bone-shaped metal I picked up in Abel's basement lab. I wish I'd studied it more carefully. Was it leg or arm bone? Was it much bigger than my limbs or the same size? I refocus and add, "But there's no scientific benefit to creating an artilect that is overly human."

"Why not?" asks Kissy, sounding almost offended.

"Human bodies are weak," I reply simply.

"Speak for yourself," quips Achilles, flexing barely-there muscles. Everyone titters, even me.

"We bleed, we bruise, we break," I explain. "They'll make something harder to destroy."

"But not impossible," announces Ling. "Which brings us to Simutech."

Ling nods to Achilles, who pulls up a holo of Simutech's main entrance. Six floors of undulating dark glass, wider than it is tall. Ling gestures at the holo. "Aevum is being developed at Simutech itself, which is located in the Hive." The holo cycles through the building's entire exterior, showing loading docks and side entrances.

"Tess?" Lana raises her hand politely. I hide a smile and nod at her to ask a question. "If this artilect is so powerful, and we don't know what it's like, isn't it a bit dangerous to try to destroy it?"

Now I can't help smiling. "It's more than 'a bit' dangerous. That would be crazy dangerous. I don't think we should destroy Aevum."

"You don't?" Ling says, momentarily horrified.

"We should destroy its power source." I address the whole room. "Mirror matter."

"Mirror matter?" Achilles repeats the words, half confused, half excited. "What's that?"

I turn to him. "Can you bring up the security stream for Innovation Lab C? It's part of the Innovation Department on Level Six."

The tech king frowns. "I can," he says cautiously. "But I don't want to lurk too long." He gestures to the holos of Simutech's exterior. "Outside is one thing, but inside is risky. They sweep for bugs and viruses more often. Can't have my identity as a Peeping Tom discovered."

"I just need a minute," I tell him, a little disappointed. It would have been helpful to watch the security streams for longer; maybe we would've found Aevum itself.

"Okay." His lithe fingers swish in the holo and the loading dock is quickly replaced by the lab. It actually looks more like a factory floor than a laboratory. The ceilings extend to the top of the whole building, maybe thirty feet. They need to be that tall to house a dozen tall, silver cylinders.

"What are those?" Ling frowns.

"I assume they're Aevum's processors," I reply. "Same ones they used for Magnus."

"But they're huge," Achilles says wonderingly. "And there are so many of them."

I nod. "Even though it's supposed to be a living thing, Aevum would still be the most powerful machine created by humans," I explain. "And those are what a powerful machine needs to run."

Achilles swishes through different angles of the spacious lab until I see what I'm looking for. "There." I point, stopping his flow. "That's mirror matter."

I'm pointing to a small glass case surrounded by a larger one. It's lit overhead by a bright white light. In the case is a baton-shaped cylinder, about six inches long. It lies lengthwise, seeming to float inside the glass box. But it's what is inside the baton that silences the room.

A glowing, brilliant silver liquid. Without a sound, it seems to hum, to vibrate, to beckon. Tiny sparks ebb and flow inside it. It looks like a million tiny mirrors that have been poured into the cylinder.

"It's…beautiful," Ling murmurs, sounding surprised.

"*What* is it?" asks Achilles.

"An extremely powerful, concentrated form of energy," I explain. "It fits into an artilect's singularix—"

"Its brain," Achilles reiterates.

"And charges it up," I say. "Think of mirror matter as an artilect's heart. Rather than it being inside their body all the time and powering them like our hearts do, artilects only need their hearts for a few hours a day. The rest of the time, it's recharging here—"

"And waiting for us to steal it," Achilles finishes, getting it.

"And because we can see it here," I add, "we know that it's powering a singularix somewhere. Aevum might not be finished yet, but it's finished enough for us to destroy it by destroying the mirror matter."

"Sorry to ask a dumb question," Achilles says. "But isn't there, like, an exit program? Some easier way to shut it off?"

"Yes, but it wouldn't be permanent," I say. "This is the only way we could destroy it for good."

"Mirror matter is life," Achilles muses. "Destroy mirror matter. Destroy life."

"Exactly," I say.

"And how do we do that?" It's Naz, sounding slightly less surly than before. "Destroy the mirror stuff?"

"Extreme cold works," I reply. "So does extreme heat. Over two thousand degrees Fahrenheit."

"Fire," Bo says, and I nod. He smiles at his girlfriend. "Burn, baby, burn."

Ling nods back, eyes shining.

"But wait, if we steal that"—Achilles points to the mirror matter in the holo—"can't Simutech just make more of it?"

I shake my head. "If we destroy that mirror matter, or if it ever runs completely dry, the singularix stops working. Permanently. Like a human brain without oxygen."

Achilles whistles. "So they'd have to make more mirror matter *and* a whole new artilect."

I nod. "I know. They're just not planning for anyone to destroy it or for it to ever completely run out of charge. Artilects," I add for emphasis, "are *living* machines. They can be killed." I point to two small boxes set into the side of the glass. "Unfortunately, we can't just open the case. You need two separate security swabs. I only have one. My uncle's."

Benji squints at the case. "I suppose we could smash it open?"

Ling frowns in disapproval. "Noisy. And dangerous." She glances at Naz. "Can we cut something like that quietly, without it breaking?"

Naz studies the stream for a second, then nods.

"So we're stealing the mirror matter, then destroying it with fire," Ling announces. "Tess, when's the quietest time to hit Simutech?"

"I'd say late on a Sunday," I guess. "Even the workaholics aren't usually there then."

"Perfect." Ling nods. "Now we just need to work out how to get past whatever's guarding the building." She turns to Achilles. "What's our best access point?"

Achilles spins in his swivel chair. He seems relieved to switch the stream from the Innovation Lab to one of Simutech's back entrances. "There are only three subs on this loading dock. It's mostly access for sanitation and cleaning." His fingers wiggle in the air and holos of the three substitutes on guard fill the room. Even in the dappled afternoon light, they look ominous.

Quicks. Just like on the Northern Bridge.

The substitutes' gleaming black-and-silver bodies look brand-new and intimidatingly powerful. Their red eyes sweep the loading dock entrance in alternating patterns: a fast sweep, then a slow one, then another fast whip around. Each Quick is set to a different cycle of movement: a strangely cold ballet.

"I don't recognize that kind," Achilles says, glancing at me. "Do you?"

"I'll tell you what kind they are," Naz answers for me. "The kind that go to robot hell after meeting Big Bad." She picks her way through the sitting bodies to slam a chunky razer onto the table. It's the size of a tree branch. "Did all the modifications myself. This'll take out a substitute in no time—wham, bam, thank you robot."

I sigh. "Wait a second—"

Naz speaks over me. "So, five on the ground team, right?" She turns to Ling. "I'll arm everyone prior to action—"

"Those are Quicks!" It's my turn to interrupt her, and I do it loudly. "That razer won't work on them."

"It will," Naz counters. "razers work on subs, and these babies could take out half of Eden."

"They're not like regular subs," I say loudly. "They're Quicks."

"Never heard of them," Naz retorts.

"Well, I have." My voice is tight. "They're made from this superstrong casing called aluminum oxy-something."

"So?"

"It absorbs laser power and turns it into energy," I tell Naz. "Shooting them would make them stronger."

"How do you know that?" she asks incredulously.

"They used the same material for a layer of Magnus," I reply, burning with irritation.

"Tess is right." Achilles glances up from a stream featuring spinning images of smooth sheets of gray. I'm impressed he found it so fast. "If it's aluminum oxynitride, then direct energy weapons will just charge them up."

"So we use straight-up fire. Toast 'em like marshmallows," Naz snarls.

"These guys are fire-, gas-, *and* waterproof." I can feel my face getting hotter. "Plus, we'll draw a lot of unnecessary attention to ourselves trying to blow some Quicks to smithereens. Forget a stealth entrance, we may as well throw a damn parade!"

"Don't tell me how to do my job, Rockwood!"

"I'm trying to not get us all killed!"

"Guys!" Ling shouts. "Stop! We're all on the same side here, okay?"

Naz and I are both on our feet, breathing hard.

"Sit down," Ling orders. I do so reluctantly, but only because the order came from Ling. "We're going to brainstorm a way to get in without using razers. Everyone," she adds, glancing around the crowded room. "I want to hear from everyone."

I slouch in my seat, focusing on the Quicks in the stream in front of me. I'm determined to come up with the answer before Naz.

"Is there somewhere the Quicks aren't guarding that we can climb over?" Benji asks hopefully.

Achilles shakes his head. "I already checked. The entire perimeter is being watched."

Everyone starts throwing ideas around, voices rising.

Gem: "What about some sort of distraction?"

Henny: "Can we forge security swabs?"

Bo: "Is there a way we could tunnel in?"

Think, Tess. What are their weaknesses?

"If only there was a way we could just walk straight in." Lana sighs, smiling at Benji. "For once, I wish a mission could be that easy—"

"Wait, that's it!"

"Everyone, shut up," Ling orders, staring at me. "What do you mean?"

"Quicks' vision is based on movement, like an animal's," I say, trying to keep the words from tumbling over each other in my excitement. "If you freeze, they can't see you."

"You just said Quicks were the biggest, baddest subs in the world," Naz says incredulously. "And all it takes to beat them is not moving?"

"Once they have reason to be alert," I say, "like after they've identified a threat or been programmed to do something, their vision changes to infrared, which is a more conscious form of cognition. But if they're just guarding a back entrance for hours on end, their vision would be motion-activated." I point to the Quicks in the holo confidently. "All we'd have to do is move when they're not looking at us and freeze when they are."

Ling nods. "We could literally walk right past them, as long as we stay completely frozen when they're looking our way."

"Exactly!" I grin.

"But it looks like they're moving randomly." Bo frowns. "We'd have no way of knowing when there'd be a blind spot."

"I doubt it's random," I say, watching the uneven ebb and flow of the Quicks' red eyes. "Machines aren't known for their spontaneity. There must be a pattern."

Achilles perks up. "Give me a minute."

He starts tracking the substitutes' movements. The room waits. No one talks. I catch Lana's eye and she smiles at me hopefully. I try to give her an equally hopeful smile back.

Achilles records each Quick individually, creating different-colored paths of movement for all three of them. The paths spread out in front of them as their eyes move, appearing as a holo above the meeting table. It looks like an oddly beautifully piece of contemporary art. Just as Ling breaks the silence by asking whether we should try a different approach, Achilles pumps his fist in the air triumphantly. "There!"

I gaze at the mess of moving color. "Where?"

He freezes the holo and points to what looks like a thin river of white between two of the Quicks, off to the far left. "They're on a cycle. And every one minute and twenty-three seconds, there's a two-second gap when this field of vision is totally clear."

"So that means every minute and twenty-three seconds, we can move, unseen, for two seconds," Ling clarifies.

"Bull's-eye!" Achilles grins, and the room breaks into scattered applause.

Ling glances over at Naz. "What do you think?"

Naz shrugs, unmoved. "I think it's risky as hell. One sneeze and we're all goners."

"They can't kill us," I remind her.

"I know," she says witheringly, "but they can nab us and deliver us to the Trust."

"I still think this is the best plan we've got."

"We can practice here," Achilles says. "And I can talk you through on the day. I like this plan." He looks right at me and smiles. "Smart."

I feel a sticky flush of pride.

"Let's move on," Ling says. "Once we're past the Quicks, we'll be outside, meaning we'll still have to get into Simutech itself. You said it was Level Six, right Tess?"

I nod. "Top floor."

The room starts throwing around some ideas. I remember there's a kitchen window on the sixth floor that's usually left open for the fresh air, which is confirmed by the holos. After that, we land relatively quickly on roping in freehand, which is what I'd seen Benji and Lana do. It saves getting past any alarms on the ground floor or having to sneak up six flights of stairs once we're inside.

"So we have a target, and we have a way in," Ling says. "Now we just need to make sure we're in control of any vision inside."

"She means security streams," Benji whispers to me helpfully. "Recording us in there."

"This is the hardest part," Lana adds. "None of us can risk being recorded on a stream."

I point to the holos of the Quicks in confusion. "Isn't that the security stream?" I ask. "You already have it."

"This is their security stream," Achilles allows. "But I can only lurk. I can't record, copy, or cut it. What I need to do is record a certain amount of stream with no one in it, then right before you go in, loop it into the system."

"So the security stream looks like it's recording empty corridors," I think aloud, "when in reality, it's not. We're in there."

Achilles nods. "To do that, I need to hack their security system. And to do that, I need to know what system they're running."

Ling glances at me. "I doubt you know that, right, Tess?"

Tell them. You're in it now. Too late to back out. Tell them.

I bite my lip. "You could see if it's the Liamond system."

Achilles whistles. "I hope not." He swings around to open a new stream with an expert swoop of his hands.

"How does someone like you know so much about their security?" Naz asks me suspiciously.

"C'mon, Naz." Ling sighs.

I shrug, affecting nonchalance. "I'm nosy."

"You're right." Achilles looks up from the stream. "They're running Liamond. Which sucks for us."

"It's impossible to hack it?" Ling asks, borderline panicked.

"Hey!" Achilles looks offended. "*Impossible* is not in my vocab. With a little elbow grease and a lot of late nights, I can get you"—he swishes his fingers and squints at a run of numbers that appear—"fifteen minutes of fake stream goodness. Ladies and gentlemen, start your mission!"

Benji whoops loudly. I feel a flash of apprehension. *Am I really ready to go back there?*

"Fantastic!" Ling exclaims. "How long will you need?"

"One month!" Achilles announces proudly.

"One month?" Ling looks pissed. "Are you kidding me?"

"Do you want to get nasty with Liamond, Ling?" Achilles stands up, offering her his seat. "Please, be my guest."

"No," she says. "It's just...a whole month?"

"It'd be quicker if there were ten of me and Simutech weren't running the Liamond system," Achilles says, almost testy. "Getting through that is like breaking through a stone wall with a toothpick."

"But things are rough out in the Badlands right now," Ling says, glancing at me. "The mission and the Kudzu stream are concrete ways to draw attention to that. I just thought we'd be doing this sooner."

Achilles rubs his eyes for a second, then grimaces. "Three weeks. And that's committing myself to no sleep and no sanity, so you owe me."

Ling socks his shoulder, grinning. "You're the best, Chilly."

"That's right," he says, sitting back down and bumping fists with Benji and Bo. "Chilly is the best."

"We'll need that time to finish the stream anyway," Gem says to Ling.

"I can't believe we're really making a stream about all this." Kissy grins, biting her lip in excitement. "People are going to freak."

"And it'll give us plenty of time to train Tess," Lana adds hopefully.

"Three weeks?" I repeat uncertainly. "You sure you want me around that long?"

"Of course we do!" Lana exclaims. "You're one of us now, Tess."

Naz coughs deliberately, and I remember what Ling said about official membership: only when everyone agrees. Still, excitement ignites in my belly at even being a guest for that long.

"So." Ling beams. "That's it! Achilles will start hacking the Liamond system, the assault team will start training, and Gem and Kissy will keep working on the Kudzu stream. Any questions?"

I am prepared for someone to press the point of *why*—why the Trust is so interested in artilects. It seems so strange to me. But the next question doesn't deal with that at all. It's worse.

"What happened to your mom?"

I freeze.

"Naz," hisses Ling.

"What?" Naz challenges, leaning forward. "This artilect thing killed Rockwood's mom. That's no secret—it's on the streams. If we're going up against the same thing, we should at least know what happened."

Ling glances at me uneasily. It's obvious that while she feels uneasy with Naz's bold line of questioning, she agrees.

"Magnus," I say his name uncomfortably. "Magnus..." I squeeze my eyes shut, feeling light-headed.

I remember waiting for her in the dark, snarling out the words as soon as the front door chimed shut.

"Where were you?"

"Tess!" Mom's hand flew to her chest, gasping. "You scared me. Why are you sitting in the dark?"

I stared at her hatefully, still stuffed into my frilly Elizabethan costume. "Where. Were. You?"

"What are you talking about?"

"Macbeth? Ring a bell?" I spat. "I was Lady Macbeth! I've been telling you about it for months!"

"Stop yelling, Tess. Don't be such a baby."

"Oh, because the only baby you care about is a machine? The only thing in the world you have time for anymore is a damn robot!"

"He's not a robot, Tess, he's an artilect—"

"Shut up, just shut up!" I screamed. "You're the worst mother in the whole world!"

"Tess?" Ling's arm on mine whisks me back to the present. "You don't have to tell us if you don't want to."

"It—he—was still in a testing phase," I say stiffly. "My mom thought he was more emotionally advanced than he was. She set up a test, at our house."

"What kind of test?" Ling asks.

I swallow, and repeat the lie I'd invented for the stunned Simutech scientists who had stood pale-faced in our kitchen, one year ago. "She told Magnus to hurt her. She was convinced he cared about her enough to refuse, despite being ordered to. That he could tell right from wrong. But she was wrong."

The room is silent. I feel cold and hard, like I'm made from stone.

Ling narrows her eyes in confusion. "Why did your mom bring Magnus home in the first place? Why didn't she just do the test at Simutech?"

I lift my head and look Ling square in the eye. I don't want to lie. But I have to. "I don't know."

chapter 8

I get home late, but Abel has dinner waiting for me. As we eat, I tell him that I spent the day at a nearby Longevity Hub. "I think I'm just going to focus on getting healthy," I tell him. "The people who work there are all really nice. Really into it." He seems surprised, but not disapproving. After I go to bed, my dreams are a frustrating mess of me trying to get into a house with no windows or doors while being scrutinized by Kudzu, who are all wearing white lab coats.

The next morning, I catch an airtrain to the filtration plant using a fake ID Achilles hooked me up with yesterday. This time, Ling's waiting for me.

"Can't wait to see me kill it at training, huh?" I say by way of a greeting.

She snorts amusement. "Or see you get your ass kicked."

I eye her with genuine surprise. "Aren't you supposed to be team leader? The one who motivates?"

"Just calling it how I see it," she says with a shrug.

"Well, get ready, Ping." I swing myself onto the floater to sit behind her, and speak directly into her left ear. "I got some serious skills, girl."

Ling's answering laugh is drowned out by the floater's engine sputtering to life.

In the dappled sunlight of Milkwood's big backyard, my training begins under the tutelage of the genetically blessed Benji and Lana. They're going to teach me what I saw them do yesterday: fast-roping, which is, according to Ling, "really hard" and therefore "really fun."

I've had some experience with climbing in the Badlands, to hunt the fat prairie chickens who like to nest in sneaky, high-up crevices. I'd never done it with a rope before, but to be honest, I'm feeling relatively confident. Up and down a rope. How hard can it be?

"Fast-roping is all about control and landing safely," Benji begins. "You want to brake with your hands, not your feet."

"Climbing isn't about upper-body strength," Lana adds. "It's all about technique. You want to know the secret?"

"Be born a monkey?" I guess.

She laughs, exposing perfectly straight white teeth. "A good foot lock."

Benji hands me a pair of black roping gloves. "Ready?"

After grabbing the rope, I'm to get it on the outside of one leg, then under that foot, then up over my other foot. I keep it in place by pinching my feet together. Surprisingly, I'm able to support all of my body weight that way.

"Now, stand up," Lana instructs. "Bend at the waist, and move your feet up a little and get the same footing."

Following her instructions, I'm able to slowly inch myself up the rope. Stand up, bend at the waist to get a new foot lock a few more inches up the rope, pull myself up, repeat. With the foot lock, I'm not hauling my body weight up the rope with my arms. Instead I can balance myself, as long as I have the rope looped between my feet.

"Got it?" Benji's just a couple feet below me, holding the rope steady.

"Absolutely." I catch Tomm's eye, on his hands and knees in the veggie garden, pulling out a handful of carrots. He gives me a friendly wave and I try to grin back, feeling like bait on a hook as I dangle in the middle of the backyard.

"Then we'll time you," Lana says, pulling out a stopwatch. "See how long it takes you to get to the top."

I glance up. "The top, as in, the top that's a million miles away?" The rope's fastened to a branch that's easily thirty feet up.

"It's closer than it looks," Benji assures me.

I see Ling and Naz over by the weapons shed, arms crossed and watching me. "Ready when you are."

Lana eyes the stopwatch. "And...go!"

The fact that I'm being timed makes me more nervous than I should be. I bend at the waist, grab rope that's higher up, then haul myself up in a quick movement.

"Find your foot lock!" Lana calls. I try to look down to guide my legs in the right place but I don't have a clear line of sight.

"Just do it by feel," Benji suggests.

I twist and turn with the rope, my forehead growing hot and sticky.

There. A foot lock. I know it from Benji's and Lana's encouraging cheers. I make sure it's firm and am once again able to get a little farther up the rope. I manage to repeat this four times in a row. My breathing becomes panting. My strength is ebbing. I must be near the top by now? But when I look up, the branch is still just as far away.

"How long has it been?" I call.

Benji's voice is a lot closer than I thought it'd be. "Just over a minute."

There's literally no way I am getting to the top of that tree without developing the ability to fly. "I'm coming down!"

"But, you've hardly even—"

The rest of Lana's words are lost in a short, sharp whizzing sound as I loosen my grip on the rope. I fall on my butt, hard. "Oof." I wince. My face feels red all over. My hands throb and sting at the same time.

I stumble to my feet, brushing leaves off my pants. "That wasn't too bad. Obviously with a couple more days of training..."

Benji and Lana are having a conversation with their eyes, then turn to give me a sympathetic, worried look.

"What?" I ask. "Well, how long will we have at Simutech?"

They speak as one. "One minute."

"One minute?" I repeat incredulously. "To get all the way to the top?"

"I think Simutech is even taller than—" begins Benji, but Lana shushes him.

"We'll get there," Lana says, putting an extremely toned arm around me.

I'm about to tell her that unequivocally, no, I really don't think so and maybe I'd be better on the ground and out of the way of the rope completely when I catch sight of Ling. Watching me with a grin, she mouths something to me across the backyard. *Skills.* My pride bristles and bucks back up. "Absolutely we'll get there. No question about it."

It's decided that we'll start with getting me into shape *generally*. I had been laboring under the impression I was pretty fit, but apparently a year of living off cheap millet and raw nerves doesn't actually produce the healthiest of human forms. Benji and Lana hit upon the idea of a multiskilled obstacle course in and around Milkwood that'll build muscle, stamina, and strength. Henny is instructed to put me on a protein-rich diet, a challenge she accepts with gusto.

While Benji and Lana get busy creating the obstacle course, I wander inside the house.

The meeting room is completely devoid of natural light. The front windows all look permanently blackened, I assume for security. The only light comes from the greenish streams Achilles is awash in. Endless yellow and black numbers fall like heavy rain in five separate security streams. Achilles orchestrates them with complex wiggles of his fingers, his tongue protruding from his mouth in concentration.

I clear my throat and he yelps. "Holy guac!" With a flick of his wrist, the five gushing streams all pause midway through their descent. He shoots me a wry smile, shaking his head at his own jumpiness. "You are not afraid of the sneak attack, are you?"

"Sorry." I grin. "I just wanted to see how it was going."

"It goes," he says. "Still waiting to see exactly how. Boss lady giving you a break from training?"

I assume he means Ling. "I thought you were a collective," I say, a little teasingly. "No bosses, right?"

Achilles scoffs good-naturedly. "We let Ling toil under that delusion. But we all know who butters the bread around here." He gestures to an empty chair next to him. "Please. Feel free to cease standing."

I sink down into the chair, eyes on the frozen streams. "So, this is the Liamond system, huh?"

"The very one. Tricky little monkey, too," he adds, rubbing his wrists. "Looks like they recently upgraded."

After what happened with Magnus, I'm sure Simutech doubled down on all security measures. "Maybe they have something to hide," I murmur.

"Maybe definitely." Achilles nods. "But don't sweat it. Achilles Zamata is on the case. The case that involves me not bathing or experiencing sunlight for the foreseeable future," he adds wryly.

The frozen strings of numbers hang in the air, looking intimidatingly impenetrable to untrained eyes like mine. "Is there anything I can do?" I ask hopefully.

"Not unless you're secretly a wizard code breaker."

I slump a little. "Nope. Just a regular non-wizard type."

"You're more than that," Achilles says.

I shoot him a *huh?* look.

"You survived the Badlands for a year!" he exclaims. "You worked out how to get past the Quicks at Simutech. You own a *knife*. And, you're helping Kudzu out—who happen to be the most awesome group of revolutionaries ever."

I want to accept Achilles' compliments, but thinking about Magnus has sent my guilt meter into overdrive. I fiddle with my necklace, searching for a subject change. "How did you find Kudzu?"

His eyes drift back to the frozen numbers. "They found me. I tried to hack a Three Towers security stream when I was about thirteen. Failed, of course, and ended up in community service, where I met Benji."

"Thirteen years old and taking on the Trust," I say with a laugh. "Consider me impressed."

"And yet, that white whale continues to elude." He sighs, stretching his neck to one side then the other. "No one's ever cracked a Three Towers stream, not that I know of. Just be glad the mirror matter isn't residing there."

Henny pops her head around the corner. "Lunch, chickens."

Achilles gets to his feet eagerly. "You'll let me know if there's anything I can do, right?" I reiterate, rising to follow him.

He nods. "Sure thing. But Tess," he adds, as we head for the hallway, "you're already doing plenty. Don't kill yourself over this. We have a strict no-kill policy when it comes to missions," he adds jokingly.

Achilles ambles down the hallway in the direction of the backyard, leaving me momentarily alone. The short, sharp word slices through me—*kill*. Kudzu and I are going to kill Aevum. For a moment, the prospect seizes me with its wrongness. What we're planning is murder. Artilects are alive. Then I pull myself together.

We're the good guys. I'm sure of it.

Lunch is a warm salad consisting of quinoa, kale, sultanas, a strong white cheese, and grated carrot. Henny adds a boiled egg to mine—the requisite protein. Lana warns me not to eat too much, as I'll be starting on the obstacle course this afternoon. I sit by Ling as I eat, and listen in on a conversation she has with Naz over weaponry. Snatches of phrases like *smoke bombs* and *contained explosions* seem surreally at odds with the peaceful, sunny vibe of the backyard.

After lunch, the symmetrical saints walk me through an obstacle course that twists and turns all around the grounds of Milkwood and out into the woods beyond. The workout they've invented would easily rival what you could accomplish on the slickest equipment at the best Longevity Hub. I'm to vault over fallen logs and swing myself over swampy patches, duck under low branches and race through the trees. Lana has already done it twice.

My first attempt kicks my ass in a comprehensive fashion. When I emerge from the woods, red-faced and muddy, Benji and Lana cheer. "How...long...did...I...take?" I ask between wheezes.

"Just over ten minutes," Benji beams.

"And...how...long...did...you...take?" I ask Lana, hands planted on my knees to help me catch my breath.

"Three minutes," Lana answers. "But ten minutes for your first time is totally—"

"Awesome," I cut her off. "Got it." I crumple to the ground and lie flat on my back. The golden-haired couple burst into laughter. They're so unflinchingly earnest, it's hard not to fall in love with them.

The afternoon speeds by as I do the course again and again and again. I knock my overall time down to eight and a half minutes, which feels like an enormous victory.

In the late afternoon, when the sun has dropped below the tops of the high city walls, sending Milkwood into shadow, Ling, Naz, Benji, Lana, and I all practice moving and stopping to get past the Quicks. We look like we're playing a kids' game. It's hard to take it seriously, even though we all know one tiny finger shake can blow our cover. We do get noticeably better after an hour, moving and freezing as one solid unit. It makes me feel united with Kudzu in a concrete way.

Eventually, twilight settles around us. Reluctantly, I tell Ling I have to get back to Abel's.

"Got to keep playing 'good niece,' huh?" she says, eyes flashing with amusement.

"The man loves a family dinner." I don't feel like explaining the tutoring session that's scheduled. Even though most people in Kudzu are about the same age as me, they seem older. The tutoring thing feels embarrassingly babyish. I just don't believe the whole thing's motivated by Abel's concern about my intellect. Maybe it's just to keep me busy and out of his way. Or maybe, I think with a jolt, it's because he has reason to distrust me. No. That's impossible. How could he know anything about Kudzu? I've been so careful.

Maybe I'll get lucky. Maybe Abel will forget about the session and leave me to my own devices. Maybe Hunter will blow it off.

Yeah, and maybe Gyan will grow wings and fly off into the sunset.

"Honey!" Abel's front door glides shut behind me with a chime. "I'm home!"

Kimiko whizzes into the center of the lounge. "Hello, Tess."

"Hello, Kimiko, darling Kimiko, apple of my eye, cream of my coffee."

"You are in a good mood, Tess," the robot observes in her smoothly modulated tone, spinning to watch me flop down onto the sofa. "I am happy to see that."

I'm still buzzing with the newness of it all. Secret headquarters and rebel ropers, stream hackers and plans of attack. I pull my boots off and let them thud to the floor. I'll probably have blisters tomorrow from the hikes and all the running. "You're not actually happy," I tell the fembot, rubbing my feet. "You don't have an artificial nervous system in order to produce the chemicals to feel happy. You'll never know the heart-pounding, knee-knocking, obsessive power of dopamine. But let's not let semantics spoil our evening."

"Are you hungry, Tess? I am programmed to prepare a variety of nutritious meals."

"I ate," I say. I prop myself up on one elbow and twist to face her. "But now that you mention it—Oh. Hey."

"Greetings." Hunter pronounces the word in the amiable tone of someone completely unperturbed by my one-hour lateness. I hadn't noticed him sitting alone at the dining room table, empty except for a single piece of scratch.

"Greetings," I echo, inwardly wincing. I was right: Abel had not forgotten about my babysitter.

"Did you want to eat before we get started?" he asks.

"No, that's okay." I sigh. "Kimiko, you are dismissed, or whatever."

"Thank you," the robot says, then whizzes off in the direction of the kitchen.

I flip myself to my feet and pad over to Hunter. He's wearing a clean white T-shirt and a calm expression of expectation. "Can I be honest?"

His eyebrows flick down in confusion. "Have you not been so far?"

"I don't need a tutor," I say, sliding into a chair next to him. "Abel thinks I do, but Abel likes wearing lady's housecoats." Hunter's mouth quirks in cautious amusement, which I take as tacit approval to continue. "Why don't we just *tell* him we're studying together, you know, without actually doing it. I can go do my thing, and you can go do your thing, and ta-da! We all do our things *separately*."

Hunter leans forward, mouth still curled into a half-smile. "And what is your 'thing,' Tess?"

I smile back. "Not doing this."

"I can't lie to your uncle," Hunter says.

"Yes, you can!" I protest. "It's easy, and it's kind of fun."

"I can't," he says firmly. "So let's just get started. I thought we'd begin with art." He goes to press his thumb into the scratch—scratch that's on-cycle.

"Wait!" I try to look nonchalant as I get my backpack, pulling out the off-cycle scratch I'd managed to get back from Ling. "Use this."

"Why?"

"It's off-cycle."

"Why do you have—"

"It was my Mom's." My voice sounds more like a challenge than I want it to, so I shrug a little and add, "She used it when she didn't want to be bothered by other people."

He purses his lips. "But you won't have a record of this session."

"I don't need a record. This is all about making me smarter right? The only record I need is up here," I say, tapping my temple.

"All right." He presses his thumb into the corner of my scratch. It glows gold. Hunter instructs, "Show me art."

The streams burst into life. Such a broad search topic brings up dozens and dozens of miniature clouds displaying art throughout the ages. Paintings, sculptures, installations, performances, and more all spin and whirl before my eyes; the old and the new jostling for our attention. The neatly presented woman who talked me through aevum begins speaking, but Hunter quickly mutes her with his eyes. An entire world of pretty, opaque information hangs above the table, like a magical mobile.

How. Extremely. Annoying.

"Your curriculum requires you to focus on one major movement," Hunter says, meeting my eyes through the stream. "What do you prefer? Contemporary? Or the classics?"

I slouch in my chair, sulking. "I don't care."

"I find contemporary art very interesting," Hunter suggests.

"Really?" I roll my eyes. "Isn't it all like, a banana in the middle of a room that's supposed to be my soul?"

"Okay, no contemporary," Hunter says, unshaken. "How about the impressionists?"

"Oh please." I snicker. "Has it ever occurred to you that they painted like that because laser eye surgery wasn't invented until a hundred years later? That Monet guy probably thought he was doing a bang-up job."

"Okay. No impressionists." This time his voice is sharp. It's very satisfying to hear the edge of irritation in his nothing-can-faze-me tone—an itch I can finally scratch. Time to let him off the hook.

"Surrealists," I say, flicking my hand over a passing Magritte. "I like the surrealists."

The surrealist stream replaces the general art one. Paintings of melting clocks and feet that turn into shoes and pipes that aren't pipes spin around us. I find my favorite painting, *Mystery and Melancholy of a Street.*

Between two white buildings, on a bright slanting street, a young girl plays with a hoop and stick. An empty wooden cart, the kind they might've used to transport horses, sits next to one of the buildings, its back doors open. In the direction the girl is running, there's the shadow of a person, maybe a man. The buildings on either side of the scene are cut with multiple archways. Small square windows run along the top of them, parallel to the roof, which is scarlet red. The sky is sea green, darkening in the foreground of the painting. Harsh sunlight hits the ground, turning what's not deep in shadow into a brilliant yellow-gold.

"Giorgio de Chirico," I announce. "This is 'my thing.' "

"Really?"

I cut him a wry glance. "Don't look so shocked. I'm surprisingly nuanced."

"What can you tell me about this artist?" Hunter asks, now in teacher mode.

"Um...He was Greek-born Italian..."

"More."

"Born in the 1880s..."

"More."

"Technically a metaphysical painter as opposed to surrealist."

Hunter raises an eyebrow. "More."

As we go on, Hunter fills in details of what I can't remember. He's surprisingly well-versed for a science geek, which admittedly is a tiny bit impressive.

"And why do you like this particular work?" Hunter asks.

"I think because it's so unsettling." I frown. "All the perspectives are off—the shadows are in all the wrong places, compared to where the buildings are. And the figure of the girl. She seems innocent, running along with a fun hoop and everything, but it's spooky and desolate at the same time."

"De Chirico painted this in 1914," Hunter says offhandedly. "Some say it was an allegory for the foreboding atmosphere of imminent war."

"An allegory for a foreboding atmosphere?" I tease. "Major geek points for that, my friend." Then, because I am genuinely interested: "Do you like it?"

"Hmm?"

"The painting." I nod as it circles slowly past me. "Is that 'your thing'?"

Hunter considers it with a frown. "I don't know," he says thoughtfully. "That's an interesting question."

"Same question you asked me."

He props his chin up on his hand and watches it drift past, eyebrows furrowed in thought. "It seems...sad to me. Lonely."

"Lonely?"

He nods. I wonder if he has many friends.

"It reminds me of Eden," I say.

His eyes dart from the painting to me. "What do you mean?"

"Just the sun, being so bright. The white buildings." I think aloud. "How what could be taken as an innocent street scene actually feels sort of creepy. Dangerous."

"You think Eden is dangerous?" Hunter sounds amused.

I recall Ling's look of horror when she found out I broke Trust law on-cycle. My quickness of subject change rivals the speed of light. "So, lonely, huh? Post-ed not bursting with friendly types?" I flick a stray crumb at him with my fingernail. "Surprised you haven't found a nerd gang to run with there. I thought the South Hills had the best science courses in all of Eden."

A peculiar expression climbs across his face. "Why would you assume," he says slowly, "that I don't have any friends?"

I've hurt his feelings. But before I can stutter out an apology, he catches me off guard.

"Why didn't you eat that food?"

"What food?" I ask, feigning ignorance.

"The food last night. When I got here, you were…angry." He pronounces the last word carefully.

The memory of that scene makes me blush. "I didn't want to."

"Why not?"

"Because I couldn't live with myself if I did."

"Why not?"

"*Why not, why not,*" I mimic him meanly. "You sound like a child."

"I'm sorry," he says immediately. "I didn't mean to upset you. I'm just curious."

I scoff. "About my eating habits?"

"About you." The eyes that could be gray or could be green meet mine in a way that feels very unprotected.

Oh no. Oh *no.* "Are you kidding me?" I exclaim, skidding my chair out from under me.

Hunter jumps, startled. "What's wrong?"

"So *that's* why this whole tutoring thing is going down?" I pace back and forth in front of the table. "Did you ask Abel? Huh? I bet you asked him."

"I didn't ask him—"

"Look, *maybe* if I hadn't just spent a year out in the Badlands, *maybe.* But where I'm at right now…" Kudzu. Izzy. My mom, Aevum, Magnus. I shudder. "It's just not going to happen."

"Tess, I'm really not following," Hunter says apologetically.

My finger jabs in his direction. "You have a crush on me!"

"*What?*"

"You heard me! And I just can't, I cannot deal with that right now—"

"Tess!" Hunter's on his feet. "I do not have a crush on you!"

I'm stopped in my tracks. "Really?"

"Really," he says emphatically. One hand is around his chin, rubbing it with alarmed concern. "I do not have a *crush* on you, Tess." He makes it sound painfully juvenile.

"You, ah, you sort of seemed like the opposite might be true, but, um, you know what, now that we're talking about it, it does seem…"

"Completely insane?" he suggests.

Hunter is at post-ed. Hunter has impressive frontal lobe capacity. Hunter is borderline attractive, for a geek.

I have weirdo plaits. I have the body of a twelve-year-old boy. I pull knives on people.

Hunter. Does not have. A crush. On me.

My cheeks go from hot to feverish.

"Tess."

Before I open my eyes, I can tell he's already cleared the room and is over in the hallway.

"Yes?" I ask meekly.

"I'm going to go. It's just—I'm going to go."

"Okay."

He turns, takes a step, then turns again. His hand is back on his chin, pawing at it frantically. "It's just—it's very important that we maintain a professional relationship. You're Professor Rockwood's *niece*." He makes it sound so inappropriate, he may as well be naming me his sister.

"I get it. Bad move," I say, cheeks flushing again. "Let's just forget about it, okay?"

He surprises me by laughing. A short, sour sound without any humor at all. "Right," he says. "Forget."

Hunter leaves me feeling so completely mortified that I'm almost angry. And I have to see him tomorrow. And the day after that. And the day after that.

My head drops into my hands, and I let out a groan.

When I emerge from the house into Milkwood's bright backyard, the first person I see is Naz. She regards me suspiciously from her position in front of the weapons shed, turning to spit when I catch her eye.

"Oh-kay," I mutter.

Ling catches it, flicking her gaze to the short, shaved one. "Don't worry about her," she says, giving my shoulder a squeeze. "She takes a while to warm up, but once she trusts you, she'd die for you."

Yeah, right. If she doesn't kill me first.

Surprisingly, I'm looking forward to the obstacle course. There's something glorious about sprinting through the woods, heart racing, legs pumping, breath rasping. It makes me feel like I am completely inhabiting my own body. On my last attempt before we break for lunch, I'm down to seven minutes and forty-five seconds. Lana and Benji are thrilled. I can't help thinking it's still double the time Lana got on her very first attempt.

Lunch is roasted root vegetables—carrots, parsnips, potatoes—served with a spicy beetroot relish. As we eat, Kudzu and I try to outdo each other with horror stories—the time they spent the night hiding in apple trees in the Farms while clueless Guiders stomped around below, trying to find who'd been stealing boxes of apples, or the week I lived on a single can of beans.

I've barely finished eating when Gem and Kissy alight around me. They're in the midst of creating the Kudzu stream that'll be released after we destroy Aevum, and they have a million questions for me about artilects and life in the Badlands. I answer them as best I can, barely finishing one answer before they demand the next. Their enthusiasm is sweet and infectious. There's something incredible about knowing my words will be used to make a stream that could expose thousands of Edenites to such strange and awful truths.

When I've satisfied their curiosity, I relax on the back steps and surreptitiously watch Naz tinker with Big Bad. She catches me looking with an immediate scowl.

"No one touches the razers unless I say so," she warns.

I nod—as if I was going to mess around with any of her swag. "Not really my weapon of choice anyway."

"Oh yeah?" She sniffs sarcastically. "And what would that be?"

I pluck Mack from the backpack at my feet, then twirl him fast through my fingers to catch the hilt neatly in my palm.

"Nice!" Lana and Benji call from the hammock.

I raise my eyebrows at Naz.

She folds her arms across her chest. "How's your aim?"

"Not bad."

She nods at the dartboard. "Go on, then."

Aware that everyone in the backyard has their eyes on us, I take aim. With a hard flick of my arm, my hunting knife flies fast through the air . . . right past the dartboard and into the vegetable garden.

"Missed!" But Naz's smug smile disappears as her eyes find where Mack has actually landed. Clean through the throat of a rabbit in the strawberry patch. Easy as a prairie chicken.

"Whoa!" The entire background breaks into applause. "Nice shot!" calls Bo.

But all I get out of Naz is an unimpressed grunt.

"Seriously?" I mutter to myself. *I just bull's-eyed a rabbit,* fuega—*give me something!*

"How'd you learn to throw like that?" Lana asks.

"When I was in the Badlands, we'd kill desert rats that way," I say. "Prairie chickens too, if you don't mind heights."

"How high?" Lana asks, eyes wide.

I shrug, trying not to sound boastful. "Sometimes twenty feet."

"Wow," Lana says.

"Impressive," Benji adds.

I smile, pride blooming inside me. "What about you guys—how high have you gone?"

Lana waves the question away. "It doesn't matter—"

"You ever hear about the ladder?" Naz cuts her off.

I glance over at her. "The ladder?"

Naz nods. "Someone painted a ladder on the inside of the city walls, and the word—"

"*Welcome,*" I finish. I had heard about that, years ago. I stare at Benji and Lana. "That was you guys?"

They both blush modestly. "We had harnesses," Lana says, sounding almost apologetic. "We weren't freehand."

I turn to stare in disbelief at the white city walls that tower over us, a couple miles north. They seem to take up half the sky. "That's got to be over three hundred feet."

"Easily," says Naz.

I wish I could take back my boast about climbing up twenty feet. My cheeks prickle with heat. "That's really amazing," I tell Benji and Lana. "Really cool."

Lana gives me a sympathetic smile, which I know is supposed to make me feel better, but just makes me feel more embarrassed. I retreat inside.

I find Henny in the kitchen, up to her elbows in soapy water. "I have a present for you," I say, holding up the rabbit by its hind legs. "Hope you like dead things."

Her eyes bug in surprise. "Fresh meat!" she exclaims, wiping her hands on her apron. "Nice work, m'lady. Usually takes a new kid a lot longer to trap something."

"Not trap. Knife," I say, miming throwing one.

"Quite impressive, aren't you?" Henny says, examining the rabbit. "I always like to see new recruits with a bit of spunk—" But she doesn't finish. Suddenly the rabbit is on the floor, and the cook's hand is on her lower back. She winces in pain.

"Are you all right?"

"I'm fine, chicken," she wheezes. "Just need to sit down for a minute."

I guide her to a wooden chair and she sinks into it heavily, grimacing.

"Should I get someone?"

"No," she says. "I'm not sick. Just a sore back. Not uncommon when you're..."

Henny's ample size isn't just from extra servings of root vegetables.

"Pregnant," I finish softly.

"Yes." She opens her eyes and looks right at me. "And it's my third."

A horrible chill cuts through me. "Your third?" I repeat dumbly. "As in, your third child?"

She nods, shifting in her chair. I'm not an expert on the female form in this condition, but she must be at least five months pregnant.

"Can you get me a glass of water?" she asks.

I all but leap toward the sink, eager to have something to do.

Henny accepts the water gratefully, and finishes it in one long swallow. I pull another chair up to sit next to her, at a loss for what to say. I know you usually congratulate pregnant women, but considering the circumstances, that doesn't exactly feel appropriate.

"Why...," I begin awkwardly. "I mean, what happened..."

"My first two children died," she says, forming the words with careful precision. "As well as my partner."

"I'm so sorry," I whisper. "That's awful."

"Yes," she says softly. "It was awful. Buzzcar crash. Fern was four, and Brandon was six and a half." She wipes her nose with her apron, her eyes red and misty. "Losing your children is like losing your limbs. The pain—it never goes away."

I swallow. "I know what you mean," I say, my voice hoarse. "My mother."

Henny reaches for my hand and folds her fingers into mine. "You know, then," she says, meeting my gaze intensely. She sits up in her chair a little, her hand on her belly. "The strange thing is, I always agreed with the population control. Two kids per couple, that seemed about right. But now..." She sighs and wipes her eyes. "I didn't know I was pregnant until I felt it kick. By then, it was too late to think about... doing right by the law." Then, with renewed passion, "I need to be a mom, Tess. I have to be. The Trust won't kill this baby, I won't let them."

"Kill?" I shake my head, taken aback. "They won't kill it, Henny. You could give it up for adoption."

Henny leans toward me. "There were nine hundred and eighty seven babies given up for adoption last year," she says. "Do you know how many people applied for them? Five hundred and eleven partnered, and three hundred and four independent."

I do the math in my head. "What happened to the other babies?" I ask.

Henny shakes her head. My stomach drops. I had no idea the population control was taken that far. A wave of nausea billows inside me. "Is that why you're here?" I ask.

She nods. "Don't get me wrong, I agree with the missions the kids run, but I'm here to have my baby. Kudzu—they'll protect me."

"Of course they will," I say, before correcting myself. "Of course *we* will."

"I know, chicken."

"And it's safe?" I say. "Having it here, I mean. No Longevity Hub, no doctors?"

"It's a lot safer here," she says somberly, "than out there."

chapter 9

This time when I get back to Abel's, I'm less whirlwind and more cautious breeze. I have no idea how Hunter is going to handle what happened between us yesterday. Somehow *lightheartedly* seems foolishly optimistic. I catch myself all but tiptoeing down the hallway and have to make myself walk normally.

Of course, he's already here because, of course, I am twenty minutes late. The sight of him knots my stomach. Tonight he's sitting on the other side of the dining room table, putting a good few feet of table between us. The chair I sat in is even drawn out a few inches in invitation, as if to say, "Sit here. No closer."

"Greetings." The word is so coolly polite, I'm not sure whether to feel annoyed or remorseful. I want to make things right between us. I want to show my somewhat stuffy but mostly decent amigo that he can trust me not to morph into an egotistical monster.

"Hey." I smile back, dropping my bag to the floor. "How are you?"

"I'm well. And you?"

"I am also well," I reply. I pause at my chair, placing a hand on it gently. I cock my head at Hunter as if to say, "Is here okay?"

He inclines his head, almost gracefully. "Please." As I sit down, he's quick to add, "Abel is in his study." It almost sounds like a warning. The idea that Abel might be here to protect Hunter from my lecherous advances makes me smile, and I have to bite my lip. "What?" he asks.

"Nothing." I shake the smile away, and meet his eyes with perfect professionalism. "Should we start on sustainability?"

For the next hour, I do a wonderful impression of a model student. I recite which materials go into which upcycling bins, how compost works, how much water a five-minute shower uses, and how to lower, restrain, and reduce consumption. I stumble a little over some of the specific bylaws of allowances—having never had a pet, I can't remember if dog food falls under Goods or Pleasure—but on the whole, I do pretty well.

As the dark blue of the evening sky deepens to black, Hunter begins to soften. His posture loses its rigidity. At first, I feel like we're performing some sort of formal interview, but after a while things become slightly more casual. I begin dropping a few sarcastic observations, which in turn invoke a flash of amusement, a smile, and then— victory!—an actual chuckle. Abel wanders in and out of his study a few times, ostensibly to get a glass of water from the kitchen, but obviously to check on us. Each time he passes, Hunter retreats into cold professionalism, but after Abel disappears, I'm able to tempt him back into behaving more normally. By eight-thirty, I feel I've definitely weakened the infrastructure of Hunter's wall of protection. Not dismantled it entirely, but caused a few spidery cracks.

"Very good work tonight, Tess," Hunter says, deftly folding the thin gold scratch into a neat square.

"You sound relieved," I say lightly.

"Do I?" he murmurs.

"I don't blame you." I shoot him a smile that's somewhere between mischievous and self-deprecating, and am relieved when I get a smile back.

"Yes. Well. I, uh..." A quizzical half smile, half frown tugs at his mouth as he continues in a low, confessional voice. "I never really know how you're going to behave."

I burst out laughing. I can't help it. There's something so endearingly honest and old-fashioned about him. His genuine confusion at my wild and wacky ways is undeniably *cute*.

Hunter sits back, bewildered. "See? That's what I mean. I have no idea why you're laughing. Was that funny, what I just said?"

"This whole situation is kind of funny," I say dryly. "Look, for the record, I'm honestly really sorry about yesterday. That won't happen again."

"I don't know. You seemed pretty confident," Hunter says, and I'm surprised to realize he's teasing me. "Maybe you know something I don't."

"No, I seemed pretty insane, as you astutely pointed out." I plant both palms flat on the table and look him right in the eye. "Can we just...be friends?"

Hunter's face is perfectly calm. "All right," he says. "Agreed."

"Really?"

"Absolutely."

I exhale loudly and close my eyes for just a second. "Thank you. I just—I just really need that right now."

"Need what?"

"Just—I don't know. Someone to talk to, maybe. Someone normal."

"And you think I'm normal?" I can't tell if he's pleased or offended.

I scratch my fingernails against the tabletop and choose my words carefully. "I've started working out at this Longevity Hub, right? And the people there are great; really cool and nice. But..."

"But what?"

"They've all known each other for ages, so it's hard to fit in. I feel like a bit of an outsider. And they're all so much better than me."

"Because they've been doing it longer," he says. "Which is why they know each other so well."

I sigh. "I guess. I mean, yes, that's right. But it's not just that." I drum my fingers on the table. "We're all training for this...triathlon. And I'm not sure if maybe I'm getting in over my head. I mean, I said I'd do it, and it's sort of like a team thing, so if I pull out, I let everyone down." I look up at him. "I'm really pushing myself. And I'm not one hundred percent sure if it's the right thing to do."

Hunter sits back in his chair, eyebrows drawn in thoughtfully. The tips of his fingers tap lightly against his mouth. He looks like he's musing over something a lot more serious than my concerns with the "Longevity Hub."

"Do you trust the people at the Hub?" he asks.

I blink fast. "Yes," I say. "Yes, I think so."

"They'd tell you," he says, "if you were in danger of hurting yourself? Doing something your body wasn't ready for?"

I have to swallow, and clear my throat. "Yes. They'd tell me."

"And you want to do the triathlon? You like that sort of thing?"

"Well, I haven't exactly done one before," I hedge. "But so far I like it. I like the training. And it seems important. Healthwise," I add quickly.

"Then I think you should stick with it," Hunter says. "It sounds like your biggest obstacle is your own insecurity. But I bet if I asked your friends at the Hub, they'd tell me you absolutely fit in and you're absolutely ready."

He's right. Kudzu have shown nothing but faith in me. Naz is prickly, but she's only one person out of a couple dozen. Everyone else just wants to help. "I just hope it's as important as I think it is," I say cautiously. "It's a lot of work for something that ends up being"—life-threatening?—"a waste of time."

"But only you can be the judge of that," he says. "And you strike me as someone who has a good grasp of what's important and what's not."

"Do I?"

"Yes. You're smart."

The hairs on my arms prick up a little. "Thanks," I murmur, smiling self-consciously. "I, um—I liked the way you said that."

He tips his head to the side, smiling at me quizzically.

"Sometimes when my best friend—or maybe, former best friend—used to say that, it sounded more like an accusation than a compliment. Even though I'm sure she didn't mean it that way."

"Former best friend?"

I wince, although a part of me knows I said that because I knew he'd ask about it. "Her name's Izzy. I caught up with her a few days ago, and it didn't end well. We had a fight."

"What about?"

I regard him, sitting very still in my chair. I'm not about to break the law again. I choose each word with precision. "About Eden," I say. "And the Badlands. We used to be the same. But now . . . Now things are different." I pinch my fingers on my forehead, pressing them into my skin. "Maybe I overreacted," I say with a frustrated groan. "Maybe it was stupid to fight. It's just—she's just—"

"Different," he supplies quietly.

"Yeah." I sigh heavily. "But we were friends for so long. How can that just change?"

"Because people change," Hunter says. "And friendship is based on shared values. It sounds like you have more in common with the people at the Hub than with Izzy." His voice softens with kindness, eyes bright with genuine compassion. "You're being too hard on yourself. People change, and a year in the Badlands would change anyone. You've had experiences your friend will probably never have. You see things differently now. Take, for example, the scratch." He gestures at it, in front of us both on the table. "What is it to a regular Edenite?"

I shrug. "I don't know—an everyday thing. Something you think you can't live without but you actually can."

"And what is it to someone in the Badlands?"

I finger the thin gold scratch, raking my fingernails over its surface to produce a soft *vvvvvv* sound. "Something you'd fight for."

"Exactly. The meaning and value you've assigned to things has changed," he says.

His face is open and warm, displaying no judgment whatsoever. People do change. I'd changed. I didn't mean to hurt Izzy. I wrap Hunter's words around me like a cozy blanket.

"I have to go," he says, glancing at the clock. "I have to go over some notes with Professor Rockwood before I leave."

I'm surprisingly disappointed when he gets up. But before he disappears into Abel's study, I say, "Hunter."

He turns to face me. In the glow in the living room light, I can see the finest spray of freckles across his nose, only noticeable because his skin is so pale. I'm not sure why I called after him, and in the absence of anything planned, I just blurt out, "I really like talking with you."

He smiles, a warm and almost delicate smile. "I like it too, Tess."

For a moment the air around us feels twenty degrees hotter. Then his expression undergoes a complete metamorphosis. A myriad of emotions seems to flash across his face at once—confusion, embarrassment, nerves. He spins around and barrels straight into the wall with a muffled crash.

"Are you okay?" I gasp.

"Fine. I'm fine," he stutters, stepping back. After another awkward glance in my direction, he turns and darts into the study.

Hunter's advice stays with me. I resolve to have faith in myself, and it makes the next few weeks of my life some of the best ever.

I love spending time at Milkwood. I love the muggy hike at the beginning of each day, and the way my boots start to find the path that Ling knows so well. I love the first glimpse of Moon Lake, and how the clear morning light makes it shine like a diamond. I love the looks of genuine enthusiasm my arrival inspires in Benji and Lana. I love being part of a mission team. I love watching Achilles work on cracking the Liamond system and listening to Bo play the guitar. I even love how much Naz doesn't like me.

The messy shared bedroom, Achilles' darkened tech room, the unwieldy veggie garden—everything about Milkwood feels more and more like home. By comparison, the clean streets of Eden seem unimaginative and sterile. As Ling puts it, we live how we want to live at Milk-wood, like the rabbits that run wild in the woods.

One day I arrive to find everyone choosing code names; Kudzu never uses real names on missions. "What's yours?" I ask Ling.

"Samurai." She grins, miming a sword fight.

Benji and Lana pick each other's; Benji is Monkey. Lana is Angel.

Naz picks Bulldog.

Achilles wants to be Big Daddy.

"No," Ling says flatly.

"Why not?" he protests.

"Because it's silly and this is serious," she says, exasperated. "Pick something else."

"Dr. X."

"No."

"Chilly Willy."

"*No.*"

"Gyan's Lovechild, Tranq 'n' Wank, Guilty As Charged, I'm With Stupid."

Ling smiles sweetly. "You can just be Stupid."

Achilles sighs. "Fine. I'll be . . . Spike."

I pick Storm. I've never seen a real storm. I think I'd like them.

After a few weeks, Gem and Kissy show me the Kudzu stream. I've never seen anything like it. Streams are soft and pretty: pastel clouds that soothe and relax. The Kudzu stream is a shove into oncoming traf-fic, a wake-up call. *No new life until all life is equal* leaps out, demanding the viewers' attention. A spiky black-and-red design tells the story, with names changed to protect the guilty. Diamond-shaped boxes make the connection between artilects, Simutech, Moon Lake, and the Badlands.

It's not just the coolest thing I've ever seen, it's also the most eye-opening. An uncensored, unauthorized stream. Edenites won't know what hit them.

Naz and Ling will have razers at Simutech. I won't. Our plan doesn't involve razers, Ling tells me, so it's unnecessary and dangerous to have me wielding the powerful weapons. When I push as to why she and Naz will have them, she allows that in a worst-case scenario, she only wants the two most experienced people on the team using them. She can tell I'm disappointed, so as a compromise, she'll teach me some basic fighting. When I tell her I already *know* how to fight—a year in the Badlands, remember?—she just shrugs. "Then hit me."

I shake my head wryly. "I'm not going to hit you."

"I know," she says, with a cheeky smile.

Okay. Challenge accepted. I pop one fist out lightly.

She whirls out of the way. "Told you."

I laugh, impressed. But this time, I'm going to try. I lunge at her again, quick as a fox. Again, she disappears from the end of my fist, spinning behind me. With a vise-like grip, she grabs my wrist and yanks it up behind my back. I gasp, relenting. "Okay, okay!"

She lets me go. "See, the thing about—"

Before she can finish, I swipe her legs out from underneath her with mine. She lands on her butt, and instantly I'm on top of her, arm against her throat. This time, I win.

She's laughing as I let her go. "What's so funny?" I ask.

"You fight like Naz." She pulls bits of leaves out of her hair, grinning at me. "Dirty."

I grin back. "Let's go again."

And so I learn how to fight. As Ling puts it, it's more about how to defend yourself or overpower someone bigger or stronger than you. I learn that if someone chokes me from behind, I'm to lean forward, pull their arms off me, then spin around to knee them in the balls. "All the power in a choke hold comes from the thumbs." Ling shows me. "But you don't want it to become strength versus strength. You want to use your speed and agility to get out of it."

When I ask her if she's ever had to do this "in the field," she just laughs. "Of course!" she exclaims, all bravado. "Guiders think they have a right to detain us, just for breaking the law."

I ask, "Have you ever killed anyone?"

Ling's smile disappears. I haven't just touched a nerve; I've mauled one. She glances back in the direction of the house, and makes an excuse about having to check in with Achilles.

I tell myself I'm putting up with Hunter's tutoring sessions to score a place to crash and appease Abel. But every night, I find myself returning home to Liberty Gardens more and more eagerly.

I've never had a boyfriend, but I've also never had a boy friend.

I like how engaged Hunter is with the world. We can talk about anything. And we do. It's easy to get us to stop studying and talk about life. All I have to do is dangle a morsel of information about myself or a particularly strong opinion I have, and he's in. And I like this. I like being the most interesting person in the world to someone.

My favorite thing about him is his eyes. Not just the color or the shape, but the way they move. Quick and darting; I can *see* him thinking. I wish I could be in his head, to know the thoughts he's examining from every angle.

And we do actually study. Abel's right about Hunter—he's a great teacher. We jump around: natural sciences, psychology, expression, health and longevity. I'm delighted to learn he's terrible at drama and music. I leap on this chink in his perfect armor, and pry it apart by insisting we perform passages from *Romeo and Juliet* out in Abel's tiny courtyard. His wooden rendition is hilariously bad. I find myself replaying the stiff way he read Romeo's flowery declarations of love for Juliet, and giggling to myself for days afterward.

Even though I hate admitting it, I'm dying to know if Hunter has a girlfriend. I keep picturing her: one of those irritatingly pretty girls who always had guys and girls interested in them and doesn't even know that's not what it's like for everyone. Or maybe his girlfriend is one of those quirky arty types who wears long skirts and has a stream dedicated to her own poetry and is called something like Vivienne or Rain.

But obviously I can't ask him about any of this. His love life feels extraordinarily off-limits. Besides, he never asks about mine.

At first, I don't know how to act around Abel, so I do my best to avoid him without seeming like I'm avoiding him. Which, for someone who should be consumed by working on making an artilect for his buddies in the Trust, is actually pretty difficult. He pins me down for breakfast most mornings. I usually recap my tutoring session with Hunter while eating as fast as I can, and this seems to suffice. The Longevity Hub I'm allegedly spending all my time at is a good cover—a kickboxing class explains any strange bruises. I'm furious at Abel theoretically, but it's hard to maintain it practically. Ling warned me not to ask him anything or spy on him at home. I find the best way to behave around him is to believe my own lies—that I really am his returned niece, grateful to be back in the city's protection and slowly moving toward a complete recovery.

The only dark times are the nights. Some evenings I'm lucky, and the day's events have me asleep before my head hits the pillow. But some nights are long. Sleep eludes me for hours and in its place are thoughts of my mother. I think about how she'd feel about what I'm doing now, if she'd approve, if she'd understand. I think about Magnus, standing to attention two floors below me. And I think about what happened. I only have to touch on it—those last twenty-four hours I spent in Eden—and I'm socked with enough guilt to know beyond the whisper of a doubt that I don't actually deserve any of this.

I don't deserve Kudzu's faith in me. I don't deserve Hunter's interest. I don't deserve Abel's misplaced love.

As the cold, gray light of dawn edges over the horizon, I finally fall asleep with one thought repeating itself.

I don't deserve love at all.

"Greetings." Hunter smiles up at me from the dining room table and my stomach does a little backflip. Seeing him makes me feel relieved and relaxed, but also strangely anxious and excited. Like I'm coming home and leaving on an adventure at the same time.

"Greetings yourself," I say, dumping my backpack on the floor.

He's been waiting out my habitual lateness by playing chess against himself, moving the floating black and white pieces with his eyes. But now that I'm here, he closes the scratch and instead focuses on me. "How are you, Tess?"

My hands are rubbed raw from a few extra hours of intense roping. I keep them closed so Hunter doesn't notice.

"I am excellent," I tell him. "Is Abel here?"

"He'll be back later," Hunter replies. "He's food collecting with Kimiko."

"So, we have the house to ourselves, eh?" I say, cocking an eyebrow at him. "Want to riffle through Abel's stuff? Raid the liquor cabinet?"

For a split second Hunter's face flinches into alarm; then it relaxes into a patient, if amused, smile. "Or," he says, "we can start on history."

"Yours or mine?" I ask innocently, and am rewarded with a stern frown.

We spend the next hour testing my knowledge of ancient and modern history, from the collapse of the Roman Empire to World War 3. I name brutal kings and psychotic politicians—all men, I point out to Hunter—who were responsible for the messed-up societies of the past. I'm not bad at history, but the year away from education has left me a little rusty on exact dates. Hunter is unsurprisingly great with them. "Let me guess," I tease him, after he corrects me for the fiftieth time. "You're a history buff, as well as being a science geek."

"I find history very interesting," he concedes. "You have to admit, Eden's history is quite fascinating."

"I just wonder if we're getting the whole story," I say without thinking.

Hunter glances at me. "What do you mean?"

Hunter and I are alone in the house. I make an educated guess that this conversation can safely remain between us.

"Doesn't it strike you as odd," I begin carefully, "that Eden has maintained a virtually crime-free city for decades?"

"What do you mean, 'odd'?" Hunter asks.

"Considering the Trust controls..." I'm about the say "the streams," but stop myself—I'd have to explain how I know that and I definitely do not plan on mentioning Kudzu. "So much of our daily life, isn't it possible they've manipulated our understanding of history? Re-created the streams to say whatever they want?"

"I suppose that's possible," Hunter says slowly. "But it seems unlikely. The Trust has no need to manipulate anything. What you're saying sounds a little paranoid," he adds, with the gentle assurance of someone who knows he's right.

"Maybe," I muse, biting my lip. "It just seems weird to me. The history of the world is this fantastically awful tapestry of wars and injustice and cruelty, and then—bang!—along comes Gyan's grandfather's grandfather and suddenly, the Trust is the first perfect system of government ever?"

Hunter shrugs. "That doesn't sound weird. That sounds clever."

"A peaceful, crime-free city, and yet we still need Tranqs?"

"Protection ensures peace."

"No member of the Trust has ever committed a corrupt act?" I push. "No Edenite has ever wanted to revolt or question the system?"

"We've evolved, Tess," Hunter says patiently. "The Trust showed everyone how to live in a cohesive harmony."

"C'mon Hunter," I say. "You can't say that without addressing Mr. White Elephant in the corner."

"I'm sorry?"

"The Trust isn't actually a perfect system, is it?"

"Why not?"

"Because they're letting the Badlands starve to death," I say simply. "No matter how well Eden functions, it'll never be perfect while the Badlands is what it is."

Hunter rubs his chin with just a hint of agitation. I can tell he disagrees with me. For a moment I think he's going to start arguing. But then he drops his hand and his face clears. "Tell me about the Badlands." His eyes pierce mine, seeming to drill right through me.

And so I do.

I tell him about peyote parties with moon worshippers, out near the shimmering Salt Flats in the west. I tell him about learning to gamble with the Yaquero, a foul-mouthed gang who ran a black market way down in the Valley, and how I had to skip town after losing a stupid $1,000 bet to them. I describe sleeping under the stars and waking up when the sun rose, majestic and brutal, over the horizon. I describe learning to handle a knife, dress a wound, and avoid being groped in a crowd. I tell him about learning Malspeak and how to steal and how not to get your stuff stolen.

I entertain him with my best horror stories. The night I sucked snake poison out of a total stranger's leg, or the week I lived on nothing but ancient sweets in an old, abandoned candy factory, but then got disgustingly sick to the point where now, just looking at a piece of licorice makes me want to throw up.

And I tell him about the loneliness. The fear. The sadness. The way my life became both so small—the sum parts of a backpack—and somehow infinite and enormous.

"I'd never felt as alive as I did out there," I say. "There was always something to do, someone to help, something going on. If anything got too much, or a routine got so easy that I had time to think too much, I'd pack up and move on."

He nods, absorbing every word.

"But a year out there felt like ten," I admit. "It wasn't home." *And*, I add silently, *neither is Eden anymore.*

"It sounds like life is pretty hard out there."

"That's putting it lightly." I snort. "All the 'problems' I used to have in Eden seemed so ridiculous when I realized how most people were living. Or not living."

"What do you mean?"

"It's not really living out there," I say soberly. "It's surviving. And most people aren't even doing that. They're just dying."

The words hang between us, heavy and hard in their truth.

I glance at the time, shocked to see it's after nine. I've been monologuing about the Badlands for over an hour. I feel exposed, but not in a bad way. In fact, it's like a huge weight has been lifted off my shoulders. I let out a sigh.

"So, back to history?" he suggests.

I shake my head. "I think we need to even the scales a bit first."

"I'm sorry?"

"You know a ton of stuff about me," I point out. "I want to know a few things about you."

He gives me a guarded look. "What kind of things?"

Asking about a girlfriend would give too much away. I try to make my voice sound playful, like my question doesn't really matter. "Tell me about your first kiss."

Hunter's face clouds over. He sits back a little in his seat, away from me. "Oh."

"Oh?" I repeat, as if I'm surprised. I didn't think he'd actually answer.

"I didn't realize that was the sort of thing we'd be talking about," he says slowly, giving me a strange look.

I'm about to tell him not to worry about it and hey, let's get back to history, when he skids his chair around the table, right next to mine. Challenge accepted. I am thrilled.

His voice is low, that of a coconspirator. "Since you asked, Emily Anderson was the first girl I ever kissed. She had red hair and freckles—"

"Aw." I giggle.

"She was the girl next door."

"No!"

"Okay, she lived across the street," he concedes.

"How old were you?"

"Ten and a half. Well, ten and eight months, to be exact."

"You would've been cute back then."

He smiles, accepting the compliment. "I guess some people considered me cute. Emily and I would swim in my father's pool after pre-ed. And one day she decided we should play pirates and mermaids."

"Sexy," I say.

"Except she wanted to be the pirate and I had to be the mermaid," he continues.

"Double sexy." I laugh.

"I informed her I would not pretend to be a mermaid—"

"Very sensible." I nod.

"And then I told her she was prettier than any mermaid I'd ever seen. And then I kissed her." He smiles. His eyes are in the middle distance, looking back on the faraway memory. I can picture it so clearly: mini Hunter, adorable in his pint-sized form, pecking this bossy redhead on the mouth and surprising them both. "It was the perfect first kiss. Sun shining through the trees, beautiful summer's afternoon..."

"So, what happened to her?" I'm distinctly aware of how much I don't want this pretty little redhead in Hunter's life anymore.

He purses his lips, thinking. "I don't know, to be honest."

This pleases me. "Well, you know what they say about redheads."

"What do they say?"

"Steal your heart then rob you blind," I tell him, poking him in the chest with my finger. "You should stay away from redheads."

"I never heard that before."

I wrinkle my nose at him. "That's because I just made it up."

He laughs. It's the first real laugh I've ever gotten out of him. It completely transforms his face, softening it. He leans toward me, both forearms on the table. "So, are you going to tell me about your first kiss, Tess?"

I bite my lip, trying not to blush.

"Come on." He nudges me playfully. "I told you."

"Okay," I relent, a little overwhelmed by how many Hunter rules he's breaking. "But this doesn't leave this room, okay?"

He nods, excited. "Agreed."

"Okay." I draw in a deep breath. This story is kind of embarrassing. "I was kissed by Joey Lucas, twin brother of the equally cute Bobby Lucas. But here's the kicker. I was the short straw."

"You were a straw?"

I explain the story. The boys both liked Izzy, and worked out the best way to get to her was a double date. Like an idiot, I thought Joey was actually into me. We got spicy noodles in Charity then watched a stream artist weave patterns of music and color. Sometime around midnight, when the night was velvety and the stars looked brighter than usual, Joey kissed me. My first kiss ever. Then he asked if I thought Izzy would ever go out with him.

"Joey Lucas sounds like an idiot," Hunter observes.

I shrug, picking at my cuticles. "Whatever. Learned my lesson there. You know," I add tentatively, "I've never told anyone that story."

"Too humiliating?" he guesses, and I nod. "For what it's worth," he says, "I can't imagine you being anyone's short straw."

My cheeks start to tingle warmly. "Thanks."

His gaze moves with uncharacteristic slowness all around my face. "You're very interesting, Tess."

"Interesting?"

"You're full of contradictions." He props his chin onto one hand, eyes narrowed in concentration. "When we met, you pulled a knife on me—" I groan with embarrassed laughter. "But you're also quite sensitive. You love your friend Izzy, but you won't bend to her will. You can be guarded; you can also be open. You seem determined to challenge the authority of the Trust yet you don't break any laws. Sometimes you seem shy. Sometimes you're the most confident person I've ever met."

"What you're saying is, I'm a mess."

"No. No!" he exclaims. "Not at all. I'm saying you're interesting." He reaches over and squeezes one of my hands. I flinch and gasp in pain.

"Are you okay?" he asks, instantly concerned.

"I'm fine." I curl my fingers inward to hide the blisters. "Just had an intense workout today."

He leans forward to get a better look at my hands. "May I?"

Oh so gently, he turns my hands over and examines them. This is the first time Hunter has touched me. He's so close I can smell him—a sharp, woodsy, clean smell. Like peppermint mixed with ash. Cologne? Shampoo? I'm not sure, but it's sort of intoxicating and makes me feel strangely hungry, even though I just ate.

Hunter runs one long finger over the reddest, sorest part of my palm. I catch myself flinching both at the soreness and the feather-light touch. "How did this happen?" he asks.

"I kind of fell down a rope," I confess. My voice isn't much more than a whisper. "Not very graceful. They're fine, really."

He glances up from my palms, studying me. But then his look changes from a fact-finding mission and into...a gaze. His eyes soften. His whole face softens, like sunlight slowly warming a dark space. His hands shift beneath mine, as if exploring what it's like to touch me. A surge of energy rockets between us, landing as a soft slow explosion in my chest. We're staring at each other. My breath trips in my throat.

Hunter drops my hands. His tenderness vanishes as fast as a buzzcar.

"If you say so," he says. The wall is back, but this time he's thrown in a moat for good measure. "We're done here." He gets up and starts heading toward Abel's study.

"Hunter!" I call after him, getting to my feet.

He turns to meet my eyes blankly. "What?"

"You don't have to be weird about it," I tell him hotly.

"About what?"

I roll my eyes. "Nothing, obviously. I just want to make sure we're okay."

"Of course we are," he replies, in a way that makes me sure that the exact opposite is true. Without another word, he turns and leaves the room.

I sink back down at the dining room table, reeling.

What.

Was.

That?

chapter 10

When I come home the next day, I'm mentally prepared to find my socially awkward babysitter encased in a metal cage surrounded by snarling guard dogs or perhaps strung up from the ceiling, armed with a pointy stick. But instead, I find...nothing. Hunter isn't here.

Or the day after that.

Or the day after that.

When I ask Abel, he tells me he hasn't spoken to him about it, but he believes Hunter is just "very busy" right now. "He has a lot of other commitments, and I suppose I was overworking him," he tells me between forkfuls of frittata. "He said to pass on his apologies."

"So, did you speak to him or not?" I ask.

Abel blinks. "I did," he says, after a beat. He squirms in his seat, clearly uncomfortable. "I'll talk to him, if you'd like—"

"Don't bother."

I focus all my energy into become a faster, stronger, and better version of myself at Milkwood. I get Ling to pick me up an hour earlier from the filtration plant. I don't spend as much time hanging out with everyone at lunch. Instead I focus on roping, running, and fighting. I get my time on the obstacle course down to four and half minutes. Lana literally has tears in her eyes when she tells me, repeating over and over again that she knew I could it.

A week ago, a bleary-eyed Achilles told us he'd have the Liamond system cracked by Sunday night. A week ago, that seemed like a long way away. But now, the future has caught up with us.

As usual, it's a flawlessly beautiful day.

When I arrive at Milkwood, I'm eager to find out whether Achilles has done it, but I'm informed genius boy has requested we do not disturb said genius. Lana and Benji decide against overexerting me, so instead I spend the morning learning a sailor's knot, which is strong enough to take a person's entire weight for fast-roping. When I point out that our plan doesn't involve me having to tie one of these, Lana shrugs breezily. "Better safe than sorry! Besides, isn't it kind of fun?"

I'm in the middle of tying that damn knot for the twentieth time when the back door bangs open. Achilles stands in the doorway, face pale and eyes sunken, arms flung open in a posture ready to receive adulation. "Ladies and gentleman," he calls, instantly quieting the chatter of the backyard. *"It is done."*

"All right, Chilly!" whoops Benji, the first of many to descend on our skinny tech king. In a blur of cheers and hollers and bumped fists, the reality of what this means floods through me.

It's happening.

Tonight.

Ling stands off to the side of the hugfest enveloping Achilles, slicing off pieces of apple with a small silver knife and chewing meditatively. She looks calm and clear-eyed. She looks like a leader. When I catch her eye, she nods at me in slow confidence.

The late afternoon at Milkwood turns quiet. Ling instructs everyone to sleep or at least rest, in order to gear up for the night ahead. She tells me she has to go over some last-minute logistics with Achilles before giving me a ride back, so with no one to talk to and nothing to do, I decide to check out Moon Lake. Henny shows me the entrance to the twisting, narrow trail that cuts through the scrub. When I make it to the water's edge, I kick myself for not coming down here sooner.

The sun is starting to set and the hazy dusk is turning everything photogram pretty in musky shades of pink and purple. Pocket-sized brown birds hop in and out of the tall reeds that grow around the water's edge. I sink down and dig my fingers into the silty mud, as rich and dark as chocolate cake. The water laps gently at the shore, rhythmic and relaxing. It is so clear I can see tiny iridescent fish moving in a school in the shallows.

"Tess!" Ling calls, breaking my reverie. "There you are!"

"Just admiring the view," I call back.

She comes over to sit down beside me. "Bo and I come down here sometimes," she says. "It's a good place to get away."

"Not exactly private up there, right?"

She chuckles. "Not exactly." A few elegant blue herons sail in overhead, landing with a quiet splash. Ling cuts me a curious glance. "What about you?"

"What about me what?"

"Any guy you're thinking about looking up now you're back?"

"No." It comes out faster and harsher than I intended.

"A girl?"

I shake my head. "No guy. No girl."

"Okay." Ling blinks, turning her gaze back out to the lake. I immediately feel bad.

"I guess there's kind of someone," I hedge. "In a very maybe kind of way."

Her eyes light up. "Really? Someone from Kudzu?"

"No." I smile. "His name's Hunter." I skim over the basics: older than me, at post-ed in the South Hills, tall, smart, shy, nice hands.

"Mmm, I love nice hands," Ling agrees. We both giggle. "So, he's an old friend of yours?"

"No, he's my uncle's assistant," I say. "From post-education. He's been tutoring me, actually, in the evenings—"

"Your uncle's assistant?" Ling interrupts me.

"From post-ed," I repeat.

"He's been tutoring you?"

"Yeah, every night." I sigh. "We just go over education topics, nothing fancy."

"What do you talk about? Just school stuff?" Ling is tense and on guard.

"No, not exactly," I reply, confused. "We talk about Eden, sometimes the Trust."

"Have you told him about Kudzu?"

"*What?*"

"Have you told him about—"

"No!" I exclaim angrily. "No, of course not!"

"How do you know," Ling asks in a tone that sounds very much like alarm, "that he's not from Simutech?"

"Simutech?" I repeat. I laugh, bewildered. "No. And even if he was, why on earth would Abel—"

"Maybe Abel's spying on you," Ling says, spookily calm. "Maybe he knows you were in his basement. Maybe he knows you're with us."

Everything stops.

No. Hunter's not from Simutech. He can't be. He's a student. But even as I tell myself this, doubt creeps over me.

Is that why Abel insisted we spend time together, so Hunter can find out what I know? Or to keep me away from Abel? Is Abel watching me?

Has Hunter been lying to me?

"He's too young," I find myself saying, my mouth coming to the realization before my brain does. "He'd have to be a post-ed graduate to qualify for a work choice like that."

"Maybe he's older than he looks." Ling shrugs. "If he's so smart, maybe your uncle had the Trust make an exception."

I shake my head. "No. There's no way. He's *Hunter*. He's a geek, he's a total nerd—"

"Sounds like the sort of guy that'd be working for Simutech."

Why did I never check this out? Why did I never ask to see his schedule or tell me who is his favorite teacher is? Why have I never seen any evidence of him having come from class?

Because I trust him.

"This might sound extreme to you, but I don't want you talking to any strangers about anything right now," Ling says fiercely. "We're all about to risk being banished if we're caught—"

"It doesn't matter," I interrupt her, my voice bright and brassy with nerves. "He's disappeared. I haven't seen him all week."

"Good," Ling says brusquely. "If I'd known about this, I would have put a stop to it. We can't compromise everyone's safety."

The more I think about it, the more unlikely it seems. If Hunter was actually watching me for a reason other than tutoring, how could he bail after a moment of whatever-that-was? Hunter just isn't into me. So much so that one moment of unexpected warmth sent him running for the hills. The South Hills. Where he is a normal science geek, just like all the other guys.

Isn't he?

"Don't worry about it." Ling reaches over to give my shoulder a quick squeeze. "You're new to this. Let's drop it."

The herons take off from the glassy surface of the lake, wheeling off into the lilac sky. A minute passes and the topic of Hunter fades with the dying light.

I glance at Ling. "Why did you join Kudzu?"

Ling is silent for a few moments. "Naz isn't the only one with family in the Badlands. I have an older sister, Sanako…" She trails off, gazing out again across the lake.

"Where is she?"

"Last I heard, she was near you," Ling replies. "Another reason I decided to go to the Badlands."

"Why is she out there?"

"Because I let her go," Ling says harshly. "Alone." There are tears in her voice. She twists to face me, eyes brimming. "Remember when you asked me if I'd ever killed anyone?"

Before I know what's happening, she's on her feet, striding off.

"Ling, wait!" I scramble to follow her, catching up in a few steps.

Reluctantly, she turns to face me. She lets out an unsteady breath, then lifts her eyes to meet mine. "Sanako predicted Gyan would cut off Moon Lake long before it was announced. She was clever that way. She could read the Trust like no one else could. She wanted to be out there when it happened. She wanted me to come with her." Ling's lower lip trembles. "I said no. I wasn't as involved with Kudzu as she was." Her voice is thick with self-loathing. "She was so much braver than I am. I should have gone with her. I should have helped."

"How long's it been since you had contact?"

"Nobody's heard from her in a year." Ling's voice is as small as the brown birds that hop quietly around the reeds. "She would've turned eighteen last month."

Sanako might be alive. It is hard to stay in touch with people in Eden without scratch and off-cycle. But both of us know the odds aren't in her favor.

"That's why we have to do this, Tess," Ling says. "Not just Aevum, but the bigger picture."

"Open the borders," I say.

She nods seriously. "Save the Badlands."

And save Sanako. Maybe. If she's still alive.

Another long moment passes. Then Ling asks me, "Do you know what kudzu is, Tess? The word, I mean."

I shake my head.

"It was a type of vine, an invasive weed. Very potent and powerful. It could grow up to sixty feet in a year. It could completely transform ecosystems." She turns to face me fully. Her eyes are flashing, and her voice is soft and full of fire. "I'm a part of Kudzu because I believe we can do it. I believe Kudzu can transform the world." Her words cause a ripple of excitement to pulse around my body.

I want to believe this passionate, impressive girl. I want her to be right.

Ling glances in the direction of Milkwood. "We should motor if we're going to get you back to your uncle's in time. But before we do, I need to know something."

Her tone is strange and serious. A chill skates through me. *She's going to ask me about Magnus.* "What?" I ask.

"Technically, this is my mission, but this is your territory. You're the expert." She enunciates every word intently. "I'll follow your lead, Tess. I'll go with your calls. I just need to know."

My hands are trembling. I ball them into fists. "Need to know what?"

Ling's eyes catch the lake's reflection, changing their dark color to a shimmering silver. "I need to know that if things get bad—I mean, really bad—I need to know I can count on you. I need to know that Kudzu can trust you."

I exhale in silent relief. My fists unfurl, no longer shaking. I reach over and thread her fingers into mine, squeezing them hard. "Yes, Ling. Of course you can trust me."

There are some things that I could never, ever have predicted I would need. Roping gloves. Stolen Simutech security swabs. An alibi.

Ling and I construct the plan together. I'll have dinner with Abel at the usual time, then feign sickness and turn in early for the night. If Abel isn't home, I'm to order food on-cycle via Kimiko, which again will be a record of my supposed whereabouts. If it comes down to it, Abel can testify to the Guiders that I was home and in bed all night. Then I'm to shimmy down the drainpipe, just like at Zhukov's, and walk to Simutech through off-cycle back streets. I'll meet Kudzu there at midnight. Sharp.

When I get back to Liberty Gardens, I'm hoping desperately that Abel both is and isn't home. If he is, my portrayal of good-but-unwell-and-secretly-duplicitous niece would test acting chops I don't have. If he isn't, I'll be worried that he's at Simutech.

"Abel?" My voice echoes as I dump my backpack on the floor. "You home?"

"Greetings."

I freeze, then turn unwillingly in the direction of the voice.

Hunter is sitting on the sofa. He's wearing a clean, white T-shirt and loose white pants: a poster boy for our great city. One finger strokes the side of his face absentmindedly, lightly scratching the slight curve of his cheek. I've never seen him so relaxed. In fact, he looks supremely happy to see me. "Tess."

"Hunter." I'm so stunned at his reappearance that for a moment, language escapes me. I finally manage, "What's up?"

"I came to see you," he says, as if it's obvious.

Hunter is not a part of the plan. Hunter might be working for Abel at Simutech. But despite this, I can't help feeling excited by his visit. What is wrong with me? I have to get rid of him.

"Well, you've seen me," I say. "Same old Tess." Then, deliberately, "Was that all?"

He rises from the sofa and strolls toward me. His eyes don't leave mine, a sensation I feel throb throughout my entire body. "I was thinking we could go for a walk."

"A walk?"

"Yes. Down by Moon River."

The prospect seems undeniably romantic. Or does he know that I suspect something?

"I can't," I tell him.

"Oh, come on. I'm supposed to be studying—I'm not even supposed to be here! But it's so nice out, and I need a break." His eyes are bright with excitement. "With you." He takes another step toward me.

I take a step back. "No. Not tonight."

"You're busy?" he asks, looking around the empty living room.

"Yes, I am," I say shortly. Then, louder: "Kimiko!"

The fembot whizzes in, spindly arms waving like a helpful, high-tech sea creature. "Good evening, Tess."

"Is Abel here?"

"Dr. Rockwood is not home."

"Can you order me some food on-cycle? I'm not feeling well, and I'm going to turn in early." There's no harm in Hunter hearing this. In fact, it's better that he does.

"Certainly, Tess," says the fembot, spinning to whiz off toward the kitchen.

Hunter frowns. "So, are you busy or are you sick?"

I fold my arms across my chest. "I'm both."

In three long strides, he closes the distance between us. Before I know what's happening, he's right next to me, raising a hand to my face. A large, warm palm rests against my forehead.

"You don't have a temperature," he murmurs. Then, with his hand still in place, he adds with unfamiliar playfulness, "Nothing some night air won't fix."

"Stop." I wriggle away from his touch. This is ridiculous. I just have to get rid of him now. "I don't want to go for a walk because I'm annoyed with you."

"Annoyed?" He sounds genuinely surprised.

"Yes. Annoyed." I set my face into a fierce expression. "You totally bailed on me last week. It was really rude."

"Was it?"

"Of course it was," I snap. Although it's not the real reason, it *is* true.

"I hurt your feelings," he says carefully. "Leaving like that."

"If by 'hurt my feelings' you mean 'pissed me off,' then yeah," I reply, eyebrows raised in defiance, "you did." I push past him, grabbing my backpack with the intention of heading upstairs. "You know where the door is. Use it now—"

"Tess, I'm sorry," Hunter cuts me off. "Wait. Please."

I sigh in annoyance. "Let me guess. This is where you apologize profusely, give a reasonable explanation for your unreasonable behavior, then attempt to win me back despite the fact you've been a total jerk?"

A smile tugs at the corner of his mouth, slowly becoming a grin. His eyes flash with mirth. "Tell me, Tess," he says in a low voice, "does it ever get tiring?"

"Does what ever get tiring?"

"Being right all the time?"

Now a smile is fighting its way onto my face too. Sometimes I feel like I am planets away from this boy, that we're different in every way possible. And other times, like right now, I feel like we have more in common than either of us have understood yet. "I don't know," I shoot back. "Why don't you tell me?"

He grins. "Come on," he says warmly. "Come with me. I want to see you. I'll apologize as profusely as you want."

I'm starting to feel genuinely torn. "Hunter, I can't."

"Why not?" Then, in the comically arched tone of a fellow schemer: "Are you meeting someone later?"

"No!" I exclaim, too loudly, too quickly. "Of course not."

"Then you're out of excuses."

Not going with him is proving harder than going. But beyond that, Hunter has an oddly powerful way of pulling me close. I want to be around him. I glance in the direction of my room, my mouth tight. I'll tell him to leave. I'll tell him right now. "Wait for me outside."

In my bedroom, I change into tight black pants and a black V-neck. Catching my reflection in the mirror, I see someone svelte and catlike. Someone criminal. I slip the pale Simutech security swab into my pants pocket, wishing I didn't have to use it, but knowing I will. Using Abel's pass incriminates him, and will probably incriminate me too.

I shake out a SleepWell sub I'd picked up on my way home with my fake ID. The little blue robot is shaped like a fuzzy teddy bear. When I switch it on, it begins snoring lightly. SleepWells are sleeping aids for little kids, but tonight, it'll be me.

Downstairs, I find Kimiko sorting through some dirty clothes in the laundry. I tell her not to worry about the food, that I'm really not feeling well and am going to bed. Then I put her to sleep so she can't hear me leave. I'd like to turn her off altogether, but it would look too suspicious. After ten minutes with Hunter, I'll tell him I'm going home, so even if Abel finds out I was with him, I can still claim I was in bed at midnight, behind my locked bedroom door.

Hunter is waiting for me, the only figure in an empty street of houses where all occupants are in for the night. Just a boy waiting for a girl.

"Hunter." My skin is alight with anticipation. "Greetings."

If the lake is natural and wild and free up around Milkwood, the part of it that becomes Moon River is stately and contained. But it's still beautiful. Streetlights spill pools of yellow light on the promenade that follows the water as it snakes between downtown Liberty Gardens, and the Hive. It's a twenty-minute walk from Abel's. I justify it by reminding myself it is on the way to Simutech. A sprinkle of stars shine through Eden's invisible dome that keeps the evening air fresh and liquid cool. Just a few miles away in the Badlands, it would still be unbearably hot.

Above us, buzzcars zip in all directions. From here, we can make out the loops very clearly. A loop allows you to fly hands free, as each one moves the cars automatically around its endless circle, until you want to exit. There are dozens of loops above all of Eden, but most of them are concentrated above the Hive. They look like interlocking bracelets of moving lights, bright and sparkling against the night sky.

"Do you know why they're called buzzcars?" Hunter asks me.

"Because their engineering is based on the visual navigation of flies," I reply. "Biomimetics."

"That's right," he says, sounding surprised. Or is it impressed? I try to ignore the hot prickle of pride that being impressive to Hunter sets off under my skin.

We sit on a wrought-iron bench overlooking the river and watch the busy interplay of the bulbous little aircrafts. The mess of curved skyscrapers in the sparkling Hive reminds me of eagle's talons, tearing at the sky.

"Someone must have dropped this." Hunter unwinds a scarlet scarf that's caught around the armrest. It's the color of Badlands soil.

"It's beautiful." A month's Pleasure Allowance slips through my fingers, as light and delicate as a sigh.

"We should find a Guider to give it to," Hunter says, glancing around. "I'm sure whoever dropped it wants it back."

Kudzu could use this. I could use this. "Or," I say, balling the scarf into my palm. "I could just keep it."

He chuckles as if I'm joking. When I look back at him blankly, his smile morphs into a quizzical frown. "But it's not yours."

"It is now."

"Ownership is based on need, Tess," he says, as if quoting from a stream.

"Ownership is based on luck, Hunter," I refute. "As in, we're lucky to be in here and they're unlucky to be out there."

"How is stealing a scarf going to help the Badlands?"

I shrug, shoving the scarf into my pocket.

Silence settles between us, but it doesn't feel uncomfortable. A light evening breeze carries the scent of something spicy: garlic and lime. I twist in my seat. There's a fancy-looking restaurant across the road behind us, the kind that'd require a fair whack of your Pleasure Allowance.

"Do you want to get something to eat?" Hunter asks.

"I'm not really dressed for it. Even with a red silk scarf."

Hunter's eyes flick around my face. "I think you're very attractive."

I stare at him for a second before jerking my gaze back to the river. *I think you're very attractive.* I replay it, checking for sarcasm, but there is none. No boy has ever said that to me. I tell myself that what he thinks doesn't matter, but my cheeks are growing warm and my head feels all swooshy. Our shoulders are touching and I'm so hyperaware of the point where they meet, it's as if my entire body is an arrow pointing at it.

"Admit it," Hunter says, glancing back at the restaurant before nudging me in the side. "You're hungry."

My palms are sticky, my cheeks are now burning. *Hunter thinks I'm pretty.* "I don't think so," I manage. "What would Kudzu say about that?" The words are out of my mouth before I can stop them.

"Kudzu?" he repeats quizzically. "You mean the terrorists?"

I stare ahead at the water, horrified. The swooshing stops, like I've suddenly been shaken awake.

"Why would you care what *they'd* think of you eating there?" he continues, confused.

"You believe in them?" I ask, trying to sound casual. "I don't even know if they're real."

"It sounds like you believe in them." His green eyes seem to glow at me, enhanced by the light of the Hive. "Don't tell me you're partial to their absurd ideas."

"So what if I was?" I ask, affecting nonchalance. "I think—I mean, I heard, they're into opening the borders and saving the Badlands. That doesn't sound crazy to me."

There's a long, slow beat as Hunter meets my eyes. For a second, I'm positive he knows everything that's happened since I came back. "Stay away from Kudzu, Tess." His voice is surprisingly harsh. "The Trust is vicious when it comes to protecting themselves and their interests. Seriously. You'll get yourself killed."

I fake a disinterested laugh. "I don't even know that much about them." My fingertips brush against the Simutech security swab hidden deep in my pocket.

"Throughout history, the revolutionary underground has made the same mistakes," Hunter continues. "They're idealists, not realists. They're more interested in personal agendas or chaos for the sake of chaos. They have no practical sense of how to achieve change."

"And you do?"

"I'm not interested in changing Eden, Tess," he says dismissively.

He sweeps his hand out at the view of the Hive. "Why would you want to change any of this?"

"Because all this comes at a cost," I snap back. "Badlanders were attacked on the Northern Bridge last month so we can take a quiet stroll by a river!"

"Or maybe the Trust kept everyone safe from a bunch of dying people desperate enough to ruin things for the rest of us," he says evenly. "Depends on your point of view, doesn't it?"

"Ruin it for the rest of us?" I'm almost yelling. "I can't believe you just said that! You sound just like the Trust!"

He blinks, looking like I'd just slapped him in the face. "I do," he says, and his words have changed from defensive to surprised. "I sound just like them."

I try to calm down. And I can't draw attention to myself, not here and not now. But I can't hide what I'm feeling. This side of him is so ugly.

"I've disappointed you," he says, watching me closely. "You really care about the Badlands."

"Of course I care about the Badlands, Hunter," I say, my throat uncomfortably tight. "People are dying every day while we live like kings."

"That is true," he says, glancing out to the water and then back to me. "I've never met anyone like you before," he says simply. "I feel like...you are changing me."

Happiness balloons cautiously in my chest before I snuff it out. This is not my focus right now. And this whole conversation should never have happened in the first place. "I have to go."

"Now?" He sounds disappointed. "I'll walk you home."

I stand to leave, hooking my bag on my back. "That's okay. I'd rather go alone." Then, on impulse, I push my hand into my pocket and twist my fingers into the softness of the scarf. "Give this to a Guider—" But my words fall short as I watch something small and white bounce to my feet. Caught up in the scarf was the security swab. I lurch forward and grab it from the promenade before anyone sees.

Hunter's voice is strangely cool. "Why do you have that?"

I freeze. Hunter didn't just ask, "What is that?" He knows what a high-level Simutech security swab looks like. How on earth would he know that?

"It's nothing," I say, shoving the swab back in my pocket. My heart pounds jerkily.

Hunter's eyes are ablaze. "Tess, wait."

"I have to go," I say quickly. "I'll see you later."

I spin away from him. Like lightning, he's in front of me again, a hand on my arm. I crash right into him in a flurry of swinging plaits and bumped foreheads. We're right in each other's faces. My heart is still bouncing wildly. His grip on my arm tightens.

I want to kiss him.

And he wants to kiss me. His eyes flick to my mouth. I feel myself gasp, short and sharp. My body is thrumming wildly with desire.

My eyes meet his. Green eyes. Open. Watching me.

What am I doing?

At the exact same moment, we jerk away from each other. My head whirls, like I just stumbled off a carousel. The almost-kiss lasted not more than a few seconds.

"I can't do this," he mutters.

"Me either." I back away.

"Tess, wait a second."

"No." I turn and start walking quickly along the promenade. My body feels like it's on fire.

I hear his footsteps behind me. I spin back to face him before he reaches me. And then, without thinking, without planning to say it, I throw a single word at him as hard and fast as I would throw a knife. *"Aevum!"*

The word stops him in his tracks. His eyes widen, stunned. He knows. He knows about Aevum. His voice is faint, all but nonexistent. "How do you know that word?"

Oh no. *Oh no.* The river and the night sky swoop crazily around me and I have to plant my hands on my knees to steady myself.

"Tess—"

I right myself. Eyes narrow. Body taut. "Stay away from me, Hunter." From across the river, bells start ringing from the Hive. Twelve bells. Midnight.

"But—"

"Just stay away from me. I mean it."

The lights from the Hive look like bright, shimmering explosions. I turn away from him, and I start to run.

part 3

chapter 11

When I jog into the darkened alley next to Simutech, the first thing I see are four parked floaters, then fidgety bodies dressed head-to-toe in black. Lana's whisper is full of relief: "There she is!"

"Tess!" Ling runs to greet me, hugging me hard. Her face is flushed, eyes bright and alive. "I was worried. Did something happen at Abel's?"

I shake my head, speaking in between gulps of air. "No....Just took...longer to get here...than I thought."

"Tess!" Benji high-fives me while Lana squeezes my shoulder, wide-eyed with excitement. Like Naz and Ling, pieces of sleek equipment hang from the harnesses they're wearing, including long loops of slim rope.

"Hey," I greet them breathlessly.

"Here." Ling hands me the protective gear everyone's already wearing. "Quick, put this on."

I strap on shin, knee, and elbow guards. When I'm done, Ling gives me a shiny black comm. I slip it into my ear and hear a tinny voice. "Tess."

"Achilles, hey," I say. "Can you hear me?"

"Loud and clear." It's comforting to know Achilles will be able to both hear and see us, thanks to the loading dock's hacked security streams.

"Rockwood." Naz hands me a thick belt with gray and red things about the size of apples strapped to it. I notice everyone else already has one on. Naz points to the gray things first. "Smoke bombs. Hold your breath, pull the pin here, chuck it a few feet, get down. Nonlethal, just a basic get-out-of-jail-free card." Next she points to the red things. "Grenades. Pull the pin here, throw *as hard as you can*, and take cover. These babies are serious explosives, okay? Only use them if you're actually *in danger.*" She points back to the smoke bombs. "Someone sneezes, I throw one of these. The smoke should let us split safely."

"Tess, don't use any of that unless you have to," Achilles says. "We blow a smoke bomb tonight, there'll be fifty Quicks on this entrance tomorrow."

Ling clears her throat. "Tess, you'll be my second-in-command—"

"What?" Naz gapes.

"She's the expert, Naz."

"But I'm always your second!" Naz exclaims bitterly.

"Not tonight," Ling says firmly. "If anything happens to me, Tess is in charge, got it?"

Lana, Benji, and I all nod. Naz spits on the ground sourly, then mutters something Ling takes as acceptance.

"This is it," Ling says with a quick, sharp exhale. "Do or die." She hands something black and misshapen to each of us. It's a stretchy mask with holes for the eyes and mouth. The skull area is hard and inflexible, like a helmet. I pull it on, then start at the sight of four masked people staring back at me. Kudzu's familiar faces are gone.

"From now on, code names only," Ling says, and I quickly remind myself who's who. Ling: Samurai. Benji: Monkey. Lana: Angel. Naz: Pitbull. Achilles: Spike. And I'm Storm. Ling's eyes meet mine. "Ready?"

We've come too far for me to ruin everything now. Besides, even if Hunter is working for Simutech—which I still don't know for sure—that won't affect what we're about to do. I just wish I hadn't mentioned Kudzu. I find the tip of my warrior necklace, cool against the hollow of my throat, and press it once for good luck. "Ready."

In single file, we creep around the corner of the alley until we're all out in the narrow street at the back of Simutech. Ling first, then Lana, me, Benji, and Naz. Ahead of us, the street continues on for another hundred feet to a plaza. I glimpse the tumbling water of a lone fountain catching yellow streetlight. Behind us, the street disappears into blackness.

The entrance to the loading dock is only twenty feet ahead. Beyond it, moonlight catches the glass windows of Simutech in small square pools of silver.

In the darkness, the Quicks' red eyes burn as they swivel left and right. They look even more threatening than in the holos; they're so *real.* My heart is thumping so hard, I'm afraid they can hear it.

Achilles' voice comes through our comms. "You're almost in the Quicks' range. . . . Almost." We creep forward some more. "Okay, stop."

Still in single file, we freeze like statues. Time passes achingly slowly as the robots' red eyes swing back and forth over us. Just as I think Achilles must have missed the one-minute-and-twenty-three-second window, I hear his calm voice in my comm. "Go."

We scamper forward a few feet. I picture us in the narrow white river Achilles showed us back at Milkwood.

"Stop."

The Quicks' gaze starts passing back and forth over us, unseeing. I'm enormously relieved to be proven right.

We keep moving like this, a few feet forward, freezing, then another few feet and freezing again. The plan is to slide past the Quick on the far left, the one closest to us. As we keep inching closer to it, I expect to feel fear, but instead my confidence surges. This is the best the Trust can do to guard their precious artilect? Ling is only a few feet away from the Quick on the far left. One more spurt of movement, and we'll be past it.

A shriek of laughter cuts my cockiness short.

The Quick on the far left whips its head around so fast I don't even see it move.

Behind me, I can hear two girls coming out of the alley.

"He was looking at *you*—"

A giggly squeal of outrage. "No, he *wasn't!*"

I am rooted to the spot. It's as if the terrifying Quick is staring straight at us. If it identifies the girls as a threat, its vision will change to infrared, and we'll become as clear as day to the machine. I hear the girls tottering up the darkened narrow street, away from us. If they have seen us or the Quicks, they don't care. Their laughter bounces off the silent buildings as their footsteps recede.

The Quick closest to us resumes its scanning. For a second my insides relax, until I hear Achilles. "Guys. Don't move." His whisper is masking low-level panic. "The scans aren't in the same pattern as before. Now you're always going to be in one of the Quicks' line of vision. Don't say anything back to me," he adds in a hurry. "You're too close, they'll probably hear you."

We stay frozen. A minute passes. Then two. Panic simmers inside me. On more than a few occasions in the Badlands, I'd been followed by a marauding gang of unsavories, so I'd grown adept at melting into shadows to hide. But I'd never had to stay this still for this long.

More minutes pass. My left arm is raised at a 45-degree angle from my body. It starts to ache. Then hurt. Then it starts to feel like knives are slicing it open. My whole body screams for movement.

"Good work, guys, just stay there. We're trying to think of something," Achilles says, sounding more worried. What can he possibly do?

I hear a small scuffle. Without moving my head, I slide my eyes to the ground. The noise belongs to something the size of a football. It's an enormous black rat.

Eden is free of pests and invasive species, but Simutech still clones rats to use for experiments. This one must have escaped. But it's no ordinary rat. This is a cloning experiment gone bad. I know because the rat has three heads.

Two heads, with separate pairs of beady eyes and twitching noses, jostle for space on the end of its thick neck. And a third head grows out of its back, around where its shoulder blades are. It is, without a doubt, the most disgusting thing I have ever seen. And I ate *pourriture* for an entire year.

The three-headed beast scampers forward, then stops, then comes closer still. The Quick ignores it. Doubtless it is programmed to ignore things like this. The rat stops at Lana's boot, all three noses sniffing it excitedly. In front of me, I can see her breathing getting quicker.

Don't move, Lana.

The rat moves past Lana's boot, and I momentarily relax. Until it stops at my boot. Then crawls up onto it.

Every instinct I possess wants to kick the disgusting thing off me as fast as I can. I scream at it silently in my head. Get off me! *Get off me!*

"Hang in there, Storm, don't move," Achilles warns. "It's probably going to leave you alone in a second."

The six-eyed rat begins climbing up my leg. I can feel it through the fabric of my pants, about the weight of a puppy. It is at my kneecaps. It is on my thigh, clinging to my pants with its sharp little rat feet.

A wave of raw disgust surges inside me and I almost wretch. *Please don't be sick, please...*

The rat crawls up to my stomach. It is like a giant, deformed baby, coming for my face.

"Don't blame me, you're the one who lost it!"

"Shut up! It must be back at the restaurant—"

The girls! The Quick whips its head around, training its vision in their direction.

I can hear them behind me, giggling as they head back into the alley.

We all remain frozen. Even the rat.

The Quick starts moving its head again. Is it back in the old pattern? I can't tell.

And then I hear the sweetest word I have ever heard any human utter. *"Go."*

Silently, we shoot forward the final few feet, safely past the Quicks.

As soon as we're through, one swift flick of my knife sends the rat arcing up off me, like a nightmarish shooting star. I give myself a second to clear my head and shake out my aching limbs. Then I gesture for the others to follow me.

Silent as ghosts, we make our way past the yawning, empty loading dock. No lights are on—a good sign. When we reach the open kitchen window, barely visible six floors up, Lana slips the rope from her torso. Benji hands her what I think is a sleek little sub, the size of a hamster. Lana fits the end of our rope into an opening in its back, then tests it to make sure it's tight. Glancing up at the window, Lana presses some buttons in its back, then rests it against the wall in front of us.

"Spike?" Benji says softly. "We're ready."

"Great. I'm about to loop the security stream. Remember, you've got a fifteen-minute window before the real stream kicks back in. Ready?"

"Ready." Gone are the goofy, grinning blondes I'd met in Kudzu's backyard. In their place are athletes ready for their star turn.

"Okay. Cut. *Go.*"

Lana takes her hand away, and the little sub whizzes up the glass wall. I watch as it zips all the way to the window ledge, carrying the rope. When it reaches the ledge, it stops. I hear a very faint high buzz. The rope shivers a little, and a fine powder falls around us. Lana tugs on the rope. It's secure. She grins. "I'm going up."

She's up that rope as quick as can be. Before I've even finished pulling on the roping gloves Benji hands me, Lana is at the darkened window, hooking her leg to slip silently inside. A few seconds later, she gives the okay sign.

Ling follows, then Naz. Now it's my turn.

Benji smiles reassuringly. "Just like we practiced."

I nod. Just like hunting for prairie chickens, but with a rope instead of rocks. I just wasn't expecting it to be so *high*. Six stories seem like sixty when you have to physically pull yourself up them, alone, on the *outside* of a building. I grit my teeth and start to climb. One hand over the other. Just like in the backyard.

Don't look down, I warn myself grimly.

We assemble in the entrance to the kitchen. I inch the door open to reveal a wide, empty hallway lit in low, overhead light. Opposite us is a water cooler, a potted palm tree, and a cart filled with what looks like pieces of human skin. Speckled blue floors, sedate gray walls. *I remember this....* I can picture my mom here so clearly it hurts—rushing over to clutch my arm, breathless over the day's new discovery. Her scent: spicy orange soap. I can *smell* it.

"I am *famished*."

"Should we order noodles?"

Two men. They round the corner, coming toward us. I just have time to see their faces before I pull the kitchen door shut. I recognize the first one instantly. Frog. The bald man with the turned-down mouth who designed the Quicks. He looks stronger than I remember but maybe I'm just scared of him seeing us. I don't recognize the other guy, Noodles: a tall, skinny man with scraggly pale hair.

"If we keep working like this," I hear Frog say clearly, "we'll turn *into* noodles."

We wait in the kitchen, still as statues, as they walk by. I really didn't think anyone would be here this late on a Sunday.

"Ah, you're finally coming around to the possibility of transmogrification." Noodles' voice starts to fade. "You're really an open-minded guy."

"I'm working on a project that's a theoretical impossibility." Frog's voice is faint now, muffled by distance. "I have to be."

And then they're gone. We wait for a good ten seconds, then crack the door open again. Nothing.

I've already told everyone exactly where to go. Exit and go right, then at the end of the hallway, we go left down a long corridor, all the way to Innovation Lab C on the other end of the building.

Ling points to the end of the hallway and mouths, "Naz."

A look of irritation flashes in Naz's eyes, but nevertheless, she obeys. Her rubber-soled boots make no noise as she runs lightly to the end of the hallway. At the corner, she glances down the left-hand corridor. She turns back to us and nods.

Our shoes make only the slightest scuffles as we hightail it down the empty corridor, past a series of departments and offices: *Exoskeleton, Sensors & Actuators, Motion & Manipulation, Biorobotics & Cybernetics.* By day, this building is busy with jargon-filled chatter, furrowed brows on brainy scientists, and overwhelmed assistants balancing coffees and reports. By night, it is unnervingly quiet. But I know this already. I've been here at this hour before.

A year ago. Before I left for the Badlands. Before everything changed. . . .

"Tess!"

I spun around, a mess of blond hair and nerves. "Howie!"

The young engineer smiled at me eagerly. "Are you looking for your mom? I think she left for the day."

"Oh—yes." I stumbled, toying with the chunky rings on my fingers. "She's usually still here now."

Howie nodded, fingering the collar of his lab coat a little nervously. "You must hardly ever see her."

No. I never see her. And when I do it's just a monologue about Magnus. Like last night—three hours on how poor, poor Magnus was having trouble creating feelings. Three hours on how Magnus should be as emotional as a teenager now.

Why do you need to make a teenager, Mom? I'm right here.

"It must be hard," Howie added. His tone was concerned and kind. I'd always liked Howie. And I could tell he liked me.

"Well, I guess . . . I guess I better go."

"Okay, Tess. You look very nice, by the way."

"Thanks." I smiled, smoothing down the short silk ruffles of Izzy's favorite skirt. "Oh—I left my comm in my mom's office. Would you mind?"

He glanced at the locked office door. "I can't, Tess."

"But it's just her office."

"No, really, I can't."

I pout and flutter my eyelashes at him. "Oh, c'mon," I wheedle, mimicking Izzy as best I can.

An amusing level of conflict twisted up his face, but still he shook his head. "I want to. I do. But it's against company policy."

"But I have to comm my mom and let her know where I am. She worries. And if she finds out you didn't help me . . ." I close the distance between us. "She trusts you, Howie. I trust you, too."

I put my hand on his arm and smiled up at him hopefully. He stared at my hand, then at me, somewhere between turned on and terrified. "All right. Just this once." He hurried over to Mom's door. "Our security system—the Liamond system—can be confusing." He was babbling, not noticing that I watched him punch in the code: 624687. Later I would work out this spelled Magnus, *making it even easier to remember.*

"Thanks, Howie." I let my voice take on just the slightest edge of huskiness. "You're really a sweet guy."

A hint of pale pink blush filled his smooth cheeks. His voice faltered. "Good night, Tess."

I waited until he had rounded the corner, shoes squeaking on the speckled blue floor, before I opened the door to Mom's expansive, messy office. Closing it, locking it. Leaning against it.

My eyes narrowed as they sported what I was here for. What Howie was too junior to know was in here, or else he would never, ever have allowed me inside.

"Tess."

"Hello, Magnus.*"*

The memory throws me. I falter. Lana, Benji and Naz crash into me like life-sized dominoes.

Naz curses me under her breath.

We have to keep moving.

We race down the corridor. The windows on our right allow us to see straight into the large, industrial room next door that we'd already seen back at Milkwood. Innovation Lab C. AUTHORIZED PERSONNEL ONLY, BY ORDER OF THE TRUST floats over the reinforced double doors. A swab reader blinks next to them

Just to be sure we're alone, Naz runs to the end of the corridor and peeks down the hallway that doglegs off to the left, past some more potted palms nestled in the corner. Coast must be clear, for she doubles back.

Ling glances from the swab reader to me. I knew I'd have to do this. But standing here before it, about to incriminate both Abel and myself, I hesitate, just for moment. Then I pass the swab over the reader.

A smoothly modulated female voice says, "Welcome, Dr. Rockwood," and the doors disappear.

The air inside the Innovation Lab is cooler than the rest of building. A low hum of invisible filters underscores everything.

"Monkey, Angel, guard the entrance," Ling instructs quietly. "Pitbull, Storm, and I will get the mirror matter."

Benji and Lana nod in unison, quickly squeezing each other's hands before taking up positions that offer views of the corridor outside, through the long windows.

"Where is it?" Naz asks, dark eyes darting every which way.

"Over here." I motion for them to follow.

We hurry past the cylinders, dwarfed by their size. Each has a small screen set into it at waist height, which whirs, beeps, and whistles endlessly, like old ladies gossiping to each other.

"Guys." It's Achilles, voice echoing through the comm. "Five minutes down, ten to go. Talk to me."

"We're in the lab." Ling presses the comm into her ear. "En route to the mirror—there it is!"

Just like in the streams, the mirror matter sparkles and shimmers from inside the clear cylinder, suspended in the case-within-a-case.

"Storm, keep an eye out." Ling eyes the case. "Let's get to work."

Using the small blowtorches strapped to their harnesses, Naz and Ling work together to start cutting a circle through the thick glass. The blue light of the torch burns as bright as the sun. It melts through the glass as if it were slicing through butter.

My heart is still pounding, but the adrenaline is making me clear and focused. My eyes sweep the room, searching for anything out of the ordinary. But we're the only ones in here. I take a second to marvel at the sight of Ling and Naz, their faces hidden by the scary-looking masks, their bodies tight beneath their stretchy black outfits, working quickly and efficiently in tandem.

"Nine minutes." Achilles' voice comes quietly through the comms.

One circle. Ling catches the glass as it loosens, and hands it to me. I place it carefully on the floor under the case. Naz starts on the second.

As soon as the tip of her blowtorch pierces the inner case, a small pop of gas escapes, like pricking a balloon. The tube of mirror matter clatters to the bottom of the case, a small sound rendered huge by the silence. We all freeze for a second. The tube rolls to a stop, sloshing the viscous liquid inside, thick as wet concrete. Then, as nothing seems to happen, Naz starts cutting again.

My eyes keep flitting around the room. I notice something.

Set into the far wall that runs parallel to the corridor and entrance we came in is a black door. A holo of a small Trust logo hovers subtly in front of it. I frown. I think that's a meeting room. Maybe there's something in there that'll help me answer the question that's been gnawing at me since Ling and I met. What does the Trust want with an artilect?

I nudge Ling and jerk my chin in the direction of the door.

She glances over, and her eyes narrow. She nods.

"Guys," Naz murmurs, directing our attention back to the case.

The second circle of glass falls into Ling's gloved fingers. Without hesitation, Naz reaches into the case and grabs the tube.

"Eight minutes," Achilles says.

We still have plenty of time.

"Get Monkey and Angel," Ling whispers to Naz, then points to the door. Naz nods obediently. She hands the tube to Ling, who slips it neatly into a loop on her harness.

There's a swab reader outside the door. I almost hope Abel's pass doesn't work. That might mean he's not as involved with the Trust as I think he is.

"Welcome, Dr. Rockwood."

With an almost imperceptible click, the door disappears. As smooth and quiet as water itself, the five of us disappear inside. The door reappears behind us, plunging us into darkness.

Slowly, our eyes begin adjusting. We are in a large windowless room, dominated by an enormous table and a dozen leather chairs. It is like the inverse of the tech room at Milkwood: coldly efficient, unflinchingly clean. The only sign of life is a long, rectangular square of plants running across the back of the room. One more step and I'd be standing in it. Looking down, I see there's a little gap between the floor and the garden, and through the gap, I can see water and plant roots growing down toward it. Ling's standing next to a large piece of scratch set into the wall like a square of sunlight.

"Where are you, what's happening?" Achilles asks calmly.

"We have the mirror matter," Ling says softly, eyes sweeping the room carefully. "Now we're in a meeting room just off the lab."

"There's scratch," I add. "I want to try turning it on."

"Is it blue scratch?" Achilles asks.

"No," I reply. "Regular."

"Okay," Achilles says cautiously. "There's no security stream where you are, but I'll run a search and try to find what you're looking at."

My fingers find the corner, pressing hard. The scratch glows gold and an intricate, crisp holo fills the table. Before any sound even begins, Ling mutes it with her eyes.

The holo is a map of Eden and the bordering Badlands, as far as the Bleached Seas circling the edges of the continent.

"Looks like some sort of presentation," Achilles says. "I'm in. We can see it here too."

Silently, the presentation begins. The words *Project Aevum. Highly Classified, By Order of the Trust* float out above everything, automatically matching to everyone's individual eyelines.

Ling and I trade a quick look. *Project* Aevum? My chest is rising and falling with anticipation. This must be it.

The map starts moving. Eden fills the table, all the neighborhoods presented in perfect miniature. The Hive, Charity, Liberty Gardens. Lakeside, and the Farms. The snaking streets of the South Hills, and beyond them, overlooking all of Eden, the Three Towers. I can almost see the palatial floor of Gyan's private quarters, right at the tip of the biggest of the three buildings.

From a single building in the Hive, a red dot glows, pulsing slowly. I recognize the location of the building—it's where we are now. I assume that dot represents Aevum.

The view pans out to display the entire continent. Now tiny whitewalled Eden is dominated by the expanse of the Badlands. Small black dots appear, labeling the human population. Numbers and graphs indicate first the two million in Eden, and then the two hundred million out in the Badlands.

It's strange to think those tiny clusters of dots represent people. I can almost make out Kep Sai'an, a thousand miles west, on the outskirts of the Manufacturing Zone. Glancing at Ling, I see she's looking at the same place. Sanako.

Then a new spray of dots appear. These are yellow. The words *Substitute Population* appear. Many yellow dots in Eden, but still quite a few in the Badlands. I can picture them easily—mostly older, clunkier models, like my old friend Robowrong. I didn't even know you could track every individual substitute, let alone what the point was.

"What the hell?" I hear Achilles mutter.

More floating words appear. *Project Aevum. Simulation.*

A large red circle spreads from the glowing red dot. It doesn't change anything in Eden, but as soon as the edges of the red circle hit the yellow dots in the Badlands, they begin to turn red. The red circle keeps expanding, turning all the clusters of yellow dots in the Badlands red until it reaches the edges of the continent. The Badlands are now almost entirely filled with pulsing red dots. It looks diseased.

Then the black dots in the Badlands start disappearing.

"Look." Naz's voice is gruff. She points to a population counter for the Badlands. It is dropping. From a two hundred million to one hundred and ninety, one hundred and eighty, one hundred and seventy, and down down down.

"The population is getting smaller," Ling says. "But how—why?"

"And why did all the yellow dots in the Badlands turn red?" Benji adds. "What's happening to the substitutes?"

More floating words. *Project Aevum. Test Case.*

"Five minutes," Achilles warns.

Lana sounds worried. "Guys, we're getting close."

The map disappears and is replaced by a holo of a group of men in what looks like a typical Badlands water bar. About ten of them sit around squat tables talking and laughing, drinking mugs of disgusting, fetid water. My stomach turns at the sight of it—I can practically taste the foul liquid. A substitute works behind the bar—an old Builder, like Robowrong.

The Builder stops pouring the water. It jerks to attention, standing stiff and still. The men glance over at it curiously.

I lean closer to get a better look at the men. The way they dress—the big brimmed hats and the coarse goat-hair ponchos—is familiar to me, but I can't remember where from.

The Builder walks out from behind the bar. The way it moves is strange: more fluid and faster than a Builder should be able to. The men look on, obviously confused that a substitute is moving without an order. It's heading for the door. One of the men calls out something to it, which makes the other men laugh. The Builder locks the door and stands in front of it. Slowly, the men stop laughing.

A man swaggers over to the Builder, reaching up to rap his knuckles on the substitute's head.

The Builder lunges for the man's throat. In a flash, the Builder's lifting him up off the ground, so his feet dangle above the floor. My chest freezes in fear. Then the Builder brings an enormous hand down hard on the man's skull. It smashes apart like a watermelon, spraying the room with chunks of brain and skull.

It happens so fast.

Lana gasps in horror, burying her head in Benji's chest. Ling gags. I feel like someone just kicked me in the stomach, but I keep watching.

Stumbling over their chairs and tables, the other men try to escape. But the door is locked and the Builder is too strong. One by one, they meet a similar fate. One has his throat crushed. One is thrown against a wall. They have no weapons, no way to protect themselves, no chance at all.

The whole thing is over in less than twenty seconds. Then the presentation disappears.

I can't move, can't think, can't breathe.

A stunned-looking Benji has his arm around Lana. Ling is supporting her weight with both hands planted on the desk. Suddenly I remember why I recognize the way the men dress. "That was in the Valley."

"The Valley?" Ling repeats. "Like—"

"The Valley of Spines massacre." Ten men in a bar, killed without rhyme or reason. I'd assumed it was an urban myth.

"Was that Aevum?" Lana asks. Her bright blue eyes are wet with tears.

"No," I say. "That was just a regular Builder. But I think Aevum was controlling it." As I say the words out loud, I realize they ring true. Kimiko is able to control all the systems in Abel's home. It's basically the same principle. "*That's* why the Trust wants Aevum," I realize with a jolt. "Because it can control substitutes."

"They call it serfing," says Achilles. "A 'serf' is a slave. But in tech speak, it means reprogramming something. Controlling it."

"Aevum can serf other substitutes," I think aloud. "It can control them."

"But substitutes can't kill people!" Lana exclaims shakily. "They've never been able to do that, not ever."

"Because humans can't program them to," I say. "But Aevum isn't human. The Trust must've worked out that artilects are different."

Ling's nodding slowly.

"And if Aevum can serf substitutes and make them kill," I go on, "then the Trust is not to blame."

"Whoa, hold up," Naz says. "How would the Trust not be responsible for this? They own Aevum. This is all their doing."

"Yeah, and even Edenites won't stand for mass murder," Ling says. "The Trust won't be allowed to get away with this."

"Because the Trust isn't doing this directly—*Aevum* is," I say. "Aevum's the perfect scapegoat!"

"It could be weeks before anyone even found out," Benji says. "The Trust controls the border crossings, and the Trust controls the streams."

"Right, and afterward, they'll probably just say Aevum malfunctioned or something," Ling adds.

"For sure." I nod. "They'll put all the blame on Aevum and then destroy it. No blood on their hands, and everyone in the Badlands is dead."

"But they've just shut off the aqueduct—why this too?" demands Naz.

I shrug. "Probably because this'll be so fast. So...effective. Whatever the reason, this is real. This is going to happen."

We stare at each other. Millions of Badlanders. Dead.

"Three minutes," Achilles announces. "Time to move."

Ling draws herself up and exhales hard. "Let's get the hell out of here. Tess—"

But her words are cut off by an earsplitting alarm. Blue lights start flashing wildly. The door snaps, locking into place.

"What's happening?" I yell. The high-pitched scream echoes through the whole building.

Ling shouts, "Spike, what's going on?"

"I don't know!" Achilles sounds panicked. "Liamond is working again!"

"*What?*" Ling yells.

Ling, Naz, and Benji struggle uselessly against the locked door. "Get us out of here!" I yell over the alarm.

"I can't!"

Shouts outside: "What's going on?"

Footsteps race for the room. A man's yell: "It's coming from in there!"

Another yell. "Override the code!" Then, just outside the door, "A drill at one a.m.? This has to be a malfunction!"

"Monkey, Angel. Left side," Ling snaps into command. "Storm, Pitbull, behind me on the right." I can barely hear her over the alarm.

Naz whips out a small razer pistol from her boot and tosses it to

Ling. A second razer materializes in Naz's hand. "Storm, get your knife."

I pull Mack. I have no idea what to do when the door opens. We haven't run a drill for this. Benji and Lana are flexing, limbering up. Ready to run—or fight. My heart is racing and on fire. Is Ling ready to kill someone? Is Naz? *Am I?*

chapter 12

The door disappears. Three Simutech scientists rush in, wincing at the piercing alarm—Frog, Noodles, and another man. They don't see us pressed flat against the wall.

"How do we turn it—" But Frog doesn't make it beyond that before Kudzu attacks.

Benji hurls his shoulder forward as he punches his scientist in the stomach. As the man doubles over in pain, Lana kicks his feet from under him, knocking him flat on his back. Benji grabs the man's wrists while Lana gets the rope.

Naz lands one, then two, square punches on the second scientist's jaw. It's Noodles, the tall, skinny man I saw earlier. He tries to hit her back but she easily ducks his sloppy attempt. He stumbles and within seconds she has one arm twisted behind his back, the razer trained to his head. He jerks, panicked. Naz pulls his twisted arm tighter. He yells out in pain. "Okay, okay," he gasps, relenting.

Ling's target, Frog, is the biggest of the three. From his position on the other side of the long table, he has a precious few seconds to size up the situation.

"Don't make me use this," Ling warns, aiming the razer steadily as she advances toward him.

Frog shoots both hands up in surrender, looking terrified. I'm thankful I'm wearing the black mask; otherwise I'm sure he'd recognize me.

"Angel?" Ling calls. "Are there any more?"

I hear a dull thump. Someone cries out. Ling whips her eyes to see what's wrong. It's Benji's scientist—Benji has flipped him over to finish tying his legs. But the second Ling takes her eyes off Frog, he punches her in the jaw. She staggers back, stunned. Before she can regain focus, he slams his fist into her stomach. The small razer clatters to the table. With a strangled gasp, Ling drops to her knees.

Frog lunges for the razer. Without time to aim, I flick Mack hard across the room. My knife plunges into his outstretched arm, pinning the sleeve to the table. Frog shouts, yanking his hand around desperately. I bolt forward and grab the stray razer. It's lighter than I thought it'd be, and I'm not exactly sure how to fire it. But pointing it at Frog is enough to make him freeze. Keeping my gaze on him, I reach over and yank my knife out of the table. "I was aiming for your hand," I tell him.

Ling limps over and takes the razer from me, then knees Frog in the groin. It's his turn to groan. "Try that again and I'll kill you," she says.

"Clear," Lana calls. "Let's go, let's go!"

Benji has finished trussing up the wrists and ankles of his scientist, who wriggles like a fish on dry land. "Tie 'em or take 'em?" He nods at the other two men.

"Take 'em," Ling says. "We don't have time."

Kudzu hustles everyone out. Ling's last, shoving Frog out the door, but as she does, I see a silver streak go flying. The mirror matter. It's on the ground, rolling toward the square of plants at the back of the room. Ling mustn't have felt it; she's already out the door. Everyone's gone. I'm the only one who even saw it fall. Diving toward the plants, I can see it, only a foot down, nestled amid white tubular plant roots. But the gap between the floor and the garden isn't big enough for more than half a hand.

"No!" I gasp in disbelief. Ignoring the pain, I try to shove my hand in farther, but it's no good. The space is too small for me to reach the mirror matter.

"Storm, c'mon!" I hear Lana call.

In a panic, I rip away at the plants and clumps of dirt but my fingers find a metal grate at the bottom of the garden. "No!" I cry again, pawing desperately at the grate. It's no use.

"Storm!" Lana reappears doorway, face incredulous. Without waiting to find out why I'm ripping the garden apart, she hauls me to my feet.

"Wait—" I start, but she doesn't.

"Go!" she shouts, shoving me out into the lab.

Naz and Ling have their razers trained on Frog and Noodles, keeping the men's arms twisted hard behind their backs as they wait for me by the door.

"Swab!" Ling yells at me angrily.

I race to join them, flicking the soft swab under the reader. Nothing happens.

"Open the door!" Naz yells at Frog.

"We can't," he growls. "Security's in lockdown—doors only open from the outside."

Acting almost simultaneously, Naz and Ling aim their razers at the long, interior windows that separate the lab from the corridor outside, and fire. Two pulses of burning white light hit the window. It shatters spectacularly into a fountain of breaking glass. I duck, shielding my face. By the time I open my eyes, the others are already climbing through the window, still with the hostages. My boots crunch through splinters of glass as I run for the window. Kicking the jagged shards out of the way, I go to swing a leg over the window ledge. "Here." Lana offers me a hand.

I grab Lana's hand, but as I do, my boot skids on some stray glass. My free hand shoots out to break my fall but as I slip, I grab a piece of glass still fixed to the window. It slices my palm. I suck in a gasp of shock, momentarily clutching both Lana's hand and the sharp glass.

"Storm!" Lana cries.

"It's nothing." I swing my leg carefully over the ledge, avoiding the shard now smeared with my blood.

Ling, Naz, Benji, and the two scientists are already halfway down the corridor. I clear the window and start running after them, Lana behind me, boots thudding as we run. I glance down at my palm. My hand is balled into a fist and slick with blood. Blood pulses from the cut with every beat of my heart.

"Guys, I can't see the Quicks from where you came in." Achilles' voice is tense through our comms.

"Where are they?" Naz yells ahead of me, all of us still running. The alarm continues to shriek painfully, blue light streaking everywhere.

"I don't know!" Achilles says. "They're gone."

The three Quicks should've found us by now. And there were more at the other entrances. *Where are they?* I catch up to the others. We're outside the kitchen—the window's still open, rope still in place.

Naz yells, "Let's get out of here!"

"But where are they?" I gasp.

"Who cares, let's just go!"

"Who are you?" Frog asks in confusion.

Benji's eyes whip past me. "Where's Angel?"

"Behind me."

Suddenly, the alarm stops. So do the flashing lights. A weird, eerie silence descends.

"She was right behind me," I repeat, looking back at the corner we'd just rounded.

Just as the thought forms that we shouldn't, we all double back to look. And then everything changes. I forget about the pain in my hand.

"What the hell?" says Frog.

"Oh no," Benji whimpers. "No, no, no."

The corridor is filled with a sea of gleaming Quicks. The two closest to us have Lana. One holds her hands behind her back. The other has a smooth, chrome hand at her throat, holding her head in place. Her mask is on the ground. She is breathing fast, eyes twitching in terror.

"I'm so sorry," she whispers. The Quick tightens its grasp, cutting off her ability to speak.

"Lana!" Benji lunges forward a step, his voice shooting high in fear. *He used her real name.*

The Quicks begin speaking, their collective voices a passionless monotone. "By order of the Trust and Project Aevum, we are authorized to act against individuals found guilty of crimes against the state." A pause, and then: "We are authorized to execute."

"No!" Benji screams.

With one flick of its wrist, the Quick twists Lana's head hard to the left. There's a soft snap, and her body goes limp. Her blond hair falls across her face as her head lolls forward. When the Quick lets her go, she crumples to the floor.

Lana is dead.

We will be next.

I whip my head to Ling. She's got a grenade and is taking aim. So is Naz. Ling's eyes meet mine. "Run!" she screams.

The grenades fly forward. I have a second to spin on my heel and take one, maybe two steps before a deafening explosion blasts me off my feet.

I slam into the wall, hitting my skull so hard I can feel every bone in my head. Smoke and the sharp, abrasive smell of burning fills the air around me. The thick sound of falling rubble—a wall collapsing. My ears are ringing with a scratchy, high-pitched whine. The alarm, the blue light, and a sprinkler system all burst into life at once.

"Run, run!" Naz or maybe Ling yells, but I can't see them through the smoke and water. I don't stop to take in the damage of the grenade or to see where the Quicks are. I scramble to my feet. There's water in my eyes. No, it's blood. A cut on my head where I hit the wall? I can't tell because of the mask. *Run.*

My cut hand bent like a claw, I half run, half stumble down the corridor. Coughing, eyes watering, I shove open the first door I can find, needing to get out of the stinking, itchy smoke before I pass out.

I am in a dark, silent laboratory. Shiny silver benches. A spinning chair. I fall into it, twirl in a circle. Another exit. I stumble through someone's office. Scratch on a desk, a silent stream of a gently flowing waterfall. A photogram of a family, two grinning kids, Mom and Dad. I'm in another corridor, passing a blue water cooler, knocking over a plant. Where am I? The others? The Quicks?

I fumble my way along the corridor, my head throbbing savagely, the high-pitched whine still invading my ears. No, it's the comm. It must have smashed when I was thrown against the wall. I pull the broken thing out of my ear. The good news is the staticky, high-pitched whine is gone. The bad news is my lifeline to Kudzu has been severed.

Out of the corner of my eye, I glimpse movement. My heart stops. A Quick? No, just a blue flashing light, circling around the corridor in a never-ending race. I back into an open doorway.

Whoosh. A set of clear doors slams shut, almost taking my nose off. I jump like a jackrabbit and spin around to face an identical set of closed clear doors.

I'm trapped.

I hear a long, low hiss. White clouds of subtly sweet-smelling gas start to fill the small space I'm in. For a second I start to panic—poison gas?—before I remember: This is decontamination gas. Standard procedure for entry into any part of the building with live specimens, like skin or hair. I know this place. It's Innovation Lab B. It only takes about five seconds, I remember now. I'm right—the inner door to the lab slides open then locks behind me once I'm through. It'll take another ten seconds or so for the system to reset. I can't open the doors again until it does.

Both doors are so thick they completely block out the alarm. Silence hangs around me like a shroud.

It's likely the Liamond system just registered someone entering this lab. But I'm rooted to the spot by the surreal sight in front of me.

Two rows of square glass cases line the room. And in each case, suspended in blue liquid, is a mutant.

That's the only word I can use to describe them. The first one, on my left, is a baby with a bulbous forehead that billows out as if holding a supersized brain. To my right, a toddler-aged boy with two heads crammed onto a thick neck. One of his faces is so deformed it looks like someone tossed his features on without looking.

They're not mutants. They must be cloning experiments. Mistakes.

The beep of the decontamination system finishing its reset cycle is enough to startle me out of my reverie. I decide not to go back the way I came—I should put as much distance between me and the bomb site as I can. I force myself to walk down the aisle of horrors to the exit at the far end of the lab.

There's something covered in so much hair it looks more animal than human. Its long, dark strands hang motionless in the liquid blue. I see a human mouth that all but covers the thing's face—a ghoulish slash of teeth and gums that stretches from ear to ear.

They all hang silently in their blue-liquid coffins, eyes closed. I have no idea if they're living or dead or something in between.

I know I should keep moving but I'm captivated by the next one. He's definitely the oldest and the most human looking, except for a long scar on the right side of his body, as if his skin has been folded inward. Even though he's completely hairless, he looks strangely . . . beautiful. I give my head a little shake, and wonder briefly if I have a concussion. But the scarred boy is lovely. My feet move toward him.

My eyes drift over a strong nose and pearly skin. The scar travels his body like a road, past his eye, down one side of his neck, his chest, all the way down to his feet.

My face is only six inches from his. I'm realize I'm holding my breath.

His eyes pop open. My heart explodes. *It's alive.*

Purple eyes the color of a bruise glue onto me. In wordless panic, I back away.

I hear a familiar *whoosh*. I know what it is before my eyes confirm it.

A low hiss fills the entrance I came through. Clouds of white steam surround the powerful bodies of two Quicks. Their blood-red eyes cut through the gas, aimed directly at me. The only thing that separates me from them is the inner glass door that'll open when the system finishes gassing them. I'm dead.

No. The other exit. I have to make it there before the inner doors open. Thirty feet away. I won't make it. I whirl around and start to run.

The mutants blur on either side of me. I hear the whoosh of the inner door opening. I hear the Quicks.

The other exit comes jerkily closer as my feet pound the floor. I'm almost there. They're almost at my back. I can almost *feel* them. Inside. The doors slide shut behind me. Their hard bodies crash against the door.

I gasp out a cry of hot relief.

Panting more out of fear than exertion, I spin around. The two Quicks are right on the other side of the doors. We stare at each other as the low hiss begins, filling my would-be coffin with cloud-colored gas. They don't try to break the door. They must know they can't, and robots, unlike humans, are never overcome with anger or desperation. No, they just wait, freakily immobile and close. I force myself to turn away. I should have a luxurious fifteen-second start on them while the doors stay locked to regas, then gas the two Quicks.

I can't go back to the kitchen. The Quicks were there and there is no way I can ride the rope down with an injured hand. That leaves the stairs.

Ready. I lower my center of gravity to get ready to run.

Set.

Go. The doors open with a whoosh. The alarm rushes my head with its awful screech.

I race out and around the corner. The corridor is empty except for a low bench and a plant. I see a red sign on a door: EMERGENCY EXIT: STAIRS. *Yes.* I shove the door with my shoulder.

It's locked.

I curse loudly and kick the door in a fury. The Quicks will be here any second.

My eyes race around the empty corridor, the walls, the ceiling.... They lock on to something. I know what to do. I yank a smoke bomb from my belt and toss it down the corridor. Instantly, plumes of woodsy-smelling gray smoke hiss out of the little bomb, filling the corridor. I watch the smoke rise, body tense. C'mon. *C'mon!*

There's a short click, then the water sprinkler system switches on, drenching the entire corridor. *Yes.*

This time when I shove the door, it swings open.

Blue lights streak everything, even in here.

I take the first flight two stairs at a time. I pass the fifth-floor landing, then the fourth, then the third. I'm back in the woods behind Milkwood, legs pounding, breath rasping. I taste blood in my mouth, warm and salty. I think it's coming from the cut on my head.

Finally, I reach Level One. I throw the doors open, the alarm reverberating through my body with its incessant high-pitched scream.

I try to run, but it's more like a lurching, staggering limp, down the empty corridor. I hear shouts. Human voices at the other end, around the corner. I hear the word *Aevum*. I turn back the way I came, noticing as I do the drops of blood. My blood. I spit out a bit more.

I round the corner and hurtle straight into a scientist.

No. It's Hunter.

I barely have time to wonder why Hunter is here, now, before he drives me back against the wall. One forearm, strong as steel, presses against my throat. I claw at it, unable to breathe.

He's going to kill me, right here in the corridor.

I am numb with shock, then I realize, *He doesn't know who I am.* I still have the mask on.

I try to choke out his name, but he just pushes his arm farther into my throat.

I can't breathe I can't breathe I can't breathe.

My eyes are wide with terror. I try to signal something, anything, with them.

I'm Tess! Abel's niece! Don't kill me! Please, please, don't kill me!

His eyes don't leave mine. Then they falter. His head cocks slightly to one side, and he isn't gazing coldly anymore, he's actually looking into my eyes. He loosens his grip, enough so I can breathe again. I choke in massive gulps of air, raspy and frenzied.

He's looking at my necklace. "Tess?" Spoken in quiet, horrified disbelief. At that exact moment, the alarm and flashing blue lights stop.

In one quick movement, he pulls my mask off. I wince as the material scrapes the cut on my forehead.

My hands clutch my throat. I wheeze, "What are you doing here?"

"What are *you* doing here?"

I pull my knife from my belt and back away from him.

"Tess, I've authorized those Quicks to kill you." He reaches one hand out—to touch or grab me, I can't tell. Without thinking, I slash my knife forward as hard as I can. It plunges straight into the center of his outstretched palm.

"Hunter, I'm sorry!" I cry before I realize he doesn't look like he's in pain. And despite my force, the knife barely pierced his skin.

A tiny drop of blood seeps from where the knife tip is stuck in his palm. It is a vibrant sky blue.

I stare at him, feeling my mouth fall open.

A clatter of pounding feet. Our heads spin in the direction of the sound. Three Quicks at the far end of the corridor, running toward us.

I wrench Mack back and yank a grenade from my belt. I pull the pin with my teeth and toss it in their direction. With lightning reflexes, the Quick shoots up a hand and bats the bomb back to me. The bomb sails back down the corridor, hitting me in the chest, then bounces to land just a few feet away. *It's about to explode.*

Hunter grabs me, putting himself between me and the bomb. For the second time tonight, a white-hot explosion rips through the world. Hunter and I are swept off our feet, shooting forward like a missile. He spins his body as we start to fall. His back crashes into the ground, protecting me. It feels like being wrapped in a brick wall. We skid across the slick floor, to a halt.

I push myself away from him, crawling on all fours, coughing. The biting smell of the blast fills my mouth and nostrils.

Hunter stands up quietly, uninjured and not coughing. "Tess..."

I see an exit sign glowing red above a door.

I pull myself up. As soon as I put weight on my left foot, a jagged spear of pain shoots through my entire body, and I cry out. My ankle.

"Tess," he says again. I don't stop. Limping over, I try the door. It's locked.

I jam Mack between the door and the frame, trying to pry it open, shoving my shoulder against it again and again and again. Panic transcends pain. I have to get out of here. Like a wild thing, I pry and shove until suddenly, almost magically, the door shoots open, and I stumble out into in the night.

I gulp the cool air, my breathing rattled and frantic.

It can't be true. But it is. I had seen it. Blue blood. No pain. The world dips and whirls around me, and I struggle to stay upright.

Hunter, always so curious, always slightly out of step with me.

The mutant with the long scar down his body. That's why I was drawn to him. He was Hunter. Hairless and deformed but he was Hunter. A version of Hunter. A mistake. A failed attempt to clone a human.

Hunter isn't human. Hunter is an artilect. Hunter is Aevum.

I draw in a shuddering breath. To my left is a sliver of brightly lit street that leads to the front entrance. Movement—half a dozen Quicks flash past the top of the alley. I freeze, my heart in my mouth. No, they aren't headed this way. I spin around and begin limping right, toward the back of the building. Smoke billows from a few open windows, its stench turning my stomach.

I am once again at the back of Simutech. To my right, I recognize the loading dock, and beyond that, the entrance of the alley. To my left, the street continues onto the empty plaza and the lone water fountain.

I force myself to run toward the plaza, each step more painful than the last. On either side of me are silent, shuttered loading docks, or the backs of other large buildings, all dark and empty.

My breath is coming in croaky rasps. My ankle throbs, already starting to swell. Then there's the deep cut on my hand, the one on my head, and my ribs feel bruised: I am a bloody, broken mess.

As I near the end of the street, I breathe in the ripe, sweet smell of oranges. I realize this is Orange Grove Plaza, one of the bigger plazas in the Hive. My foggy mind tries to put the geography together.

I need to find Kudzu but there's no way I can find Milkwood on my own. The only place they'll know to look for me is Abel's. It's not safe there, now that Hunter and presumably Abel know I'm with Kudzu, but it's my only option. I have the vague impression I'm heading west. If I keep going in a straight line, I should eventually clear the Hive and be in Liberty Gardens.

Like most plazas in Eden, Orange Grove is circular with a large white water fountain in the middle. Boutiques in beautiful stone buildings, now all closed, ring the empty plaza. Running straight across feels too exposed. I wait ten seconds to make sure no one else is around. Then I slink up to the first set of boutiques and begin moving in front of their curved windows, making my way to the other side of the plaza. I have to clear about ten storefronts to get all the way around.

Almost immediately, I hear a quick, rhythmic tapping. It's the sound of Quicks running. They are coming this way.

I could never outrun them. Freezing won't work either, not when they're actively searching for me. I'm in front of a florist shop, but of course it's locked.

My body won't move.

Run.

But I have nowhere to go.

chapter 13

The tapping becomes a drumming. Like a swarm of nightmarish insects, Quicks spill into the plaza. They begin to fan out in a meticulous, symmetrical formation. There are at least fifty of them. It's only a few seconds before one of them sees me. A spike of fear, right through my heart. The entire sea of gleaming black heads swivel as one to face me. Glowing red eyes lock into mine. They surround me so quickly, I don't have time to move a single step.

My arms are forced behind my back. The powerful hand at my throat is ice cold. They are too fast and strong for me to escape in the ways Ling taught me. Without a human body's weakness to exploit, I am helpless.

A chorus of emotionless voices begins. "By order of the Trust and Project Aevum, we are authorized to act against individuals found guilty—"

"Help!" I scream hoarsely. "Somebody help—"

The grip around my throat tightens, muting my cry. This can't be how I am supposed to die. Alone in an empty plaza, surrounded by a flock of robots that won't even notice my blood on their hands.

Faces flash at me. Ling, Benji, Lana, Naz, Achilles. Abel. Hunter. Yes, even Hunter. A strangled choke of terror escapes my throat, but then I steel myself. I will not die crying.

"...We are authorized to execute."

I gaze up at the sprinkling of diamond stars above the plaza, pinpricks of light that traveled so far to meet my eyes.

Here I come, Mommy. Here I come.

And then...nothing. My entire body is tense, ready for pain. Still nothing.

"Just get it over with," I wheeze, my voice strangled through their immobile grip.

As one, the Quicks' eyes change color. They switch from red to white. My arms and throat are released. I almost collapse, doubling over and gasping for breath. The robots all turn away, going from the plaza, their feet drumming loudly on the clean stone inlay.

Then they are gone. I stand, dumbfounded, alone but for the gentle burble of the water fountain. *Why did they stop?*

A lone figure emerges from the shadows, walking slowly toward me. It is Hunter.

His green eyes seem to glow. No. They *are* glowing, pulsing with some kind of power that has never been human.

"Th-That was you, just then," I stutter in disbelief, my hand still rubbing my throat protectively. "Those Quicks—you serfed them."

His face is devoid of expression. "Yes."

My survival instinct kicks in. "Someone might see us. Someone human." I gesture behind me. "These boutiques are all locked—"

The sound of the door unlocking cuts me off. Without a word, he strides past me and opens it, walking inside. A moment to take this in—Hunter as masterkey—and then I follow, closing the door securely behind me.

The fresh perfume of flowers hangs heavy in the air. Dozens of beautiful bouquets spill out everywhere—enormous white lilies the size of buckets, full red roses that smell just like chocolate, a bird-of-paradise with bright feathers growing from its stem.

A huge oval mirror hangs above a glossy pink counter. I lock eyes with a beast. I start in fright before realizing the beast is me. Dried blood cakes one side of my face from the cut on my head. My skin is darkened with smoke and dirt and rubble. The ends of my hair and parts of my eyebrows have been singed off. Red marks shaped like fingers bracelet my throat.

My tronic glows in the dim light, four words embedded under my skin: *No feeling is final.*

Hunter comes toward me. I don't know if I should be scared of a killer or thankful for a savior. His voice is just a murmur. "You're hurt."

A thin hypodermic needle plunges into my forearm.

"Ow!" I try to wrench my arm away, but Hunter holds it securely, pumping cool, clear liquid inside me. "What is that?" I ask in a panic.

"Nanites. A form of microrobotic technology—"

"I know what nanites are!" I exclaim. "Why am I chock-full of them?"

"They'll help you heal faster."

He extracts the needle carefully. As I rub where it had pierced my skin, I can't help but stare at him. I look like a war zone. He just looks like Hunter.

This must be a mistake. A huge and terrible mistake. Maybe Hunter does work for Simutech but he can't—There's no way he's actually—

There's one question that'll answer this. My voice is not much more than a whisper. "Who is Emily Anderson?"

Shadows pool around his face, his expression still completely unreadable. "A memory I wrote," he replies quietly.

I spin around, away from him, one hand clamped over my mouth to stifle a cry. I grab the counter for support.

"You're not my uncle's assistant," I say.

"No."

"You're not a student."

"No."

"You're…" I can't look at him. "You're…"

"Say it," he says, in a strangely urgent voice.

I squeeze my eyes shut, hard, then force them open. I turn to meet his gaze coldly, channeling my most mechanical self. "You're a combination of human clone tissue and machine. You have an artificial nervous system, powered by robotic neuron and glial cells. Your DNA sequences are genetically engineered. You're not human. You are…" I pause. "You are an artilect. You are Aevum."

In the darkness of the boutique, I catch the faintest glimpse of a smile on his mouth. "Right again, Tess Rockwood."

A flood of memories pours over me. Hunter's fingers running up Mack's handle the day we met, the way his eyes darted so quickly to mine. The pleasure of discovering Malspeak. The questions, the curiosity, the awkwardness. The endless repertoire of facts and figures and information. Magnus was connected to the streams. He could see everything. That's why Hunter knows so much about art and history. He was in the streams the whole time. How could I not see? How could I not realize what he really was?

"But—But you were always at Abel's," I stutter. "How is that possible? Why weren't you locked up at Simutech?"

Hunter's eyes slide sideways. "That information is classified."

"Screw classification!" I exclaim. "Hunter, it's me, it's Tess."

His eyes flit to mine before flitting back to the floor. After a pause, he says, "Abel told the Trust the reason Magnus killed your mother was because he was not socially conditioned, and that I must be allowed to operate in society as a normal boy in order to be safe. The Trust refused. A compromise was made."

"You could be at the house," I say. "You could travel to and from Abel's home."

The walk by the river. That's why he was so excited. That was the first time—I shake my head, almost unable to comprehend it all—that was the first time he'd even been to the river.

My feet move toward him to get a better view. He looks *exactly* like a normal boy. His hair, his skin, the color of his eyes. *A perfect clone. Of whom?*

I wonder. "You're amazing," I breathe, stunned. I can't believe Abel did it. My fingers reach to touch his skin—skin that doesn't rip or tear, skin that doesn't seem to feel pain, skin that looks human but must be improved somehow, modified, strengthened—before I remember where I am. Who I am. Who Hunter is.

"The presentation," I remember. "Hunter, I saw the presentation at Simutech."

Nothing. He's silent, unmoving.

"I saw the Builder kill those men," I continue, my horror growing with every second. "You did that. You took control of that Builder and you killed them."

I will him to say no.

"Yes," he says. "I did."

I'm having trouble breathing. "I can't believe you did that. I just—I just can't believe that. You're a murderer!" I cry, before catching myself and dropping my voice to a frenzied whisper. "You're a murderer. You killed ten people."

"Yes, I did."

"And you're supposed to carry out Project Aevum. You're supposed to"—my voice wavers; I snatch it back—"*kill* everyone in the Badlands."

"Technically, I'm anticipating a ninety-six point seven percent success rate," he muses quietly. "But essentially, yes."

"That's why the Trust created you." My mind is racing, trying to pull everything together. "Project Aevum wasn't your idea, you're just ... you're just the means to the end. You can make subs kill people."

"Yes."

I swallow hard, panting with adrenaline. "Okay. Okay. We'll go back to Abel's together," I think aloud. "We can wait there for Kudzu. Once we find Ling, she'll know what to do."

"Kudzu?" Hunter blinks before his face clears into understanding. "That's why you used the off-cycle scratch," he murmurs. "You're part of Kudzu. That's who broke into Simutech."

There's not point denying it now. "Exactly."

"If I'd known that..." A subtle grimace touches his features.

"What?" I ask in alarm. "If you'd known that, what?"

Hunter looks momentarily lost in thought. "I might not have sent in all those Quicks."

Hunter sent in the Quicks. The Quicks who killed Lana. It was him. *He* authorized the Quicks to kill. For a moment I can't bear to look him. *He didn't know,* I remind myself fiercely. *He's a puppet. You have to save him.*

I grab his arm and pull him a few steps toward the door. "We have to get out of here."

"Why?"

"Because otherwise the Trust will force you to kill millions of people," I snap, more out of fear than annoyance. "We have to get out of here now!"

Hunter pulls his arm easily from my grip and steps back to put a healthy distance between us. His voice is dead calm. "The Trust isn't forcing me to do anything, Tess."

"What are you talking about?"

"I am choosing to perform Project Aevum," he says simply. "Removing the human element from the Badlands is the most effective course of action for the ongoing prosperity of Eden. You saw what happened on the Northern Bridge. The Badlands are a threat. It's very fortunate I can stop it."

I'm dumb with disbelief, before I choke out, "You can't really think that, Hunter. I mean, you can't actually *believe* that."

"Yes, I can."

"But these are people's lives. You'll be ending people's *lives*."

"What's the alternative, Tess? Everyone starves to death?" Bizarrely, his voice switches to my voice, an octave higher than his. "*'It's not really living out there. It's surviving. And most people aren't even doing that. They're just dying.'*"

I said that to him. They're my exact words.

"I'm not sadistic, if that's what you're thinking. Project Aevum is designed to be humane," he continues in his regular voice. He turns and wanders away from me, his voice echoing around the darkened shop. "That's why the Trust built me to be able to do this. A human would be pointlessly distracted from the task by emotion. I see the problem. I fix it."

"But what you're doing is wrong!" I cry.

"Perhaps according to your morality," he allows. "But not to mine. Eden is the pinnacle of human evolution, Tess. It's a society that has been thousands of years in the making. Project Aevum will allow it to be fully realized."

I can't believe he is justifying this, so cold, so calm. "Hunter," I say, trying to keep my voice even, "there's no need for drastic measures, okay? Let's just—let's just talk about this."

He smiles, amused and intrigued. "What an interesting thing to say," he says softly. "I can't imagine anyone in Eden who's taking more drastic measures than you right now. Do you assume you are better placed to make this decision than I am? I may not be human, but I am conscious. Just because you don't like what you hear doesn't make it immoral."

"Yes it does!" I snap, throwing up my hands. "What you're talking about is absolutely *insane*."

He is wholly unperturbed by my anger. "You've studied the world's history, Tess. You know I'm not the first person to decide the fate of millions. They had their reasons. I have mine."

"Those men were all monsters," I say harshly. "You really want to be in their ranks?"

Hunter's eyes move around my face with austere assessment. "Anger," he muses softly. "Such an interesting emotion."

"Yes, lucky you're not 'distracted' by that," I snarl sarcastically. I flash on Hunter holding my sore hands across Abel's dining room table. "How can you even say that? You have emotions, Hunter, I've seen them!"

Hunter's face drops into complete blankness, as if I'd just switched him off. "No," he says flatly. "I don't."

Hunter's been faking his emotions. Simulating them. A murderer playing a boy to manipulate me.

Just like I did. This is karma.

In the dim light of my mother's office: "Hello, Magnus."

"Tess. You are not permitted to be here." His deep voice rumbled and I put one finger to my lips.

"Shhh."

Obediently, his voice dropped to a low murmur. "I am glad you are."

I giggled, cocking my head to the side. "That's me, little boomerang girl. Always coming back." I made my way over to the hulking man-machine in the corner.

"Do you like what I'm wearing?"

His large head moved down, then back up as he looked over Izzy's come-hither outfit.

"Yes."

A shiver of electricity ran through me as I put one hand on his huge bicep. It was cold and hard. "Can you feel that?"

"Yes."

"Do you like how it feels?" I murmured, letting the cool of his exterior absorb steal the heat of my hand.

"Yes."

I started running the tips of my fingers up and down his arm, tipping my head up toward his. I know he can feel it, my fingerpads racing up and down, up and down. "Do you like that?"

"Yes."

"Tell me. Tell me that you like it."

"I like the feeling of your hand on me, Tess."

"Do you want me to continue?"

"Yes. I want you to continue."

"What about this?" I whisper, pressing more of my body against the bulk of his. "Do you like this?"

"Yes. I like that very much."

I stopped and quickly pulled myself away.

His deep voice rumbled immediately. "Please continue to do that."

"Who is in charge of you?" I asked sharply.

"Simutech and Doctor Francesca Rockwood," he replied. "Please continue to touch my arm with your hand."

I hovered a few inches from him, looking deep into his dull, silver eyes, barely able to stop my voice from becoming a snarl. "Who. Is. In. Charge. Of. You?"

I can almost see the processes whirring clunkily in his singularix, as his excited nervous system battled with his logic circuits.

"You are, Tess. You are in charge of me."

"That's right." I exhaled, flushed with success. Guess what, Mom? Lowering your little project's logic circuits to maximize his emotional susceptibility? Big-time success.

With a smile full of secrets as dark as witches', I pulled his head down to meet mine.

Stumbling, I knock over a vase of roses. It crashes to the ground, scattering the flowers across the polished floor. Roses and thorns crunch under my feet.

"Tess?"

I wish I could burn these memories out of my brain. I used the feelings Magnus had for me with a callousness I can't bear to recall. But his feelings *were* real.

Breathing hard, I look Hunter right in the eye. "You were designed," I say, "to have emotions. You should be able to feel things. Correct?"

He's silent. But I'm right. I know I am.

"Why did you tutor me?" I ask suddenly.

"Abel ordered me to."

"Why?"

Hunter remains inscrutable. "I don't know," he replies.

"You must have a theory. If you're really so *smart*."

His eyes dart to mine, then shoot away. A crack. A crack I can get through. "Abel wasn't getting you to watch me," I think aloud. "Abel didn't know about Kudzu."

Then why insist we spend time together?

"Does Abel know," I ask, "what the Trust intends to do with you?"

After a moment, Hunter nods. "He does."

"And does he disagree?"

"He's not permitted to say."

"What do you think?"

Hunter's gaze draws away from me. "Abel does not approve," he says softly.

I'm remembering things. Abel watching me refuse to eat the mushroom risotto. Abel asking me about my time in the Badlands.

"Is it possible," I continue, "that Abel thought I could—I don't know—help? In your development? That I could be a . . . good influence?"

As the words leave my mouth, I feel certain I am right. Abel didn't support building a genocide machine. He was using me to expose Hunter to a different way of seeing things. Or to make Hunter feel things.

What was it my mom said defined consciousness? Free will. Morality. Empathy. Hunter has free will, or so he believes. And he believes he is acting morally. But empathy? No. You need emotions to feel empathy, and he doesn't think he has those. Abel wanted me to help Hunter feel things. Yes. If Hunter did feel empathy, maybe he wouldn't be able to go through with Project Aevum. If he cared about the Badlands like I did, maybe he wouldn't be able to destroy them.

Time is running out. I have to convince Hunter to come with me. I have to do it now. And to do that, I have to get this boy-machine to feel.

"Why did you save me from the Quicks?" I whisper.

Again, my question is met with silence. I move slowly toward him, keeping my voice soft.

"Why did you save me back at Simutech? You could've killed me. Why didn't you, Hunter?" His eyes are on the floor, staring at the space between us. I feel so incredibly exposed. My face burns. My heart thumps. "Is it because you care about me?"

Still, nothing. But he's not moving away. Slowly, I reach for one of his hands. He flinches. "It's okay," I whisper, stopping for a second. "It's okay."

My fingers find his. They are warm, pulsing with genetically altered blue blood, powered by mirror matter. Gently, I lift his hand until it's near my face. I press his fingers onto my cheek, so he can feel my skin. Finally, finally, he lifts his eyes from the floor and lets himself look at me.

In those eyes is so much confusion and pain and fear, it breaks my heart. "Hey." I smile.

His eyes don't leave mine. His voice, just barely audible: "Hey."

This tiny word floods me with an ocean of hope. I press his hand harder onto my face. "Do you remember," I whisper, "when you held my hands that night at Abel's? They were red and sore, and you asked me what happened to them? Do you remember?"

"I do."

"And do you remember earlier tonight?" I move closer still to him, until I can feel heat radiating from his body. "Right before I left. At the river. Do you remember that?"

"I don't forget anything."

I move my hand from his, and miraculously, his stays in place, holding my cheek. "I thought you were going to kiss me."

He's silent, searching my eyes with his.

I stare up at him. Even now, even knowing what I know, I feel attracted to Hunter. No. More than attracted. Connected. "You have feelings, Hunter. You have them for me."

His eyes dart cautiously between my lips and my eyes. He wants to kiss me. My spine prickles. "How do you know?"

"Because," I tell him honestly, "I have them for you."

He blinks, stunned. "For me?"

I nod.

His eyes are darting between mine; left, right, left, right, left, right. "I felt scared," he says haltingly. "When I saw you at Simutech. You were bleeding, and the Quicks were after you, and I felt scared. Not for me. For you."

"Yes." I nod again. "I was scared."

"And that's...normal?" he asks, sounding embarrassed.

"Yes." I place my palms flat on his chest and draw myself closer. His body twitches under my hands and I can smell him—mint and ash. "That's *empathy*."

He starts, jerking away from me. His eyes narrow into slits. "Is that what this is?"

"Hunter—"

"No." He backs away from me, out of my reach. "You're trying to manipulate me. For your cause. You're just trying to stop me."

"No, Hunter," I say desperately. "I feel those things for you, *I do*."

A noise interrupts us. Through the front windows, I see three floaters prowling in the shadows. Kudzu is looking for me.

I meet his eyes again. "Kudzu has to stop Project Aevum, Hunter."

"You can't," he says, voice soft but sure.

"We can if you come with us." I run to the door and open it. Ling, Naz, and Benji are on the other side of plaza. My heart sings with relief. "Hey!" I call softly.

They see me and swing their floaters in my direction.

I race back inside the shop to find Hunter hidden in the shadows on the far wall. "Come with me," I plead. "Once everyone finds out what you've done, Edenites will turn on you and the Trust will betray you. They'll kill you, Hunter."

He says nothing. I hear Kudzu zoom across the plaza.

"Do you care about me?" I ask. "Do you?"

He just stands there, still as a statue. "I...can't. The Trust will be at Simutech within the hour. I have to go with them."

"Tess!" Ling calls quietly.

"Hunter, we can't let Project Aevum happen," I repeat, my voice rising in desperation. "I mean it. Come with me."

Nothing. No reaction.

His eyes cut through the darkness. "Are you going to try to kill me?"

"We're going to try to stop you."

His words are low, almost a growl. "What if I stop you first?"

My heart skips a beat. "Could you kill me, Hunter?" I take a step closer, to less than an arm's length away. Goose bumps race up my arms. "Could you?"

He doesn't answer. His face remains frozen.

Ling calls urgently from outside. "Tess!" The floater engines rev impatiently.

With one final, desperate look back at him, I run outside. The plaza is empty and painted in silver moonlight. I swing myself onto the back of Ling's floater and she guns the motor.

Glancing over my shoulder, I can just make out the ghostly form of Hunter in the florist window, watching us as we ride away.

We head out of the Hive, across Moon River, then north through Liberty Gardens. Ling leads the way, keeping under the speed limit and always on the back streets. We need to stop and regroup, but everywhere there are houses full of people or any number of service subs who could easily be on-cycle. Now that the Trust has identified us as terrorists, the sleeping city feels like a trap ready to snap shut.

We approach a park with a large nature reserve spreading out behind it. "There!" I point. Ling drives off the street and straight through a manicured flower bed. We shoot past swing sets and slide toward the pine trees at the back. Naz and Benji are right behind us.

As we approach the safety of the trees, Kudzu cuts their motors. Wordlessly, we hop off and start jogging, guiding the floaters forward until trees tangle together into a small forest. The ground becomes soft and springy underfoot.

When we can't see the street or darkened houses anymore, Ling stops. "This is far enough." She presses her comm into her ear, speaking to who I assume is Achilles. "We just need a minute."

The floaters fall to one side. For the first time, I get a good look at the others. They look like they've been hit by an airtrain. Skin smeared with smoke and dried blood from scratches and cuts, bruises beginning to deepen, hair matted and burned. Naz has a deep gash on her head, Ling has one on her lip that is still bleeding. Benji looks the most unharmed, but his eyes are glazed and unseeing. He's the first to speak, his voice sounding thick and strangled. "They killed her. They broke her neck...Oh, Lana!" he cries out, voice breaking. Ling rushes over. He buries his face in her neck and starts to sob.

Naz pulls a tightly rolled cigarette from her pocket. Her hands are shaking so hard she can't get the lighter to work. She swears softly under her breath.

I go over and cover her quivering hand with mine. I hold it there until the shaking stops. Then I take the lighter, and after a few tries, light her cigarette. She sucks in deeply and exhales a steady stream of thin gray smoke above my head.

"It doesn't feel real," she says gruffly. "What just happened. I feel like I'm dreaming or something."

"Has that ever happened before?" I ask in a whisper. "Has anyone ever...died...in a mission?"

Naz shakes her head. It makes sense. After all, subs couldn't kill people—until now.

"How'd you get away?" Naz asks me.

I recount everything from the first bomb up until the Quick batting the grenade back to me.

"So why aren't you smeared on Simutech's walls right now?" she asks.

I can't bring myself to tell Kudzu about Hunter. The whole thing is just so impossibly weird. So impossibly wrong.

"Guess you survive one grenade, you can survive them all," I mutter softly.

She snorts. "Pretty hard-core, Rockwood. You're lucky to be alive." She tells me the three of them made it down the rope and, after escaping some Quicks at the bottom, got away on the floaters. From the sound of it, I'm the one who suffered the most injuries. But when she asks to see my palm, I'm shocked to see that the cut has already closed over and is starting to heal. "Doesn't look too bad." She sniffs, giving me an unconcerned once-over. "You say that grenade exploded right at your feet?"

The nanites. I can't believe how fast they're working. "Sort of," I backtrack. "It was pretty close."

Naz rolls her eyes in disbelief and I flush with embarrassment. "So in between all that, you didn't see Aevum?"

"What do you mean?" I ask nervously.

"Aevum," Naz repeats. "The thing. We still don't know what it looks like, right?"

"Yeah. No," I stumble. "No. We don't. I didn't see it."

Benji has stopped crying. Ling lets him go. She takes a long, deep breath and then looks around at us all evenly. "So. What do we do now?"

As Naz and Ling begin debating between taking the back roads to Milkwood or staying in the city, I think about what I want to do. I know we should lay low. But this is the only chance we have. As soon as the Trust arrive at Simutech, it's all over.

Which brings me to the question I've had ever since Hunter's blue blood stained the end of my knife.

Can I kill Hunter?

The thought threatens nausea and I work hard to contain it.

If I tell Kudzu about Hunter, they'll freak. The only way we go back is if I tell them later. Yes, I care about Hunter. More than I've been willing to admit. But I can't let my feelings get in the way of what I know is right.

So when Ling asks me what I think we should do next, I respond by asking if Kudzu has a weapon that'll heat the mirror matter to over two thousand degrees.

"Oh, Tess." Ling looks at me, totally crestfallen. "I can't believe I didn't tell you." She gestures to herself forlornly. "I lost it. It's gone."

"No, it's not." I quickly explain where the mirror matter actually is—the bottom of the indoor garden in the meeting room. "No one else knows it's there," I say. "That room wasn't on the security streams."

This isn't entirely true—I don't know if Hunter knows it's there. As far as I know, Magnus couldn't track his own mirror matter, but Magnus could barely do the dishes. Hunter might have it, right now, fitted back in his artificial brain. But that won't stop me. I will get it from him and I will destroy it or I will die trying. I have Lana's blood on my hands now. I have to. *I have to.*

"So," I say again. "Does Kudzu have a weapon that'll heat the mirror matter to over two thousand degrees?"

Naz thinks about it for a moment, then nods curtly. "It's doable."

"Then there is only one thing we can do," I say. "We go back. Right now."

"What?" Ling gapes at me.

"Look, the Trust will be there within the hour—"

"How do you know that?" Naz asks incredulously.

"I heard the scientists talking. After we got separated." I'm not about to tell them Hunter had let that slip while we were in the florist shop. "The first thing they'll do is relocate Aevum to the Three Towers." The Three Towers are the most heavily fortified buildings in all of Eden. It is impossible to get in or out unless you're Trust.

"She's probably right," Naz says gruffly. "And that's game over for us."

"But every Quick in the city is after us," Ling says. "Authorized to execute, remember?"

"Can you think of another plan?" I ask.

Ling is silent.

My voice sounds steely and cool. "We go back now, and we destroy the mirror matter while it's still at Simutech. Who's on board? This only works if everyone's in."

Naz flicks her cigarette butt high up over our heads. "I am. I think I know how to wipe out those Quicks too."

"Excellent." I breathe in relief.

"I am," Benji says. His eyes are still dull with grief, as if part of him died with Lana. Right now he looks more like a substitute than a human.

"Are you sure you're up for it?" I ask. "Maybe you should—"

"I'm going."

Ling is shaking her head, trying to process what I know sounds like a death-wish of a plan. "I can't guarantee everyone's safety," she says. "Not after what happened to Lana."

"We've only got one shot at this, Ling," I say quietly. "If we want to destroy that mirror matter before it's moved up to the Towers, if we want to stop a massacre out in the Badlands, we have to act now."

Ling meets my eyes. She trusts me. Right or wrong, Ling has always trusted me. She presses her comm back into her ear, looking right at me as she speaks to Achilles. "How long before you can get the rest of Kudzu to the Hive?"

We are going back to Simutech. We are going back to kill Hunter.

chapter 14

The next half hour passes in a blur. In the forest, Naz barks off the weapons she needs while Ling issues calm, fast orders, creating a plan of attack on the fly. Benji pockets his comm and drifts away from us to stare silently at the moon. When I catch his eye as we prepare to leave, I shiver. His gaze, once alert and joyful, is dead and empty.

Our ride back is slow and surreally calm. Again, we stay off main roads in favor of silent suburban back streets. We weave past sleeping homes winking with reassuring night-lights. Past empty boutiques and beautiful parks. Through the midnight-quiet streets of the clean and gleaming Hive.

The alley next to Simutech will be crawling with Quicks, so we decide to meet the others in a twenty-four-hour parking garage on the other side of the Hive. We park our floaters, then assemble quietly in the eerie garage, which is full of empty buzzcars stacked one on top of another. The space is lit by moody red light and feels monumentally creepy.

"Hey, Tess." Ling opens her palm to reveal a Kudzu necklace—the silver K on a thin red string. It's an offering.

I glance at Naz to see if she objects. Then I lift up my ponytail for Ling to tie it around my neck, but she shakes her head. "No. Leave it with one of the others. Just in case..." *Just in case we're caught. Just in case we don't make it back.*

Ling circles her arms around me for a quick, hard hug. I catch the scent of the burning bombs in her hair. "Thank you," I say, my throat a little tight.

Benji gives me a bland smile, and even Naz nods her approval. "But throw away another muesli bar," she warns, "and I'll rip it off you myself." I get the impression she's only half kidding.

I squeeze the necklace tight in my fist. I'm Kudzu now. I'm one of them.

Seeing the rest of Kudzu ride into the sinister red light of the parking garage is a wake-up call. Gone is the playful, lighthearted crew. Now the grim young rebels look ready for warfare.

Bo beelines for Ling, pressing his lips on her dirty forehead, before Ling breaks away to address the small crowd. "Okay, listen up. I know Achilles filled you in on what happened." She pauses for a second, then continues in a clear, unwavering voice. "She was the best of us. And we're not taking this lying down. It's okay if you're not in. But this is about stopping a massacre. And this is about Lana."

Ling breaks us into three assault teams—Alpha, Beta, and Gamma. Gamma is on getaway, keeping the floaters safe from Quicks and ready to pick up everyone after we destroy the mirror matter. Those are mostly the non-fighters, including Henny. Beta team will draw fire from the Quicks and Tranqs, clearing the way for Alpha team. Ling assigns the Beta team: Gem, Kissy, Bo, and Tomm. Naz, Benji, Ling, and I are Alpha.

"I need one more volunteer for Alpha," Ling says, surveying the quiet group.

No one speaks. No one is under the illusion that Alpha's task isn't the most dangerous.

"I'll go." It's Achilles.

Ling frowns at the not-exactly-muscular boy. "Are you sure?"

"No," he replies. "But you need me. Security's still on lockdown. Anything I could do remotely, from Kudzu, would take days. But I can hack the Liamond system on site with this." He pulls a square of scratch from his pocket and opens a stream with his eyes. The stream is a series of different-sized falling blocks, which remind me of a kids' game where the aim is to make the different pieces all fit together.

"What is that?" I ask.

"Think of it as a really complicated key," he says. "I call it . . . a Key." He explains he can use this stream to lock and unlock all entrances and exits, but only from the main security desk in the foyer. "That means I have to physically get inside with you."

Ling's eyebrows draw together in concern. "Achilles, are you sure? You've never been on the front line."

"Again, big-time no," Achilles says. "But unless you limit the number of subs and people after you, you'll never make it. You'll need the exits sealed off, and you'll need all the doors inside unlocked."

I can see from Ling's expression that she knows he's right. She turns to Naz, and nods.

Naz flips open a piece of canvas I'd seen Bo unpacking to reveal a dozen or so air rifles.

I stare at the guns in front of me: bulky, unsophisticated things with large metal canisters strapped to the bottoms and long barrels that taper forward like a pointed finger. "We're going against the Quicks with *air*?"

Naz picks up one of the rifles and fires at a nearby upcycling machine. We all jump as it flies back, crashing loudly onto the concrete thirty feet away.

"Naz!" Ling hisses in horror as the machine skids noisily to a stop. "What happened to stealth?"

Naz throws me a dirty look and snarls, "Someone said no razers."

"I didn't invent that rule because I wanted a challenge, Naz," I shoot back. "I was just telling you what I know—"

"Guys!" Ling warns.

We both shut up.

Naz shows the Alpha and Beta teams how to aim and fire the rifles. A solid posture is key, so as not to lose your balance on the kickback. Just one hard pulse of air. Aim for the chest or legs. The upcycling machine proved the air rifles are powerful. But powerful enough to knock down a Quick coming straight at you?

"Should be."

We also get small razer pistols. If it comes down to it, the razers are for human targets. Naz hands me the weapon, almost inconsequential with its light and easy grip.

"I wonder if I'll be able to go through with it," I say.

"Go through with what?"

I swallow hard. "Killing someone."

"It's not killing someone," she says matter-of-factly. "It's protecting yourself and your team."

Because of the noise both weapons make, I won't even have a chance to test them before using them for the first time. I mutter this to Achilles as he fits me with a new comm.

"Yeah," he responds, straight-faced. "Being a revolutionary is amazetown, huh?"

"What about you? This your first time firing with air?" I wave the rifle at him and he flinches, dropping the comm. I raise my eyebrows as he bends to pick it up.

"I'm not really…into guns," he says apprehensively.

"Seriously? What are you doing in Kudzu?"

"Hey, I'm tech," he says defensively. "Geek boy, remember? Kind of out of my element here."

So only four of our five will actually have weapons? I try to ignore the sour feeling of foreboding that's bubbling inside me. "What about the mirror matter?"

Naz holds aloft an enormous flamethrower. "I'm packing this baby," she announces, kissing the weapon's huge barrel dramatically.

"And it'll get above two thousand degrees?" I ask.

"Just need a clean shot," she replies, oozing confidence.

Ling raises her voice. "Time to go. Everyone ready?"

Our mission leader stands before us, jutting her chin defiantly, sweat beading her brow. In a loud, clear voice, she says, "Our minds are better. Our hands are faster. Our hearts are stronger." She pauses, and the last words are spoken by us all, echoing around the parking garage: "We are Kudzu."

I want us to sound strong. But our voices waver for a fraction, out of sync, and instead we sound slightly unsure.

"Alpha team, remember to wait for my signal," Ling announces. "Let's move."

Everyone in Alpha and Beta finds the backseat of a floater driven by someone in Gamma.

"Chicken." Henny pats the seat behind her. "Ride with me."

I hand her my Kudzu necklace. "Can you keep this safe?"

"I'll have it waiting for you," she says.

We take off like a flock of dark avenging angels. I find myself holding on to Henny's warm and comforting body tighter than I need to. This may well be the last time I ever get to hold another human being.

HOW THE FUTURE FEELS.

Simutech's slogan stretches above the front entrance, illuminated in a jerky dance of flashing lights. From our vantage point across and down the street, crouched behind a parked buzzcar, those of us on Alpha team can see the front entrance. Any hope that it might be easier to get in than we thought is instantly dashed.

At least fifty Quicks form a protective barricade around the entire building. Local Guiders have already arrived and are talking to some dazed-looking Simutech scientists. Another buzzcar full of Guiders arrives, landing in a quick vertical descent. Several bright red Longevity Hub buzzcars are also parked out front. Frog is being treated in one by a Hub doctor, a blanket around his shoulders and a stunned look on his face. For a moment I feel sorry for him—seeing a pretty young girl murdered by a bunch of Quicks probably wasn't how he planned to spend the late shift. Then I remember him punching Ling in the face, and my sense of empathy vanishes.

Where is Hunter now? Already at the Three Towers?

I shake the thought away, focusing again on the main entrance.

"The good news is, it doesn't look like the Trust is here yet," Ling murmurs into her comm. "I can't see any Tranquils."

My heart stops. *Oh no.* I nudge Ling, and nod at the man she'll recognize too. Uncle Abel. He's arguing furiously with an irate Guider. "But how could it've been one of *my* security swabs? I've *just* gotten here!"

"Sir, I can't let you in the building."

"But I'm the head of the project! I'm in charge!"

"I can't let you in the building," the Guider repeats, louder.

"But—But—" he stutters. "I have to assess the damage! Someone broke in? Why?"

I feel a pang of sympathy when I see how upset he is. But I can't let it blossom into anything more. The Guider refuses to cave, and a moment later, Abel throws up his hands and storms off. I sigh with relief.

Ling presses the comm into her ear. "Beta team, are you ready?"

A volley of yesses echoes into our comms.

"Go."

From the opposite end of the street, Gem and Kissy emerge, tottering toward the hullaballoo of Simutech. Both wear elaborate golden masks decorated with peacock feathers—the kind people wear to the burlesque shows in Charity. They stop on the corner, giggling.

"Hey," Gem calls to the line of Quicks. We can hear her perfectly through our comms. "What's going on?"

A Quick turns its attention to her. "By order of the Trust, you are instructed to move on."

"What?"

"By order of the Trust, you are instructed to move on."

Gem and Kissy come a few feet closer, still giggling. "What's going on here?" For all intents and purposes, they look like two cute young girls coming home from a night out.

"By order of the Trust, you are instructed to move on. Vacate this—"

"I can't understand you." Gem shrugs.

"Hey!" One of the Guiders—a pudgy guy in an ill-fitting blue robe—notices them both. "What are you girls doing? Get out of here."

"What's going on?" Kissy asks innocently, tucking her hair behind her ear.

"Are you deaf as well as stupid?" he barks, striding over. Five Quicks follow him. "Go on home, by order of the Trust."

"This has to do with the Trust?" Gem asks, impressed. "Do you know anyone who works in the Three Towers?"

"I bet you do," Kissy adds. "You look like someone who's pretty powerful."

The Guider looks down at Gem and Kissy. They smile back up at him suggestively. He shifts his weight and squares his shoulder. "Yeah, I got a couple buddies in the Towers," he brags.

The Guider begins flirting with Gem and Kissy, who ooh and ahh at everything he says. In less than a minute, a second Guider wanders over for a piece of the action. Another five Quicks tail him like dogs.

"Tomm, Bo—go," Ling instructs.

From the same end of the street, Tomm and Bo swagger toward the scene. They are both wearing standard issue upcycle worker masks, the kind that covers their mouths and noses.

"Hey!" Tomm yells at a different group of Guiders. "I got an upcycle truck parked over on Main that I can't move because the street's blocked off! What the hell is going on?"

"You!" a Guider calls. "Get out of here, this is Trust business—"

"Oh, Trust business, is it?" Tomm calls back mockingly.

"Better shut down Eden if the Trust is involved," Bo adds sarcastically.

"We got a thousand houses to pick up upcycling from *tonight*," Tomm says. "Who's going do it if we can't move our truck?"

"You know, you *should* be using subs to do your work!" a Guider snaps at them as he strides over, followed obediently by a pack of Quicks. "We *should* be phasing out people working menial labor."

"*Menial* labor?" Tomm and Bo ask together in delighted outrage.

Success. An argument is suddenly in full swing. Between that and Gem and Kissy's flirtation, the line of Quicks is broken.

"Alpha," Ling says, looking at us as well as speaking into the comm. "Let's move."

Naz, Ling, Achilles, Benji, and I start crossing the road, now visible to anyone who cares to look over. We are all wearing cream-colored lab coats that someone brought from Milkwood. They're a different cut from Simutech's—as well as being pretty dirty, while Simutech's are snow-white—but I can't imagine the Guiders will know the difference. Because we can no longer hide our faces, we're not using code names this time. I can't bring myself to worry about this—I'm sure Abel knows it was me who used his swab anyway. My heart is bouncing wildly in my chest, mouth sticky and Badlands dry. But with all the distraction the Beta team is causing, we might be able to slip right in—

"Hey." A Guider stops us. "Where do you think you're going?"

"We are working on Project Aevum." Ling smiles prettily. She's changed her voice to sound softer and more precise. "We were instructed by the Trust to begin relocating Aevum's processors."

He glances over at us, looking tired and disinterested. "All right. Hurry up." It worked. We just passed as scientists, even with Naz toting a huge flamethrower strapped to her back under her lab coat.

We continue toward the main entrance. Fast, but not too fast.

A scream from Gem cuts through me. My gaze rockets to her in a panic. Her hand is on the Guider's chunky arm, and she is doubled over in pseudo-hysterics. It was just a scream of laughter. But a Quick has caught me looking. Glowing red eyes lock into mine. I freeze. Suddenly, all the Quicks, wherever they were, swivel their heads toward me. The Quicks speak as one; flat, monotone voices ringing out together: "Terrorist identified."

The Guiders stop flirting and arguing, confused.

Ling doesn't need to give the order.

As one, we whip out the air rifles and razers that are hidden under our clothing. The rest of the Beta team emerges from their hiding places. They quickly move to either end of the line of Quicks and Guiders. Now both Beta and Alpha are in front of Simutech, facing the street.

"What the—" cries the sweat-stained Guider before a suddenly sober Gem sends him flying with a hard pulse of air. He knocks into a couple of Quicks and crashes onto the concrete.

It's on.

Kudzu begin knocking down Quicks and Guiders with air rifles. The noise is deafening. Scientists scatter haphazardly, their shouts of fear adding to the chaotic soundtrack. On either side of me, Naz and Ling pick off their targets with a steady hand, one by one. Across the street, Gem, Kissy, Bo, and Tomm do the same. Achilles darts past me, racing inside the building.

"Start firing!" Naz shouts.

I grasp the heavy air rifle, trying to remember what Naz had said. Steady posture, weight spread evenly on both feet, low center of gravity—

"Tess!" Ling yells.

Looking up, I see a group of Quicks running straight for me. In a panic, I pump the trigger. The force of the gun knocks me off balance, and I stumble back a few feet. I blow one Quick back but there are still more coming. I regain my posture and raise the gun again. I grit my teeth, steady my hand, and begin firing. One. Two. Three in a row.

"Nice!" yells Ling.

"You want this?" Naz growls as she blasts her targets backward. "How about you, you want a little of this too?"

I catch a glimpse of Benji's face and feel a sudden flash of fear. It is cold and hard, set into a mask of pure hatred.

A flare of white light blows a smoking hole into the front of the building, and we all flinch. The Guiders have started returning fire with razers. I've never seen Guiders with weapons before. "Rockwood, watch out!" Naz yells. "Don't get smoked!"

"Beta, fall back and cover us!" Ling orders. "Alpha, start moving in."

Beta scatters, still firing as they run. We start backing toward the building.

"Hurry up, Achilles," Naz mutters. We keep edging into the building, now past the doors, which are still wide open. "Whatever you're doing, do it fast."

Outside, Guiders lie strewn everywhere, knocked unconscious from the fall or too hurt or scared to move. Others blast razer fire at us from unseen vantage points. And no matter how many Quicks we blow away, they keep picking themselves up and coming for us.

"Kissy, retreat!" Ling yells.

Kissy struggles under the weight of her heavy air rifle, screaming as she blasts Quicks and Guiders.

"Kissy, *retreat!*" Ling yells again.

The Guider she'd been flirting with returns fire on her viciously, white pulses of light missing her head by inches.

"Kissy!" I hear Gem scream in terror through the comm.

Slinging the air rifle over my back, I whip out the small razer pistol. It feels featherlight in my hand. I aim for the Guider shooting at Kissy. At the last second, I drop my aim from his chest to his leg and fire. Dead on. I'm panting hard as he hits the street, clutching his leg and shrieking in pain. Kissy glances over at me, breathless and wild-eyed, then sprints off into the darkness. I glance at Naz, nervous she'll berate me for not killing the Guider. But she just gives me a quick nod, and we turn our attention to the madness before us.

"Got it!" calls Achilles. The huge front doors begin closing, coming to meet in the center. Slowly. No whip-fast disappearance like upstairs.

"Beta, retreat! Gamma, fall out to collect, then await instruction!" Ling yells, still firing at the approaching Quicks.

But the doors aren't closing fast enough. With Beta not blowing away the Quicks coming after us, we don't have enough power to stop them.

"Hurry up!" The robots just keep coming, wave after wave after wave. There are so many of them—their red eyes drilling into us, their black-and-silver bodies moving impossibly fast.

The doors are almost closed. At the last second, a Quick forces itself into the doorway.

"It'll be crushed!" Naz yells. But it isn't. It's too strong. The doors stop closing, grinding but not moving, and effectively holding the thing in place by its torso. We all start firing on it. But our air rifles achieve nothing.

Black-and-chrome hands appear in the gap between the two doors above the Quick.

"They're pulling it open!" The Quicks are wrenching the doors back: a quarter inch, then a quarter inch more. The Quick in the doorway struggles, almost free.

"Hold your fire," Ling orders.

"If they get that door open..." I can't finish the thought. Without the support of Beta, we're dead. There are fifty Quicks outside ready to kill us.

"Hold it," Ling says.

A quarter inch more.

"Now!" All four of us fire at once. The doors are open just enough to free the Quick, and we blast it cleanly backward, taking out the Quicks behind it.

In a rush of released pressure, the doors slam closed with a booming crash.

The five of us stand panting; shocked into momentary inertia.

Simutech's wide, open foyer is dotted with green plants and a few bright orange sofas for waiting visitors. It's surreally calm. The sound of a round of razer fire on the heavy front doors jerks me back to high alert.

"Let's go!" Naz shouts.

"Stairs!" I lead the charge. My ankle twinges with every step, but it'll hold out: Hunter's nanites make sure of that.

Guns drawn, we bolt across the squeaky blue floor toward the stairs. We don't see a soul. I know there are probably Guiders and scientists in here somewhere, but hopefully they'll be hiding from five crazy kids with air rifles and razers.

We round the corner. The corridor looks like a wrecking site—exploded walls exposing the offices behind them, rubble everywhere. Part of the ceiling has collapsed. This was where the second grenade exploded. Where Hunter wrapped me in his arms and saved my life.

"Your handiwork, Rockwood?" Naz asks as we pick our way as fast as we can through the debris.

"Yup," I reply, eyes scanning the walls for the entrance to the stairs. "My day isn't complete without at least one explosion."

I see rust-colored spots of blood on the floor. Probably mine. And then, so small it's barely noticeable, a splash of sky-blue. Hunter's blood. "Stairs!" I point with my gun.

I ram the door with my shoulder. It opens—Achilles' key is working. Instantly the shrieking alarm and flashing blue lights we'd become so familiar with begin again. It doesn't really matter now—our presence is no secret, nor is what we're after.

Level Two.

Level Three.

Level Four. My legs are starting to shoot battery acid instead of blood.

Level Five. My head spins with the exertion; sweat pours down my temples.

Level Six. I shove open the door, legs on fire, trying to work out which way we need to go.

"There!" Ling puffs. A sign reading INNOVATION LAB C with an arrow points the way. We stagger down the corridor, heaving with exertion.

Around another corner. Jackpot! We're back at the entrance to the lab. The shards of glass that had covered the floor when we'd last been here are gone. But the long window that Ling and Naz had shot with their razers is still broken.

"Careful with the glass," I pant. Maybe I can use the butt of my gun to smash away some of the leftover pieces that cling to the bottom of the sill. Benji moves past me to help. No, he keeps walking past the window. "Benji?"

I look up ahead of him, along the corridor we'd first run down earlier tonight. I can see the aftereffects of the two grenades Ling and Naz hurled into the sea of Quicks that'd filled this corridor. Walls and parts of the ceiling have been blown away, but the rubble has been cleared. But it's what I see at the far end of the corridor that makes my heart stop.

Lana.

White tape cordons off the area around her, but apart from that, she looks as if she's sleeping. Hair the color of ripe wheat fans out around her.

"Benji!" I yell, running after him. "We don't have time." I grab his arm to stop him but he shakes me off.

I stumble back. He keeps moving like he's sleepwalking. I refocus on what we're here for. The mirror matter.

I'm careful as I swing myself over the jagged ledge. As I run back to the Trust meeting room, I can hear Ling behind me. The door is already open. I burst in, and stop short. The garden is gone. A ragged, gaping hole is all that's left, and even though I don't need to fall to my knees to confirm that the mirror matter is gone, I do anyway. Ling's in the doorway behind me as I turn, stricken. "It's not here."

"C'mon." She pulls me to my feet. "Not over yet."

We race back through the lab. How is it not over? Hunter has it, I know he does.

Back in the corridor, I see Benji, a walking corpse, drawn hopelessly to the body of his girlfriend. I jog a few steps toward him, confused and panicky. The alarm screeches. The blue lights keep flashing. Naz joins Ling and asks, "Not there?"

"No," Ling replies. "Tess, come back here—"

The alarm and flashing blue lights stop. And then we are plunged into total darkness.

I widen my eyes as much as I can to soak up any scrap of available light, but the darkness is all-encompassing.

"Hey!" Naz yells.

"Where is everyone?" Ling calls.

"I'm here!" I say. I sling my rifle onto my back and put both hands out in front of me to move gingerly in the direction of her voice. I know what the blackness means.

The Trust has arrived.

I hear a scuffle. Something falling. Something heavy. *"Oof."*

"Benji?" Ling calls, voice rising in fear. "Benji?"

No reply. I pull my knife but have no way of defending myself against an attacker I can't see. My breathing is shallow and panicked. The darkness magnifies every sound, and I hear swift but heavy footsteps. We are not alone.

A fumble, a click, then a tiny flare of orange light. Ling and Naz are right next to me, Naz holding her lighter. Illuminated in the darkness are a circle of four razer tips pointed straight at us. We are surrounded.

"Lights," orders a tinny voice.

I wince at the sudden brightness.

"Drop your weapons," the voice says again. Blinking my eyes open, I grasp the full horror of our situation. Naz, Ling, and I are surrounded by four Tranqs; the human guards of the Trust. Helmets cover their entire faces, giving them night vision. Farther up the corridor, Benji is on the ground, a fifth Tranq pointing a razer straight at his head. "Away from you," barks the voice again.

Naz, Ling, and I slowly put our weapons on the ground. Where is Achilles? I flick my eyes to Ling. She returns my gaze, steely and even, but with no suggestion of what to do except obey.

"All of them. And your comms."

The razers. The rifles. The flamethrower. Smoke bombs. Grenades. The Tranquils crush our comms with their boots. A wave of panic hits me. How are we going to coordinate our escape? Then I realize how stupid that is. We aren't *going* to escape.

"Hands behind your head. Now!"

"L-Look guys," I stutter, my mouth making decisions without first consulting my brain. "There's obviously been a misunderstanding—"

"Shut up," barks one of them, slamming the side of his gun into the cut on my head. Warm blood flows into my eyes. My head rings like a bell with the pain.

"Tess!" Ling cries, reaching for me. A brandished razer stops her. Slowly, she puts her shaking hands behind her head. Naz does the same.

"How does Gyan want them?" one of them asks, and I'm surprised to hear it's a woman's voice.

"Preferably alive. Dead if they give us any trouble."

A snort. "I'd say these lot qualify as troublesome."

Ling lets out a low growl and the Tranq immediately aims her weapon at her. I lunge forward to put myself between them. "Really?" I snarl through gritted teeth. Blood drips from the bottom of my chin onto the floor. "You'd kill three unarmed teenage girls? Your mothers would be so proud—"

"I said *shut up!*"

The cold tip of the razer presses into my sweaty forehead. I squeeze my eyes shut, anticipating pain. I hear the loud sound of razer fire and exhale, hard. Nothing. No pain. Opening my eyes, I see smoke coming from the female Tranq's body. Her gun slips from my forehead and her body drops to the ground. Behind her, a wide-eyed Achilles stands holding a razer pistol. He looks completely terrified.

Before the rest of the Tranquils even have time to turn around, Achilles shoots another one, hitting him right in the back.

Mayhem explodes around us.

The Tranquils spin to return fire. Achilles lets out a shriek and flees back around the corner. Pulses miss him by inches, exploding the wall behind him. Naz, Ling, and I drop to the ground, scrambling desperately for our razers. From the corner of my eye, I see Benji whip his leg up to kick his captor hard in the side of the head.

Naz is the first to grab her gun, rolling out of the way of a blast of white light, then returning fire while still on her back. Another Tranquil collapses—but not before his last blast of fire hits the top of her right arm. Naz screams in pain, eyes rolling back. The gun falls from her hand. Ling dashes to grab it.

I grab my razer and scramble to my feet, head pounding savagely from the reopened wound. A Tranquil darts in front of me and I take immediate aim. At the same time, another Tranquil takes aim at me. Movement in the corridor stops.

Benji is on his feet, his gun trained on the Tranquil who is aiming at me. The Tranquil I'm aiming my razer at is aiming at Benji. The four of us stand in a tense square: enemy, friend, enemy, friend. Ling is on her feet, her razer switching focus between the two Tranquils.

"Don't do anything stupid, kids," the Tranquil aiming at Benji warns. "Surrender now, and no one gets hurt."

"You just said you wanted us dead or alive," I mutter, my aim steady. "You'll forgive me if I don't take your word for it."

Naz cries out, clutching her arm. She can't help. Achilles has disappeared.

Unsure of what to do, I catch Benji's eye. He gives me a small, sad smile. "Benji, *no*—" I cry.

Before I can move, Benji pulls his trigger. The Tranquil aiming at me screams in pain. Quick as a flash, I shoot the Tranq aiming at Benji—but not before my target fires off one shot at Benji. Both Tranquils and Benji fall to the floor, bodies smoking. I'm the only one left standing, gasping for breath, every muscle taut.

"Benji!" Ling races to him and flips him over. Smoke drifts up from his skin in wisps, forming a delicate garland. At least his death was quick. But Benji really died hours ago, in this same corridor.

Naz is still writhing on her back, clutching her arm and making a low, guttural sound.

"Achilles!" I yell, scooping up my knife then running over to help Naz. "Let's move!"

The slightest sound of shoes on the squeaky floor has me whirling around and taking aim. A petrified-looking scientist whom I don't recognize stands with his hands sky-high, hiding behind a potted palm tree.

"Don't shoot!" he cries.

"Don't give me a reason to," I say, hooking Naz's good arm around my neck and hauling her to her feet. "Just tell me where I can find the mirror matter."

"Wh-What's that?" he stutters.

"You know what it is!" I scream, brandishing my gun at him. "Tell me where it is!" We do not have time for this—soon this floor will be teeming with more Tranqs than we can possibly handle.

Ling strides past me, heading straight to the petrified scientist. She shoves the tip of one of the Tranquil's huge razers under his chin, forcing it up. "I've seen two of my best friends die tonight," she says, her voice spookily calm. "Killing you would really help with the healing process."

Ling is over the edge. I'm not sure if this is a good or a bad thing.

"The roof," he whispers, pointing up. "It's on the roof. We're moving it to the Towers."

Naz reaches for the flamethrower, moaning in pain as she tries to strap it across her body. There is no way she'll be able to aim that thing properly with a dud arm.

"I've got it." Ling snatches the flamethrower from Naz.

"You know how to use it?" Naz croaks.

Ling aims the weapon up the corridor and fires. With a deep *whoooosh*, a massive stream of orange flame shoots out in an uncontrolled burst. It knocks her back a few steps and sets fire to the wall.

"I'll learn," she says. "Let's go."

Achilles is on his hands and knees scooping up the smoke bombs and grenades.

"Leave them!" I yell back, starting to run toward the stairwell we'd come from. "Just get the razers and the rifles!"

Naz barely lets her injured arm slow her down, even though she must be in excruciating pain. We move as fast as we can up the stairs, Ling and Achilles behind us. We are only one flight from the roof.

The blood from the cut on my head keeps getting in my eyes. In desperation, I shove my hand into my pocket, hoping to find something to staunch the flow. My fingers find silk. All the chaos and pain stops for just a second as I pull out the red scarf Hunter had found by the river. It is exactly what I need right now. I don't have time to ponder the irony. Wrapping the scarf once, twice around my head, I tie a quick knot, but not before his face flashes in my mind.

Where are you now? Do you know Kudzu is back?

I told myself I would be able to destroy Hunter. People I care about have died because I said I could go through with this.

You can do it, Tessendra. You have to.

We reach the top of the stairs. The door in front of us is marked ROOF ACCESS. Beyond it is the sound of humming motors and people yelling orders.

"Stay here," I tell Naz.

"Screw you, Rockwood," Naz mutters through clenched teeth. "I'm covering you."

"Okay." I thrust my razer at her and grab the one Ling throws to me. "Don't get smoked."

She snorts and checks the sights.

I tell Naz to watch the stairs. Then Ling and I cautiously push open the door, no more than an inch.

A flurry of activity greets us. Scientists, Quicks, and a dozen-odd Tranquils, all in the process of moving equipment and boxes and messy stacks of scratch up the wide ramp of a huge blue-and-white Trust cargo ship that's parked on the far side of the roof. Everything is being transported from a freight elevator that opens directly onto the roof about fifty feet from where we stand. The cargo ship's motors whip a dirty wind around the roof, sending loose pieces of scratch flying. White steam pours out from inside it—refrigeration or decontamination gas.

I can't see Hunter. But I also can't see the mirror matter. Are we too late?

"Careful, careful," I hear a scientist cry in a panic. "That specimen is extremely delicate!"

It's the scarred mutant boy I saw in the cloning lab. He's being transported onto the ship by the Tranquils, his case now horizontal, his pale body sloshing in the thick blue liquid.

"Who—what is that?" Ling asks, staring at the mutant. "Is that Aevum?"

I don't want to lie, so I say nothing. The concerned scientists shuffle with the case toward the ship, and suddenly, I see it.

The mirror matter.

On a cart, about halfway between our doorway and the ship. It's in a case within a case, but this one must be new as the sides are all intact. Scientists hover around it somewhat uselessly. I nudge Ling and nod in its direction, heart pounding. Ling shifts the flamethrower from her back to her front, eyes fixed on the mirror matter. "Found you," she murmurs softly.

"Five agents down on the sixth floor!" yells a nearby Tranq. "Fugitives on the loose. Fall out!"

The mass of Tranquils races for the rooftop door. Adrenaline surges through me, white-hot and powerful. *They're coming straight for us.*

Ling's eyes meet mine, pulsing with grim fire. Her words come through lips smeared with dark blood. "Child's play."

Ling bursts through the rooftop door to meet the Tranquils head on.

With an animalistic scream, she shoots out a massive wave of orange fire. The first three Tranquils light up, flames finding instant purchase on their uniforms, and they drop to the ground. I'm right behind Ling, managing to take out one more Tranquil with my razer before they realize what's happening. Immediately, the roof lights up with blasts of lethal razer fire. As reliable as the sun, the gleaming black-and-silver Quicks come for us, a frightening display of precision and speed. Using air rifles, Achilles and Naz blow away both the oncoming Quicks and the Tranquils.

A blast of razer fire shatters the mutant's case. In a gush of blue liquid, he flops out onto the roof, a fish on a dry land. "*No!*" A gaggle of scientists rushes to his side.

Achilles shrieks, his cry piercing the roar of the ship's motor. He's been hit. His rifle drops to the ground as he clutches his thigh.

"Get back in the stairwell!" I yell at him. Achilles slides his razer to Ling, who has her hands full with the flamethrower.

The sound of exploding glass. The mirror matter case. It's been hit by razer fire, causing more squawks of panic from the scientists. Through the smoke, I see the baton of silver liquid hit the ground and begin rolling toward the edge of the building.

"Naz, cover me!" Amid flying rounds of razer fire, I sprint across the roof for the mirror matter. It is almost at the edge. I dive forward onto my stomach, *just* as it goes over, *just* before it starts to fall. My fingers reach out and grab it. *I have it.* I scramble to my feet. With a sudden fierce joy, I realize that we can stop Project Aevum. The power to do it is literally *in my hands*.

"Ling!" I whip around triumphantly.

That's when I see him. Standing at the top of the cargo ship's wide ramp, amid the billowing white steam.

Hunter.

For a second, I just stare. Then a blast of razer fire forces me to take cover behind a large metal container on wheels.

"Tess!" Ling brandishes the enormous flamethrower in my direction. "Drop it! I need a clean shot!"

Risking being hit by a razer, I glance back at Hunter from the edge of the container.

Our eyes lock. His face is frozen in pure shock.

"Rockwood!" Naz picks off another Quick, shooting it over the roof's edge. "What are you waiting for?"

I hold the brilliant silver baton out in front of me, ready to toss it at Ling's feet. But I can't drag my eyes from his.

I can't do it.

I can't kill him.

"Tess!" Ling screams. Her eyes dart wildly between Hunter and me, expression changing from confusion to horrified understanding. "Drop it! Do it now!" Then, in anguish: *"Please!"*

"I'm sorry," I gasp, dropping to my knees. "I can't."

"Dammit Rockwood!" yells Naz.

"Tess!" Hunter's voice cuts through the chaos. He races down the ship's ramp toward me.

Ling swings the flamethrower at Hunter.

I scream "No!" but it's too late. Hunter runs straight into a giant burst of flame that encapsulates his entire body. *"Hunter!"* He's on fire.

Through the flames, I catch a whirl of yellow robes disappearing into the mouth of the ship.

This is the last thing I see before a razer blast smashes me in the chest, flinging me backward.

Then there is pain.

Then there is darkness.

part 4

chapter 15

A strange, shimmering swirl of blue and green emerges from the fog. Such beautiful, brilliant hues; colors that move. Groggy and weak, I blink, trying to see through the hazy mist. Feathers? My eyes sharpen, and the soft, fuzzy swirl finally comes into focus.

A peacock is looking at me. Its beady black eyes blink curiously. It takes a few unhurried steps toward me, its claws click-clacking on a polished marble floor.

The air is as cold as a crypt and just as silent. I am coming to in a stylish if uncomfortable chair, made of what feels like glass.

As soon as I move my head, I feel an absence. My hair. It's gone. My head has been shaved. I'm dressed in a white shirt and white pants that look and feel clean. My skin is clean; no traces of dried blood or dirt or smoke. My hand flies to my throat and I feel a sharp surge of joy—I still have my mom's necklace.

I scramble for the last thing I remember, and I fight the urge to cry out his name.

Hunter.

Hunter yelling my name and starting to run for me across Simutech's roof. Running to save me? Or save himself?

Ling setting him on fire, a horrifying beacon burning against a dark sweep of night. Did that kill him? Yes. Of course it did. Not even Hunter's strong skin could've survived that. Had Ling and Naz and Achilles been killed on the roof too?

I remember Lana's body falling almost gracefully at the Quicks' feet. I remember Benji, sacrificing himself to save me. And I remember Ling's gut-wrenching look of betrayal. A wave of shame and guilt crashes over me.

The peacock gazes at me, unafraid. Its long swoop of a tail hangs out behind its sleek blue body, trailing the floor like a roll of rich, embroidered silk. Beyond the bird is a floor-to-ceiling window. And through the huge window, far, far below, beyond the white walls of the city, is the Badlands. Hard red earth lit by the equally harsh midday sun. It is blinding. I groan a little and have to look away. I know where I am.

"Curtis." A man's voice echoes around the high ceilings, self-assured and mellifluous. I know that voice. Every Edenite knows that voice. "It sounds like our guest is awake. Now, come here, Curtis." A rattle, like the sound of dry beans in a can. The peacock blinks in the direction of the sound, glancing between me and the owner of the voice. "Come on." Another rattle.

The truth of the situation flies at me like knives I am too weak to dodge. I am alive. I am in the Three Towers, in Gyan's private quarters. I touch the cut on my forehead and feel an inch of stitches, bumpy and foreign under my fingertips. The thought of the Trust operating on me without my knowledge induces a spike of terror.

Another sharp rattle makes me jump. The peacock decides the noise is more interesting than I am. With a slow, relaxed stalk, it begins walking toward it. The chair suddenly swivels a full 180 degrees, revealing the head of the Trust, the most powerful man in all of Eden: Gyan. He is feeding a peacock.

In his trademark yellow robes and flat straw sandals, Gyan is standing in front of a polished wooden desk, twice the size of Abel's dining room table. As I glance around, I see everything about this space is large and airy and impressive. I try to take it all in without looking like I'm scoping it out for potential weapons or an exit, which, of course, I am. It doesn't give me much hope.

The walls are high and white and hung with artwork: loops of snow melting on black rock, a pretty painting of colorful dancers swirling through a plaza. A large handblown glass vase sits on a low coffee table, filled with fresh flowers.

Various plants of all shapes and sizes are scattered throughout the room, hanging from the ceiling or arranged on polished wooden shelves. It all feels sophisticated and alive and completely terrifying.

"Good boy," Gyan murmurs appreciatively, dropping a few pieces of grain on the floor. The peacock pecks at them, its beak hitting the floor with short, precise clicks. Gyan addresses me casually, as if talking to an old friend. "Aren't they magnificent? They can live up to forty years, you know. Obviously, I could have clones modified to live longer, but there's something much more satisfying about raising a real peacock from birth." A pause as he scatters more pieces of grain onto the floor. "Would you believe they come from the same family of birds as *chickens*?"

Beyond Gyan, on the wall opposite the windows overlooking the Badlands, is another floor-to-ceiling window overlooking Eden. I'm sure I'd think it was beautiful if I were here as a sightseer: the impressive white-walled city visible in its entirety from our high vantage point. We are at the highest peak of the Smoking Mountains. My heart sinks. The only way in or out of Three Towers is by air. The treacherously steep, snowy mountains offer no pass for even the most experienced climbers.

Both windows stretch all the way to the far end of the room, where there is a large piece of light gold scratch on the wall, and next to it, a single unmarked door. No handle. No lock. Nothing.

"All right, that's enough fun for one day," Gyan says to the bird fondly. "Papa has work to do." He looks up, voice suddenly booming. "Enter!"

The door at the far end of the room disappears with a soft *shick*. Two pale silicon substitutes appear. They are surreally lifelike in appearance, with two arms and two legs, but their oval faces are inhuman: blank except for the slightest indents for a nose, mouth, and eye sockets. They wheel a large, empty cage. For a horrifying moment, I think the cage is for me, but then the two placid subs make their way toward the peacock.

"Back to the aviary for you, old friend," Gyan says, taking a seat in the huge chair behind his desk. The subs gently shoo the bird into the cage. Once it's inside, they wheel it back toward the door. "Not too fast!" Gyan calls after them. "He doesn't like it."

Obediently, the subs slow down. The door reappears after they leave.

"Has the feeling returned to your legs?"

I run a quick physical check. Yes, I am pretty sure I have feeling in all of my limbs. I frown a little at the tops of my knees, like I'm willing something to happen, before giving them a few punches with my fists. With a curt shake of my head, I indicate no.

"It will in time. Are you hungry?"

I definitely am, but the food could be poisoned, although that wouldn't make much sense if some doctors had gone to the trouble of fixing me up. Food will make me mentally and physically stronger. But the thought of taking anything from the Trust feels wrong. I go to shake my head no, but then a half-formed plan emerges. Slowly, I nod.

"Bring in some food for Miss Rockwood," Gyan announces. He has both elbows on his desk, fingers meeting each other lightly to form a triangle. "You are a very interesting girl, Tessendra Rockwood. You intrigue me." He gazes at me with dark eyes that are almost black. "I am not easily intrigued."

"Tess," I spit out.

"Pardon me?"

"Just Tess," I mutter, my voice croaky and hoarse. I cough and clear my throat. "Only my family calls me Tessendra."

"All right." He permits himself a small, amused smile. "Just Tess. Now, Tess, I have a feeling you're under the impression that I am your enemy. Is that correct?"

I say nothing.

"Because that is absolutely untrue." The edges of his eyes crinkle as he smiles warmly at me. "We have a lot in common, you and I. We both share concerns—deep concerns—for the well-being of Aevum. But you see, Tess," he continues, rising to wander around his desk, "it's very important for a person in my position to have all the facts, to be in control of everything. Otherwise, it's very difficult for me to make the right decisions and to properly care for everyone." He casually leans against the edge of his desk. "I'm going to ask you some questions. And I'm sure if you're honest with me, then whatever happened before today can be forgotten, and you can go home to your uncle. How does that sound?"

It sounds like a load of crap.

Shick. The door disappears and one of the blank-faced subs reappears with a small cart. On it is a tall glass of water and a plate of food: some artfully arranged raw vegetables, a hunk of white cheese, and a sprig of crimson berries.

The food appeared sooner than I'd expected; I wanted more time to work out my plan. As the cart wheels closer, I see—just as I'd hoped—real silver cutlery. A fork. A *knife.* That makes the decision for me. This might be my only chance for escape.

The blank-faced sub is halfway across the room. And like before, the door is still open. I focus on taking slow, deep breaths. In. Out. Stay. Calm.

"So, Tess—" Gyan is beginning to talk to me but I am so focused on what I am about to do, I can't hear him properly. I clench and unclench the muscles in my arms and legs.

The substitute is almost here. Gyan's voice throbs around the cavernous space.

Not yet.

Not yet.

The sub positions the cart next to me.

Now.

In one swift movement, I spring to my feet, grabbing the silver knife, then shoving the cart into the sub. After an initial stumble, I find my footing and start running for the door. I hear a thud and a splintered crash behind me—the plate, glass, and cart hitting the ground. My legs are weak but they work. Feet pounding the cold marble, adrenaline pumping through me—and yes, the door is still open! The knife feels good and solid in my hand; it'll work as a weapon. I am almost there, almost out—

Suddenly and from nowhere, pain explodes inside my head. With a gasp, I fall to the ground, knife clattering out of my hand. My head is in a vise, being squeezed until it will pop. I cry out, rolling into a ball. Pain is behind my eyeballs, squeezing them, wringing me out like a washcloth. I want to scream but I can't speak. I can't see or move except to make animalistic, choked noises. After what seems like an age, but is probably only a few seconds, the pain starts to subside.

Nausea billows up inside me. I vomit yellow bile on the clean marble floor.

"Well," Gyan says calmly. "Evidently the chip works."

In the same unhurried voice, he orders the sub to pick up the cart and the food, then clean up "Miss Rockwood's...mess."

Evidently the chip works.

There's a chip *inside* me? Something the Trust put there when I was under?

The pain is subsiding. Within a minute it is gone, just leaving a dull, throbbing ache. I claw the floor, stunned, useless.

"Miss Rockwood. *Miss Rockwood.*" I force myself to look up at Gyan, hate radiating from every pore. "I wish you hadn't done that. It makes it very hard for me to be your friend, if you're not going to be mine."

"I am not," I wheeze, "your friend."

He shrugs, scratching his beard absentmindedly. "As you wish." Then he indicates the chair I'd been sitting in. "If you please."

The substitute pauses by me to clean up my small pool of vomit with a napkin. It offers me a hand, which I swat away. Wiping my mouth with the back of my hand, I slowly stalk to the chair.

"You said the feeling in your legs hadn't returned," he murmurs as I sit down again.

I shrug, eyes hard. "I lied."

This time, there is no amused smile. "I wouldn't recommend doing that again," he says softly. "We have inserted a chip into your brain that can be activated with this." He holds up a sleek rectangular device with a single red button. "Obviously, it is not the only one, so there is no point attempting to steal it. I am going to ask you some questions. They are very important questions, so I would encourage you to answer them as comprehensively and honestly as you can. Is that clear?"

My fingers rake my head until I find it. At the base of my skull, a long, vertical scar held together with neat stitches. That is where they put the chip. I drop my hands to my lap, immobile, my face a mask. I am afraid any movement will give away the sheer hopelessness and terror I am feeling. Gyan holds the chip's controller aloft, his forefinger on the red button. "I said, is that—"

"Crystal." My voice is barely a mutter.

"Good." He stands up and strolls over to gaze out over Eden, his back to me. "How did your mother die?"

I blink, surprised—and then scared. If he's asking me, it means he doesn't believe the cover story.

"Tess." He swings around to face me. "I asked you a question."

Haltingly, I begin cobbling together the story: a test that should never have happened, a tragic accident. He listens intently, waving off the end of my monologue with an impatient flick of his hand. "Yes, yes, I've heard this version." He pauses and lightly presses the tips of two fingers into one ear. I notice a tiny comm fitted neatly in there. After a moment, he takes his fingers away to let them rest, casually, by his side. "While I very much wish to discuss this with you further, unfortunately, we have more pressing matters to attend to."

I exhale thankfully. Good.

"Where is the rebel group Kudzu based?" he continues, his tone so light it's almost blasé. "I know they are here in Eden, and I assume you've been there. Where, exactly, are they?"

If he wants to know where Kudzu are, that must mean not all of them are dead. My chest rises and falls in sudden happiness. Gamma team and maybe even Beta must've gotten away. Maybe even Naz and Ling and Achilles escaped too.

I wonder if this means Project Aevum *hasn't happened yet.* If it had, I doubt Kudzu would be enough of a priority that Gyan himself would be questioning me.

Of course it hasn't happened. Because Hunter is probably dead.

"Tess?" Gyan's finger lightly taps the red button.

I stiffen in fright. "I don't know," I say. "I don't know where they are."

He cocks his head, obviously not believing me, finger lifted to press the button. Sweat breaks across my forehead in tiny little stabs.

"I don't," I repeat urgently. "They blindfolded me whenever we went to their HQ. I was only ever indoors. They were paranoid about security."

"Your desire to protect your cohorts is admirable, Miss Rockwood, but misinformed," he says. "They are not protecting you in the same way."

I don't know what that means—just an empty threat? Or are more Kudzu locked up and betraying me? No. Kudzu would not betray me. But then, they think I betrayed them on the rooftop....

"Let me ask you again, Miss Rockwood, and this time, please: no lies." His finger hovers deliberately over the red button. "Where. Is Kudzu?"

I look him straight in the eye. "I. Don't. Know."

Gyan regards me with profound disappointment, as if he just caught me breaking curfew. "Then you leave me no choice," he says, and presses the red button.

A tidal wave of pain. I lurch forward, spasming into a ball on the floor. Pain splits me open, white-hot and acidic. My vision blackens and I hear myself make a choking cry.

"The Trust was willing to tolerate Kudzu's pathetic little pranks, but now you've overstepped the line and you will all face the consequences." Gyan's tight voice is just barely audible above the war in my head. "We have streams of you and the girl Ling pulled from various traffic substitutes. Never a blindfold. We will find Kudzu, with or without your help. But might I suggest you start cooperating." I hear him sigh, sounding almost wistful. "Because that's what civilized people do, Tess. They cooperate."

Once again, nausea snakes its way inside me and I wretch. Thankfully, I'd emptied my stomach the first time.

"Come now," he says with a touch of irritation. "Up you get. We're not done yet."

I hold my broken, poisoned head, whimpering. I want to tear the stitches open and pull the chip out with my bare hands.

"Tess," he warns, "don't make me do this again."

Tears prick my eyes but I force myself to crawl back up into the chair.

"Why didn't you destroy the mirror matter when you had the chance?"

This question catches me totally off-guard. My head is aching so much it's hard to think. He repeats the question, pronouncing each word with cutting precision.

"Because it would kill Hunter," I reply, unable to think of anything except the truth.

"But wasn't that the point?" he asks incredulously. Then, after a pause, "Answer me."

"Why don't you ask him?" I wheeze, trying to stall.

His lips pull tight into a hard white line and my immediate impression is he *can't* ask him.

"Answer the question," Gyan says softly.

I can't answer this without explaining my feelings for Hunter.

"Answer the question, Miss Rockwood. Why didn't you destroy the mirror matter when you had the chance?"

I say nothing.

Gyan's voice drops to a subzero temperature. "Answer me."

I raise my head to meet his gaze. My eyes are dead. My mouth is completely dry. "Screw you, Gyan."

A wolfish snarl of rage, a colossal slam of pain, and then, blackness.

chapter 16

I come to sluggishly, feeling a damp washcloth wipe my forehead. "There. There," a soothing female voice croons. "There. There."

"Mom?" I rasp. "Mommy?"

"There. There."

The inhuman face of a Nurse is hovering over me, a caring if crazed-looking smile on its pale pink chrome face. I gasp in fright and try to move away, but I am tucked firmly under a starched white sheet and only succeed in shifting a few inches. There's an IV in my arm.

"No. No," the Nurse says gently. "I am here to help you, Rockwood, Tessendra."

"Get away from me," I say hoarsely, but I'm tempering my kneejerk reaction of fear. Nurses are just medical robots. They aren't a threat. I glance around, taking in a white hospital bed in a small, nondescript room, bathed in a comforting, warm orange light. Curtains make the fours walls around me. To my left and right, I can hear the muffled sound of other Nurses, all speaking in the same gently rolling cadence, designed to soothe the sick and scared.

"Are you thirsty?" it asks.

I nod, scooting myself up. I am beyond just thirsty. My tongue feels like a ball of dust.

With a graceful sweep of its arm, the Nurse plucks a glass of water from a small bedside table. Gently, it lifts the glass to my lips. I chug the whole glass, water spilling down my front.

"Thanks," I mumble when I'm finished, wiping my chin. I'm still in the white clothes I'd been wearing in Gyan's quarters.

"You are welcome," the Nurse replies musically, elegantly setting the empty glass on the bedside table.

"Where am I?" I ask, hoping against hope I am, for some reason, back in Eden proper.

"You are in the Stay Well Center in the Three Towers." My heart sinks. "How are you feeling, Rockwood, Tessendra?"

"Fine," I mutter. I wiggle my toes—great, feeling in my legs. I'll need those to walk, or, more specifically, run. If I can ever work out an escape plan.

"Wonderful." It rolls away from me to interface with what I assume is my chart—holos of graphs and numbers—that springs up at the end of my bed.

"What am I doing here?"

"You are resting."

"No, I mean, why am I here?"

"You experienced damage to your cerebral cortex." The chip. Three bursts is enough to land me in hospital. Gyan didn't mess around.

"How bad was the damage?" I ask nervously.

The Nurse floats its head up to look at me. "The damage was minimal."

"Is anyone else here that I know?" I ask impulsively.

"I do not know who you know—"

No, of course not, I say to myself, trying to think of how to rephrase the question. "Is there anyone my age here?"

The Nurse smiles at me. "I am not authorized to answer that."

"Can you remove the chip that caused the damage?"

The Nurse gently takes the IV out of my arm. "I am not authorized to do that." A long shot, but you can't blame a girl for trying. I wonder what the range is for the remote Gyan has. Probably extensive.

"Goodbye, Rockwood, Tessendra. I am glad you are feeling better."

"Goodbye?" I repeat. "Where are you going?"

"I am not going anywhere." I hear the sound of heavy boots coming toward us. "You are going to the Holding Cell," it continues, as cheerily as if I were going to a birthday party.

The white curtain is yanked aside.

"Get up," snarls a Tranquil.

No fewer than four burly Tranquils drag me out of bed. I'm allowed to slip on a pair of white hospital slippers before they wrench me into handlocks and start marching me out of the small room, surrounding me in a square.

"What's the Holding Cell?" I ask. "How long will I be there? I need to comm my uncle. Hey! I'm talking to you!" But unlike the helpful Nurse, the Tranquils don't say a word.

We pass a dozen curtained rooms in the little medical center, then a check-in desk manned by an identical Nurse, who waves and calls a cheery goodbye.

We burst through a set of glass double doors. The light changes from warm orange to cold blue, the temperature dropping at least twenty degrees. We're in a wide, stark corridor. The curved steel-blue walls are stamped with enormous emblems of the Trust. There are no windows, and even though I have no way of knowing, I get the feeling we are underground, buried deep in the cold earth of the Smoking Mountains.

Everywhere is busy with Tranquils, blue-robed Guiders, and the odd man or woman dressed like a regular Edenite, in swaths of flowing pale cloth. I double-take when we pass a Tower Official: an imperious, hawk-nosed man in a white robe edged with yellow. I've never seen a Tower Official in the flesh before, only ever in holos—standing behind Gyan during a speech or milling about at official Tower receptions. They are true Trust, living here in the Towers, unlike Guiders, who live in Eden with their families.

I'm marched into a silver elevator. We're on floor –36. A Tranq punches in the last button—the letters *HC* in a circle, one floor below –86. My stomach flies into my mouth as we shoot down. The doors open and the din of hundreds of people all talking and yelling at once meets my ears.

Then the smell hits me. Human waste, rotting food, and dank, musty air. The small reservoir of courage I've been cultivating promptly vanishes.

"Welcome to hell." One of the Tranqs sneers.

In my mind, the phrase *Holding Cell* conjures up something small and clean, sort of like my hospital room but without the comfy bed. A Holding Cell—somewhere I'd be held temporarily. This, however, is much, much different. The elevator doors have slid open onto a large platform above an enormous cage; it's the size of several football fields. There must be over a thousand people in there. Through the rusty bars, I see beds made of scrap wood, an old lounge chair covered in stains, even a very old piece of scratch beaming up a flickery entertainment stream. Kids dressed in rags run through the adults' legs, playing tag. This doesn't look like a Holding Cell where people spend a few hours. It looks like the prisoners have been living here for years.

The Tranquils hustle me down a flight of metal stairs. People close to the bars start yelling at me.

"Hey, Newbie—"

"Pretty girl, my lucky day—"

"Newbie!"

"Oi! Oi! *Oi!*" A man covered in botched, tasteless tronics with a mouthful of what looks like animals' teeth leers at me. "Got a boyfriend?"

My insides shudder and I set my gaze coldly, trying to hide my rising panic.

The Tranquils march me around the corner of the cell and into a small office, lit by a single overhead light that flickers. In here, the din from the huge cage is merely a muffle. A large woman with ebony skin, bucketloads of silver eye shadow, and a hot pink cardigan over her tight blue robes sits behind a desk. A sign marked REGISTRATION hangs above her. She is flicking aimlessly through a fashion stream and looks supremely bored. Two red-eyed Quicks stand silently on either side of the desk, like dark, evil knights.

A small wave of relief flutters through me—a woman, a regular *person.* I can't reason with a Tranquil or a Quick. But I can reason with a person.

"Another one for you, Shanice," one of the Tranquils says, finally uncuffing me. I rub my wrists in relief, rolling the sore muscles in my shoulders.

"Mmm-hmm," she says, not taking her eyes off the stream.

The Tranquils turn and march out.

Silence. The woman doesn't even acknowledge my presence.

"Hi," I say gingerly. Nothing. No movement from her or the Quicks. "I'm not supposed to be here. Oh, I guess you hear that all the time, but—look, I need to comm my uncle right now. Dr. Abel F. Rockwood."

Nothing. It's like I'm not even here.

"It's important. It's actually a matter of life and death." I raise my voice and take a step forward. "Are you listening to me? A company called Simutech has created something called Aevum. It's an artilect, an artificially intelligent being that looks like a person. It's going take control of all the old substitutes in the Badlands and kill everyone. I'm trying to stop it, that's why I'm here. Lock me up, I don't care, but we need to stop this." I plant my hands on her desk. She looks up from her stream, looks at my hands, then raises her eyebrows in slow disapproval. I take my hands off her desk.

"Shanice," I say. "You look like a reasonable person. You seem like someone who would care about the fact that everyone in the Badlands—"

"Name."

I'm so surprised, I stutter. "That—that everyone in the Badlands will die if—"

"*Name*," she repeats, giving me a look of complete disinterest.

I exhale in annoyance. "Tess Rockwood."

With the speed of a turtle, she flicks out of the fashion stream and begins entering my details into a system on another stream. "Shanice, I just need to use a comm for five minutes—"

"Age."

"Just five minutes—"

This time she doesn't even bother repeating herself. She just looks at me with those same raised eyebrows.

"Sixteen."

More flicking in the stream.

"Project Aevum. It's called Project Aevum," I babble desperately. "People *I know* have already been killed trying to stop this thing. *Millions* of people are going to die if we don't—"

"Arm."

"What?"

"Give me your arm." Glancing nervously at the two Quicks, I extend one arm reluctantly in her direction. She sees my tronic and sighs. "Other arm."

I obey. She flips it so my wrist is facing up and aims what looks like a very old version of a tronic gun at it.

"This won't hurt...," she mutters.

The tronic gun emits a flash of light. I flinch with the sudden snap of pain.

"Much."

A strange black branding has appeared on my arm, a series of dots and dashes of various thickness, about six inches long. It reminds me of a cityscape—the black dashes could be buildings, except they're square instead of curved. Spots of blood ebb through the blackness. I squeeze it, eyes watering. "Is that permanent?"

Shanice does not answer me.

From underneath her desk, she pulls out a threadbare towel covered in tea-colored stains. On top of it is a roll of rough-looking toilet paper and a lump of gray soap.

"I'm going to give you some advice, since you obviously consider me such a trustworthy friend," she says, her words dripping with sarcasm.

"Okay," I say, bewildered.

"One. That's the only toilet paper you're going to get, so make it last. Two"—she slows her words down and leans forward. Her enormous cleavage is everywhere. "You are never going to get out of here. *Registered!*"

She yells the last word so unexpectedly that I jump. On hearing it, the two Quicks spring into action, each grabbing an arm.

"No—wait!" I shout as they pull me out of the small office. "I have to comm my uncle. I have to stop Aevum. Wait, *stop!*"

"Mmm-hmm..." is the last thing I hear before they drag me out.

Stark fear grips me. My feet try to dig into the bare concrete, but it's no use. The Quicks are far stronger than I am. "No, no, no," I hear myself saying. "No, no, no!"

With a rusty shriek, an outer door is wrenched open and the Quicks haul me into a closet-sized space. As soon as the door smashes shut behind us, the inner door to the cell is flung open. Amid jeers and hoots from the other prisoners, I am pushed inside, the door clanging shut loudly behind me. I land on my hands and knees in a shallow puddle of what I can only hope is water. The old wounds on my knees sting painfully.

"Hello, Newbie!"

"Look at your nice *skull*—"

A hand touches my head and I slap it away, panicked. I instantly leap to my feet. I've never wanted my knife so badly in my life. People crowd around me—scary-looking people. A man with open, leaky wounds on his face is blowing kisses at me. A woman swings a rope in circles—no, it's her own long plait of hair, stuck with pointed pieces of metal. A couple of sharp-eyed kids no more than ten or eleven circle me like hyenas. Everyone looks like those creepy deep-sea fish that don't get any sunlight.

Forget stopping Project Aevum. I'll be lucky to make it through the next hour.

"Give us a kiss, love." The man with the weeping wounds pulls me toward him. Dropping my towel, soap, and toilet paper, I spin into his grasp and slam my elbow into his stomach. He groans and sinks to his knees, to yells of amusement from the ragtag crowd. Fingers grab my throat from behind. With a shout, I whip them off, spinning around.

My attacker's a fat man with piggy eyes. I grab his shoulders and knee him in the balls as hard as I can. He makes a thin, pathetic noise and stumbles back a few steps, knocking the people behind him. The hyena kids dive in and snatch my dropped belongings, disappearing into the mob of prisoners before I have the chance to stop them.

Fists raised and panting hard, I whip around for whoever's next.

"Well, well, well. It appears today's newbie is a fighter. How *delightful*." The crowd parts for a man dressed in a hodgepodge three-piece suit: bright green pants, a faded pink jacket, and a purple vest. Gaudy rings crowd his fingers while a tangle of mismatched chains—gold, silver, a string of bright green stones—circles his neck. His irises are an unearthly light yellow. His hair is slicked back with enough oil to choke a whale.

He doesn't walk so much as stroll, oozing confidence. A smile plays on thin lips, beneath an equally thin mustache. He's flanked by several shirtless thugs with droopy faces.

Pink Suit stops a few feet away from me and makes an elaborate show of bowing deeply. "Hello," he says, positively simpering. "I'm Myrtle. Myrtle Beach. And you are?"

"Tess Rockwood," I supply, somewhat uneasily. This guy is a Class A weirdo.

"Welcome to the cell, Tess. You'll come to know me as one of the top dogs around here." At the phrase *top dog,* a few people in the crowd howl like dogs. Myrtle permits this for a moment, then silences the crowd with a curt wave of his hand. "Someone with whom it pays to be friends. I like to think of all of us cell mates as *friends*. And friends always look out for each other, don't they? I will look out for you, if you, angel-pet, look out for me."

"And what exactly does that mean?" I ask suspiciously, fists still raised.

"Oh no," Myrtle says with a smile. "I can see what you're thinking. Women are not *my* weakness. My weakness, angel-pet, is *beautiful things*." He circles me, speaking in an impassioned whisper. "Luxurious creations, things that shine and sparkle and call to your soul, 'Touch me! Wear me! Love me and display me for others to see!' Objets d'arte created in dreams, crafted by the blessed." He pauses in front of me. The dank prison light glints off his chains. "Beautiful things. Just. Like. This." He slips a pointed fingernail under my necklace.

I swat it away. The crowd oohs, enthralled. "That's not for sale."

Myrtle's icy eyes lock onto my necklace as if it has him under a spell. He licks his lips nervously, spittle bubbling in the corner of his mouth. "Of course, I would offer you a trade. New towel and soap?"

"No."

"Guaranteed safety in the shower?"

"Don't think I'll be showering in here."

"Place to sleep."

"I'll find one myself."

"Or how about"—his effeminate voice drops to an ugly snarl—"I just don't cut off your ears."

Four thugs grab me.

"Hey!" I struggle against them. "Let me—"

A dirty rag is stuffed in my mouth. I gag on it, retching.

The crowd taunts me ecstatically, a cavalcade of deranged freaks. Myrtle dances around, relishing every moment. To my horror, I see he has a switchblade. What? How are the prisoners allowed to have knives?

"Hold her still!" he orders the thugs. He holds the blade to my ear. "This is what happens when rude little girls don't listen to Myrtle," he snarls. Gone is the weirdly charismatic top dog. In its place is a sociopath ready to cut off my ear. I can't scream. I can't move.

"Cut it off! Cut it off!" the crowd yells.

The blade bites the top of my ear and I shriek, my scream muffled.

Cut it off! Cut it off!

"Bye-bye, little ear!" he whispers, eyes glittering manically. "Maybe you'll listen better next time, angel-pet—"

"Hey!" A strong voice behind him rips through the crowd. "Leave her alone, Myrtle. She's with me."

Myrtle hisses in displeasure, but after a moment, he takes the knife away from my ear. I almost die with relief. My legs collapse so I'm held aloft only by the strength of the thugs. Myrtle narrows his lemon-colored eyes angrily, and spits the word as if it tastes like metal. *"Naz."*

With another hiss, Myrtle swings away from me. Naz. Shaved head, cargo pants, tank top, and scars. There's one significant difference that hits me in the pit of my stomach. Naz has only one arm.

"I've been here eight years, *fuega*," Myrtle spits. "What makes you think you can call the shots?"

"Because my girls kicked your ass yesterday and we'll do it again if we have to." Naz raises her one good hand casually in the air. From out of the shadows behind her, a gang of the toughest-looking women

I've ever seen emerges. Many have shaved heads, just like Naz, and the same dark, hard eyes, and muscular builds.

What the hell? Naz couldn't have been here more than a week, depending on how long I was unconscious—how had she managed to form a gang?

At the sight of the women, Myrtle's thugs bristle. The crowd quietly starts to disperse.

Myrtle growls again, thin, ring-covered fingers twitching. "What's my trade?"

She tosses something in his direction. He shoots his hand out and catches it. It's a pink-and-yellow ceramic unicorn: a collectible. Cute, if useless. He grunts, quickly examining it from all angles. He holds it up to the light. He sniffs it. He even touches the tip of his tongue to its pointed horn and smacks his lips. His gaze flits between my necklace and the unicorn, obviously torn.

"Good trade?" Naz pushes.

He glances back to the unicorn, unable to stop a small smile of excitement from creeping onto his face. "Good trade."

The thugs let me go. I fall to the floor and pull the dirty rag out of my mouth.

With his flock of thugs surrounding him like a cape, Myrtle spins around and swirls off. Naz's women melt back into the shadows, and just like that, it's all over.

Naz strides toward me. "Rockwood," she growls, eyeing me with displeasure. "I knew you'd be back to screw up my life again."

I hold my arm out so she can help me up but she just scowls at me and turns to stalk off. But just as she does, something on my arm catches her eye.

"What's that?" She grabs my arm and looks closely at the black code Shanice had just burned into my flesh.

I wince, then use her iron grip to steady me as I get to my feet. "Don't you have one too?" I ask, the metallic taste of the rag in my mouth.

With her eyes on my branding, she flips her arm over and shows me. It's not as long, and the dashes are much thinner than the thick ones of my cityscape. "Yours is different," she says accusingly.

I take a closer look at the brandings of the other prisoners' arms and see she's right. Different isn't good. Did Shanice mark me for some reason? Does it have to do with the chip in my head? I twist my arm out of her grasp and nervously wrap my fingers around the strange pattern.

Naz gives me a long look of dirty suspicion. "You owe me a pack of smokes for the horse."

"Actually, I think it was a unicorn."

"Whatever." With a final glare, she turns and heads off into the cell. I have no choice but to run after her.

"How long have you been here? Who were those women? Are the others here? What happened"—I was going to say "to your arm" but chicken out at the last minute—"on the roof after I was shot?" I can't stop the questions from tumbling out of me as we weave our way deeper into the cell, away from the entrance. As we keep walking, I notice the cell is changing. It's less freak show and more, for want of a better word, neighborly. It's cleaner, for a start. A huge overhead light brightens the surrounding area. We pass families living in tent houses, complete with thin mattresses, chairs, even a few dogs curled up and sleeping. The atmosphere is much calmer.

"I've been here three days," Naz says, threading her way easily through the crowds of people.

"How are you so connected?" I ask. "Isn't there some kind of hierarchy?"

"I got family here."

"Your family is here?" I'm stunned.

"My cousin Lopé. Thought that crazy *fuega* was still out in the Badlands. Turns out she's been in here five years. I'm probably related to half the screwups in this joint."

That explains the gang of women. "Who are all these people?" I ask, bewildered by the sheer numbers.

"Low-level crims. Hustlers. Anyone who makes the Trust look bad."

"Why weren't they just banished?"

Naz shrugs. "Guess they want to keep an eye on us."

"Naz," I say, trying to catch her eye as we move deeper into the cell, "thank you. For stepping in back there. Especially after..." My words trail off.

She grunts, flashing me a dark look. "You screwed up bad, Rockwood, and I still don't get why. But that doesn't mean I'll sit back and watch Myrtle cut off your ears. That crap makes it more dangerous for everyone."

I nod, accepting this.

"I'm not forgiving you," she clarifies, stopping and glancing around. "It's just, this isn't the time and place, you know?"

I nod again. "I'm so sorry, Naz," I say quietly, "about this." I place my hand gently on the shoulder of her absent arm, now just a dirty bandaged nub.

She stares at the ground for a long moment, then looks up at me. I am shocked to see tears shining in both eyes.

"Yeah, so am I," she whispers hoarsely. There is so much sadness in her voice that my eyes instantly grow hot with tears too.

Then she exhales noisily and pushes past me, striding off.

I follow her to the front of a large tent with a wide opening. Big pieces of green fabric are strung up to form three walls and a roof. Inside, the floor is covered in faded straw mats. A few blankets are folded neatly in one corner. Cupboards made from old boxes line the walls, filled with various odds and ends: a sticky brown bottle marked MEDICINE, a green-handled hairbrush, a salt shaker. "This is Lopé's place," she announces. "Home, shit home."

The dozen people sitting inside and around the house look up at me. I feel a sharp stab of recognition. Ling and Achilles are among them.

"Tess!" Achilles exclaims. "We thought you were dead!"

"Yeah, I get that a lot," I reply, grateful he's pleased to see me. Ling, however, remains seated and stone-faced.

Achilles hops up and limps over. I'm surprised when he goes to hug me, but find myself hugging him back.

"Love the haircut, really brings out your bruises." He shakes his head in astonishment, eyes marveling at me. "Are you sure you're not a cat? You got more lives in you than most."

"I'll say," Naz mutters.

"You should talk," I say, gesturing at his leg. "Saw you take a hit on the roof."

"And I've got the limp to prove it. Come sit down." Achilles gestures. "I can't *believe* you survived that razer shot! Right in the chest! Amazetown!"

"I think we've all got stuff to talk about," Naz adds darkly. She looks over at Ling, who, after a long moment, nods wordlessly. Apprehension coils in me like a snake.

Naz asks everyone else to give us some space and we soon have the tent to ourselves. She unrolls the front flap and lets it fall. Green light makes everyone look sick and ghoulish.

We sit cross-legged, the even corners of a square. I notice the brandings on Achilles' and Ling's arms are like Naz's. I probably don't want to know why mine's different—I doubt I've won a lucky door prize. I can feel Ling's sharp brown eyes boring into me, but I can't bring myself to meet her gaze. Instead I ask Naz what happened after I was shot on the roof. She lights a cigarette and matter-of-factly tells me they were captured, taken back here to the Three Towers and then separated for questioning as to Kudzu's whereabouts. "We all gave them a false location," Naz finishes.

"A far-flung spot in the Farms," Achilles adds. "It'll take them a few days to work out we were lying. Buy us some time."

"What happens when time's up?" I ask.

"No idea." Naz blows a line of dirty-smelling smoke above my head. "Maybe something. Maybe nothing. What about you?"

I tell them about coming to in Gyan's quarters, the chip, the questioning of Kudzu's location, the hospital, everything up until being thrown in here. I work out I'd been unconscious for two days after being shot on the roof, and another night after Gyan put me in the hospital.

"And you didn't say anything to Gyan about where Kudzu are?" Naz presses, sounding like she didn't really believe me.

"No! No, of course not. That's why I ended up in the hospital! No, wait," I backtrack. I may as well be as honest as I can. "That wasn't the question that put me in hospital."

"What was?" Naz asks.

I take a deep breath. "He wanted to know why I didn't destroy the mirror matter when I had the chance."

A long, painful pause.

"And that, ladies and gentlemen, is the question on everyone's lips," Achilles says softly.

I force myself to look at Ling. She is staring at me unflinchingly, her gaze all icy venom. "That was Aevum, wasn't it?" she says. "On the roof. The boy I shot with the flamethrower."

"What happened to him?" I ask urgently. "What happened after I was shot?"

"I burned him to a crisp!" Ling spits. "That was him, *wasn't it?*"

"Yes," I whisper. So it's true. Hunter really is dead. Because of me.

Ling spreads her hands in an exaggerated gesture, not needing words to ask the question everyone in the dank, smoky tent is asking: *What. The. Hell?*

When I start speaking, my voice is pinched and nervous. "I met Hunter the night I arrived at my uncle's—"

"Wait—*Hunter*?" Ling interrupts. "The guy you liked? Your uncle's assistant?"

I flush. "Turns out he was more like my uncle's special project."

"But you said artilects couldn't look like people," Achilles says.

"I was wrong." Haltingly, I start at the beginning: How I'd come to know the green-eyed boy who was the catalyst for our current circumstance. His role as my tutor, and as my friend. "He saved me at Simutech. After we lost each other, he saved me and that's when I worked out who he was. He was in the florist shop, where you found me—"

"He was there?" Ling cries. "With you?"

I nod. "He doesn't believe he feels any emotions, and I was trying to help him." I explain my theory about Hunter needing to develop empathy, which was why Abel had us spend time together, but Kudzu aren't interested in that. They're interested in the fact that I betrayed them.

"So, you knew Hunter was Aevum when we made the plan to go back," Naz clarifies.

"And you knew you had"—Ling shudders—"*feelings* for him."

"Feelings that ended up compromising the mission," Achilles finishes.

Shamefully, I nod, creating an angry ripple of collective disbelief. "I thought I could go through with it. I really did, right up to—"

"Right up to the moment we all got captured by the Trust," Ling says sarcastically.

"That would've happened even if we'd destroyed the mirror matter," I mutter.

"I can't believe you sold us out like that." Naz spits the words darkly. "We trusted you. We took you into our home—"

"Naz," Achilles says, voice strained. "She didn't know Hunter was Aevum until that night. And by then she knew him. They were...friends."

"She should've told us as soon as she found out!" Naz yells. "I *knew* she couldn't be trusted, I knew it right from the start!"

"I tried to convince him to come with me," I say beseechingly. "He was close to saying yes, I know it."

"Come with you? What, with us? On the floaters?" Ling looks at me as if I'm stark raving mad. "Aevum was a *killing machine*, Tess. Built to *murder people*. And you wanted him to come with us?"

"Well, yeah," I say helplessly. "I thought I could get him on our side."

Ling shrugs sarcastically. "Guess he was still on theirs. Until I killed him."

Her callousness renders me speechless. Grief-stricken. Hunter is gone.

"Well, we'll have a lot of time to mull over the specifics of it all," Achilles says. "Unless they torture us to death first."

"What do you mean?" I ask. "How do we get out of here?"

Achilles looks at me in surprise. Then, pity. "We can't, Tess," he says softly. "According to the Trust, we're terrorists. They can lock us up for as long as they like."

"What? That's crazy!" I exclaim in disbelief. "We need to get ahold of Abel!"

"Have you got a comm?" Ling's words are biting.

"No. But isn't there something we can do?" I scramble for options. "Maybe the others can get us out of here. Maybe we can break out!"

Achilles slowly shakes his head. "How? The only way out is by air." His head drops tiredly, his hands pressing into his eyes. "Why do you think they're letting us be in here together, Tess?"

"I don't know. Why?"

"Because we're not a threat," he replies quietly.

Ling reaches over to rub his back, her shoulders hunched. Naz's eyes are fixed in the middle distance, empty and glazed, one hand holding her stub protectively. No one says anything.

A clanging bell rings out, matching the panicked thump of my heart.

"Damn." Naz scowls. "Dinner's on. We'll be at the end of the line now."

The three rise quickly to their feet. "You coming?" Achilles asks, limping toward the flap. "The food's maggots-to-non-maggots ratio rises steeply toward the back of the line."

My voice is hoarse. "I think I'll stay here."

"Suit yourself," he says, ducking under the flap. "Be back later for the post-meal vomit."

"Ling." I grab her arm as she goes to follow Naz and Achilles. "Wait."

She shakes my hand off, but still turns to face me. Her arms fold across her chest. "What?"

"I'm sorry," I whisper. "I'm *so sorry*. I let you down and I lied to you, and now we're . . . in here. Please forgive me."

Ling's arms drop to rest uneasily on her hips. She rocks back on her heels, swallowing hard and tipping her chin up, looking like she's trying not to cry.

"Please," I beg, my voice cracking. I hold out one hand toward her, willing her to take it. "Ling, *please.*"

Ling lowers her chin and exhales with a long, shuddering breath. "I'm sorry, Tess," she says. "I can't." Then she turns and leaves the tent. I'm left alone, one hand still pathetically raised after her.

The naked horror of spending the rest of my life locked up like an animal with a chip in my head for the Trust to use whenever they want sucks the breath out of me. I'm never going to feel the warmth of the sun or sleep in my own bed ever again.

I curl up in the corner farthest from the entrance.

Later, I hear the others return. The smell of rotting garbage—presumably the "food"—fills the musty air. I don't move from my corner.

After a few hours, the hubbub of the cell mutes to the occasional yell or angry exchange. Someone drapes a thin blanket over my shoulders. At some point, the huge overhead light is shut off.

I was expecting the tent to be cold, but the body heat of the dozen people keep it reasonably warm. I'm pulled down into a dense and heavy slumber.

Morning comes quickly. First, restless movement and low murmurs between people in our tent. Then the enormous light is turned on. People start rising. I hear the front flap being tied up. The clang of breakfast. I stay where I am, my back to the tent. I have nothing to get up for.

"We should we wake her," Naz mutters.

"Let her sleep," Achilles replies.

"But Lopé says the new ones are supposed to keep guard."

"Naz," Achilles says, "just let her rest."

I hear them leave.

I feel myself start to turn inward. My heart feels like a raisin, dry and useless in my chest. I feel myself growing hard.

Days pass.

chapter 17

The front door is ajar: an invitation. I push it open, knowing this is dangerous, knowing it could be a trap.

"Abel?" I call, breathless and bleeding. "Abel!"

The house is cold with moonlight, darkness crouching in every corner.

"Tess." His voice is like an arrow. Hunter, tall in the shadows; a beautiful streak of white light.

"Hunter!" I run to him and I'm shivering and scared but he's here, he has me.

"Tess." Arms reach out for me and I fall into them like a child, clutching his shirt, his arms, the back of his neck. He's real, he's here, he's mine. "Tess, I'm sorry."

My eyes are streaming and I pull back to see his face. When did Hunter grow a beard?

His arms whirl me around. Kimiko advances, her metal fingers spindly as snakes. "I'm sorry," he says. Her snakes encircle my throat, hissing and cold and tight. "Get up."

But I can't stand. I'm on my knees, my throat is crushed, I can't breathe, I'm dying, I'm dying, Hunter standing over me and he's smiling, he's smiling—

"Get up!"

I wake with a shout, yanked into consciousness. Two Tranquils stand above me, razers aimed at my head.

"Gyan wants to see you."

Through the open flap of the tent, I see Ling, Achilles, and Naz, stone-faced and cuffed, watched over by a couple of Quicks.

After some prodding by the sharp tips of their razers, I drag myself to my feet. My body is so unstable, the ground feels like it's undulating beneath me.

The cell is unusually quiet when the four of us are hustled out. I stumble as we ascend the metal stairs, pushed toward the elevator.

I catch sight of myself in the warped shiny surface of the elevator walls, then instantly wish I hadn't. I'm a freshly dug-up corpse. Purplish circles under both eyes, lips that are cracked and pale. My skin feels tight over my ribs. My white hospital clothes are stained with sweat and dirt. "You stink, Rockwood," Naz mutters.

I try to stand stoically but the thought of that hellish pain slamming into my head again makes my stomach twist into a nauseating mess.

The elevator shoots up to Floor 100. We're marched down a twisting, unfamiliar corridor where the air is frigid and smells like disinfectant. A couple of blank-faced subs press themselves against the walls as we pass. We stop at a set of double doors that disappear with a whisper-soft *shick*.

An enormous oval table with a slick mirrored surface dominates the sparse space. Like Gyan's quarters, one wall is all window, looking out over Eden. But the wall opposite is made of water, like an aquarium. A long, white shark gently cruises through the clear water, its tail fin swishing slowly from side to side. Its small eyes are dark pink, reminding me of a Quick.

The bright sunlight glinting off the distant Moon Lake makes me squint. It is, as usual, a relentlessly glorious day.

My uncle is sitting in one of the twenty-odd chairs surrounding the table, flanked by two Tranqs. His head jerks at our entrance. "Tess!" The strangled relief in his voice is pronounced. I try to say his name but it just comes out as an unintelligible choking noise. He rises, only to have two razers cocked at him in warning. Slowly, he sinks back into his chair, eyes seeming to take in every detail about me.

"Tess Rockwood, Naz Rodriguez, Ling Sun-Yi, Achilles Zamata." Gyan's hands are folded casually in front of him, facing us from the other end of the table. "Please. Have a seat."

"What have you done to these children?" Abel asks in horror, as we're shoved toward empty chairs. Tranqs and Quicks stand behind us.

"Please, Dr. Rockwood," Gyan says, one soft palm raised calmly. "Let's not get emotional."

"Emotional?" Abel repeats incredulously. "How can I not get

emotional when—" Razer tips aim in his direction and he falls silent. He must know by now that I was the one who used his Simutech swab, that I was part of the failed mission to destroy Aevum.

Gyan's deep, cultured voice commands the huge space effortlessly. "I have some questions about Aevum. As you can appreciate, I am a busy man overseeing an important transitional period in Eden's evolution, so please, let's keep this brief and to the point. Agreed?"

Abel's low voice radiates disgust. "I assume you're referring to your barbaric plan to destroy life in the Badlands."

The nod Gyan gives the closest Tranq is almost imperceptible. In a blur, the butt of the Tranq's razer smashes down on my uncle's hand. Abel shrieks in pain.

Gyan frowns at his cuticles. "Answer the questions and nothing more. Understood?"

Abel rocks back and forth, clutching his hand, shock all over his face. He hisses, "Senseless violence? Why am I not surprised."

Gyan enunciates his words again, this time slower and more threatening. "Answer the questions and nothing more. Understood?"

Abel's eyes are on me as he mutters through gritted teeth, "Understood."

Gyan clears his throat perfunctorily. "I am making the educated guess that you encouraged your niece to spend time with Aevum in an effort to"—he twirls his fingers, searching for the right phrase—"undermine Project Aevum. Correct?"

Abel shakes his head. "I was trying to get Hunter to develop emotionally, as he theoretically should have done. What he did after that was up to him."

"Did you know, Dr. Rockwood," Gyan asks, placing his fingertips together and tapping them lightly, "that your niece was brought back to Eden by the rebel group Kudzu?"

I duck my eyes. Abel's voice is faint. "Not at the time," he replies. "But over the past few weeks, I've come to suspect as much."

"Interesting," Gyan murmurs, before shifting his gaze to Ling. "Miss Sun-Yi, now that you've had some time to enjoy life in the Holding Cell, I wonder whether you've reconsidered your answer as to the whereabouts of your fellow terrorists?"

Ling snorts, eyes steely. She shakes her head slowly. "No."

Gyan glances to Achilles and Naz. "No? No takers?" Then, staring at me, "What about you, Just Tess?"

I stare back at him blankly.

"Very well." Gyan strolls to the window, hands twined casually behind his back. The hem of his yellow robe swishes over the spotless floor. "I see now that the relatively long leash I gave Simutech in the development of Aevum was a mistake."

Abel's voice is dangerously passionate. "What you intend to do with Hunter is categorically inhuman—"

"*Aevum* is making its own decisions," Gyan retorts. "We aren't forcing it to do anything."

"Of course you are!" exclaims Abel. "You haven't shown him another way of thinking!"

"It's a *machine!*" Gyan shouts, voice cracking like thunder. He stares down at my uncle, quivering with rage. "All of the problems we've tracked with Aevum have been a direct result of its involvement with your niece. Letting her escape at Simutech, the reprogramming of fifty Quicks in Orange Grove Plaza—"

"What?" Abel asks in confusion.

"It doesn't matter," Gyan says angrily. His dark eyes swing to me viciously. An electric shiver spikes through me. Gyan takes a deep breath through his nose. Then he snorts a little laughter. "It doesn't matter," he repeats, but this time, it sounds like he means it. "Ah," Gyan smiles at something behind me. "Speak of the devil."

I swing around in my chair. Standing in the doorway is Hunter.

I can't do anything but stare at him, jaw unhinged, as he strides confidently toward Gyan. He is dressed in all white, a crisp button-down shirt and pants. His hair is neatly combed. New white boots squeak on the spotless floor. He looks thoroughly and unmistakably Trust.

I was wrong. He's alive. Maybe his skin was fireproof, maybe he was rebuilt somehow, I don't know. But he's right here. *He's alive.*

"Good morning, sir," he says, shaking Gyan's outstretched hand.

"Hunter." The word steals out of my throat, too low for anyone to hear. My eyes drink him in. "*Hunter.*" This time, he can hear me.

He looks at me, a quizzical frown creasing his smooth forehead. He cocks his head at me, and my heart leaps painfully. Hunter: curious and calm and kind. He turns back to Gyan. "How does that girl know me?"

Gyan's lips curl upward, revealing snow-white teeth. "Excellent," he breathes.

"Sir?" Hunter asks again. "Is this what you wanted to see me about?"

"Yes, Aevum," Gyan says to Hunter. "But there's nothing to be concerned about. These are the people who were compromising your development." He stares at me, his expression pulsing with power. "The ones we had removed from your memories. That's why they know you, but you do not recognize them. I'm glad to see the process was a success."

I turn to my uncle in fear. "Did that really happen?"

My uncle's words feel as cold as snow. "Yes, Tess, I'm afraid it did. Myself included."

I look back at Hunter, my throat constricting. "You don't...remember us?"

"No," Gyan answers. "He doesn't." He sighs, brushing his fingers down Hunter's arm almost wistfully. "That's what I love about technology. It's so efficient. So exact."

I direct my words at Gyan, rage boiling inside me. *How could you. How could you treat him like...like a machine you can do whatever you like with?*"

"Aevum *is* a machine I can do whatever I like with," Gyan snarls back. "Aevum is the property of the Trust."

"No!" I cry, ignoring the restraining hands on me. "He has a mind! He's alive! Now you've destroyed..." My words falter, catching in my throat. "Now he won't remember..."

"What?" Gyan's words are urgent. "What doesn't Aevum remember that's so important to you?"

I stare at Hunter: mysterious, clever, sweet Hunter. He looks back at me curiously. "How do we know each other? Do you work for the Trust?"

Behind him, the white shark drifts endlessly back and forth in the water. "Now he doesn't remember the feelings he had for me," I say meekly.

A few long beats of awkward silence. The look on Gyan's face is a perfect mix of incredulity and disgust.

"Tess," Abel says softly, "artilects don't have feelings like we do. Not even Hunter."

"That's not true!" I choke, tears welling in my eyes. "They do. That's why Mom was killed, that's why Magnus killed her, it was because of *me!*"

A Tranq shoves a razer into my back, but Gyan stops him with a lifted hand. His eyes don't leave mine. His voice is low and intense: "Tell me why your mother was killed."

I say nothing. I've held on to that secret for over a year. I'm not breaking, not even now.

Gyan slips his fingers into his robe and extracts the remote for my chip, holding it up like a prize.

"Do your worst," I mumble sourly. At least the Nurses will be nice to me when I end up back in the hospital. Change of clothes can't hurt either.

Gyan slits his eyes. "Tell me why your mother was killed and I'll pardon one of your friends from execution."

Naz, Ling, and Achilles all stare at me, eyes round with shock. None of us even knew the Trust executed prisoners, let alone that we were on the list. "Works for me," murmurs Achilles.

I close my eyes, steadying myself on the edge of the table with outstretched hands. The truth about Magnus. A secret I swore I would take to my grave. But now it can save someone from theirs.

I open my eyes. Everyone is staring at me. Even the Tranquils and Quicks look as if they're listening. I say, haltingly, "Magnus killed my mom because he thought he was in love with me."

"What?" cries Abel in disbelief. "What are you talking about?"

My gaze lowers to the table. "I wanted to punish her. For spending so much time away from me. I was so jealous of him..." Blood rushes to my face. "It was stupid, and it just got out of control. I didn't realize how much it was affecting him, I swear, I didn't know."

"How *what* was affecting him?" Abel says in confusion. "Magnus barely spent any time with anyone, that was the problem with Frankie's approach. Why would Magnus think he was in love with *you?*"

Hot tears drip onto the table in front of me. "C'mon, Uncle Abel," I say with a sad smile. "Isn't it obvious?" Abel's look of noncomprehension forces me over the edge. "Magnus...and I...were..." I suck in a deep, shuddering breath. "Involved."

There it is. The secret I'd let banish me to the Badlands. The secret that had not only destroyed me and my mother but Magnus as well. He wasn't anywhere near as evolved as Hunter, but it was still wrong. He was still alive in some strange, undefined way. He was alive, and because of me, now he isn't. I am the one who used his feelings for me to get him out of Simutech and into my *house.* Where we were caught.

My bedroom light made the copper color of his artificial skin look like it was on fire. "How much do you love me?"

I could just hear the soft electric wheeze of hidden mechanics as Magnus revolved his head toward me. "I do not understand the question. I cannot define emotions in a quantifiable way."

I laughed and rolled onto my stomach, fumbling for the bottle of white nail polish on my crowded bedside table. "It's just an expression, dummy. Rhetoric. Tell me you love me more than there are stars in the sky."

"I love you more than there are stars in the sky."

My fingers found the polish. "How many stars are there, anyway?"

"Seventy sextillion."

"Sextillion, huh?" I giggled. Unscrewing the small bottle, I carefully dab at my fingernails with the fine brush. "Tell me you love me more than Mark Manzino loves his stupid dogface girlfriend."

"I love you more than Mark Manzino loves his stupid dogface girlfriend."

"Thought so." I snickered softly. I finished my nails and rolled off my bed to twirl across my bedroom floor. I've let my room get insanely messy. I don't care.

Izzy said love made her unstoppable. But you don't need to be in love to feel that way. Just being loved did the trick. And Magnus loved me more than any of Izzy's boyfriends or girlfriends ever loved her. This thought made me tingle all over. For once, I'm the one with an obsessed boyfriend. Me.

"What do you love about me?" I asked with a sigh, eyes closed, wanting to feel giddy.

"Everything."

I opened my eyes. The room spun. "Be specific."

A pause. "I love the color of your hair."

I giggled, stumbling over to collapse into his lap. "Yes, that's interesting, isn't it?" I folded my legs up under me and snaked one hand around the back of his thick, cool neck. His huge size made me feel tiny. "I read men are genetically programmed to find women with blond hair attractive because they look younger," I said. "Younger equals more fertile, and more fertile equals greater chance in producing offspring. You'll never get anyone pregnant, and you're still into blondes."

Or maybe, you're just into me.

I stroke one side of his mathematically square jaw with my fingertips. He made a low whirring sound that conveys what he experiences as pleasure. My man-machine. Mine. Magnus would do anything for me. I thrilled at the power I had over him, a wicked and glorious and dangerous power that made me feel so deliciously alive.

"How much do you love me, Tess?"

His large, strong hands cradle my back, exactly where I've told him I like it. He never forgets. I arched my back like a serpent. "More than anything in the world." The lie swirled from my lips like a delicate wisp of smoke.

The front door slammed. My head jerked in the direction of the sound.

"Tess?"

She's supposed to be at a conference.

"Don't come in here!" I leaped to lock my door, but Magnus held me in place.

"Please keep touching my face with—"

"Shut up," I whispered furiously. "And let me go. Now!"

"Tess?" She sounded panicked. Damn—did they realize he was missing? It's only been an hour. Or so?

"Don't come in here!"

I flew across the room. My hand on the knob just as she pushed it open, knocking me back.

"Tess, have you—" She saw him. Shit. Shit. I'm grounded for the next year. Her protracted look of disbelief was so comical, I almost laughed.

My mother's voice, a hoarse whisper, alien in its terror: "What is he doing in the house?"

I watched her alert, flushed face answer that question for herself.

The fact was I'm wearing nothing but a t-shirt. The Simutech transport in the driveway. The unusual changes to Magnus' singularix she couldn't understand. My late-night visits where I'd "forgotten" she wouldn't be there, relayed to her by helpful Howie. And the fact I'd stopped asking for her attention, months ago. It all spoke for itself. The expression on her face made me realize how much I relished the power I had over her, too.

Now I have your attention, don't I?

"*Tess, go into my bedroom and lock the door.*"

I rolled my eyes. "*Mom, relax. It's fine—*"

"*Now!*"

"*Don't tell me what to do!*"

"*Tess, you are upset.*" Magnus rose from my bed, far too big, far too tall.

"*Magnus, I want you to follow me downstairs,*" Mom said slowly. "*I'm going to take you back to Simutech.*"

"*I want to stay with Tess.*"

Her eyes snapped to mine in shock. Smugly, I took a few steps toward him, folded my arms, and shrugged. "*He wants to stay with me, Mom.*"

"*Magnus,*" Mom said louder, looking directly at him. "*I'm going to take you back to Simutech. I'm going to take you back there right now. Everything is going to be fine.*"

"*It's been more than fine, Mom,*" I sneered. "*I've been showing your little project the real world and he loves it—*"

"*Dammit, Tessendra!*" Tears shone in her brilliant blue eyes. "*This ends now, whatever it is! Magnus, get downstairs!*"

"*No. I want to stay with Tess.*"

"*I said, get downstairs!*" In a furious panic, Mom hurtled toward me and tried to wrench me away from him. In one swift movement, Magnus latched on to her wrist. I heard the crunch of breaking bones. My mother gasped then cried in pain, a terrible, nightmarish sound.

"*Magnus, stop! Stop it!*" He immediately did, standing upright, right beside me. Substitutes can't hurt people. But Magnus isn't a substitute. Magnus is something else.

"*Get away from Tess.*" My mother gasped, clutching her arm to her chest, afraid to touch me. I stood stock-still, frozen by shock. Things were unraveling and I didn't know how to stop them. "*Leave the room. Now. That's an order.*"

"*I will not. I love her. I love Tess.*"

"*Don't say that!*" my mother cried. "*This is wrong, but I can fix it.*"

"*But I am not broken.*" His voice was changing. His words were coming quicker.

"*Magnus, come here!*" Mom ordered.

"*No, Mom, stop!*" I cried.

"You cannot stop me from being with her—"

"You bastard!" The words ripped out of her, possessed by a force greater than all of us. "I'll destroy you myself if I have to!"

"No!" *Magnus shouted.*

"Magnus!" I screamed, hysterical and sick. "Get away from my mother!"

But I cannot stop him from grabbing her. I cannot stop him from picking her up. And I cannot stop him from throwing her, sickeningly hard and fast, across my bedroom.

The splintered crash of a mirror breaking.

"Mom!" I screamed, falling onto my hands and knees. I crawled to her like a baby. I slipped in the blood. "Mommy!" I rolled her over and my heart stopped. She was broken. Her eyes were unseeing. There was so much blood. "No! No, no, no," I whimpered. It was the only word I could say.

And then, his voice.

"No one will separate us. I love you, Tess."

Three long, drawn-out words bring me back to the present. "How. Extremely. Interesting," breathes Gyan.

I open my eyes to see everyone staring at me, dumbstruck. My cheeks are hot and wet—I didn't realize I'd been crying. I wipe at them with the back of my hand, which is shaking uncontrollably.

Now everyone knows the truth. But the truth has spared the life of someone in Kudzu.

Hunter sits next to Gyan, spine as straight as a ruler. Unlike everyone else, his face is as blank as a substitute's. If my story had any impact on him, I can't tell.

"Right," Gyan announces. "Now that I finally have all the facts, I'm satisfied we can safely begin Project Aevum. Immediately."

"No!" I gasp. "You can't!"

"Take them all to the Interrogation Room," Gyan continues. "If they don't wish to divulge the real whereabouts of their coconspirators, you have authority to execute."

"What? No!" shouts Abel, who is instantly restrained and gagged.

"What?" I gape at Gyan. "You said you'd spare one of my friends. You said it!" I shout. "You just told me!"

Gyan places one hand possessively on Hunter's shoulder. He regards me as if I am an ant he'd take great pleasure in squashing. "I lied."

Two Tranqs haul me out of my chair. The rest of Kudzu are in front of me, screaming and cursing. Gyan begins speaking with Hunter as if we weren't there. "I assume, Aevum," I hear him say, "that you're expecting a one hundred percent success rate?"

I'm the last one at the door, about to be shoved out by a Tranquil. "No!" I yell. "He's not!" Gyan ignores me, but Hunter glances in my direction curiously. "He expects a ninety-six-point seven percent success rate," I gasp desperately.

Hunter's jaw loosens in surprise, his thick eyebrows drawn close. "How did you know that?"

Two Tranqs lift me to pull me from the room, but I grip the door frame, babbling frantically. "You told me, Hunter! You care about me, you know you do! You can't do this! You can't kill all those people!"

Hunter is staring at my arm, stock-still and almost trancelike. He's looking at the cell branding—the strange markings that don't look like the other prisoners'. My eyes flit from the branding back to him. His head snaps up to find my gaze, fast and almost desperate. For the first time since he entered the room, there's something alive in his eyes. Is it recognition?

"Hunter!" I scream, but it's too late. I'm out of the room and he's gone.

My feet skip and slide across the shiny floor as the Tranqs drag me along. Far off in the distance, I hear the horrible caw of a thousand crows. Then I realize it's the sound of Kudzu, yelling in protest. The long, low doglike moan is me, a sound I wasn't aware of making.

Shick. The neat whisper of a door disappearing reveals white light and colorful scribbles of movement. The Tranquils let me go and I fall like a puppet cut loose from its strings.

Silence. No. Not silence. A soft and gentle fluttering.

"What the—" says Ling.

"Where are we?" Naz sounds nervous.

"They're not really going to kill us?" Achilles asks, petrified. "That's just rhetoric, right?"

"Tess?" Fingers pull my bottom eyelid down. A burn of white light. I flinch and pull away. Ling says, "She's conscious. Help me sit her up." Hands try to lift me, my back slumping against a wall. "Where are we?"

"I don't know," Achilles says nervously. "This is...weird."

"C'mon, Rockwood. Don't be such a baby," Naz growls.

I moan.

"There you go."

I am sitting up. And because I don't want to be a baby, even now, I make myself open my eyes.

We are in a bright, white, square room, empty except for us. In the four walls that surround us, and yes, even in the roof overhead, are butterflies.

Hundreds and hundred of butterflies—iridescent green, black-and-yellow-striped, electric blue. Some are as large as dinner plates, some as tiny as moths. They are fluttering around what must be a huge butterfly sanctuary, open except for the cube of space we are in. Looking through the clear wall I'd been leaning against, I can see out about twenty feet before the sanctuary ends, but because the walls are all painted white, it's impossible to get a clear perspective on the space. Except for the butterflies, it is distressingly barren. No weapons. Not even a chair. And, like the rest of the Three Towers, it is absolutely freezing.

Naz pounds the white door we must've come through with her only fist, swearing. She runs her fingers around the edge of it, but the gap between the door and the wall isn't wide enough for even a pinky. She slams her fist into a glass wall. It is so thick, it barely makes a sound. "Hey! Let us out of here! *Hey!*"

Achilles massages his wrists nervously. "Not sure 'let us out' is going to win them over at this stage. Besides, didn't your parents ever tell you tapping on the glass disturbs the animals?"

"My parents are stuck out in the Badlands, about to be killed! Just like us! I've got bigger problems than some stupid butterflies," Naz snaps, kicking the glass hard. I flinch. That looked painful.

"That's not helping anyone—"

"Shut up, Zamata!" she says tearfully, kicking the glass again. "Shut up!" Another kick. *"Shut up!"*

"Stop!" he cries. "You're just hurting yourself!"

Naz paces the room in circles for a few moments, then stops, huffing air. We wait, tense, expecting something to happen. Nothing does. After a few moments, Naz turns to me and scowls. "Quite a story you told back there, Rockwood."

"You want to cut me down, Naz?" I hiss. "Go ahead. I'll even get you started. Disgusting freak girl who fools around with artilects—"

"Whoa, calm down," Naz interrupts. "You got a 'bot hot for you to piss off your mom. Don't be such a drama queen about it."

I stare at her, bewildered. "My mom's dead because of me."

"You didn't know he'd do that," Ling says. I look at her in surprise. She looks directly at me for the first time in what feels like forever.

"You're speaking to me?" I say without thinking.

"I can't condone your betrayal," Ling says. "But telling the truth about Magnus in order to save one of us? That's honorable." Her eyes explore the space carefully as she continues. "And as far as the whole Magnus thing…I mean, you probably shouldn't have done it—"

"*Probably?*" I repeat in disbelief.

"Okay, you shouldn't have done it, but weren't you just"—she bites her lip, gaze still sweeping the sea of butterflies—"experimenting?"

I can't answer. I can't believe Ling is being so blasé about it.

Ling looks back at me evenly. "We're probably all going to die, Tess. You may as well stop beating yourself up."

"And for the record," Achilles adds absentmindedly, "Hunter? Yeah. I get it. That guy's serious boy butter. You know," he adds quickly, "if he wasn't a technically advanced mass murderer."

I look at the three of them in shock. "But don't you think that's gross? Being with something that isn't human?"

Around us, the whisper of a thousand butterfly wings. Ling shrugs. "There's just no point going to your grave with that on your conscience. There's nothing wrong with you, Tess. You're just…human."

"*Attention prisoners.*" The calm, modulated voice sounds as if it's coming from right here in the room. I move closer to Ling. Our fingers find each other, squeezing hard. "Where is the rebel group Kudzu?"

We glance at each other. My fingers move back to the bumpy cut at the back of my skull, heart rate rising.

"Screw you, we're not telling you crap," Naz says loudly.

A pause.

I am sweating and shaking. Ling glances at me in alarm.

"Very well."

A screaming wall of pain blasts inside my brain.

I lose control of my muscles and fall into a ball.

"Tess? *Tess!*" Ling's voice breaks in panic.

"Stop it! Stop hurting her!" Achilles shouts.

The only sound I can make is a strangled, choking cry, like an animal in pain.

"Where is the rebel group Kudzu?"

Tears break through my eyes, and I gasp. In blotches, my vision starts returning.

"Don't tell them," I whisper through gritted teeth, forcing myself up onto my hands and knees. My eyes are watering and I wretch.

"We don't know," Ling says uneasily.

"Very well."

Another explosion. The pain falls on me like a building collapsing, crushing me flat to the floor.

"Dammit, *stop!*" Naz shouts.

"Where is the rebel group Kudzu?"

No one says anything.

Another burst of pain.

Then another.

Rolling attacks, like monster waves doggedly pounding the shore, one after the other after the other. Savage. Hateful.

Now I have no words left. No mouth. No voice.

"You're killing her!" Ling screams, the words tearing out of her throat. *"You're killing her!"*

In the vastness of space, planet Earth is a speck of red dust on an endless desert plane. I understand this unfathomable hugeness for the first time. The idea of distance being measured in light-years and the size of the sun in comparison to the planets surrounding it suddenly becomes very clear to me.

I see myself, and the three people around me, and then my vision spins out and up—above the Three Towers, above Eden, above the Badlands, above Earth and then farther away, until Earth is no longer visible. I just keep traveling, farther and farther and farther away into the deafening silence of space. Into blackness. Into the void. And then, finally, thankfully, into nothing.

No feeling is final. Except for your last.

Blackness.

And then, something.

Movement.

Voices.

"What's going on?"

"I don't know. Is she dead?"

The soft *shick* of the door disappearing. With enormous effort, I am just able to crack open one eye. Everything is dark, except for a figure in the doorway, standing in silhouette. Light streams in from behind it. It steps into the room and says, "Hurry. We don't have much time."

Hunter.

chapter 18

Hunter is here. Is this really happening? Or are these the dreams of the dead?

Two arms scoop me up. They're strong and warm and when I'm pressed against his chest, I smell something sharp and clean. Mint and ash. My head pounds ferociously and I can't move my limbs. But I think this is real. I think I'm still alive.

"Come on. Now."

"Wait," I hear Ling say. "Why should we trust you?"

"Because I'm the only one who can get you out of here."

"He's right," Achilles says. "Let's go."

We're moving. Hunter holds my head close to his body, cradling my skull protectively. My vision is slowly returning, and I glimpse the bodies of fallen Tranqs. Everything is surreally quiet. The only sounds are the smacks of my friends' feet and the raspy rhythm of their panting.

Voices. Tranqs yelling, not far away. "Security's all down! Nothing's working!" Hunter pulls to an immediate halt.

I hear the heavy sound of boots hitting the floor, but they're not coming this way. I still can't move; I'm still only half conscious. I shift in Hunter's arms. He responds by holding me tighter.

"We need to get to a flight deck," Hunter says, voice low. "I've jammed the elevators, we'll take the stairs."

"Are you coming with us?" Ling asks.

"Yes," Hunter says. "But I need to get the mirror matter first."

"Okay," Naz says. "Where are—"

Her words cut off by the sound of razer fire.

"Get behind me!" Hunter yells. Holding me tight, he swings his body in a semicircle. I feel his back spasm as he takes the full force of three razer blasts.

Ling cries out in shock.

"I'm okay." Hunter runs back around the corner, putting me down as carefully as he can. "Stay here. Give her this."

I try to move, to speak, but I'm limp and nearly lifeless.

I'm aware of Ling crouching over me, something in her hand. "Tess? Tess, he said to give you this." I feel a pinprick of pain in my arm and wince. A needle.

Cold seeps into a vein.

And then... *Bam!*

Electric energy slams through me. I gasp, bolting upright. I'm coming up for air after drowning, heart racing a million miles an hour, the needle still hanging from my arm. Ling is staring at me openmouthed. "What was that?"

I can see everything. My vision is diamond-sharp, my focus clear as day. "Adrenaline," I pant, as if I'd just finished a sprint. Adrenaline and who knows what else.

I'm back.

I scramble to join Achilles and Naz. From our vantage point at the end of a corridor, we watch Hunter race toward six Tranqs. His skin absorbs their razer blasts as if they are no more than sunbeams. He easily wrenches a razer gun from one of them and turns it on the others. Half of them run, half of them try to fight back, but in less than five seconds, all six bodies lie smoking on the floor. I'm still panting as his eyes whip to meet mine. Relief courses over his face when he sees me upright.

"Let's go!" Ling yells. She darts for the smoking bodies, snatching up a gun. Naz, Achilles, and I do the same. When I pry the razer from the Tranquil's fingers, another surge of power hits me. *I am so ready.*

"This way!" Hunter gestures, and we're running past the Tranqs, through the blue, windowless corridors of the Three Towers. We have razers. We have Hunter. For the first time since I woke up here, I'm filled with real hope. I glance at Ling, running next to me, and I know she feels it too. Her eyes are alive with fire, her mouth set in fierce determination. It's the old Ling, the one who believes she can change the world. She catches my gaze and we grin at each other.

We zip around a corner—and straight into the oncoming path of a dozen Quicks. We yell in fright, almost falling as we try to stop short. In a panic, I swing my razer in front of me. It's only as my finger pulls the trigger that I remember razer power charges the Quicks.

"Stop!" yells Hunter, but it's too late—my razer blast hits a Quick clean in the chest. Its legs blur as it sprints toward us.

"Run!" Ling yells, swinging in the other direction, but Hunter grabs her.

"It's okay," he says. "They're with us."

The Quicks reach us, but instead of attacking, they assemble into a silent semicircle.

"What?" Ling asks, backing away from them.

"He's serfing them—reprogramming them," Achilles says, staring at the Quicks. "Look at their eyes."

"They're white," I note. "Not red." Just like outside the florist shop in Orange Grove Plaza.

Hunter nods quickly. "Figured we'd need backup."

The sight of the white-eyed Quicks suddenly becoming our allies is bizarre. But it doesn't take Ling long to make the mental leap. "Get an army's worth!"

Hunter shakes his head. "I'll lose too much power. Let's keep moving."

With the Quicks forming a protective wall around us, we keep running down the corridor. "But what about Orange Grove Plaza?" I ask Hunter, panting as we run side by side. "You serfed fifty Quicks there."

"No, I just erased their memories of seeing you." Hunter is not panting, his words coming as evenly as if he were walking. "Full serfing takes a lot more power."

Something swoops low and fast over my head. I start in fright. It's a crimson parrot, flying above us down the corridor. Another, then another fly after it, all squawking loudly. It takes me a few moments to realize where they came from. With the security down, Gyan's pets are loose.

"Look!" Ling points at an open meeting room. Two gold-and-black cheetahs are poised, ready to spring. One crouches on the floor; the other, a large table. As we run past, the two animals jump at each other, meeting midair in a snarling crash of teeth and claws.

"Here!" Hunter pops a heavy door open with one slam of his fist. "Down, all the way down!" The Quicks and Kudzu shoot past him, down the stairs.

"Are you sure you're okay?" he asks me, as I pause for a second to catch my breath. "Are the nanites working?"

I nod. "Nanites and adrenaline. Killer combination."

Hunter grazes my cheek with his hand, sending a flurry of tingles down my spine. "Tess." His voice is full of emotion, eyes distressed. "What have they done to you?"

"I'm okay," I say. "Let's go."

I lose count of the flights of stairs after about twenty, but soon after that, I barrel into Ling, Naz, Achilles, and the cluster of Quicks. Everyone's waiting at the bottom of the stairwell in front of a door stamped with the words FLIGHT DECK 15.

Hunter quietly pushes the door open.

The large expanse of the flight deck looks empty except for nine blue-and-white Trust cargo ships parked in a neat square. A handful of regular buzzcars are behind them. The space yawns out toward the opening of the hangar, which lets in pale lemon sunlight. Even from our position at the doorway, I can see the townships of Eden, located far beyond the mountains we're in now. An icy wind blows in from the mouth of the deck, sending stray handfuls of snow in a dance around the cavernous space.

"Can't see anyone," murmurs Ling, sounding surprised.

Hunter nods. "They're running the internal procedure for an attack. That means they'll be directing personnel to start closing the larger flight decks first—this is one of the smaller ones."

Movement on the deck. We all freeze—but it's just a spotted deer, galloping gracefully across the empty expanse. Ling and I exchange bemused glances. The sound of its hooves echoes musically around the enormous space.

Hunter pushes the door open, speaking quietly. "Cargo ship in the front on the far left."

Still surrounded by our Quick bodyguards, we run for the ship. The clatter of the Quicks' metal feet hitting the hard surface of the flight deck seems terrifyingly loud. My body is clenched, waiting for someone to fire at us, but there doesn't seem to be anyone around.

The ship's nose faces the hangar's opening, ready for takeoff. It's the same kind of ship we saw on Simutech's roof: a good, sturdy ship that'll easily fit all of us. The entrance is around the back, facing the flight deck, but it's disguised by the crowd of other ships around it. Naz punches the ramp Exit button with her one good fist. The entrance slides open and a ramp extends down toward us.

"Achilles, see if you can get the ship off-cycle," Ling says. "Naz, check what weapons they have and make sure this thing is charged."

"I'll get the mirror matter," Hunter says.

My words tumble. "But how do you know where it is?"

He gives me a complicated look. "Same way I knew where it was at Simutech."

"How long will you be?" Ling asks him.

"Three minutes," he replies. "If I'm not back by then, leave without me."

I'm too shocked to even protest. Leave without him? He just saved our lives.

"Then I better start her up," Ling says. "We'll be ready to roll as soon as you get back. Tess—"

"I'm going with Hunter," I interrupt, before she can give me an order.

Hunter's reaction is immediate. "No."

I open my mouth, but Ling stops me with a raised hand. "We don't have time for an argument. Whatever you do, do it fast."

The white-eyed Quicks start streaming up the ship's ramp. Ling runs to join them.

I sling my razer over my back and hurry to follow Hunter as he strides away from the ship.

"Hunter—" My words are cut off by the ship's huge engines spluttering to life. "Hunter," I call, grabbing his arm. "I'm coming with you!" Part of me knows this isn't the best plan, but I can't help it.

"No!" he calls back, gently pulling my hand from his arm. "Stay here!"

"But what if they serf you like you're serfing the Quicks?" I demand. "What if something happens to you? What if I never see you again when—" I can't finish the sentence: *when I just got you back.*

Hunter grasps my shoulders firmly, as if to pass me strength. He holds my gaze calmly. "Please don't worry, Tess. I have to go."

"Okay," I whisper. He pulls me close and presses his mouth to my forehead. His lips are warm and unexpectedly soft. For a split second, the fear disappears. But before I can even raise my hands to touch him back, he's gone, racing away from me between the blue-and-white ships.

I should get back to the others. But I need to see him leave safely. After a moment's hesitation, I dash past the last parked ship.

As I clear the ships, I freeze. The flight deck is no longer empty.

Tranquils.

Quicks.

Guiders.

Naz, Ling, and Achilles, weaponless and rigid with fear. Ling and Achilles are cuffed. Naz has her arm behind her head. A dozen razers are trained on each of them.

Hunter stands stock still in front of it all. He is staring at someone.

Gyan's honeyed voice rings out over the roar of the cargo ship's engines. He says to Hunter, "I assume you're looking for this," opening his palm to reveal the glowing mirror matter.

The roar of the engines begins to die; our escape plan being powered back down. No one moves. I glance at Ling. She widens her eyes a little, nodding behind me. No, not behind me. At the razer that's still slung on my back. I might get one shot before they return fire. Before I can decide what to do, Gyan pulls out the device with the red button. I ready for a question or a demand. But neither come. With the ghost of a smile, Gyan presses the red button.

I brace myself, but instead of a slam of pain, I only feel a dull, heavy ache. Painful. Distracting. But not enough to stop me. I catch Hunter's eye and he's nodding a little, looking grimly relieved. I wonder if he has something to do with this, if he jammed it somehow. Breathing hard, I stay upright. I can take this. In one swift movement, I sling the razer off my back.

"Get the girl!" Gyan yells.

Bodies rush for me. I catch Hunter's eye and hurl him the razer. As soon as it leaves my hands, I'm tackled to the ground. The wind is knocked out of me, palms and knees bashing against the concrete.

I hear a mass of Quicks and Tranquils crash into Hunter. I'm hauled to my feet, hands twisted so painfully behind my back that I cry out. But Hunter is fighting everything off, tossing the Quicks like toys and firing once, twice at the Tranquils with my razer. A wave of white-eyed Quicks, the ones Hunter is still serfing, race toward us, ready to do battle.

"Stop!" Gyan shouts. "Or we kill the girl."

Hunter's head snaps up. He freezes. The white-eyed Quicks stop dead in their tracks.

I yell, "No!" but a Tranq clamps a white-gloved hand over my mouth. Red-eyed Quicks move swiftly to hold Hunter in place. He could easily fight them off. But he doesn't. He's not fighting back because of me. Once again, we are prisoners of the Trust.

"Interesting," Gyan murmurs, glancing between Hunter and me.

His words are barely audible above the final splutters of the cargo ship's engines. "I had no idea…" His words trail off, but I can guess why he is surprised. The power of an artilect's emotions. Desperately, I will Hunter to keep fighting, not to sacrifice himself for me. But a part of me knows it's hopeless. Hunter, like Magnus, will act illogically, even recklessly, for love. Just like a human.

Hunter's voice shakes with anger. "If you hurt her—"

"Silence!" Gyan orders. Hunter's words stop. Gyan spins to face me, his gaze dark and victorious. "You were right. It is surprisingly powerful, their ability to *feel things.*" He spits these last two words out as if they taste disgusting. "But it's just another level of control, isn't it?"

White-robed Tower Officials spill from the stairwell, brandishing thick, long prods and armfuls of wire net. The ends of the prods spit white light. The officials fan out to approach Hunter warily, but he can't see them; his body is angled toward the hangar's opening. They're going to capture him like an animal. I try to shout but the hand over my mouth muffles my cry.

The officials rush Hunter. As soon as he realizes, he throws the Quicks holding him off, but the officials surround him with prods. They stab at him, white light crackling like spitting oil. He's thrown to his knees. I cry out again. *He can't feel it,* I tell myself desperately. But it still brings tears to my eyes, watching someone so beautiful and strong be overpowered so cruelly. The wire net flies above him, spreading out like the wings of a great gray bird. It falls heavily, clattering onto the flight deck. Hunter writhes beneath it, yelling and tearing at the wire, but it's too much for him. Too many prods, too much netting, too many officials, too many Quicks.

Gyan glances at the Tranq holding me. His words are clipped and perfunctory, as if he were wrapping up a meeting that had run far too long. "Execute the rebels at once. Starting with her."

Ling, Naz, and Achilles cry out. Every razer on deck swings toward my head or my heart.

I try to find Hunter's eyes, so his gaze can be the last thing I witness. But I can't see him through the wire net. My breath steams in front of me, like the razer smoke that'll surround my corpse. I hear sobbing: Ling. It echoes around the deck and fills the quiet corners with defeat.

I close my eyes.

I was right about Hunter.

I did the best I could.

I am not afraid to die.

A sharp, deep cry. My eyes fly open. Gyan clutches his hand, the one holding the mirror matter. There is something embedded in the soft flesh between his thumb and forefinger. He pulls it out, and both the mirror matter and a small, ceramic unicorn drop to the floor. Its horn is smeared in Gyan's blood. The mirror matter rolls away. The razers aimed at me waver in confusion, as the entire ensemble searches for the unicorn's origin.

From the balcony that circles the flight deck, Myrtle's pale eyes glitter, locked on the mirror matter. "Pretty shining," he snarls.

With a collective howl, hundreds of wild-eyed cell mates pour onto the flight deck.

In less than five seconds, the Trust is outnumbered ten to one. In ten more seconds, it's twenty to one, and it can't even be a fifth of the total prison population. The security systems. Hunter said he'd shut them all down. Which must mean Gyan's other zoo—the cell—was unlocked as well.

Razers fire wildly. Shouts punch the air. The Tranquil who has me lets me go as an enormous bald woman three times his size tackles him to the ground. I crawl on my hands and knees, trying to get to Hunter, but I can't see him through the throngs of people. In no time at all, prisoners have prods and razers. I duck out of the way of a barefoot boy swinging a prod to clear a circle around his small body. Cargo ship engines roar to life. People want to escape. We have to get a transport before they're all gone.

"Ling!" I yell, crawling through the chaos in Hunter's direction. "Achilles! Naz!" I have no idea if they can hear me, or if they're still alive.

I find a spare razer on the ground and use it to blast a Tranq out of the way. As his body hits the floor, I see the writhing mass of gray wire. *Hunter!* I shove people out of the way, stumbling toward him.

"Hunter!" I fall to my knees and begin tearing at the metal wiring.

"Tess!" His muffled voice tells me where his head is.

The metal net cuts my fingers. "Hunter!" I cry desperately. "The wire's too thick, I don't know how to cut it!"

"Get a razer and blast it!"

Gripping the gun securely, knowing I can't hurt him, I aim for his head and squeeze the trigger. The blast makes me flinch, but when I refocus, a small, smoking hole has appeared in the layers of wire net, its edges singed black. "Yes!" I cry, shooting my hand through the small space. I can feel part of Hunter's body, maybe his cheek.

"Do it again!"

With one eye on the fighting around me and one eye on him, I keep firing methodically, circling out like spiral. Soon I see an ear, his nose, his eyes. I hear a cargo ship take off in a monstrous roar, and then another—I have to hurry. I'm almost done when a strong hand grabs my shoulder. I jerk it off, and swing the gun around. "Naz!"

"Don't shoot," she says wryly. Crouching next to her are Ling and Achilles. They must still be in handlocks as their hands are behind their backs.

I turn the gun back to Hunter and keep firing, talking quickly as I do. "We have to get a transport. I'm almost done." I fire one last blast. "Can you make it out?" I call to Hunter.

Hunter's broad shoulders wriggle free from the netting, the singed wire scraping his skin. It's so sharp it'd slice open a human, but with Hunter it doesn't seem to penetrate more than a few millimeters. The blue blood that stripes his cheeks and arms look like delicate lines of paint.

"Watch out!" Naz points at an oncoming buzzcar; some prisoners had commandeered it, but they've lost control. The little car plows through the crowd toward us. Everyone scrambles to get out of the way. I struggle to pull Hunter free of the netting. The car is coming right for us. "Move!" I yell at Kudzu, and they scatter.

Hunter's arms finally pull free. With seconds to spare, I drag him from the netting and we throw ourselves from the car's path. It explodes against a far wall with a fiery crash. Hunter's pulling me to my feet even before I've processed that we made it.

"The cargo ships are all taken," he says.

"Buzzcar," I say, coughing through the smoke. The explosion is actually a good distraction; part of the flight deck's wall is on fire. "Get the others into one. I'll get the mirror matter."

"But—"

"You've got to stay out of sight, and so do they," I say. "Don't argue, go!"

I dive back into the crowd. I keep low, scanning the ground methodically. I wonder if Gyan is still here, if he had a chance to grab Hunter's life force before the prisoners attacked.

I'm in a moving tableau of bare feet, Tranquil boots, and smooth Quick legs. A layer of smoke fills the top of the deck, but as smoke rises, the ground is thankfully clear. I step over bodies and avoid splatters of blood. More buzzcars zip up and out.

Just as I'm about to give up hope, I see it. There, spinning around on the ground, being kicked every which way. I drop my razer and lunge for it, miss by inches, then dive through the crowd. There, again! In the far corner of the deck, out of the way of everyone. I race to snatch it up—but I'm too late. Someone steps from the shadows and scoops it up, seconds before I can.

"Pretty shining," Myrtle coos happily, holding the mirror matter up to his eyes.

"Myrtle!" I gasp, thankful it's him and not someone from the Trust. I snatch at the mirror matter. He pulls it back. Then he slips his long fingers into the pocket of his pink jacket and pulls out a small razer gun. My chest freezes. "Myrtle, I need that. It's not a beautiful thing, it's a power source—"

"What's my trade?" He cuts me off derisively, spittle spraying in my face. "Hmm? Trade? You have nothing to trade for the pretty shining?"

But I do have something to trade. My mom's necklace.

I can't change the past. But I can choose the future.

I snap the chain off my neck and hold it out to him. "Remember this?" Myrtle's yellow eyes light up. He does. He glances between the mirror matter and the necklace, his thin lips twisted in confusion. He mumbles something under his breath. "You can't wear the pretty shining," I cajole. "But you can wear this."

"Pretty shining." Myrtle mutters, sniffing the cylinder. "But pretty necklace too."

"You've got three seconds to decide," I snap. "Three. Two. One—"

"All right." Myrtle thrusts the mirror matter at me and snatches the necklace from my fingers.

For the second time in my life, I have the glowing, sparkly, shimmering mirror matter. *I have it.* I turn in the direction of the buzzcars, and I run.

I duck and weave through the thinning crowd, slipping past prisoners and Tranquils, across the deck in the direction of the buzzcars. There's only one left. Ahead of me a Tranquil and a tall toothless man covered in tronics grapple for control of a razer. I dodge past them but lose my balance, stumbling into someone else, who catches my arm as I fall. It's a man in a bright yellow robe.

I am face-to-face with Gyan.

I'm so shocked I can't speak. Neither can he.

His eyes drop to the mirror matter. A smile crawls its way onto his mouth. "Well, well, well," he says softly. With a jerk, he twists my arm behind my back. Pain explodes in my shoulder, and I cry out. I'm barely conscious of the mirror matter clattering to the ground. My legs give way and I'm forced to my knees. "Look what you have for me, Just Tess." He twists my arm even more and I shriek again, short and sharp. The pain is hot and stabbing and won't let up. Struggling makes it worse. *He's going to break my arm.* Gyan's voice is a soft snarl in my ear. "Let this be a lesson to—" But he never finishes his sentence. There's a flash of white light, and his body spasms. Razer fire.

Gyan drops to his knees, squealing in pain and letting me go. I scramble to my feet, my shoulder burning and singing with relief. A second later, his eyes roll back in his head and he crumples to the concrete. Unconscious? Dead? I'm hoping it's the latter.

Grabbing the mirror matter, I scan the crowd for the shooter. Standing a few feet from the stairwell entrance is Abel. The razer in his hand is still aimed at Gyan.

"Tess!" On the other side of the hangar, Ling gestures at me to hurry to the buzzcar.

"One minute!" I call through the chaos, then sprint toward my uncle.

"Tess, I'm sorry, I'm so sorry." He's pleading as I reach him.

"Do you have a way out?" I pant, drawing us close to the hangar wall.

"No. Yes. I'll be fine," he stutters. He looks so broken and strung out that my heart almost breaks. "Do you?"

"Yes. A buzzcar. But it's—" I can't bring myself to say *full,* but it is. Buzzcars only take up to five people: any more and they won't fly.

Abel nods in understanding. "Tess," he says nervously. "There's one other thing. One other thing about Hunter."

"What?" I gasp, glancing back at the car where Ling is waving at me furiously.

Abel's eyes dart from the buzzcar and back to me, flustered. "Nothing. Nothing important."

I frown, now curious, even worried, but there's no time and we both know it.

Abel pushes me gently toward the car. "Go. I'll be fine."

A round of razer fire smashes into the wall a few feet from our heads and we both flinch. "How?" I ask. "How are you getting out of here?"

Instead of answering my question, Abel takes my chin with bandaged fingers. For a second, he holds my gaze tenderly. His eyes are warm and wet with tears. "I am so proud of you, Tessendra," he says. His voice cracks saying my name. Then, in a firmer voice: "Go."

I pull him close for a hug. Then I turn and bolt for the car.

"Let's go, let's go!" Naz is yelling at me. The car's already moving toward the hangar's opening as she helps pull me in. Ling and Achilles are squashed next to her in the backseat, yelling at me to hurry up. Hunter's in the driver's seat, silent and focused. His eyes flick to take in the mirror matter, then meet mine in relief.

As the car door folds shut, I twist back in my seat. Abel stands where I left him, pale as a ghost. He's smiling bravely and holding up one hand in a shaky farewell. I hold his gaze, as sure and strong as I can.

Then we shoot out fast over the edge of the hangar, flying away from the Three Towers.

part 5

chapter 19

Below us, the Smoking Mountains are a blur of white snow and black granite. Hunter takes the tube of mirror matter from my white-knuckled hands and places it carefully on the dashboard. The little car's displays beep and whirl fluidly.

"Are we off-cycle?" Ling asks breathlessly from the backseat.

"Yes," Hunter replies.

In an explosion of sound, Ling, Naz, and Achilles immediately go crazy. They're hysterical with relief; laughing and yelling as they recap our ordeal.

"I thought we were done for!"

"What about when he serfed the Quicks—"

"The unicorn—"

"The butterflies—"

"The net!"

I stare straight ahead, but my eyes aren't seeing the sweeping view. I am completely overwhelmed, barely able to process what just happened. *We made it out*, I think numbly. *We escaped.* My heart rate starts to slow. My muscles start to unclench. A tiny tear of relief slides down my cheek. I turn to the boy next to me. "Are you okay?"

Hunter's brow furrows, thinking hard about the question. But when he looks at me, his face becomes peaceful. "Yes," he says softly. "Yes, Tess, I am."

Ling leans forward. "What's the plan?"

"I'm taking us to the loops," Hunter replies, instantly professional. "We can decide what to do there."

"Good idea," Ling says. "We're not out of the woods yet." She's right. With the Trust after us in a city that has eyes everywhere, our escape has just begun.

We clear the lower half of the mountain and start flying over the houses of the South Hills. From up here, the large houses with their blue swimming pools and wide decks look like toys. The sun burns directly above us, reflecting in the shifting surfaces of the pools. It must be about midday. "Izzy lives down there," I murmur.

Hunter follows my gaze. "That must feel...strange."

Strange is an understatement. Just over a year ago, I'd been sunning myself by Izzy's pool while we complained about the lack of decent dresses in the boutiques or hot guys in education. The Trust was a vaguely annoying presence I didn't really consider and the Badlands was somewhere exotic and dangerous I had no intention of ever visiting, except maybe overnight on a dare. Now I feel grateful just to be alive.

"How did you remember me?" I ask Hunter. "I thought they wiped your memories."

He reaches over and starts to slide his fingers up my right arm.

"Hunter!" I push his hands back to the two control sticks in alarm. "You're still flying."

His mouth quirks into a crooked smile. I realize that we are still flying, even with his hands off the sensitive controllers, even with his eyes meeting mine. He's flying the car with his...powers. My lips part in amazement, and then promptly snap shut as he starts moving his fingers again. They trace over the black cityscape on my arm, making it tingle. "This," he says. "This is how I got you back."

I frown. "The cell branding?"

"When I found out what the Trust intended to do, I created a code that would unlock a hidden backup of my memories and entered it into the cell security system under your name. I knew you'd end up there, and I knew Gyan would let me see you again, to see for himself that the memory erasing worked."

"So Shanice was in on it?" I ask in disbelief.

"No." Hunter smiles. "She had no idea."

"That's why Rockwood's was different from ours," Naz pipes up. "I knew something was up."

"That is so totally amazetown." Achilles sighs. "You're like a superhero for nerds."

We approach one of the busier loops that circles above the southern part of the Hive. "But what if I'd been wearing something long-sleeved?" I ask Hunter. "What if you didn't see it?"

"Then you wouldn't be here now." Noticing my look of horror, he adds, "The odds were in my favor. It was a calculated risk."

My stomach drops as we shoot into a loop. In the buzzcars around us, I glimpse Edenites talking animatedly to each other or flicking through the streams, no longer having to pay attention to flying. Hunter relaxes a little and turns around to face us. Clearly, we're all thinking the same thing. What now?

Ling leans forward confidently, looking every bit a leader even though her wrists are braceleted with handlocks. "There's only one thing we can do." She pauses to meet each of our gazes individually. "Fly to the nearest border crossing and rip it apart."

Naz exhales in triumph and pumps her fist. "Yes! I'm ready. Right now."

I start in alarm, and say, "Wait a second," but Ling barrels over me, eyes burning with excitement.

"Hunter can serf the Quicks and take out the Tranqs. We go now, right now, hit them before they know what's happening."

Naz whoops ecstatically, just as excited as Ling. "Let's do it! Let's go!"

"Can you really do that?" Achilles, sandwiched between the two electrified girls, blinks at Hunter nervously. "Serf more Quicks—do you have enough power?"

"I could," Hunter says calmly. "But I won't."

Silence fills the car. We reach the end of the loop and start to take it again.

"What?" Ling's question drips acid.

Hunter looks unfazed at her anger. "I don't believe opening Eden's borders will create a hospitable living environment for the people of the Badlands."

"What, and *murdering* everyone will?" Naz spits. "Let's not forget who we're dealing with here!"

Ling's body turns rigid. "He never said he's not going to do Project Aevum," she says, voice suddenly tight. "He never said that." For a moment, she reels back, anger meeting fear. "Is that what you're going to do?"

"No!" Hunter and I chorus the word at the exact same time.

"No," Hunter repeats firmly. "That's why we're all here."

"Yeah, chill out," I snap. "And don't talk to him like that. Hunter just saved our lives." I run my teeth over my lower lip before adding, "And I happen to agree with him."

"You do?" Ling's mouth drops open in surprise.

"Yes, I do." I twist to face Kudzu fully. "Guys, we just saw what happened when Hunter opened a border, back on the flight deck. Chaos. *Dangerous* chaos. It'd be the same in Eden."

Achilles nods. "I think she's right."

"So, we just run and hide for the rest of our freakin' lives?" Naz asks incredulously. "You saw what he did back there. We have to *use* him—"

"He is not yours to use!" I exclaim furiously.

Ling finds her voice. "And you're not in a position to decide what Kudzu does! This is what we've been been working for, and this is what we're going to do. I don't care if you don't like it, Tess. I don't care if you're too chicken." Her voice reaches a fever pitch, hands balled into fists. "We're going to open a border now!"

The words tumble out of my mouth before I have time to stop them. "Opening a border won't get Sanako back!"

Ling freezes, stunned, as if I just sucker-punched the entire car. Ling's face looks as if it's burning hot and icy cold, all at once. Her voice is a low, predatory growl. "How dare you say that to me."

"I know you want her back," I say, my voice full of desperate passion. "And I know you blame yourself for her leaving. I know what it's like to lose someone." I reach for her hands but she flinches, yanking them back. Her eyes are on fire. "But you're a leader, Ling," I continue. "You have to make decisions that are best for everyone, not for one girl who may or may not be out there. A girl who made her own decision about her own life and has to face the consequences herself. You can't save her."

The world whirls by our little car as we reach the end of the loop and start it again. Below us, Eden glitters like a treasure chest. Ling hisses roughly, "It's not about her."

I can't make Ling see what I see. My voice is quiet, but not weak. "Isn't it?"

A tear spills from Ling's lower lid and streaks down her cheek. Her voice is cracked and hard. "I want to help the Badlands. Not just her."

"I know. And so do I," I tell her. "But we're not ready to open a border now. We've no backup, no weapons, and no plan for how to make sure a lot of people don't end up dead."

Ling blows her bangs out of eyes and exhales loudly. Naz and Achilles stare at her, waiting for her decision. I'm sure I'm right. I recognize the crazed look in her eye and the impossibility of her plan. That was me fleeing Eden for the Badlands.

After what seems like an age, she turns her head to meet my gaze. "You're right," she says evenly. "This isn't the right time."

I sag in relief.

Naz sniffs, disgusted. "So we do nothing?"

"We're escaping," Achilles points out. "That's not nothing."

My eyes flicker to Hunter, then back to Ling. "We can't stay in Eden, can we?" I'm framing it as a question, but I already know the answer.

"No," Ling says flatly. "Whatever happens, we'll have to leave for the Badlands. Tonight. We'll have to be gone by dawn."

Achilles looks as if he's just licked something sour. "Really?" he asks. "All of us?"

Ling nods curtly. "What other option do we have? Stay at Milkwood and never leave? It's not completely self-sufficient, and I bet the Trust would find us eventually, even if it were."

Silence settles into the car for a moment as we absorb what this means. Leaving Eden. Returning to the Badlands. "I know we escaped," I say slowly. "And I know we stopped Project Aevum. But somehow..."

"Scurrying over the border with our tail between our legs totally sucks?" Achilles suggests.

I wince. "Exactly," I mutter.

Ling sighs angrily. "I just wish there was something we could do."

So do I. I glance at Hunter. He cocks his head a quarter-inch, eyes serious and, somehow, committed. He nods, just slightly. He's up for something. My heart swells—of course he is. Of course he'll help. My mind begins whirring frantically.

Ling continues, "Something that means Benji and Lana didn't die for nothing."

"Something badass," grunts Naz.

"Something involving Hunter," Achilles chimes in, sounding smitten. "I mean, c'mon, the guy's six kinds of awesome." He raises his shackled hands, offering one palm to Hunter for a high five.

Hunter frowns at Achilles, unsure.

"He wants you to hit it," Naz explains.

Hunter blinks, just once. Achilles grins and nods encouragingly. Hunter slaps Achilles' open palm. Hard. Achilles flinches, emitting a tiny yelp of pain.

"Too hard?" Hunter asks in concern.

"No," Achilles replies hoarsely, dropping his hands into his lap to rub his palm against his pants. "You got it, buddy. You got it."

My loose idea finally solidifies into something whole. "Actually, there is something we could do."

Ling, who'd been staring morosely out the window, jolts to attention. "What?"

I face everyone in the car, feeling excited, nervous, and almost incredulous that I'm actually going to suggest this. "Just before Ling brought me back from the Badlands, the Trust built a dam. A thick concrete dam, one hundred feet tall and fifty feet wide. The dam that stops Moon Lake from flowing through an aqueduct to become Lunalac in the Badlands." I pause, glancing around at the four sets of eyes that are glued on me. "We're going to blow up that dam."

Ling's expression slowly transforms. "The aqueduct," she whispers. "We can blow up the dam."

Naz whistles, low and long. "Damn, Rockwood. You're hard-core." She nods in approval. "I like it."

"Blowing up the dam will flush the Badlands with thousands of gallons of fresh water," I continue. "It'd change lives, *save* lives." I picture the little kids who used to crowd outside Zhukov's bar, and the looks on their faces when fresh water starts to flow from the taps again. "We could never do it on our own," I add. "But if Hunter agrees to help..." I trail off, glancing over at him, knowing he'll say yes.

"It won't fix the problem in the long-term," Hunter points out. "But it's far more achievable and less dangerous than opening a border. You can count me in."

A giddy wave of adrenaline bubbles up inside me, making my heart beat faster. I tell Hunter, "There's about a hundred Quicks on guard—"

"How do you know all this?" Ling demands.

"Remember the off-cycle scratch you gave me?" I ask. "I didn't have much to do after my 'tutoring' sessions." I put air quotes around the word *tutoring*, and Hunter flicks me a wry smile. "I was curious. But I could only see what was on the streams, nothing that official."

"Bo can help with explosives," Ling begins, before catching herself. "Assuming..."

Assuming Milkwood is still standing. Assuming the Trust hasn't killed our friends.

"We have to go back to Milkwood." I say it, but I know I'm also speaking for Ling, Achilles, and Naz.

"Milkwood?" Hunter asks.

"Kudzu's base," I explain.

"Our home," Ling adds.

Hunter shakes his head firmly. "No. It's too dangerous. The Trust could be waiting for us."

Ling opens her mouth in immediate protest, but I stop her with a quick glance. Instead, I turn to Hunter. His face is set in a look of resolve. "Tess," he says, "you can't go back. I can't put you in danger like that. I want to…" He pauses, and glances furtively at the others in the backseat. The look strikes me as odd, and a second later, I realize why. He's nervous about them overhearing. It's so unexpectedly vulnerable and impossibly human that a little shiver of something electric and warm races through me.

"You want to what?" I ask quietly.

He looks back at me, and the expression on his face reminds me of when he told me in the florist shop he was scared for me, asking me in that soft, embarrassed way if that was normal. "I want to protect you," he finishes in a low voice.

Ling makes a noise from the backseat that could be a scoff or an *aw*.

I reach out to take his hand. Our fingers intertwine. Even though I initiated it, I have to suppress a gasp. Every nerve ending sings and sparks and shoots pulses of energy up my arm. I try to focus. "Hunter, our friends are there. People we care about. We have to see if they're okay." I squeeze his hand, and another flurry of that feeling, that strange, electric feeling, floods through my veins. "Can you understand that?"

He glances down at our fingers, lips parted. I wonder if he's feeling what I am. He nods. I squeeze his hand again, then pull away.

Hunter straightens in his seat and asks, "Should I access the official schematics on the dam now?"

"You can you do that without going on-cycle, right?" Achilles asks, awestruck.

"Yes. Trust schematics are never on-cycle," he replies. "They're not for the public to see. I can't go on-cycle at all now," he adds. "Not unless we want the Trust to know where we are."

"Yes, stay off-cycle," Ling says, a little imperiously. "Don't let them find us through you."

"Don't worry," he says. "I know what they're looking for. I will remain"—he shoots me a sly, sideways look—"impotent."

We hold each other's gaze for a second longer than necessary, long enough to feel my cheeks buzz with color. Someone in the backseat laughs.

"Hey." I frown, reaching for the mirror matter. "This isn't full, it's maybe ninety percent." I glance back at Hunter. "I don't want to"—I purse my lips, searching for the phrase—"run you down. How does this recharge?"

He smiles unevenly, taking the silver tube from me. "Sun works," he says, putting it back on the light-filled dashboard. "Not as quickly as the recharging stations at Simutech and in the Towers, but sun works."

"Solar." Achilles nods approvingly. "A classic for a reason. You can recharge yourself wherever you are."

"How long will it take to fully recharge?" I ask. Hunter's involvement in anything we do from now on is key.

"A day," he replies.

"We won't have a day," I say, alarmed.

"Right," adds Ling. "We can only risk blowing up the dam tonight. Any longer and the Trust will track us down. We have to leave Eden before dawn."

I glance at the sun and do some quick math, remembering that we lose the sun earlier at Milkwood because of the high city walls. "We probably have only six hours of direct sunlight left."

Hunter doesn't look bothered by this. "I'm okay for now. I just need to keep this in the sun for as long as possible."

I nod. The silver mirror matter glints and shimmers on the dashboard: a life force in a tube.

"What can you tell us about the dam?" Ling asks.

Hunter relaxes, unfocusing his gaze. His eyes start to glow, as if someone switched on a torch behind them. They're the color of cut kiwi fruit. "One hundred and eight Quicks," he murmurs. "The dam wall is ten feet thick, and yes, one hundred feet high and fifty feet wide. The entrance to the aqueduct is also one hundred feet high and fifty feet wide, shaped like an oval. The space between where the dam ends and the entrance to the aqueduct is forty-three feet—"

Suddenly he stops. His eyes lose the inhuman glow and he makes a small sound of surprise. "What?" I ask anxiously. "What did you see?"

Hunter shakes his head. "Nothing." His hand moves to rub his chin, distressed, eyes meeting mine. "I just lost access."

"What does that mean?" Ling asks.

"It means the Trust just cut me loose," he replies ruefully. "I knew it was going to happen eventually. I was hoping for later rather than sooner."

Panic flares inside me. "Are they going to shut you down? Serf you? Wipe your memories?" Horrific scenarios of Hunter seizing control of our buzzcar and flying us back to the Trust laughing manically explode into my imagination before I see him shaking his head emphatically.

"They can't do that. I'd have to be there for them to modify my memories, and they're nowhere near powerful enough to serf me or shut me down. It's the equivalent of losing my security clearance."

I shake my head, confused. "But what about the exit program? Surely they can shut you off remotely?"

"Actually, that's what Abel originally wanted," Hunter says. "It was Gyan who insisted I be more independent. I guess," he continues, tilting his head thoughtfully, "that's what you'd call irony."

"Did they know you were looking at the dam schematics?" I ask urgently. If they did, our plan is as good as dust—we could never hit the dam if the Trust knows we're coming.

"No," Hunter replies. "They can't have known that."

"So, what does this mean?" Ling asks.

Hunter's face darkens. "It means I can't serf the Quicks."

"Oh." I sink back into my seat. "Oh."

Could Kudzu take on all those Quicks ourselves? No. That's way too dangerous. Outside, the sun beats down relentlessly as we start to take the same loop again. "What do you need?" I ask Hunter. "What do you need to serf the Quicks?"

"Something called a root processing algorithm," he replies. "The RPA."

"Well, where is it that?" I ask. "How can we get it?"

He frowns, running one hand through his hair. "We could go back to the Three Towers—"

"*No,*" the backseat choruses.

"I am officially passing on that idea," Achilles adds.

"It might be in official scratch," Hunter thinks aloud. "I can't check now. It's actually very frustrating—"

"Wait!" I exclaim, sitting up. "Official scratch, like blue scratch?"

He nods. "Possibly. Probably. Ugh." He makes a face, musing to himself. "This uncertainty is extremely disconcerting. I'm used to having access to everything, all information, everything in the streams. This is what it must be like to be human—"

I whack him lightly. "Hunter, shut up." I turn to the others, grinning. "I can get blue scratch."

Ling looks at me disbelievingly. "What?"

I quickly explain that Izzy's father is a Guider. "What day is it?" I ask Hunter.

"Monday."

"She'll be at education now," I say, "but if we come back later tonight, she might give it to me."

"Might?" Lind asks warily.

"We didn't part on the best of terms," I say. "But it's worth a shot."

It's all Ling needs to hear. "Right. We're on. Let's get to Milkwood, we'll work out the rest on the way." She pauses, glancing at us in an uncharacteristically mischievous way. Then, in a low, almost conspiratorial tone: "Our minds are better."

Achilles grins, holding up his shackled hands. "Hands? Definitely faster."

Naz and I trade a look. For the first time ever, it is a look of equals. We grin widely, then chant together, "Our hearts are stronger."

Then, all at once, we raise our voices and shout with delirious abandon, "We are Kudzu!"

Our laughter is high and wild, and when I catch Hunter's bemused look, I laugh even harder. Tears prick my eyes, and joy fills me from the boots up. My friends, my crazy, brave, passionate friends, are going to blow up a dam. In our little stolen buzzcar, we howl and we shout and we laugh. We are Kudzu.

We land south of Milkwood, near the entrance to a hike that circles around the lake. It's uncommon, but not unusual, for Edenites to buzz up here from any of the townships. We can't take the regular path back to Milkwood because we can't risk the Trust seeing a buzzcar land so far north. We'll have to beat our own path back.

Naz busies herself trying to cut the Trust handlocks off Ling and Achilles with a stone, telling Hunter and me that if she can't do it in a few minutes, we'll just have to help them hike to Milkwood without the use of their arms. I know Hunter could break the handlocks, but he doesn't offer, which makes me assume he's saving his power. And besides, I've already asked so much of him; I don't want him feeling like some sort of garden tool. Instead, I ask quietly, "Can we talk?"

As the dull clang of rock on metal echoes out around us, Hunter and

I move into the scrub. The fallen leaves form a soft mulch that's spongy underfoot. We stop after passing a large elm tree, putting it between us and the others. Honey-colored light fills a small clearing. I find a safe spot for the mirror matter, a low, wide tree fork drenched in bright sunlight. It catches the light and sparkles like a thousand tiny diamonds.

Before I open my mouth, Hunter surprises me. "I have something for you." He leans down and draws a bundle out of his white boot. It's about the size of the mirror matter, wrapped in tough black fabric. When I flip the fabric back, I gasp. "Mack!" My knife! My beautiful, strong hunting knife that I was sure I had lost forever. I flip it fast through my fingers, thrilling at the familiar feel. "But where was—how did you—"

"I had it when I rescued you from the Interrogation Room," Hunter says, taking in my rapt face with clear satisfaction. "I forgot about it until now."

I grin up at him. "I thought you never forget."

I say this because I remember him saying it in the florist shop. The shop. Suddenly the pleasure at Mack's return wavers, and I'm reminded of what I need to speak to Hunter about. Carefully, I wrap my knife back in the black fabric and move to balance it on the tree fork, next to the mirror matter. But even after I put the knife down, I can't drag my eyes to the boy behind me.

"Something is wrong," he says. "What's the matter?"

I frown, my hands twisting into each other anxiously.

"Are you nervous about the dam?" he tries again. I shake my head no. "Tess. Look at me. Please?" Reluctantly, I turn to face him. "I find humans hard enough to understand when they're being direct," he says seriously. "Removing speech makes comprehension significantly more difficult."

"I didn't want to say anything in front of the others," I say, glancing in their direction. "I didn't want them to worry."

"Worry about what?"

My stomach twists with nerves. "Well, what if you change your mind? About helping us? What if..." I exhale hard, my body tense. "What if we have a fight and you decide Project Aevum is the best way to go?"

Hunter blinks, surprised. "That won't happen, Tess."

"But it might," I insist, taking a step closer to him. "It could. The only thing stopping you is your feelings. How do I know you won't just change your mind again?"

Hunter runs his fingers through his hair, bewildered. "Tess, I just saved your life. And defied the Trust, the people who made me. How can you even suggest that?"

I show him my tronic, the curled letters softly glowing in the afternoon light. "Because no feeling is final, Hunter. People change."

He stares down at me, his lower lip parted in an expression of confused astonishment. I stare back defiantly, not giving an inch. I care about Hunter and I don't like telling him I don't trust him. Because honestly, I do trust him. Almost beyond my own will, I feel I could trust Hunter with my life. But I can't be naive.

Hunter's words are halting but sure. "Abel was right about me, Tess. As soon as I let myself admit how I feel about you, everything changed. Now the idea of killing even one person in the Badlands doesn't seem efficient. It seems barbaric. Insane." He takes a step back, one hand rubbing his jaw with stark concern. "I can't even believe you're still speaking to me after what I said I'd do. What I've already done." His eyes widen with horror, voice rising in panic. "That girl. The girl the Quicks killed. You knew her. She was with you. She was with Kudzu, wasn't she?"

"Hunter—"

"Wasn't she!"

"Yes."

His eyes grow wild, hands bunching into fists at his side. "I helped kill her. I authorized the Quicks to kill your friend!"

I move to him quickly, reaching up to take his hands. "You didn't know that—"

"I killed her!"

"You did not," I say firmly. "The Trust killed Lana, not you." I unclench his fists to hold both hands tightly. "Listen to me. What's done is done." I try to make my voice as soothing as possible. "Okay? We can't change the past. You just can't ever do it again."

"I have no intention," he mutters. "Believe me."

I do. We stand in silence for a few moments, until his shoulders lose their tightness and he looks somewhat normal again.

Then he says, "I don't entirely agree with you."

"About what?"

"About no feeling being final." Hunter's hands move to rest on my shoulders. They feel solid and warm. His eyes drill into mine. "My feelings for you won't change."

I'm in clothes that literally stink. My head is shaved, and I'm covered in cuts and bruises and dried blood, not all of it mine. The idea of anyone, let alone Hunter, having real feelings for me seems absurd. "What feelings?"

A quizzical, happy smile sneaks onto his face. His words sound innocent and unflinchingly honest. "I'm in love with you."

I feel as if someone just threw a bucket of water over me.

"You didn't know," he says, studying my reaction. "You are surprised. You are...unhappy?"

"N-No, Hunter," I stutter. "You're not in love with me."

"Yes, I am."

I cross my arms over my chest. I can feel my heart hammering through my shirt. "What you're feeling is just...excitement. That we made it out."

"No," he says. "It's not."

"It'll fade," I insist. "What you think is love is just a chemical called dopamine and that doesn't last. Whatever you're feeling will be gone in a week."

"No. It won't." He looks like he always does: curious, calm, utterly fascinated by me. "How do you know all this?" he asks. "Have you ever been in love?"

I exhale noisily. "We should get back to the others."

"Tess, have you ever been in love?"

I bite my lip and stare at the patchwork of leaves on the ground. "I don't know," I confess, somewhat unwillingly. "No, I guess."

"Then how do you know this isn't love?" Hunter closes the distance between us, and suddenly his arms are around my waist and lifting me up as if I weigh no more than sunlight.

A squeal escapes me before I can stop it. "What are you doing?" I sound strangely giggly and not at all like myself.

He deposits me easily on a tall, moss-covered tree stump. "Sweeping you off your feet?"

"That's a metaphor." My cheeks are growing warm. He's standing between my legs, hands resting lightly on my waist. My hands lie sweaty and tense in my lap.

"Is it?" he asks. His eyes move around my face, taking in every part of it. He touches the neat scar on my forehead, a light touch so impossibly gentle. His eyes meet mine again, and he smiles. "You really are very beautiful. I think you're the most beautiful girl that I've ever met."

"You haven't met that many girls," I reply, trying to sound matter-of-fact. "You're a rogue science experiment."

"Okay," he relents. "You are the most beautiful girl that has ever entered my consciousness in any form. And I can write my own memories, so..."

"Emily Anderson." I narrow my eyes.

"Let's not dwell on a fictional ten-year-old." He continues to stare at me. I've never noticed how soft his lips look. "You know what my favorite thing about you is?"

"My many scars?"

He smiles. "Your eyes." Then, off my look of surprise: "What?"

"That's one of the things I like best about you," I murmur.

"I can see you thinking," he says softly. "And I like it. I like the way you think. That's what makes you beautiful." He presses both hands into my hips. "You're like a fascinatingly complex algorithm."

"An algorithm?"

"Yes." He nods. "Who also feels beautiful, and sounds—" He frowns. "Well, you do a lot of yelling."

I giggle, feeling oozy, like my bones are made of wet clay.

"You make me malfunction, Tess," he continues, leaning forward to murmur shivery deep into my ear. "That's how beautiful you are."

I can no longer stop my arms from moving up to circle his neck. I twist my fingers into his dark, slightly coarse hair, scratching an itch I've had for weeks. Then my finger trails down the back of his neck and cautiously, so cautiously, down his jaw and to his lips. A smile lifts the corners of his mouth as my fingertips trace over the bow of his upper lip, the half-moon of his lower. I wonder how it is I never noticed he doesn't breathe. When my fingers finish their journey, they sneak back into his hair, twisting, playing, feeling every texture. My forehead comes to rest against his, and my skin is flushed and alive. I close my eyes, every nerve in my body singing.

"Can I be honest, Tess?" he whispers.

"Have you not been so far?"

"I really want to kiss you."

I can't concentrate on anything except him: in my arms, me in his, his face so close to mine. My answer is barely a whisper. "I think I want to kiss you too."

"No, I really, *really* want to kiss you," Hunter replies, eyes on my mouth. "That desire is overtaking every other function I have, except for standard programming and security, but they never shut off."

"Robot." My lips are just half an inch from his, so I speak the words directly into his mouth. "That's my new nickname for you. Do you like it?"

I feel him smile, our lips a millimeter apart. "I love it."

"Guys!" Ling's voice cracks through the clearing. Hunter and I jolt away from each other, just as she appears. "Naz couldn't—oh." She stops abruptly, eyes bugging at the sight of our entanglement. Naz and Achilles are right behind her.

My entire face feels blood red. I bumble my way off the tree stump. "We were just—" My command of the English language deserts me completely.

"I bet you were," Ling says, then holds her wrists up. "We couldn't break them. Let's just go."

"Yes." I cough. "Go. We should. Now."

Hunter follows me toward the others. He takes both of Ling's wrists and jerks them apart in one fluid motion. Ling gasps as the metal hand-locks snap easily. Then he does the same to Achilles.

"Could you do that the whole time?" Naz asks, dropping the rock she'd been using in irritation.

Hunter glances at me, somewhere between guilt and elation. "You needed to rest before the trek," he says unconvincingly, moving into the scrub. I'm rewarded with a scowl from Naz, raised eyebrows from Ling, and a high five from Achilles.

chapter 20

We start moving north. Ling and Naz lead the way. Hunter follows, shifting heavy stones and holding aside thick branches. I carry the mirror matter, obsessed with trying to keep the silver liquid in the sun as much as I can. It feels warm and safe in my hand; but then, I'm just feeling warm and safe, period. The memory of my almost-kiss with Hunter replays in my head constantly.

The hike feels easy, even enjoyable. The air smells fresh. The dappled afternoon light is alive with insects and birds. I notice things about the foliage that I never have before: the way twisting silver snail tracks look like a child's drawing or how moss feels like damp carpet and is the same color as Hunter's eyes.

After a while Ling falls in step beside me at the back of the group. "So all's good with you and—" She nods at Hunter, who's lifting a delighted Achilles up a steep incline ahead of us.

I shrug and make a noncommittal noise, but I can't keep a silly grin off my face.

"He seems nice," Ling says, stumbling just slightly over the pronoun.

"He is," I agree. "And if nothing else, he's going to make this whole dam thing happen. If...everything else falls into place." Both of us know that what we find at Milkwood will decide for us what the plan actually is.

Ling nods and wipes a smudge of dirt from her arm.

I pause, one hand tight around a low-hanging vine. "I am really sorry, Ling." I find myself saying. "I'm sorry I lied about Hunter. I'm sorry I betrayed Kudzu. I should have told you about him as soon as—"

"I get why you didn't." Ling stops me with a dismissive wave of her hand. "It was a tight spot to be in. Plus, you remember my stance on grudges."

"They're for whiny bitches," I remember.

"Yup." She sighs, stretching her neck left and right before fixing her gaze back on me. "We do crazy things for love. That's just what happens."

"We're not in love," I correct her quickly. "We're just...friends."

Ling dips her eyebrows in disbelief. "Friends who make out?"

"We didn't," I say awkwardly. "I mean, I don't know if I should. He's...and I'm..."

Ling's eyes are sharp. "Do you trust him?"

"Yes," I say immediately. "I do."

"Do you want to jump his bones?"

"Ling!"

"Do you?"

I fight a blush, eyes on the ground. "Maybe," I admit.

"Then be open to it. Good guys are few and far between."

"You've certainly changed your tune."

"I'm not an idiot," she says matter-of-factly. "He saved our lives. And I see the way he looks at you." She hooks up an eyebrow and leans toward me, voice deep and breathy. *"I want to protect you."*

"Shut up." I whack her arm, but we're both giggling.

Ling shoots me a smile. "I'm just really glad you're okay, Tess."

Out of nowhere, pain billows into my head. The chip. I suck in a gasp.

"Are you okay?" Ling grabs me, helping me stay upright.

"Tess!" Hunter calls. He must still be jamming it because it's nowhere near as painful as before. It feels more like what happened on the flight deck—painful, but not completely traumatic.

I pull myself upright, breathing as deep as I can. "I'm fine," I call back. The pain ebbs. "I'm okay," I tell Ling. "Let's keep moving."

You'll need more than that to stop me now, Gyan.

It's late afternoon by the time we reach the outskirts of Milkwood. The sky is a dramatic palette of pink and purple, rose and gold. Naz waves at us to stay back as she scopes out the front of the coffee-colored building. It's quiet except for the calls of unseen birds. She jerks her head at us to follow her around back.

From the edge of the scrub, we see the backyard is empty too. No folding chairs, no stray musical instruments.

"Is anyone even here?" I whisper.

Hunter's darting eyes take everything in. "I'm not picking up anything on-cycle."

"We're not on-cycle," Achilles says. "What about comms or off-cycle scratch?"

Hunter shakes his head. "Nothing."

"Weird," Naz mutters, crouching in the dirt.

"Where is everyone?" Ling sounds worried. "You don't think . . ."

We're too late. The Trust has already found them. *The Trust is here.*

"Let's get out of here," Naz says suddenly. But just as she does, a girl's voice calls out—thin and trembling.

"Naz?"

Our heads twitch in the direction of the voice. It came from the house.

"Gem?" Ling says hoarsely. She bolts upright, even as Naz pulls her to get back down. "Gem!" she screams.

"It's Ling!" someone yells deliriously. The back door is thrown open and members of Kudzu push their way out. Bo, Tomm, Henny, Gem, Kissy, even Carlos, who bounds across the yard, barking joyfully.

"Bo!" Ling screams, sprinting toward him. She falls into his arms and begins sobbing uncontrollably. He holds her tight, and he's crying too, kissing her wet cheeks over and over again.

"Achilles! Naz!" Everyone is shouting at once, crying, screaming, hugging. Even Naz is shaking as Gem and Kissy throw themselves on her. They kiss her cheeks and cradle the nub of her arm. "Your arm. They took your arm," Gem is gasping, "but they didn't take *you.*"

I lock eyes with Henny. Wordlessly, she opens her arms, eyes shining with tears. I fall into them, and she wraps me up in a huge hug. I'm crying too, out of exhaustion and relief, and also from sadness. There are two people missing from this reunion: Lana and—

"Benji?" Tomm asks, looking around wildly. "Where's Benji?"

Ling shakes her head slowly, wiping her cheek with the back of her hand. "He didn't make it. He just . . . He didn't make it."

With this, the questions start. Where have we been? What happened to us? Did we get the mirror matter? Did we destroy Aevum? And, of course: "Who are you?" Gem calls to Hunter, who has been standing off to the side a little awkwardly.

I gesture for Hunter to come closer to me. He stays where he is, uncertainty written all over his face.

"It's okay," I tell him. "They won't bite." I reach out my hand. He comes forward to take it, slowly. As soon as our fingertips touch, a flurry of electric shocks scoot up my arm and I have to stop myself from drawing in a breath. I give his hand a reassuring squeeze. He squeezes back. Then I turn to face Kudzu. My words are slow and measured. "This is Hunter. He is Aevum."

There's a long pause as everyone stares silently at us both. Kissy points at our fingers. "Are you guys...together?"

Hunter replies without pause, "Yes."

Which is at the exact same time I exclaim, "No!" I drop his hand immediately. It hadn't properly registered we were holding hands the way couples do.

"No," Hunter corrects himself, taking in my expression. "No. We don't even like each other."

Longing for the day when his ability to read social cues becomes a little more sophisticated, I shoot Ling a confused look. As Bo pecks soft kisses on her cheeks, she frowns at me as if to say, "Be open to it."

"We...like each other," I tell everyone. I instinctively want to add "but we're just friends," but I stop myself. I glance at Hunter, who's looking at me with equal parts expectation and confusion. I grab his hand and pull us out of the weight of Kudzu's collective stare, my cheeks burning red.

Leaving Naz, Ling, and Achilles to explain our entire unwieldy adventure, I drag Hunter behind Naz's weapons shed, mirror matter in hand. After keeping it in the sun all afternoon, I'm disappointed to see the tube is still only three-quarters full. "Here," I say, handing it to him. "The sun's down. You may as well keep this."

He takes it from me, looking a little apprehensive.

"What?" I ask nervously. "Are you worried there's not enough?"

"No," he says softly. "I just—" He breaks off, unable to meet my eyes.

"What?" I repeat insistently. "Hunter, there's a lot of really crazy stuff going down right now, and worried looks aren't helping me stay calm."

He raises his eyes to mine, thick eyebrows drawn together in consternation. "Are you sure you really want to see?" he asks. "How it... goes in?"

"Of course I do," I say eagerly. "How does it work?"

Relief and pleasure chase each other across his face before he swivels away from me. His fingers find a small mole, a few inches below the bottom of his hairline. "Here," he says. "Can you feel that?"

My fingers replace his, and I'm surprised to feel the mole is hard, like a bead. "I can feel it," I say.

"Press it. Hard."

I do. A circle of skin a little bigger than the size of the mirror matter tube flips down neatly. I squeak in surprise, than lean forward to get a better look. There's a hole in Hunter's head, a slanting space for the tube of mirror matter. Through the opening, I glimpse silver machinery, sleek and gleaming, and little lights blinking. Blue blood bubbles in clear tubes. It's everything I saw in Abel's basement lab come to life. I never got to see inside Magnus's head like this. "That is so cool," I say, giddy with excitement. "That's a singularix! That's your singularix!"

"Has anyone ever told you," Hunter muses as I continue to stare openmouthed in fascination, "that you're not like other girls?"

"Yeah, you, all the time," I reply, my skin tickling with delight as I see another slosh of blue blood race up a tube. "I'm an algorithm, apparently. Want me to put this in?"

"Are you sure you want to?"

In reply, I raise the tube of mirror matter to the opening and begin inserting it as gently as I can. It's no more than an inch in when I feel a slight pressure. The tube is sucked from my fingers, disappearing inside. The flap of skin rotates back in place, and suddenly the hole is gone. I can just make out the thin circle of its edge, but it's no thicker than a piece of hair, and you'd have to really be looking for it to see.

Hunter turns back around to see me grinning like an idiot. "You liked that," he observes, eyes shining.

I nod enthusiastically. "I did."

The air around us is warm with the memory of sun. Hunter stares down at me, a funny little half-smile on his mouth, and cocks his head to one side. The sight of it makes my heart leap like a gazelle and a little noise escapes my throat; I am thoroughly and completely *undone* by the gesture. It's all I can do to resist throwing myself at him, hungry to feel those soft, dark pink lips press against mine. But instead I make myself say, "We need to get back to the others."

He nods, looking disappointed. "Lead the way."

"I always do." I smirk at him, which becomes a laugh as he rolls his eyes at me. *I taught him how to do that*, I think proudly.

Ling has called an immediate meeting, so we all jostle into the front room. Hunter and I take the last two seats, which I realize with a sharp pang are Benji and Lana's. Ling runs over the plan we'd invented in the buzzcar, and announces the first point of order is procuring the blue scratch. We decide that Hunter will fly me to Izzy's in the buzzcar we stole from the Three Towers. A floater would take too long and I can't fly—I'd left for the Badlands before I was old enough to learn.

"Be as quick as you can," Ling emphasizes. "We're running out of time."

Ling turns to address Gem and Kissy brusquely. "You guys will need to make some modifications to the Kudzu stream. Explain what Project Aevum was, and change the stuff about artilects being so dangerous. Work with Hunter." The sisters nod, glancing at Hunter a little nervously. "Right," Ling continues. "Explosives. I need Bo, Achilles, and Naz. And I'll need maps!" As I appear to be dismissed, I leave the others and steal five minutes to bathe in Moon Lake.

It's with wild joy that I ease myself out of what I'm wearing: the white hospital shorts and shirt I woke up wearing in Gyan's quarters. They are stained in shades of brown, yellow, and red: an artist's canvas of filth and pain.

I wade into the river naked, cupping clear water to splash my face and arms. Soon I'm deep enough to duck under. Emerging for breath, I sigh with happiness. The water is cool and clean. The lake is still but not silent. Birds call from the trees surrounding the edges, keening and plaintive. In the distance I hear soft splashes: fish jumping or herons landing.

As I swim, I rub at the dirt on my skin, watching it disappear. The stitches in the cut on my forehead and at the back of my head have finally dissolved, leaving two ragged scars. After a few minutes, I head back to the shore. I dry myself with a thin cotton towel and change into a simple khaki top and pair of blue-gray pants Henny found for me. The pants are a little long. With a start, I realize why. These are Lana's clothes.

A flood of memories whirls around me: Lana and Benji lighting up whenever I arrived at Milkwood, cheering me on as I took the obstacle course. Lana roping into Simutech, quick as a spider monkey. Benji helping me to do the same. Lana grabbing my hand as I slipped on the glass. Lana, eyes wide, being held by the Quicks. Her body crumpling to the ground.

My breath stumbles in my throat. Tears prick my eyes.

"Tess?"

I spin around to see Hunter standing at the entrance of the path back to Milkwood. He's changed his clothes too, now in a black T-shirt and pants. "They sent me to find you. You have to leave now to meet the buzzcar. Ling doesn't want it landing anywhere near here."

A tear runs down my face, and I swipe it away quickly. "I'm coming," I call unsteadily.

Hunter lopes through the grass. "What's wrong?"

Another tear rolls down my cheek. "You're very hard to hide things from," I chide him shakily.

He studies my face with bewildered anxiety. "I want to understand you," he says plaintively. "I care about you."

He says this with a sincerity that reminds me of Benji and Lana. I bury my face in the towel and start to cry.

"Tess?" Hunter sounds pleading and agitated. "What can I do?"

I lift my head from the towel. "You can hold me."

He reaches over and grasps one forearm firmly. "Like this?" he asks hopefully.

Now I'm laughing and crying at the same time. "No, silly," I tell him between hiccups. "Like this."

I drop the towel and wrap my arms around his neck, pulling myself close. His arms move across my back, stiffly at first, then softening into a hug. I close my eyes and rest one cheek against his shirt. I want to stand like this forever, holding the boy I care about, even if he's not technically a boy.

But I know I can't. Because now I have to convince Izzy to risk being banished to help me.

When I leave Milkwood, it looks as if someone has turned it upside down and shaken everything out. Half-packed boxes of clothes and gear and food are strewn around the backyard. Everyone's scurrying, planning, trying not to panic.

A while later, I'm flying over the twinkling lights of Eden alone. Except I'm not alone. Hunter's voice comes through the comm fitted snugly in my ear while he simultaneously flies the little buzzcar we've commandeered. I run my fingers over the blinking controls, wishing I could touch Hunter himself. But I am touching him. Sort of. He's *in* the car. He's inside its insides. It feels surreally intimate to know that part of what makes him alive is flying me now, in the power that surges beneath my fingers.

"I don't understand how you can fly without seeing," I say, pressing the black comm into my ear.

"But I can see," he says, his voice tinny and distant. "There's vision inside and outside your car."

"So, you can see me too?" I ask, wiggling my fingers in the air.

"Yes. You're doing something very strange with your hands. Ah," he continues, as I hold up my middle finger. "And now you're doing something rude with them."

I grin and settle back, letting the familiar sensation of flying relax me for a few moments. Then I ask, "What's it like?"

"What's what like?"

"How you see things." I gesture out to the traffic zipping around us. "Like the buzzcars. What's it like seeing everything like you can?"

There's a pause and for a moment I think I've lost him. Then I hear him say, "It's like...It's like the traffic is one living organism; incredibly complex but also beautifully simple. And I'm right in the center of it. I'm part of it, but also outside it at the same time."

I close my eyes to chew this over, wishing—not for the first time—that I could see things that way. Be in the streams all the time, have every piece of knowledge at my fingertips.

Suddenly I notice that Hunter's taking me the wrong way, heading toward Charity instead of straight over the Hive. "Hey," I demand. "Why are we—"

"They're checking cars ahead," he replies.

"What?" I peer out into the mess of jerking lights. Far up ahead, there's a blob of flashing blue hovering at the entrance to the loop we should be taking, stopping every buzzcar momentarily and consequently causing a long traffic jam. Guiders.

"Don't worry," he says. "I can get you there safely. We just won't have as much time."

My nerves are on high alert, but I'm not going to work myself into a panic. I try to think of something to distract myself. "My chip," I say. "Do you know what it is? How it works?"

"It's a silicon chip," Hunter replies. "When activated it sends false messages of pain to your thalamus, which is then relayed to the parietal lobe, the limbic system, and the cerebral cortex."

I shiver, running my fingers over the long cut at top of my spinal column. "I hate it. And not just because it opens a can of whoop-ass on me. I just can't believe they did something so dangerous. It's my *brain*."

"Neural circuitry isn't particularly dangerous," Hunter muses. "Doctors use the same principle to treat various degenerative disorders—"

"Hunter," I interrupt, "I have a chip *in my head*. Right now I want sympathy, not a science lesson."

"Understood," he says, sounding pleased. "I am sorry this happened to you, Tess."

He sounds so formal and obedient that it doesn't sound like real sympathy at all. I shake my head, a confused smile on my face.

"What?" he asks. "That was sympathy, correct?"

"Yeah, but you have to mean it," I say.

There's a long pause on the other end of the comm. "I am beginning to think," he says slowly, "that escaping the Trust will not be the most complicated task I am to undertake."

"Oh yeah? What is?"

"Understanding you," he replies sincerely.

It's another half hour before we're flying low over the South Hills, making us well and truly late. As we begin our vertical descent to Izzy's street, sad, sweet nostalgia twists inside me. Summervale Drive, with its grand glass-and-steel houses, hosts a thousand memories of hot summer days and long summer nights.

"I'll be back as soon as I can," I tell Hunter after we land. "I'm going to switch the comm off now." Having Hunter listen in would be needlessly distracting.

"Okay," he replies. "Good luck."

I switch off the comm and climb out. The door closes behind me, like a wing folding back down. The insides of the car go dark.

Izzy's street is empty except for a distant figure walking a dog. Parked buzzcars catch silver light in their windshields from a bleached white moon.

The lights are all on in Izzy's home. I don't ring the doorbell in case her parents should answer. Instead, I climb over a side gate and steal down a narrow stretch of grass along the right side of her house. Like most of the houses here, Izzy's front door is level with the street, with the rest of the house stretching out on top of tall poles that prop it up level on the sloping hillside. Izzy's bedroom is toward the back of the house—toward the killer view. I can see her bedroom window about twenty feet above me.

I find some pebbles and start throwing them lightly at the window. The first one misses. So does the second. I curse under my breath, and take careful aim with the third. This stone strikes directly in the center of her window, cracking it soundly into a spiderweb of jagged lines.

Izzy's head appears at the window, face screwed into anger. "What the f—" But she stops short, squinting down at me the darkness. "Tess? Is that you?"

"Shhh!" I put one finger to my lips, then point to the front door. "Let me in. Don't tell your parents."

Without giving her a chance to argue, I run back toward the front door.

I hover at the side of the house, waiting. A minute later, light spills from inside. Izzy creeps out onto the porch. "Tess?" she whispers.

I stay half hidden in shadows. "It's me. Are your parents home?"

She nods, looking stunned. "Yeah, they're in the lounge. What's going on? Where have you been?"

"Can you sneak me into your room?"

She hesitates, glancing back inside.

"Please?" I say. "It's important."

"I guess," she says, jiggling from one foot to the other. "But I'm not alone."

Of course. It was naive of me to assume that. "Can you get rid of them? And turn off anything on-cycle?"

Izzy squints at me in disbelief. I know I'm being beyond a bad friend, but I don't know what else to do. She exhales noisily. "Wait here. You so owe me."

Another minute passes before the door opens again. I'm almost looking forward to seeing what poor dope Izzy has wrapped around her little finger this week, but when I do I almost yell out in surprise.

"Joey Lucas," Izzy purrs at the boy in the doorway. "What can I say? You just know how to tire a girl out."

"It's not even nine," Joey mutters sourly, all slouchy disappointment. He's sprayed with acne and wears pants five sizes too big for him. That was the boy I let be my first kiss? Fail times a million.

"Need my beauty sleep." Izzy pouts, reaching up to kiss him on the mouth. She lets her lips linger for an excruciatingly long moment, which I can't help feeling is to make me jealous. It doesn't work. "See you at education," she says when they're finished.

"Yeah, whatever." He sighs, then lopes up the drive.

As soon as he's gone, Izzy gestures at me furiously. "This better be good," she hisses. But when I emerge fully from the shadows, her face transforms from irritation into alarmed concern. Her gaze travels around my bald head, my scars, and the many bruises that paint my skin in lurid yellow and purplish blue. "What happened? Who did this to you?"

I wave at her to be quiet, and point inside.

In her always messy bedroom, a single lamp sets a seductive mood. Rose perfume hangs in the air, a telltale hookup sign. I couldn't count the nights we'd spent in here, tucked into furry blankets and scarfing down butterscotch ice cream until we both felt sick. Part of me aches to curl into those soft blankets right now and drift into the sleep that I so badly need. But I'm already late.

Izzy brushes her fingertips against the scar on my forehead.

"I'm fine, really." I take a deep breath. "I need a favor. Sort of a big one."

Something flickers behind her eyes. "A favor?"

If I had more time, I'd ease into this more delicately. "I need your father's scratch." I say this as simply as if I was asking for one of his shirts. "His Guider's scratch."

Izzy's eyes pop out at me. "Right," she says with a laugh. "And I need an unlimited Pleasure Allowance and a swimming pool full of chocolate."

"I'm not kidding," I tell her. "Can you help me?"

An uncomprehending expression fights its way onto Izzy's face. Her huge, round eyes lose their softness. "I'm sorry," she says slowly. "I don't think I'm getting this." She clears her throat, eyes now steely. "You disappear for a year. Then you come back, only to disappear *again*, then you reappear, finally, but you don't want to see me, you don't want to hang out with me, you just need a *favor*?" She starts pacing before me. "A favor, I might add, that's against the law and could get me kicked out of Eden *for good*." She stops to stand directly in front of me, both hands planted on her hips. "Is that right? Am I reading this situation correctly?"

There's something undeniably adorable about Izzy, five feet two of nothing but cute, standing in the middle of her girlish bedroom with a narrowed-eye expression of pure fury. But to point that out now would not be a wise move. She is monumentally pissed. "Yeah," I say feebly. "That's about it."

"Ten years of friendship, Tess. *Ten years*. For Gyan's sake, does that mean nothing to you?" Her voice cracks, making her words sound more than a plea than an accusation. "Do I mean nothing to you?"

"No! Of course not," I argue. "You mean a lot to me. That's why I'm here, because I know I can trust you."

"What's it for? What do you need it for?"

I open my mouth but no words come out.

"You can't tell me," she concludes, almost smugly. "So, you show up out of the blue not to see how the hell I'm doing without my best friend in the whole world, but to *use* me, and you don't even have the balls to tell me why? Wow." She laughs coldly. "Way to trust me, Tess."

"I can't tell you because I'm protecting you," I tell her urgently. I'm out of time. "Look, remember how I said I wanted to 'do something about it'? 'It' being...the unfairness of the world? Well, I'm doing it. But I need your help. And yes, the way I'm asking totally sucks, and yes, I am a bad friend. But please, please trust me when I say I'm only asking because I have to." I take a step toward her. "If you've ever felt anything for me, please—can you get me your dad's scratch?"

Izzy draws in a deep breath through her nose, then exhales. She takes a half step toward me. I can feel her breath, hot and sweet, as she smiles up at me. Then the smile becomes a snarl. "I would rather die than help you, Tessendra." She pronounces my name as if it is venom, black and toxic. "I. Hate. You."

I reel back, feeling like she'd slapped me. Izzy stares at me unflinchingly, mouth set in a hard line, eyes as cold as stones.

Blindly I reach for her doorknob, willing myself not to cry. I open the door quietly and check that the coast is clear before turning back to her. She's still standing frozen in the middle of her room, watching me with a complicated expression that could be victory or could be anguish. "Well, I love you, Izzadore," I tell her honestly. "And I always will."

The night air is a welcome relief to my burning skin. I place both palms on the exterior of the buzzcar and try to calm myself down. I'll just have to be professional. I'll just have to get back to Milkwood and tell them the mission's off. I imagine Ling's face when I tell her we have to flee Eden not as heroes, but as victims. Because of me.

I pop the door open and find the comm where I left it on the dash. Gritting my teeth, I slip it back in my ear and switch it on.

"Hey," I say. "I'm back."

Instantly, the car's displays and lights come alive. "Hi." Hunter sounds surprised and unusually eager. "How did it go?"

I drop my face into my hands. My voice is muffled in my fingers. "I didn't get it."

"What? I can't hear you."

I lift my head, feeling dull and beaten. "I didn't get the scratch."

"Oh." There's a long, painful pause. "Oh."

"I'm sorry," I whisper. "I bet you're all ready to go by now."

"Yes," he replies. "We're waiting for you."

I squeeze my eyes shut. "Just get me home, okay? Just get me—"

A sharp rap of knuckles on glass interrupts me. Twisting in my seat, I see Izzy outside the buzzcar. I pop the door open in disbelief.

"Izzy—" I start, surprised. She's clutching her dad's blue scratch.

"Here." Izzy presses the roll of scratch into my hands. Her face is flushed. "I love you too, Tess."

I'm so stunned I can't say anything more than, "What?"

She smiles, her face happy and alive. "I said, 'I love you too.' "

"Thank you," I manage. "Izzy, thank you so much."

She kisses me softly on the cheek. "Be safe," she whispers. And with that, she turns and runs lightly back down her drive.

chapter 21

The buzzcar darts up so fast that I have to grab the dash to steady myself.

"Sorry," Hunter says. "We have to hurry."

"Did she get it?" Ling's voice echoes through the comm, sounding like she's standing behind Hunter.

"Yes," Hunter tells her. "I'm bringing her back now."

"Do you want me to open it now?" I ask. "The scratch?"

"No," Hunter says. "It'll be faster for me to do it back here."

"Bring her straight back to Milkwood," I hear Ling say. "We'll leave as soon as we can for the dam."

"What about the Trust?" I ask. "We could lead them right to us."

"We'll just have to risk it," she replies tensely. "We're out of time."

The buzzcar descends neatly in the fields beyond the veggie garden. As soon as it does, I'm out of the car and running through grass that shimmers silver in the moonlight. Instantly, I'm back in Benji and Lana's obstacle course, racing through the woods like a nymph. But I don't feel sad at the memory. I feel alive.

A lone figure waves from the back steps. It's Ling.

I burst into the backyard. The half-packed bags and boxes are all gone. All that's left are four backpacks lined up against the back of the house.

I catch sight of Naz and Bo near the weapons shed. They're crouching intently over some thick red circular things, no bigger than dinner plates. Bombs? Relief flits across their faces at the sight of me.

"Meeting room!" Ling flings the back door open, and I half run, half stumble inside. We barrel through the bare bedroom, past a stripped kitchen, and into the front room. Most of the equipment is gone. The rest of it is in the process of being packed.

Hunter springs to his feet when he sees me. I try to catch his eye but he's looking at the scratch in my hand. Panting, I hold it out. Achilles pops his head up from behind one of the desks, a screwdriver in his mouth. It clatters to the ground when he sees Hunter about to smooth open the bright blue scratch.

I've never seen anyone use official scratch before, and from the rapt looks on Ling's and Achilles' faces, I don't think they have either. With swift, careful movements, Hunter unrolls the scratch and presses his thumb and forefinger into the corner. It glows a gorgeous sapphire blue. A holo of a Trust logo bursts out, glittering like diamonds. It's surprisingly lovely, spinning grandly in the near-empty room. I'm about to ask what exactly we'll see when the logo disappears and a strange wall of patchy color replaces it. It's not a stream—at least not anything I'm familiar with. I glance at Hunter and am stopped short by the sight of his eyes. They are moving so fast that they're quivering, they're *blurring* beneath his lids. I'm about to nudge Ling, but before I can, the wall of color vanishes. Hunter has folded the blue scratch closed.

"What just happened?" Ling asks in confusion. "Didn't it work?"

"I'm finished," Hunter announces. "I looked through everything, and—"

"You looked through everything, just then?" Achilles' voice shoots high in disbelief. "It didn't even take a second!"

Realization hits: the wall of color was the entire scratch, moving too quickly for us to make sense of. I ask, "Was it all there?"

Hunter lifts his eyes to mine reluctantly. "No. I'm sorry. I thought it would be there. I was wrong."

I'm momentarily paralyzed. I am literally unable to comprehend what he just said.

"Wait." Ling throws her hands up. "What do you mean you don't have it?"

"It wasn't there," Hunter repeats. "It must be restricted."

"Restricted," repeats Achilles softly, sinking into one of the empty chairs that circle the table.

"Then we're screwed!" exclaims Ling.

"Who's screwed?" Naz appears at the end of the hall, Bo right behind her.

"We are," Ling tells her. "The RPA wasn't in the Guider's scratch."

"What the hell?" Naz thumps the doorframe in anger. "The robot said it'd be there!"

The word *robot* sets off Ling, Achilles, Bo, and even Hunter. Everyone is yelling at each other.

"Hey. Hey! *Hey!*" I shout over the din. Everyone stops arguing and looks at me. I suddenly feel extremely parental, glowering at them all angrily, my hands on my hips. "Look, we're tired and we're stressed. But we're still a team. There must be another way we can get it."

For a second, I think Ling is going to bat an insult back at me, but instead she exhales slowly and joins Achilles and Hunter at the table. Naz and Bo follow suit.

"Okay," I say, turning to Hunter. I'm trying to be as professional as I can. I'm trying not to look too intently into his eyes. "Where else is the RPA stored?"

Lines crease his forehead. "I could extract it from a Quick physically, with the right equipment."

"We can't get close to one without you serfing it," Ling huffs. "What else you got?"

"Simutech designed the Quicks," Hunter muses. "It's probably in the official schematics that are kept there."

The humans at the table trade glances. Another impossibility. "They're there," I confirm. "But going back to Simutech for a third time—"

"Is a bloodbath no one wants a ticket to," Achilles finishes. "Plus, we wouldn't have time to get there and back, *and* blow up the dam, *and* cross the border at dawn."

"How do you know they're there?" Hunter asks me.

"I saw them last year," I say. "But I barely remember what they looked like then, let alone—"

"You saw the schematics," Hunter interrupts. He's suddenly alert and alive, like a cat who's spotted prey. "You remember seeing them?"

"Yes," I say slowly, "but you can't expect me to remember an algorithm. I'm not like you. I barely remember what happened last week."

"No, I don't expect that." Hunter's eyes haven't left mine.

"What?" I ask, suddenly infused with hope.

His eyes flick fast around the table. All five of us are leaning toward him, expectantly. The seconds of silence feel like years.

"Hunter!" Ling explodes. "Tell us!"

"No," he says, shoulders sagging. "It's nothing."

"What was it?" I demand.

"It's nothing," he says firmly. "It's too much to ask."

"I don't know if you've noticed," I tell him dryly, "but I have more bruises than hair right now. And I would love to even the score with my hairdresser from hell." I raise both eyebrows at him deliberately. "*What's* too much to ask?"

Hunter rubs his chin in a familiar wide-eyed expression of alarm. "Achilles," he says eventually, in a way that sounds almost painful, "do you have something that would work as a conductor? Anything that could transmit energy?"

Achilles nods. "Sure do."

Hunter turns back to me. "Human memory is imperfect, often a mix of actual and imagined realities. You're positive you saw the schematics for Quicks?"

"Yes," I say, a little hotly. "Why?"

"Do you remember how I told you that your chip sends messages to your thalamus?"

I nod.

"That's near the hippocampus and the amalgams, which control memory. You might not be able to remember seeing the RPA," he continues, "but, using that chip, I can."

I shake my head in confusion. "You can find that memory? You can *see* it?"

"That is so awesome!" exclaims Achilles, but Hunter shushes him with a pointed glance.

"I can make a copy of your memories and download them into me," Hunter says. "If you saw the schematic, and I see what you saw, then we have the RPA."

"And just that memory, right?" I clarify. "Just that minute?" That doesn't sound too bad. In fact, this actually sounds like a solution.

Hunter shakes his head. "That's why it's too much to ask," he says. "I can only do it by copying all of your memories, Tess."

No one says anything. My blood turns to ice. All of my memories? Everything that's ever happened to me?

Achilles whistles, long and low. "That would be embarrassing," he says. "For me. I'm sure your memories are all—"

I shut him up with a scowl. I can hear my heart thudding in my ears. "I can't do that," I mumble sourly. "I just can't."

"I know," Hunter says. "I told you. I shouldn't have suggested it."

I can feel Kudzu watching me. Willing me to agree. Tension claws its way around the table. The idea is insane. I can't show Hunter everything about me. Every time I cried myself to sleep or went to the bathroom in a Badlands "toilet."

Everything I did with Magnus.

Ling rises to her feet, voice awkward. "We're all just going to..."

"You can't expect me to do this!" I cry.

Ling lifts her hands in quick surrender. "I don't. Tess, I really don't. We're just going to give you guys some space." She glares at the others, who get hurriedly to their feet.

"I'd do it," I hear Naz say with a sniff, as they head to the backyard.

I raise my eyes to Hunter. He's watching me carefully, waiting to take my cue.

"Would you do it?" I ask. "Would you let me see everything you've done?"

He doesn't even hesitate. "Yes. But that doesn't matter."

Somehow, it does. I kick my chair out from under me and get to my feet. I need to move. I run my fingers over the prickly hair that covers my skull. Somewhere, deep in its squishy, wet insides, holds the key to saving the lives of hundreds of thousands of starving Badlanders. I half groan, half cry. "It's just, you'd see everything!" My voice is shaking. "You'd see it all."

"What scares you the most?"

I close my eyes. I breathe. "Magnus," I say. "And my mom."

"You've already told me. You were lovers—"

"But you'd *see* it!" I cry. "You'd see us together. You'd see what we did, what I made him do. You'd see my mom die and you'd see—" My throat is hot and scratchy. *Don't cry. Do not cry.* "You'd see it was my fault."

"Tess." Hunter comes toward me but I stop him with an outstretched hand. "Tess. What happened to your mom wasn't your fault. It wasn't Magnus's fault and it wasn't Simutech's fault."

"So it was her fault?" I snap.

"No!" he exclaims. "No, it was no one's fault. No one was to blame." His voice sounds calm and slow and kind. "It was an accident. It was awful and tragic, but it was just an accident. And I never knew your mom, but I'm certain she wouldn't want you to continue punishing yourself for it."

I stare at Hunter, who's looking back at me expectantly. "No," I say faintly. "She wouldn't."

"You said it yourself," he says softly. "What's done is done. You can't change the past. You just can't make the same mistake again."

I sink back into one of the chairs. He sits down next to me and I reach over and take his hand. Our fingers thread easily, almost automatically. I press our hands into my cheek for a long moment. Then I let his fingers go. "My mom always said," I say cautiously, "that artilects could save the world. I mean, it was hyperbole, but she meant it. And I always thought"—I look at him—"that it was something *you* would do. Alone. I never thought..." I exhale heavily. "I never thought it would involve a person."

"And you never thought that person would be you," he adds sagely. I smile feebly. "No. But it is. Isn't it? It's me."

He nods. "It appears so."

I sit up straight and swallow hard. "How long would it take?"

His eyes widen a bit before he answers, "Twenty seconds. Not even."

I get to my feet. "Will it hurt?"

He rises too. "No."

"But you..." I stumble. "You, wouldn't feel any differently..." I pause, shaking my head. "I can't ask you that. You have no idea how you'll feel after walking down my memory lane."

His lips melt into a smile. "I do know. I know already." Hunter raises his hand and traces one finger lightly down my jawbone. "There is nothing I could find out about you, that would change how I feel."

I'm about to turn in the direction of the backyard. "Just be careful with me," I tell him. "Afterward."

"Of course," Hunter says. "Of course I will."

When Hunter presses a smooth, coin-sized piece of metal against each of my temples, all feelings of impishness vanish. I'm sitting at the tech table, attended to by Achilles and Hunter. I'm trying to stay calm, but I can taste bitter adrenaline in my mouth. It races maniacally around my insides like a caffeine overload. Naz, Bo, and Ling watch from the far side of the room with the fascinated, horrified expressions of people about to see open-heart surgery for the first time. The cool metal headpiece that presses into my temples is the conductor Hunter asked Achilles to bring. More wires are affixed to the inside of my wrists and the pulse point in my neck.

"Where do these wires go?" I ask, holding up the ends of what's attached to me.

In response, Hunter's fingers find the invisible button that opens the back of his head. Again, the flap of skin flips open neatly. Achilles swears, joyous. Hunter pops the mirror matter out. It slides out neatly, and he hands it to me.

I snatch the sparkling tube in alarm. "It's less than half full!" Flying me to Izzy's used more power than I'd anticipated. "Are you sure you have enough to do all this? You can't recharge until after we blow up the dam."

"It's okay," Hunter reassures me. "Don't worry about it."

Hunter gives the ends of the wires to Achilles and directs his excited assistant to attach them to various ports inside the circular gap the mirror matter fits into. He's talking to us both, explaining how the electrical surges send my memories to his singularix, but I can't concentrate. I'm about to show someone everything about me. Every embarrassing moment, every cruel act, every flaw, every fault. Every secret. Everything.

Suddenly I'm seized by the urge to rip the conductors from my temples and flee into the inky night. My eyes pull to Hunter's, panicked beneath a cool exterior. As if reading my mind, he stops his science babble and we share a moment of loaded eye contact. Without saying anything, he calms me down. I know what he is thinking: *You don't have to do this. I won't judge you. I care about you.* And just like that, my fear is back in check. I don't even think the rest of Kudzu noticed.

"Okay." Hunter sits down across from me. "Just relax, Tess."

I try to obey. My palms are drenched with sweat. I let go of the mirror matter, letting it rest on the table. I'm afraid of clutching it too hard once we start, and breaking it. "This is safe, right? You're not going to wipe me clean or anything?"

He shakes his head and smiles. "Worst-case scenario is it just doesn't work. Are you ready?"

It takes a second, but then I nod.

"Okay. Close your eyes."

I do. The cool metal of the conductor starts to feel tepid. In fact, my entire head starts to feel warm, like I'm standing in the sun. I open my eyes. Hunter's gaze has turned inward, his eyes no longer seeing. Strange twitches jerk his face and arms. I flinch as his body spasms, seemingly beyond his control. The conductor changes from warm to hot, searing my skin. My nails cut into my palms.

Hunter starts speaking. But it isn't his voice. It's a little girl's. "Mommy! I want it!" I flick my eyes to Achilles in alarm, but Achilles isn't looking at me, he's staring at Hunter, open mouthed. Seconds later, the girl's voice is older and less babyish. "But why?" The voice keeps aging, and I know, of course, that it is my voice. Now Hunter sounds about ten, and extraordinarily petulant. "Pink. Izzy said it had to be pink!" A peal of laughter becomes a pained cry. "All you talk about is Magnus!" I recognize the voice as my age now. Hunter screams, "Mom!" and I jump, with a sharp cry. *"Da, danke bolshoi."* I sound guarded now, speaking with vigilance. Then words I remember quite clearly, recent words that run into each other without stopping: "How did you get my DNA he told me himself he'd quit Simutech it's so *beautiful* his name's Hunter we have to go back you've got three seconds to decide I think I want to kiss you too!"

The conductor's temperature starts dropping from hot back to cool. I let out a breath I hadn't realized I was holding. Slowly, Hunter's eyes start to come into focus, as if he is waking up from open-eyed sleep. I'm staring at him. Frozen. He blinks, once, twice, and raises his hand to rub his eyes. He's back. And he has my sixteen years of life with him.

Naz's drawl startles me—I'd forgotten the others were here. "Well, that's the freakiest thing I've ever seen."

"Did it work?" Ling asks.

Hunter's hand drops back to the table. He hesitates, just for a split second, then says, "Yes. I have the RPA."

"You have it?" Bo repeats.

"You're kidding!" gasps Ling. "No way!"

"I can serf the Quicks," Hunter confirms.

Achilles, Naz, Bo, and Ling explode with victory, their shouts and cries filling the small room. But I'm silent. Something's wrong. Hunter isn't meeting my eyes. I lean forward through the mess of wires and grab his hand. It feels stiff and unyielding. "Hunter, what's wrong?"

He shakes his head, voice low. "Nothing."

"You look like you've seen a ghost," I say, trying not to sound worried. "That pink phase was pretty unfortunate, right?"

His eyes finally rise to meet mine. In them is distance. Caution. Regret. He takes his hand out of mine, as unemotionally as if he were taking back a piece of scratch. "Let's get ready to go."

My blood curdles in my veins. It's *my* worst-case scenario: Hunter's seen the real me, and he didn't like it.

He slips the conductor from my temples, which are now burning again. But not from the metal, which has turned ice cold.

When Ling suggests I practice fast-roping while the others finish packing, I do it without question. I am focused and efficient. But I'm faking it. In reality, I'm a mess. Hunter saw something in my memories that he didn't like. Was it Magnus? The feeling of my warm lips on his cool ones? Was it something to do with Izzy? My mom? How could I have been so stupid as to let someone in like that? It's more than anyone, human or otherwise, can handle.

As I scamper up and down Benji and Lana's thick old rope, I watch Hunter carry the four bulky backpacks to the buzzcar. His tall, slender frame moves with a sharp gracefulness through the darkened backyard, illuminated only by the light spilling from inside. But he doesn't look at me.

Because Naz can't rope down with only one arm, she won't be coming with us. Instead, Ling, Bo, and I will set the bombs on the dam wall, while Achilles and Hunter run security and tech. After we leave, Naz will run one final check of Milkwood before abandoning it for good. Then she'll meet up with the rest of Kudzu, who are already on their way to the Northern Bridge border crossing. If all goes according to plan, we'll meet them a few miles from the crossing before dawn. I'm disappointed to hear we're leaving Naz behind, a decision that was made while I was on my way to the South Hills. "Don't worry, Rockwood." She smirks, handing me half a dozen air rifles. "You'll have plenty of time to piss me off when we're out in the Badlands."

"Good," I say. Having Naz by my side definitely makes me feel safer.

She looks a little thrown by my reply, and then her eyes widen. "Almost forgot." She shoves her hand into her pocket and pulls something out. It's a Kudzu necklace. The little silver K on the bright red string. "Henny said to give you this."

I rest the air rifle butts on the ground so I can tie it around my neck. "Thank you," I say, looking her right in the eye. "For everything."

She responds by brusquely clearing her throat. "You're all right, Rockwood."

"You're pretty badass yourself." I smile. "You know—for a chick with one arm."

She's startled for a second, then her face relaxes and she actually chuckles. "Go put the rifles in the car before I show you how a chick with one arm fights."

Ten minutes later, our little buzzcar is packed and ready to go. The backpacks belong to Ling, Achilles, Bo, and, surprisingly, me. "Gem packed it," Ling explains. "Otherwise you'd be leaving with nothing." We also have all of Benji and Lana's roping equipment, a duffel bag of protective gear, the air rifles, some razers, and nine handmade explosives.

Ling's in the driver's seat to save Hunter's strength, although he'll still have to use his power to keep the car off-cycle. Bo sits next to her.

Achilles climbs into the backseat. "Guess I should sit in the middle," I say to Hunter as we approach the car. "That way we're together."

"Sit wherever you like." His words are cool and detached, like they were when we first met. "It doesn't make any difference to me."

I forget how to breathe.

As we take off from Milkwood into the jet-black sky, I can just make Naz out, waving goodbye, shouting, "Don't get smoked!"

We fly fast and low, following the silver curve of Moon Lake around to the north. Below us, Eden is dark and indistinct. Even now, jammed next to him with our hips and thighs touching, Hunter and I are apart. I keep screaming at myself, *It does not matter; it is not your focus right now.* But I can't stop thinking about it. My mind scrapes obsessively over my deepest, darkest secrets, wondering which one pushed him away.

We're in the air less than ten minutes before Ling takes us down to the banks of Moon Lake. Unlike the rich black mud that covers the riverbanks at Milkwood, here the water greets the land at a narrow strip of pale yellow sand. The vegetation is less lush. A forest of thin white birch trees only as thick as my arm crowds the shore. We are close to the white city walls—they loom over us, only a stone's throw away. The Three Towers are too far to see, and the handful of buzzcars above the Hive are no more than tiny darting lights.

In my mind's eye, I can see where we are: the northernmost tip of Eden, the only place where the lake just kisses the city walls, or used to, before the dam was built. I assume some kind of Divers built the dam, working from the bottom of the lake up. I picture their weird open mouths sucking out water from around the newly formed dam as it rose from the lake's murky depths like a tombstone.

We leave the backpacks in the car but take everything else. Ling leads the way up a narrow, sandy path through the trees—an animal track. It's quiet and still, somewhere between peaceful and sinister. The ground rises as we jog, and eventually we start to curve around so that we're no longer heading toward the white city walls, but are bending around until the walls are next to us. Finally we come out into a clearing at the bottom of a small hill. The grass rises before us, too steep to see what's on the other side. We all know it's the dam.

"I'm going to use a white-noise frequency to scramble the Quicks' hearing," Hunter says quietly to Ling. "That way they won't hear us. But let's stay out of sight for now. I won't start serfing them until we absolutely have to."

"Good idea," Ling replies. "Everyone, leave the gear here. We'll scope it out, then come back."

We do as she says. Following Ling's lead, we get on our bellies and use our elbows and knees to snake up the hill. When we come to the top, I can see both the dam and the aqueduct.

The entrance to the aqueduct is set in the city walls—a huge, yawning oval hole. At first, the Trust tried to block up the aqueduct itself, but it wasn't structurally sound, so in the end, they built the dam. I remember the size of the dam from seeing it on the streams: one hundred feet high and fifty feet wide. Before the dam was created, the entrance to the aqueduct would not have been visible, as it is set below the water level. But now, water no longer flows through it. The tall, concrete dam stops the lake from entering the aqueduct. This is what we'll be scaling down, and decorating with red bombs.

Ling nudges me and jerks her chin toward the top of the dam. There, it is about ten feet wide. You could walk the length of it easily, with the lake on one side of you and the long drop down on the other. A sturdy waist-high railing runs along both edges of the top of the dam. She's pointing for two reasons. First, because this is obviously where we will tie our ropes in order to scale the dam face and set the bombs. Second, because one hundred and eight Quicks are stationed along it, their red eyes sweeping endlessly back and forth.

Hunter is studying everything carefully. He's chosen to watch from the other side of the group, putting Ling, Bo, and Achilles between us.

Ling snaps her fingers lightly to get my attention, jerking her head to the bottom of the hill. I follow her as we all slither down.

Back in the clearing, Ling nods at the collection of circular red bombs. "Show Tess the merchandise."

Bo hands me one of the bombs, which I accept somewhat gingerly. It's maybe four inches thick with a flat surface on one side and a large handle, like the kind on a suitcase, on the other. "We call these Red Devils," Bo says. "The Devils are armed by a two-phase system. Ling, you, and I will set the first phase." Taking it from me, he lays it flat on the grass with the handle running vertically. He begins explaining how they work, but I'm distracted by Hunter, who's sitting opposite me. How could he pull away like this? His words ring in my ears: "There is nothing I could find out about you that would change how I feel." *Liar.*

"Tess?" Ling hisses. "Are you even listening?"

I snap myself back and try to focus on what Bo's saying. "Sorry. Can you say that again?"

"Twist the handle clockwise so it's horizontal," he says patiently. "Then it'll attach to the wall. I won't do it now, or it'll try to attach to the grass. You must make sure the Devil is perfectly flat against the surface of the dam before you twist the handle. If there are any gaps, it might fall. Once it's attached, the bomb is set."

I nod. Twist the handle. Attach it to the dam. The bomb is set. Got it.

Bo fishes in his pocket and pulls out a slim black box with a counter set to 120 and a small yellow switch. "When all nine bombs are in place, Achilles will activate them with this."

"How long do we have once they're activated?" I ask.

Bo points to the 120 setting. "One hundred and twenty seconds. Two minutes. Once the bombs have been activated, they cannot be switched off." He stresses this last part, then addresses Achilles. "So you must only activate them once we are all off the dam."

Achilles nods, taking the sleek control even more gingerly than I took the bomb. "No trigger finger. Got it."

"Any questions?" Bo asks. "No? Then let's gear up."

I start strapping on the guards I wore at Simutech: knee, shin, and elbow. The climbing gloves feel hot and itchy on my sweaty hands. I hesitate with the mask: our identity is no longer secret, and I don't like losing so much peripheral vision, but the protective helmet still appeals. In the end, I slice away a large hole for my face, leaving the skull intact. Bo helps me loop three Red Devils across my body, secured by a thin chain. When I feel the weight of them, so close to my heart and powerful enough to crack concrete, the adrenaline kicks in for real. My heart rate picks up even more as Bo hands me the rope. I consciously try to slow it down. I can do this. Benji and Lana showed me how.

We rise to stand in the clearing. Ling, Bo, and I are decorated with Red Devils and ropes. Achilles has the control and a stopwatch.

Hunter stands a little away from us.

"Tess?" Ling appears my side, making me jump. "You sure you're up for this?"

I swallow hard and lie. "Of course I am."

Her eyes slide suspiciously between Hunter and me. "Right. Achilles, Bo, and I are going to run a perimeter sweep, make sure there's nothing we haven't planned for. We'll be five minutes." When she turns back to me, her almond-shaped eyes flash deliberately.

I nod in anxious understanding. Their three figures melt into the scrub, leaving Hunter and me alone.

I close my eyes for a long moment to steel myself. The sky is turning a dirty gray, no longer true night, not yet morning. A light breeze carries the soft *splish splish splish* of the lake hitting the top of the dam. Then I say his name. He rotates toward me. "What's going on?"

"Nothing," he replies, voice strained. "Nothing we should talk about now."

"Considering it's my memories that are freaking you out," I snap back, "I'll decide when we talk about them. And I'm saying it's now."

His mouth works with anxiety, but no words come out, his gaze directed far above my head.

"Hunter," I plead, moving toward him. "Talk to me. I can't handle you being like this. Not here, not now."

His eyes drop from the treetops down to mine. "All right," he says at last. "It's just that I don't know if..." He drifts off, looking like he's lost in some terrible thought.

"Hunter." I grasp his shoulders firmly. They are solid and strong beneath my fingers. "Just talk."

When he finally begins speaking, his voice is low and confessional and makes me want to shudder. "You had an aunt. An aunt who died when you were very young."

"Pascuala," I say, dropping my hands. Abel's only partner.

"She died in childbirth. You went to her funeral. One of your first memories of sadness."

"Yes, I suppose so," I say, bewildered.

"Did you know the boy survived?"

"No." I gape. *Abel has a son?*

"For ten days," Hunter clarifies. "Just ten days. You remember some of the conversations the adults were having at the time, but they didn't make any sense to you back then. Seeing them now, it was clear—"

"So what?" I shake my head. "Abel had a son who died. So what?"

Hunter's face as is bleak as death itself. He answers my question as if it physically pains him to do so. "Abel never told me who I was cloned from." His mouth tightens. "Tess, you've seen photograms of Abel when he was my age."

I don't really remember these, but I'll take his word for it. "And?"

"We look exactly the same," Hunter says. "Tess. I think—no, I am sure—I am cloned from Abel's son."

My mind whirls. "Which means... Which means we're cousins?"

"I'm a clone of your cousin," Hunter clarifies quickly. "I am not a human being, so we are not cousins."

"You're a clone of my cousin," I repeat, the words thick and slow in my mouth. The ground seems to undulate beneath my feet, I can't stop myself from saying the word a third time. *"Cousin."*

Hunter studies my face, positively stricken. "I knew it," he says, more to himself than me. "I knew you'd feel this way."

I shake my head, trying to put this in perspective. A clone of my cousin. That's not the same thing as cousin. But it's not nothing.

I look up at Hunter and suddenly I see Abel in his face. The same sharp nose, same piercing eyes. Add some lines and pounds and gray hair and—"Abel," I breathe, horrified, "you look like Abel."

A low, distressed noise sounds from deep in his throat. "I didn't want to tell you," he says anxiously, "until after."

"So you just push me away till then?" I cry.

"I didn't know what to do!" he shouts, then drops his voice tersely. "It's not exactly something they put in the 'Welcome to Being an Artilect' stream."

"There's a welcome stream?" I blink, then realize that Hunter is finally learning sarcasm. "Well, you shouldn't have turned to a block of ice like that. You really scared me."

"I'm sorry," he says intently, taking a step toward me. His eyes are burning, almost emerald. "I just... I just don't know if this changes anything for you. Does it?"

I rake my hands over my sweaty scalp. My face feels like it's on fire. "I don't know," I moan. "I don't know. How can I know?" My hands are trembling. "I'm about to blow up a dam. Hunter, how could you tell me this now?"

"Because you told me to!" he exclaims, flinging both hands toward me in accusation. His cheeks are almost purple and in a flash I realize that's because his blood is blue, not red like mine. He drops his face in his hands and groans with irritation. "How can you handle all these feelings?" His head snaps back up, hands balling into fists. "I'm experiencing a lot of very strange physical urges right now."

"To do what?" I ask, alarmed.

He thinks for a second, lips pressed tight. "Hit something. Not you," he adds quickly. His eyes light up with a realization. "Maybe another boy."

"Hunter, stop turning into a teenage guy," I order him. "That's really not helping right now." I exhale, short and fast. "We have to do this," I continue, gesturing to the three Red Devils that are still strapped to my chest. "We have to make this work."

"Right," he says. "You're right."

"Let's just talk about it afterward, okay?"

"Okay." He nods.

I wrench my thinking back to the bombs, to the dam, to Hunter serfing the Quicks.

"How much mirror matter do you have left?" I ask.

"Enough to serf the Quicks for six minutes," he replies.

"Really?" I'm surprised. "It was half empty at Milkwood. Are you sure?"

He nods. "I am."

Glancing behind me, I see the others returning. "Okay," I say, but I'm worried. I can't get in perspective how much energy Hunter needs to perform certain tasks. Is he lying to protect us?

"Bo had an idea," Ling announces to Hunter as the three of them rejoin us. "Why don't you get the Quicks to set the bombs, instead of us?"

Hunter shakes his head. "They're not dexterous enough to climb the rope."

"What are you going to do with them?" asks Achilles curiously.

"Putting them all to sleep is the only way I can do it with the power I have left," Hunter replies. "But I'll move them to the far side of the dam, to the scrub on the other side of the lake."

"Okay." Ling nods. Her eyes flick between us searchingly. "Are you ready?"

"Yes," I reply, meeting her gaze evenly. "Hunter can serf the Quicks for six minutes."

Achilles whistles. "Not much time. We need to be in the air by then, meaning you guys only have four minutes to set the bombs."

"We can do it." Bo and Ling speak at the same time, and trade a confident grin. Ling says, "Four minutes to set the bombs, then Achilles activates them, giving us two more minutes to leave before they explode." She turns to Achilles. "Ready?"

Achilles holds up the black-and-yellow controller and the stopwatch. "As I'll ever be."

Ling exhales slowly, rolling her shoulders. Bo jogs on the spot, cracking his neck.

"Get to the top," Ling says to Hunter. "Then give us a countdown of five before you start."

"Got it," he replies. And that's when he steps toward me. I don't know if he means to kiss me or touch me or just wish me good luck. But I flinch. It's an almost imperceptible freezing, but he sees it. Our eyes lock. Hunter's face is a mask of surprise, of sadness, but also of a terrible sense of inevitability, as if he knows he's lost me. My eyes fly to Ling. "If anything happens—"

"We meet at the safe house," she says, swinging her arms in a circle. "There's an old cottage in the Farms, between a lemon grove and a strawberry field, a few miles from border control. And if not there, I guess we meet in the Badlands. Any suggestions?"

Hunter is walking slowly up the hill, away from me. "The Salt Flats," I say softly. "In the west. We can meet there." But even as I say *we*, I am struck by the feeling that Hunter will not be with me, no matter where we go.

Ling says, "On the dam wall, you take the left. I'll take the middle, Bo will take the right. Let's try to space out as evenly as we can." I nod. She tips her head to indicate I should stand next to her. "Then get ready."

Hunter pauses near the top of the hill, just out of sight of the Quicks. Bo and Ling take their marks, eyes ahead of them, bodies low like sprinters ready to run. My heart is galloping in my chest. I close my eyes for second. *Please, don't let anyone die.*

When I raise my head, I see Hunter, as strong and certain as a beacon, standing at the top of the hill. He raises his hand, all five fingers spread wide, and uses them to silently count us down. Five fingers become four.

Three. Adrenaline charges through me like a street fight.

Two. I can hear Ling next to me, already panting.

One.

His arm whips down to his side. Hunter shouts, *"Run!"*

chapter 22

We burst forward. Our feet rip at the grass as we streak up the hill. When we reach the top, I see the Quicks shuffling like sheep away from us, toward the scrub on the far side of the dam, eyes a piercing white. Hunter is serfing them, but I do not have time to look at him as I run past. We slip and skid down the incline and race toward the top of the dam.

I find my place on the left. Ling is already next to me, fifteen feet between us, and tying the end of her rope in a secure knot around the iron railing. I drop the long spool of rope at my feet and start to tie the end in a sailor's knot, my fingers finding the twisting, complex pattern with ingrained muscle memory.

I catch an arc of movement: Bo's rope sailing over the edge. Ling is one step ahead, swinging herself over the iron railing and pulling back on her rope as confidently as if she were climbing over a fence. A loud *vvvvvvvvvvvv* echoes through the cavernous space below us as she shoots down on the rope. A few moments later, I hear another. Bo.

I finish the knot, and pull back on it to test my weight. It tightens, creaking as I pull. It's solid. I toss the spool of rope over the edge. It seems to unfurl in graceful slow motion as it tumbles to the bottom. Ling and Bo are already down there, yanking Red Devils from their chains.

Holding the rope tight, I swing one leg over the railing so I'm sitting on it, one leg dangling over the edge. I don't look down. Still, the vertigo makes my head spin. I am so terrifyingly far from the ground. I grit my teeth and lean back on the rope until it takes my whole weight. Holding tight, I swing my other leg over. Both feet are planted on the bottom of the iron railing. Below me is nothing but empty air for a hundred feet. Behind me is the aqueduct, open and empty.

I drop my feet from the railing and let my arms take my entire weight. I wait for the rope to settle, and then get a loose hold of it between my feet. If I'm dangling too wildly, I'll smash into the dam on the way down. All I focus on is holding the rope exactly as Lana showed me: not too tight but not so loose that it does nothing to break my fall. The rope steadies. I loosen my grip.

Vvvvvvvvvvvv! The world blurs around me as I shoot down, down, down. My hands burn, even with the roping gloves. My stomach shoots to my mouth. I'm going too fast.

"Slow down!" Ling screams.

I tighten my hands on the rope, pain whipping through me. The ground slams into me, knocking the wind out of me.

"Five minutes!" Achilles' voice rings out. He sounds neutral; totally calm.

"Are you okay, Tess?" Bo calls.

"Yes!" I call back, stumbling to my feet. I'm delirious with elation, even though my hands are smarting with pain. I can't believe I made it down. The top of the dam looks like it's on top of the sky from here. "I'm okay!"

Ling and Bo already have their first Red Devils stuck in place, and have started climbing back up. I yank the bottom Devil off the chain and hold it flat against the dam. Then, with one quick flick of my wrist, I turn the handle hard to the right. I hear a click, and when I pull my hand away, it stays there. The first Devil is set.

I hop back up the rope and start climbing. I climb fast, buzzed from the jump down. My feet find the rope like it's an extension of my body. I'm moving as smooth as a snake through grass.

"Stop there, Tess!" Bo calls from below me. Ling and Bo are still climbing. I'm the first to the middle, but only by a second. Holding the rope with my left hand, I jerk the second bomb off the chain around me. The rope sways a little with the movement and I have to stay still for it to settle. Then I press the bomb flat against the dam. The arm supporting my weight starts to shake with the exertion. I grind my teeth, remembering what Bo said about the bomb needing to be exactly flat against the dam. I twist the handle to attach. For a second I think I haven't laid it flat enough and that when I let it go, it'll slip past me and fall to the bottom. But when I take my hand away, it sticks like a limpet to the wall.

"Four minutes!" Achilles' voice, again.

Now for the top. I'm starting to tire. I glance up, just once, and see Achilles' head poking over the railing. Sweat pours down my brow as I climb, finding the foot lock, pulling myself up, finding the foot lock again. My breath comes in great wheezes, and my arms ache so much it's as if they've been shot by a razer.

"Stop there, Ling!" I hear Bo call. Looking up, I see Ling, a good distance above me, attaching her last Devil to the dam.

"Tess, *hurry*," Bo calls. I pull out every last reserve and finally make it in line with Ling's and Bo's bombs. Once again, I perform the ritual. Lay it flat, twist, release.

"Three minutes!" Achilles calls. There's the slightest note of anxiety in his voice.

Ling is over the railing. Bo isn't far behind.

I'm so tired. My arms hurt so much. I dangle for a moment, teary-eyed from pure exhaustion. But I have to move. My body screams at me with every pull of my arms, but it's not enough to make me climb like before. But I am climbing. I'm nearly at the top.

"Tess?" Bo calls.

"I'm okay!" I wheeze. Finally, *finally*, the railing comes into view. Bo grips my forearms and in one swift, strong movement, he hauls me over the railing. My feet are unsteady on firm ground and it takes me a second to find my balance. We did it. We're out. Ling stands panting, bent over with her hands on her knees at the top of the ridge, next to Achilles. Hunter is all the way over in the scrub on the other side, surrounded by white-eyed Quicks. He's grouping the robots as far from us as possible.

"Achilles, activate the bombs!" Bo orders.

I hear a series of tiny beeps. When I glance down at the dam, I see all the bombs have lit up. They almost look beautiful, all nine glowing ruby red in a nearly perfect square.

"Two minutes to impact!" Achilles calls back.

Bo yells, "Everyone out!"

We sprint back to the clearing. Success courses through my veins, hot and wild and real. When I reach our gear, Ling and Bo are already scooping up the air rifles. I glimpse Achilles disappearing down the animal track, back toward the parked buzzcar. The sky has turned pearly, the clearing no longer in shadow. Dawn is coming.

"Tess, go!" Ling yells.

"Where's Hunter?" I pant, glancing at the top of the hill.

"Go!" she repeats, pushing me in the direction of the track.

"Hunter!" I scream. "Where are you?"

I hear his voice: it sounds as if he's still on the other side of the lake, and as if it's taking him a great effort to call to me. "Get...to the...car..."

Bo follows Achilles, racing into the birch trees. The slow beeping of the bombs echoes from the dam wall below.

"Tess, c'mon!" Ling grabs my arm. "No time!"

I twist out of it. *Where's Hunter?* Before she can stop me, I'm racing back to the top of the hill. When I get there, my heart stops.

The hundred-odd Quicks are clustered together and immobile, still with their eyes safely burning white. But Hunter is no longer standing. He is on the ground, his hands pressed into the earth as he tries to drag himself away from them, his long legs paralyzed and useless. "No!" I cry, starting toward him. "Hunter!" He lifts his head wearily and moves his mouth, but no sound comes out. Then, as I watch helplessly, he collapses to lie lifelessly in the grass.

As one, the Quicks' eyes change. Snow white becomes blood-red.

"No," I whisper, horrified. "Oh, please, no."

I'm still standing there, inert on the hillside, when their heads swivel in the direction of Hunter's fallen body. I'm still standing there, chest rising and falling in unadulterated fear, as they move to surround him. And I'm still standing there when the closet Quick bends down to pick him up as if he weighs nothing at all.

His head lolls back, arms and legs dangling. The Quick turns in the direction of the aqueduct and in a smooth, easy motion, tosses Hunter's body over the edge. I stifle a cry, clamping my hand to my mouth. *This must be a nightmare.* It doesn't feel real to see Hunter's body sail down, down, down, one hundred feet to the bottom of the dam. At the last second, I have to squeeze my eyes shut, because I cannot survive watching him smash into the concrete. Instead, I see my mom's body, hurtling through space, smacking against my bedroom wall. I hear a soft thwack and then a tiny clink. I open my eyes and see the clink was the mirror matter. I can just make it out, a tiny scrap of movement spinning across the concrete. Hunter's body lies motionless near the mouth of the aqueduct. Blue blood pools around his head. His arms and legs are splayed like a corpse.

He is a corpse.

I have seconds before the Quicks see me.

When the dam explodes, Hunter will be washed into the Badlands, separated from the mirror matter forever. He needs it to recharge. If he doesn't recharge, he's dead. But he's probably dead already; if he's run himself completely dry, if there's nothing at all left in that tube, he's dead and I can't save him. With the Quicks no longer being serfed, they'll execute me as soon as they spot me. *He's dead, Tess. He's gone.*

I have to leave him.

But I can't. I remember the look on his face when I flinched after he tried to touch me. So sure that he'd lost me. My hands ball into fists. He cannot die believing that.

As soon as I start running toward the rope that's still tied to the iron railing, the Quicks see me. They cover ground five times faster than I can. I'm only a few feet from the rope and already they're flocking fast across the top of the dam wall toward me. I reach the rope, heart snapping like a rubber band, and swing myself over the edge. Black-and-silver hands grab for me. I cry out as they miss by millimeters. Then I'm dangling, once again at the top of the rope. I loosen my grip and begin to slide. The bright red bombs flash past me on both sides. One, two, three, all of them beeping an unstoppable countdown. I tighten my grip as I near the bottom, then I hit the ground with a hard thud. Scrambling to my feet, I race for the mirror matter. My steps echo around the bottom of the dam. The tube looks empty, but I don't have time to study it. I snatch it and race back to Hunter, dropping to my knees, drenching them in blue blood. He's on his stomach, the hole in the back of his head wide open, spilling blue liquid. No lights blink inside. When I edge the tube in, it's not sucked in like last time; I have to close the flap of skin myself, pressing it into place until it seems to stick shut. I look to the top of the dam and see the Quicks lined up along the railing, watching me with eyes that cut paths of crimson light through the early dawn. I have no plan for what I'll do at the top. But we need to get out of here before the dam explodes. The Devil closest to me flicks from forty seconds to thirty-nine to thirty-eight.

I haul at Hunter's body and am shocked then overjoyed to find he barely weighs fifty pounds. I cry out in relief. I can lift him! I'm on my feet and wearing him like a cape, holding his arms across my chest. My hands are sticky with blue. I run for the rope and realize that I don't know how I'll climb and keep him on my back. Then I hear a clatter behind me. Metal on concrete. I whirl around. A dozen Quicks are behind me. A dozen more leap down to land squarely on their feet, their arms spread out for balance. They fan out and begin to advance.

I shrink against the dam wall, fumbling for the rope. "No," I gasp, my voice rising in fright. "Get away from me!"

They're ten feet away. Then five. Like lightning, I pull Mack from my belt and stab him out in front of me. The Quick closest to me pauses, eyes moving to assess this threat. It's not a threat, but I thrust it forward again like it is. The Quick raises its head again and I almost see smugness in its red eyes, although I know this is impossible. It knows I have nothing to fight with. It takes another step, now only an arm's-length away. I scream as it lunges for me, impossibly fast—then it jerks back and flies across the dam floor with a crack. A second one follows, hurtling away from me.

I look around wildly. Ling and Achilles are aiming air rifles at the Quicks from our buzzcar, which is hovering above me. Bo is at the controls. A length of rope lands at my feet.

Ling calls, "Grab it!"

Shoving Mack back into my belt, I dart for the rope, hearing but not seeing more of the Quicks get blown back by the air rifles. The pops from the rifles keep them at bay. Heart crashing in my ears, I gather up the excess rope to make sure the Quicks can't pull me back down with its end, then twist my hand for a solid grip. I use the other hand to cling to Hunter's ragdoll body.

I scream, "Go!"

The buzzcar darts up, just as dozens more Quicks leap down. It's only by pulling my feet up that they miss snatching my legs. But we move so fast, I almost lose my grip. "Careful!" I shout, and the car slows. I see the timers on the bombs. Eleven.

Ten.

Nine.

We're halfway out. We're going to make it.

My hand slips. Hunter's sticky blue blood threatens my grasp. "Hurry!" I scream. "I'm slipping!"

Eight.

Seven.

Six.

We're three-quarters of the way out, almost even with the top of the yawning aqueduct. Below me, the Quicks leap and jostle like a pack of hungry dogs, ready to devour their prey. My hand slides another inch down the blood-slick rope and I scream, again. *"Ling, I'm slipping!"*

Five.

Four.

Three.

Two things happen at once. I hear a tiny chorus of beeps. They form a high, single note, like a heart monitor signaling the end of someone's life.

And I lose my grip on the rope. I tumble, with Hunter in my arms, through empty air toward the waiting Quicks.

Then a colossal and deafening explosion rips the world apart.

A roar of air scoops us away from the Quicks, blasting us toward the open mouth of the aqueduct. The sky is below me, above me, below me again. And then I hear the water.

Hold your breath.

I have a split second to suck in one great gasp before a wall of water explodes around us, driving us forward. Instantly, we're submerged and blasted into blackness.

We're in the aqueduct.

I can't move, can't see. All I know is the roar of the water, rocketing us forward. I'm clutching some part of Hunter's body as hard as I can, but my grip is clumsy and the water is an angry live thing that wants to pull him from my fingers.

We slam into something hard—the side of the aqueduct?—and bounce off again in a sick spinning whirl. I need to breathe. My lungs burn. If I breathe now, I drown.

We shoot forward like a bullet, racing blind. The water has its claws in me, ripping at me viciously.

I want to breathe, I need to breathe, please, let me breathe—

We're being sucked down, and then up? Are we going up? I squint my eyes and the rushing black water is turning dark gray, light gray—

Bright light bursts around us and we pop like a cork out of the water. I take a huge, gut-wrenching gulp of air. We splash back down. We are in the open air, racing along like a buzzcar. I feel thick, soupy heat. I catch snatches of ochre earth. I'm underwater again before I realize it and take in a mouthful of water. I'm coughing as we bob to the top again, gasping for air.

I grab for Hunter and catch a terrifying flash of green eyes, wide open yet unseeing. The sightless stare of the dead. My legs kick wildly. I hook my arms around his torso, trying to hold on to his body and keep my head above water at the same time. The raw pink of dawn fills the sky that is above us, next to us, above us again. The river flips us around, and I see a streak of white—Eden's city walls, receding.

I am in Lunalac. I am back in the Badlands.

On either side of the river, people in flea-bitten sun robes gape at the gushing water. A range of expressions flash past me: fear, shock, disbelief, delight. A little girl points at me and yells, *"Acqua azul!"* We race past her entire family, dumb with sleepy surprise, gathered on the banks of the river. She's grinning from ear to ear.

Finally the force of the water lessens. Kicking hard, I pull us diagonally toward the shore. My feet find purchase on the banks. In a few heavy, ungraceful lunges, I drag Hunter's body out of the new river and drop him flat on the bone-hard earth along the shore.

"Hunter!" I slap his face, hard and then harder still. "Hunter!"

Nothing. Mouth-to-mouth? No, he doesn't need air to live. He needs mirror matter.

Please don't let it have gotten lost in the river. Near me, I hear cries of delight as people begin jumping and wading into the river, but all I can focus on is finding the circle of skin at the back of his head. It opens easily. The empty tube falls into my fingers. I laugh, wild with relief that it made the journey. But is it empty? Is he dead? My eyes can't find silver. I turn it around, studying every part anxiously. It looks empty.

Glancing up, I see the sun's first rays breaking over the horizon, creeping toward us. I hold the tube of mirror matter in my palm. My hand is shaking so badly it rocks the glass. I grab my wrist and try to steady it but I can't, so I put it on the ground next to us.

"Please," I whisper, watching the sun warm the empty cylinder. "Please let there be something left."

Around me, people are yelling and laughing and splashing in the river, their voices joyous. But all I feel is dread.

Then I see something in the tube. A silver stain, no bigger than a hair. But will it be enough? I grab the tube end and, with trembling fingers, insert it back into Hunter's head.

"Hunter," I whisper, searching his face for any sign of life. "Hunter?"

A minute passes. Nothing. It wasn't enough. Did he know serfing that many Quicks would kill him? Yes. I'm sure he did. We broke the dam. We brought life back to the Badlands. But Hunter sacrificed himself in the process. And now I am alone in the Badlands once more. *I am alone in the Badlands.* No friends. No food. No money. And no Hunter.

"Please," I choke. "Please let him live."

His face is unmoving. His eyes are flat.

I collapse on his chest and start to sob, my shoulders shaking, my soul broken.

Something moves. I jump like I've been shot, jerking up hard. "Hunter?" I stare into his dead, unseeing eyes, my jaw loose. "Hunter?"

He blinks.

"Hunter!" I scream. "Can you hear me? Hunter!" I'm babbling, my eyes all over him. "Are you alive? Please, please be alive. Hunter! Hunter!"

In a flurry of tiny twitches, life returns to his face, as beautiful as any sunrise. He blinks again, and his sight returns. He focuses on me. He sees me. He croaks, "Tess?"

"I'm here," I say, stroking his face gently. Tears drip down my nose and splash onto his face. "It's me. I'm here."

His face contorts, and he says something I can't make out. I put my ear to his mouth. "What? I couldn't hear you."

He clears his throat. "More. Soon...I'll need more sun."

"Okay," I tell him. "Soon." For now, I just want to hold him to make sure he's really still alive.

"Thank you." He winces, trying to sit up. "My legs..."

"Here." I put my hands under his ams and help him into a sitting position.

"Lucky I'm so light." He gives me a crooked grin. "Or maybe you're just strong."

I'm laughing and I'm crying and my heart is singing, singing, singing because Hunter is alive.

He glances around, taking in his surroundings. Unpaved roads piled with garbage and rows of rundown, colorful shacks. Children run barefoot toward the river, naked or in rags. By now thousands of Badlanders are by the roaring river—wading, drinking, splashing in the shallows. The sultry morning air is alive with the sounds of laughter and one word ringing out over and over and over again. *Acqua.* Water.

"We are in the Badlands," Hunter says.

"Yes," I nod, wiping away tears.

"And you are here with me."

"Yes," I breathe the word. "Yes, I am."

He studies my face, reaching up to wipe something off my cheek. "And you are still alive."

I hiccup a laugh, my tears finally starting to subside. "Defies belief, doesn't it?"

"No one knows how to stare death in the face like Tessendra Rockwood," he says with a slow, gentle smile.

I stare at him, lost. Lost in the gaze of the boy who saved my life, and whose life I saved. One hand raises to graze my cheek and I shudder. His fingertips spark electricity under my skin, bringing my body back to life. I raise my arms to circle his neck, pulling myself as close as I can to him, my head buried in his neck. For a long moment, we just hold each other and all I can think is *thank you thank you thank you.*

I pull back so I can see his face again. His usual expression of calm curiosity has been replaced with something more intense. Something alive and hungry.

"Tess?"

"Yes?" I ask, my thumb pads drawing slow circles on his cheeks.

His mouth quirks, lips parting. "Is this really just a chemical called dopamine?"

I smile broadly, feeling as warm and full as the sun. "No. It's not." I look into his eyes, his beautiful green eyes gazing back at me steadily. "I love you. I love you," I say it again, and I can't stop myself saying it a third time. "I love you, Hunter."

As my lips move to his, I feel him sigh, the words almost lost over the roar of the river. "I love you too, Tess."

Finally, finally our lips meet. At first his lips just brush mine, no more than a butterfly wing, no more than a ray of sunlight. But even this whisper of a movement sparks an explosion inside me; a feeling that is at once wholly new, and also an expectation met. I lean back, and see Hunter's eyes are still closed, his expression rapt. When he opens them, they are glowing and so extraordinarily alive. He says, "More."